Body of Truth

Doubleday
New York
London
Toronto
Sydney
Auckland

David L. Lindsey

Body of Truth

PUBLISHED BY DOUBLEDAY
a division of Bantam Doubleday Dell Publishing Group, Inc.
666 Fifth Avenue, New York, New York 10103

DOUBLEDAY and the portrayal of an anchor
with a dolphin are trademarks of Doubleday,
a division of Bantam Doubleday Dell Publishing Group, Inc.

Book design by Anne Ling

Library of Congress Cataloging-in-Publication Data
Lindsey, David L.
Body of truth / David L. Lindsey.
p.   cm.
I. Title.
PS3562.I51193B63   1992
813′.54—dc20   91-28713
                                                                                    CIP

ISBN 0-385-24814-8

For Joyce,

the wrong girl who became the right woman
after walking through the wrong door
at the right time.

We perceive an image of the truth
and possess nothing but falsehood . . .

Blaise Pascal
Pensées

Body of Truth

Chapter 1

Haydon stared out through the rain-spattered windshield of his car, past the uneven, foggy margins that had formed around the edges of the glass in the cold January afternoon, and waited for the woman to gain control of her emotions. She was not a woman who showed her feelings easily, nor was she inclined to invite demonstrations of tenderness from others, so that even in her grief, which for so long she had refused to disclose, Haydon did not feel free to comfort her. Until now, her dejection had been a closely held sorrow, a concealed anguish. As he sat beside her in the front seat, his hands on the cold steering wheel, wishing for a cigarette, though he hadn't smoked in years, he imagined that their closeness in the car, his intimate witness to her loss of self-control, must be costing her dearly.

Germaine Muller was fifty-six, ten years older than Haydon himself. He had known her and her husband exactly three months to the day, having met them when he investigated the disappearance of their daughter, Lena, who had gone to the Rice University campus, not far from where they were now sitting, to meet a friend. She did not come home.

Lena had graduated from Rice three years before she disappeared. She had majored in philosophy and six months after graduation had joined the Peace Corps and spent two and a half years among the Ixil Indians in northwestern Guatemala. She had completed her term of service in the Corps and had been home only six weeks when she disappeared. Germaine and George Muller were convinced that their daughter had gone to the university campus to meet a young free-lance journalist she had gotten to know in Guatemala named John Baine, an American who traveled throughout Central America. He had shown up at the Muller home unannounced five or six days earlier. They said their daughter seemed to have been upset by his visit, and when he showed up again the next day, George Muller had told him to leave and had threatened to call the police. Baine had left, but only after a bitter quarrel between Lena and her father that George Muller blamed on John Baine.

The investigation had been an awkward one from the point of view of satisfying Lena's parents. After a lengthy inquiry, Haydon had come to the conclusion that there had been no foul play. In fact, Haydon believed that Lena had disappeared voluntarily, probably with John Baine. It had not taken Haydon long to learn that George Muller and his daughter had a complicated relationship, one that—before Lena had left for the Peace Corps—had come full circle from inseparable (and, some had said, "unhealthy") to intolerable. Lena's disappearance had all the signs of flight, not abduction.

George Muller, however, could not abide this reading of his daughter's disappearance. As abrasive a man as his wife was stoic, Muller insisted from the beginning that the Houston Police Department was misreading his daughter's disappearance. He was convinced she had been murdered. He had badgered them, tried to pull political strings, tried to put pressure on everyone in the department, from the chief on down to Haydon himself. He had written letters to the editors of both major dailies complaining about incompetence and neglect within the homicide division. He was certain John Baine was a murderer, despite the total absence of any evidence. Muller was outraged that his daughter's disappearance could not be resolved, and in the fog of his own frustration he found fault with everyone.

Because of Muller's high-profile protest and the lack of a conclusive resolution to Lena's disappearance, the story had a long run in the newspapers and the television nightly news. Lena Muller was a pretty girl, her parents were well-to-do, the university from whose campus she had disappeared was a prestigious, private institution. In a way, from the media's perspective, Lena's disappearance was even more intriguing than if her body had been found. It had all the ingredients of a melodrama. In fact, this morning both Houston dailies had done follow-up stories: THREE MONTHS LATER—WOMAN STILL MISSING, and MULLER'S DISAPPEARANCE STILL A MYSTERY.

Germaine Muller opened her purse to get tissues, and a faint, sweet smell reached Haydon in the close confines of the car. He had opened the purses of many women over the years, and most of them had had in common something of a similar fragrance, the subtle hint of cosmetics. A strawberry blonde going gray, Germaine was an attractive woman, always well dressed, always ready, her dove pale eyes prepared for any jolt. She did not like being caught by surprise. Lena had been her only child.

Haydon waited, looking across the manicured lawns of the university campus, the wet winter day foreshortening the distances of the heavily wooded grounds with a veil of suspended mist. He took a hand off the steering wheel and touched his moustache. It was three weeks old, just getting to the point that it reflected to its best advantage the crisp, clean lines that he wanted it to have. It was darker than his hair, which had been going gray at the temples for several years. He didn't know why he had decided to grow the moustache. One morning he simply had looked at himself in the mirror and didn't shave his upper lip.

Germaine's raincoat made a muffled crinkling noise as she moved in the leather seat, wiping at her nose, clearing her throat, digging in her purse for something, he didn't know what, something she needed. He had no idea why she had called him at home on this drizzly afternoon and asked him to meet her here. When she had pulled up behind his car as he waited for her at this isolated campus drive, she immediately had gotten out of her car, walked up to his Jaguar, and gotten in. She had said, "Thank you for coming. I'm sorry to get you out on a Sunday. I

3

really ought—" and then she suddenly, uncharacteristically, had broken down, and for the next ten minutes he had listened to her weep uncontrollably. It was a long ten minutes, every minute a full sixty seconds, and she had slumped over against her door, leaning her head against the window as she hunched her left shoulder defensively as if she thought he might be moved to touch her, as if this was a gesture to keep it all to herself.

Haydon was uncomfortable. Anyone in this much pain easily evoked his compassion, and he usually said what he felt, did what came naturally, a firm hand, empathetic words. But Germaine Muller was complex. He did not want to offend her, and he wasn't sure that she might not find such a gesture too intimate, somehow unwarranted.

He waited as she began to regain her composure, and he wished for some other sound to concentrate on other than the detailed ones of her poignant effort to recover her demeanor of equanimity, a practiced behavior that he imagined she had used all her life to keep the world at arm's length. Haydon thought about the odd phenomenon of self-image, about how so many people had it wrong, and about what it did to the lives of those who were slaves to it. Germaine Muller lived her life by it and, sadly, had tried to mourn by it.

"Jesus God," she managed to say, her voice thick with emotion and tears. "This was masochistic. I could have met you anywhere."

It was like her to believe she was being masochistic, rather than sentimental, to have asked him to meet her so close to where her daughter had last been seen. He looked at her.

"You're too hard on yourself," he said. "It's been a stressful three months. You owe yourself a little self-indulgence, even a lot of self-indulgence."

4

Her head was bowed and her eyes began to flutter, and he thought she was going to start crying again, but she didn't. She steadied herself. She hadn't looked at him since she'd gotten in the car.

Haydon's eye caught a movement in the rearview mirror, and he looked up and saw a girl on a bicycle approaching them from behind on the narrow lane. She was wearing a forest green plaid skirt and a pastel yellow sweater and high socks pulled past her calves, and when she saw them in the car she stopped pedaling and let the bicycle coast. Just before she got to the car she began pedaling again and looked at them as she passed, the wheels of her bicycle making a swishing sound on the wet pavement, her breath a vaporous streamer trailing from her mouth. Germaine had not known the girl was coming and flinched as she passed them, then kept her eyes fixed on the cyclist as she rode calmly around a curve and disappeared into the mist and woods. Haydon wondered what the girl must have thought they were doing. An affair, probably. She must've been close to Lena's age. Could possibly have known her. Rice wasn't a large university.

Germaine Muller continued to stare at the swirling mist where the girl had vanished.

"I know you must've seen the papers," she said.

"I did, yes."

"That was bad," she said, turning a little in her seat now. "I wasn't prepared for that. Oh, they called. The reporters called, but I couldn't talk to them. So I knew what they were doing. Still . . . it was . . . shocking."

The word sounded quaintly outdated, though it was entirely consistent with her personal moral rectitude, a frame of mind that seemed so out of place in the last decade of the twentieth century when so few persons had the time, or the innocence, to be "shocked" by anything. Haydon almost wished the word still meant for society what it meant for Germaine Muller.

She held the wad of tissues to her nose and tilted her head back for a moment in a gesture of emotional exhaustion. Then she straightened it in resignation.

"Apart from all the . . . heartbreak,"—Haydon was surprised at this word too—"the publicity . . . the loss of what was ours being ours alone, has been unnerving."

Haydon had no way of knowing how much the Mullers had known about their daughter's personal relationships, but the newspaper reporters, every one making an "investigative" effort to bring the story alive on their paper's pages, had made it abundantly clear that Lena Muller had been a child of her times. Her sexual involvements while she was at Rice could have been described as promiscuous, though that word, too, had lost some of its potency and had fallen into disuse in the wake of the sexual revolution.

"You must have found us to be odd people, George and I, during these past months," she said. "We've felt odd, to tell you the truth. Not ourselves. It's . . . been humbling. For me. George, of course . . ." She shook her head, her shoulders moved, the beginning of a shrug that never developed. "Being affluent, well, you can afford to isolate yourself from so much, can't you, from the disarray that seems to characterize so much of other people's lives. You believe you are someone who avoids the stupid muddles other people get themselves into, you avoid scandal and tawdry episodes. You begin to believe that you do this all by yourself, because you are better educated, more intelligent, wiser. If you think like that long enough, keep it up for decades, most of your life, you actually begin to believe you're . . . above the foibles of others. You know, 'God, I thank thee that I am not like other men. . . .' Maybe you don't come right out and say it, but you believe, deep down, that you're somehow superior." She was pensive, and then she whispered, "Such . . . hubris . . ."

Haydon looked at her profile against the fog on the window beside her face. Germaine Muller was a woman in confrontation with the immutable frailties of human nature and with the realization that she, after all, shared them with everyone else.

"I've read every word printed in the newspapers about us during these past months," she continued. "Secretly. George didn't know it. For him, I've pretended to be above it all. Aloof. But I read all of it. I've clipped every snippet, however minute, even those Crime Stopper things that appeared from time to time. I was hypnotized. It was as if I were seeing myself from outside my body. A very peculiar experience. There were times when it seemed that I was reading about someone else, while at other times it was clear I was reading about us—George, myself, and Lena—but we didn't seem . . . distinctive. Our names easily could have been interchangeable with anyone's name. There was nothing there, inherent in our lives—and the reporters seemed to have discovered a great deal about us—that distinguished us from anyone else. In fact, we, our lives, seemed terribly common. We could have been . . . anyone."

6

She stopped, suddenly aware of how much she had been talking. Haydon said nothing. What could he say to such a surprising monologue? Nothing was expected of him.

"I imagine that sounds strange to you, maybe even naive, coming from a woman my age," she said, looking down at her hands, but then returning her attention to the foggy lane in front of them. "But it was so . . . revelatory, and so sad. For Lena, all they wrote about her. They shouldn't have. She was a child, really, at twenty-one, all of them are children. Her work in the Peace Corps didn't seem to carry as much weight with them, not as much as the way . . . she lived in college." She shook her head wearily. "Something is out of proportion, isn't it. The way we see things, the way we think, the way we live, what we require of others and of ourselves. Too much, too little. Ill-proportioned lives."

Germaine Muller had undergone a sea change during the ninety days since her daughter had disappeared, but Haydon would have been hard pressed to say whether it was a slow turning toward something finer.

"Lena's alive," she said bluntly, without prelude. "George has found them."

Haydon was caught off guard. When Germaine had said "George" had found them, she was referring more precisely to her husband's obsessive resolve. The person who actually had found them was a private investigator named Jim Fossler, whom George Muller had hired almost three weeks earlier.

"In Guatemala?"

She nodded. "But Mr. Fossler says they are not living together. He doesn't believe they ever did." This was an important point for Germaine Muller, a kind of evidential furtherance of the fact that her daughter was not an obsessively sexual creature. And it had merit, coming from Jim Fossler. He was a good man, an ex-cop, a forthright, persistent investigator who was proficient at what he did.

"When did you hear from him?"

"He called me last night."

"You?"

"Yes, he called on my line. George never answers my line. He doesn't know yet." To explain, she turned toward Haydon for the first time, her colorless eyes swollen from the crying, her face drawn. Fifty-six was not old, but Haydon could see the old woman in her skull, the one she would one day become. Grief, as it so often did, was giving him a glimpse of the future.

"At the very beginning, when George hired Mr. Fossler, I met with him privately," she said. "He's a perceptive man, not that you need great perception to see what kind of man my husband is. It's because of how he is that we've come to this. Everyone knows that but George. That's why he has so much antipathy for you. You told him that right up front, in so many words. You'd . . . you'd think that after a young girl had gone through college, after she had spent two and a half years in the Peace Corps, with all the self-assurance that requires, you'd think that after all that she would be able to claim some independence. But you don't gain independence from a man like him. When she came home, he was all over her again . . . I'm sorry. God."

George Muller was the wealthy founder of a petrochemical company, a man who knew what he wanted and what was required to get it, and whose forceful and unyielding personality had made him a fortune. He was greatly admired by other successful men, men who were like him and who saw something of themselves in Muller's strong-willed triumphs. But George Muller's insistence that his self-centered will should never be denied, neither in his professional nor his private life, had not been without a price, a price that must have caused him much dark pain in those secret moments that occur in all men's lives when they confront the naked reality of their own culpability. His preoccupations with himself had withered his wife's love and alienated his daughter forever.

"Anyway, I resolved that if we ever again made contact with her I wouldn't let him . . . ruin it. I went through all this with Mr. Fossler, a long, honest, detailed conversation. He seemed to be very understanding. I simply asked him to let me know first."

"And he called you last night."

"Yes. He said . . . he said that there might be a chance of persuading her to come home."

Might-be-a-chance. Haydon studied her. Desperate people could sustain themselves on such airy nourishment.

"But, apparently, he's concerned about something," she said. Germaine Muller's voice quavered slightly, and she leaned her head back against the window and took a deep breath before going on. "He said he thinks she's in some kind of trouble. That she and that boy are in some kind of trouble."

In the entire time Haydon had known her, Germaine Muller had never said the words, John Baine. He was always "that boy" or "him" or "that young man." Something primitive in her kept her from saying his name. George Muller, on the other hand, spoke it all too often, spitting it out like a curse word, "Baine . . . Baine . . . Baine." He was bedeviled by "Baine."

"What are their circumstances?" Haydon asked. "You said they're not living together?"

"Lena is living with an American woman in Guatemala City, someone she met during one of her weekend leaves in the Peace Corps. Apparently they had become close friends."

"And Baine?"

"I don't know. He's just on his own, I guess."

"What kind of trouble?"

She shook her head. "I don't know. He said Lena was fine, she's safe, but something . . . Frankly, I was angry with him—Mr. Fossler—for being so vague, but he said he could be all wrong. He said he wanted to talk to you but wanted to clear it with me first."

"Why me?"

"When I had that first conversation with him and I recounted everything that had happened during the investigation, how helpful you had been despite George, he said he knew you. He had good things to say about you, that he respected you. I guess when he ran into something unexpected . . . you had handled the investigation . . ."

"You know that if he contacts me, I'll be dealing with him in an official capacity," Haydon said. "I'll have to write a supplement to the investigation into Lena's disappearance. This can't be off the record."

"That's what he said you'd say. That's why he was asking me, wanting to know if I wanted to keep it unofficial. I understand that. I'd like to have your help."

Haydon looked at Germaine Muller's tortured eyes. She was looking at him, too, wanting some kind of reaction. His blessing, maybe. Or guidance, or simply assurance that she was doing the right thing. He hated to think what the Mullers' lives must have been like since their daughter's disappearance. Westerners, at least those of Anglo and Germanic stock, weren't given to dramatics in their grief, not the kind of wailing, flailing exorcism of sorrow one sometimes sees in other cultures. Their psychology demanded a gravity that concealed, rather than revealed. In their own way, George and Germaine Muller were still in the calamitous throes of their loss. It had been a mighty lamentation of silence.

"Did Fossler say how Lena was feeling about being found?"

Germaine turned around in her seat and looked out the window again, but it was too foggy for her to see anything. She looked through the windshield to the wet, leaf-strewn lane where the girl had disappeared into the mists.

"I asked him that," she said. "He said she was upset. He said that she had cried. But . . ." She looked down at her purse, saw her hands gripping the wadded tissues. Slowly opening her fingers, she turned over her hands and regarded her rings, the diamond cluster, the emerald, the costly black pearl, with a detachment that reduced their value to smoke. "He said—and I was struck by his sensitivity to this—he said he wasn't sure how to 'understand' it."

9

Haydon watched her, sensing her discomposure more than actually seeing it. It was as if he were witnessing an emotional implosion.

"You haven't the remotest . . . inkling . . ." she said hoarsely, stopping to swallow as she raised her gaze to the window again, her empty eyes on the gray beyond the glass. "You haven't the remotest inkling of the desolation I felt when he said that."

Chapter 2

"*Colpa non perdonata dal genere umano, il quale non odia mai tanto chi fa male, nè il male stesso, quanto chi lo nomina.*"

Haydon flipped through his Italian dictionary and studied the verb forms once again. They made no sense within the context of the Italian sentence, at least as far as he could tell. Without completely understanding the entry, he made a stab at the translation anyway. "Mankind does not forgive fault, or hate so much one who is evil, nor evil itself, as much as one who names it." His rendering was literal enough, he thought, but it was not graceful, and he wasn't sure how far he could go in improving the style without distorting the meaning. He studied the sentence a few more moments and then turned to De Piero's translation: "Men do not so much hate an evildoer, or evil itself, as they hate the man who calls evil by its real name."

He laid down his pen in the center of his well-worn copy of Giacomo Leopardi's *Pensieri,* its broken spine allowing the book to lie as flat as unbound sheets, sat back in his chair, and stretched out his legs to rest his feet on the thick cross-brace of the old refectory table. The subdued light of the winter afternoon suffused the library and Haydon's clutter of Italian dictionaries, papers, and notebooks with a tenuous, hoary sheen. A copy of Leopardi's *Operette morali,* still in its cellophane wrapper from Blackstone's from whom he ordered most of his books, lay to one side. Forgetting his inept translation for the moment, he let his attention drift to the recording playing in the background, to the serene, seraphic voices of an a cappella requiem mass by Giovanni Pierluigi da Palestrina. Normally he couldn't work with music playing, a personal quirk that he often regretted, but these masses were so extraordinarily ethereal that they offered no resistance at all to concentration.

His eyes wandered to the slightly frosted glass panels of the French doors through which he could see the bare terrace and the dead winterscape beyond, across the lawn and down to the two greenhouses visible through the naked branches of the trees. It was a desolate setting, and to him winter was a desolate season that he scarcely could tolerate, brief though it was along the Texas coast. He hated the effects of winter's killing touch that stripped the trees and burned the summer vines, turning their graceful rambles to a bare and brittle unloveliness. Normally this was not a scene he had to contemplate very often, but this year had been exceptional. Just before Christmas a series of numbing northers had driven deep into the South and well into Mexico, hurling sleet and snow across the subtropical landscape with a stunning viciousness that was not seen but once or twice in several decades.

The freezing nights that followed had devastated Haydon's tropical gardens. The sluggish sap in the lime trees that clustered in a loose orchard down near the greenhouses—where the bromeliads, at least, were safe—swelled as it froze in the plummeting temperatures, bursting the bark in long, serrated wounds that exposed the tender core of the trees. The towering and lacy-leafed flamboyanas at the far end of the terrace near the sun-room, two trees that Haydon had grown from seeds he had brought back from the Yucatán more than fifteen years before, had met the same fate, as had the lank jacarandas, visible now just outside the French doors, below the terrace stairs. The storm had filled the terra-cotta pots of bougainvillea with tiny white kernels of sleet that had lain with the woody stalks of the old vines in a cold and destructive embrace and had left the wild trumpet vines along the high rock walls stunned and dying without their blossoms. Near the bathhouse, the skeletons of the ebony and persimmon trees stood brittle and glazed in pale ice. Though only spring could confirm the lasting effect of the damage, the ever-varied, evergreenness of the subtropical plants, which served as the rich foil for their own gaudy efflorescence, was already reduced to the umber and bister sameness of winter.

The snow itself had not remained long—two days, a trace of it on the third day, a ragged, dusty blue line of it next to the footing of the stone wall that surrounded the garden and the lawn—but Haydon was plunged into an unshakable gloom by the sudden plunder. To get his mind off the dreary setting, which was made even more somber on this January afternoon by the damp, lowering sky, he had taken out his dictionaries and his two collections of Leopardi, a questionable choice since the Italian poet-scholar himself had a cold eye and was given to sober moods that colored all his writings.

Haydon had turned to this kind of diversion before, and although he wasn't very good at it, he stuck with it, battling verb forms, wrestling with the baffling rules of grammar and grappling with a system of sentence structure that seemed to fold back over itself. The lines accumulated, the stanzas multiplied, and the paragraphs became pages as he unlaced the finely woven garment of Leopardi's eloquent language and listened to the clear, contrapuntal voices of Palestrina's *Messa per i defunti*.

13

This was what he had been doing when Germaine Muller had called, and this was what he had come back to when he had left her sitting alone in her car on the foggy lane in the woods of the Rice campus. But it wasn't any good now. He couldn't concentrate, couldn't even complete a sentence without his thoughts wandering back to the sad image of an alienated woman refusing consolation as she slumped against his car door, and to the unexpected news that Fossler had found and talked to Lena Muller.

"How are you doing over there?"

Haydon started. The library was quiet; Palestrina's *Lacrimosa* had ended, and he hadn't even been aware of it. He turned around and looked at her. Nina was sitting behind him on a small leather sofa, her feet shoved up under one of the cushions as she rested her back against the padded arm. Wearing a black vee-neck sweater of ribbed cotton with the sleeves pushed up to the elbows and a pair of black pleated pants, she had been reading an article in *Progressive Architecture.* Her reading glasses had slipped slightly down on her nose, and she was looking at him over the rims, just over the tops of them so that it seemed as if her pupils were hidden exactly behind the thin border of the tortoiseshell frames. The magazine was propped against her raised thighs, and she was holding it open with one hand while the other hand had gathered up her long chestnut hair, holding it up off the nape of her neck.

"Not bad," he said. He looked at her, olive skin and dark eyes and common sense. He relished moments like this when, by some oddity of perception, he unexpectedly saw her anew, as if for the first time again. Everything about her was fresh and surprising, her dusky coloring, her manner of becalmed curiosity, and her air of self-understanding that projected an emotional stability that was a rare and fine treasure. Even her sexuality, which stemmed from a harmony of all the other attributes together, was an orchestration of qualities of which he had never tired.

"Not bad," she said, raising her eyebrows and pushing up her glasses as if she were considering what to do with such a feeble response. He knew that she had caught him with his mind wandering and was curious about what was preoccupying him.

For the most part, Nina could live with Haydon's protean frames of mind. That was the great thing about her and the bad thing about him. If she had been the kind of woman who needed to know what he was thinking every moment, needed to be included in his every waking thought, needed to have an explanation for every queer mood of his nature, or felt slighted by his sometimes introverted temperament, the marriage would never have lasted. Additionally, if Haydon had had to make any fundamental changes in his personality to save the marriage, he couldn't have done it, though it would not have been for his lack of desire or willingness to do so. It was only that the peculiarities of his character were not susceptible to radical change. He could have willed himself to make the effort; he could not have willed himself to succeed. But neither was Haydon given to self-deception. To his credit, he held no illusions about himself and gratefully acknowledged the good fortune that had come to him in marrying her.

Nina, on the other hand, would have been equally willing to make a change to save their marriage if it had ever been necessary, but where Haydon would have failed, she would have succeeded. She was a survivor, a woman of strength and resilience, who did not have a personality in conflict with itself. She did not find it necessary to steel herself against invisible threats, nor did she create dreadful fictions that compelled her to do battle with Hydra-headed "what ifs"—apprehensions that Haydon lived with as though they were psychic siblings. She perceived life through a clear and finely ground lens, not through the cloudy-green refractions of an old bottle. If she had needed to change to save their marriage, she would have been good for the sacrifice, and she would never have looked back with second thoughts.

It was not that neither of them hadn't made sacrifices. No two people could remain together for eighteen years without experiencing disappointments in the other, without discontents and the painful renunciation of selfish ends, both significant and incidental. But none of their sacrifices had been beyond their ability to make, or more importantly, greater than their regard for each other. The true good fortune of their marriage had been that by virtue of the incalculable odds of serendipity, they had chanced upon that famed, but all too rare, felicitous paradox: the true compatibility of opposites. That, and the fact that they never had forgotten all that was good and exceptional about their beginning.

Still turned in his chair, Haydon crossed his long legs, rested one arm on the chair back, and with the forefinger and thumb of his other hand, lightly touched his moustache, unconsciously checking the preciseness of its trim.

"I don't understand *fa*," he said.

She nodded slowly, her eyes still on him. They looked at each other a moment, and then they both smiled at the same time.

"I know what we need," Nina said. "How would you like a cup of coffee?"

"Perfect."

"What kind?" She put down her magazine and took off her glasses, which she laid beside the lamp on the mahogany table behind the sofa.

"Something dark."

"Colombian Supremo?"

"Okay, that."

"Strong."

Haydon nodded. "Grind an extra spoon of beans."

"That'll make it too strong," she said. But he knew she would do it.

"And some Lindt's too, okay?"

"You're self-indulgent," she said. "Too self-indulgent. It ought to bother your conscience."

"It does," he said.

She looked at him. "It probably does," she said, shaking her head. She stood and ran her fingers through her hair as she leaned back in a twisting stretch, then relaxed and straightened her sweater, her loose, thick hair falling back around her face. With the wan winter light of late afternoon turning the rich hues of the library into muted colors, it seemed to Haydon that he was looking at an Italian baroque canvas in which Nina's modern face and form had been set in anachronistic, but perfect, consonance with the seventeenth-century painting.

"Be back in a little bit," she said.

Haydon watched her walk out of the library and listened to her footsteps as she crossed the marble hall to the dining room and into the kitchen. Within moments he heard her talking and then heard the liquid, Colombian lilt of Ramona's voice. It had been a little over two years now since she had come to live with them as a favor to her uncle, a homicide detective Haydon knew in Bogotá. A long-legged girl with an easy smile and the eyes of a woman twice her age, Ramona had been a freshman at Rice University then, and though the arrangement was supposed to have been only for one year while she got used to her new surroundings, Nina and Gabriela, and even Haydon, had grown so fond of her that they invited her to stay on. Listening to snatches of their conversation, a polyglot of English and Spanish in which they interchanged the words of the two languages with a careless freedom that Haydon never had achieved, he heard them discussing psychology and grade-point averages and prerequisites. Ramona was in the midst of midterm exams, and Nina, who was especially fond of the girl and treated her like a younger sister, was wanting to know how she was doing.

Suddenly aware of a chill on his feet, Haydon wiggled his toes in his well-worn suede oxfords. He hated having cold feet, and in the old house with its limestone and marble floors it was something he constantly fought during the brief few months that constituted winter. The old shoes were favorites because they were just sloppy enough to allow him two pairs of socks. He got up from the refectory table and walked over to the fireplace, took several logs from the copper-lined bin beside the bookcases and stacked them on the grate. Taking a match off the limestone mantel, he lighted the gas jet under the grate and watched the blue flames from the jet lick up the rough sides of the logs from the bottom, watched the logs begin to burn until he smelled the first sweet wafts of the oak fire.

Chapter 3

The telephone in the library had been altered so that its ring was little more than a soft mutter. Haydon, stirred from his thoughts in front of the fireplace, walked over to his desk and picked up the receiver.

"Hello."

"Stuart?"

"Yes."

"This is Jim Fossler."

Haydon could have bet money on Fossler and not been afraid of losing a dime. He was dependable and methodical. Common sense was high on his personal list of virtues, a list he took seriously. Fossler was a lanky man of fifty-four with a quiet disposition, thinning black hair, a permanent five o'clock shadow, and slightly bulging eyes that didn't miss anything they weren't supposed to miss. Low key, but often impatient with the frequent wrongheaded thinking of a municipal bureaucracy, he took an early retirement when the second of his two sons graduated from college, and started his own investigation agency. His wife, Mari, a talkative and bright Filipino whom Fossler had married after the death of his first wife, while the boys were still in high school, quit her position with an accounting firm and used her keen eye for business to help Fossler build his agency. After five years, Fossler's work was distinguished by his high success rate and his preference for keeping a low profile. As Fossler saw it, he was basically in the information business and you didn't get information by attracting attention to yourself. He was very good.

"I was hoping you'd call tonight," Haydon said. "I hear you've had some luck down there."

"Then you've talked to Germaine Muller?"

"This afternoon. A few hours ago."

"Good. I'll tell you, I'm not at all sure what the hell's going on down here," Fossler said, his voice calm. He must have been calling from a pay telephone, because he seemed to be speaking close to the mouthpiece, and Haydon thought he heard traffic. "Long story about how I finally got to the girl, which we can get into some other time, but I can tell you this, nothing in this country is simple. I went from coast to coast and border to border before I found her right here where I'd started out. Which was a surprise."

But Fossler didn't sound surprised. Not only did he have a personality that some would consider unexciting, he was also unexcitable. Day in and day out he could make you want to climb the walls, but in a fast-breaking situation, in a squeeze, he was steady on, the kind of man you prayed for.

"Listen," Fossler said, "before I even get started here I want you to take down a couple of names and addresses. I'll get to why in a minute. You got something to write with?"

"Yeah, I do. Go ahead."

"Okay. John Baine." Haydon wrote down the address.

"Janet Pittner." He gave her address and telephone number. "She's the woman Lena's living with, been living with her almost the whole time she's been gone. This woman's older than the girl by ten or fifteen years, I'd guess. Wealthy American, socially connected. Everybody in the American community here—which is pretty big—knows her, and she knows everybody. Good looking, but kind of crazy, I think. High strung.

"Dr. Aris Grajeda. He works in the slums here, no telephone, and no street address except somewhere in a shantytown called . . . I'll spell it: M-e-z-q-u-i-t-a-l. I haven't met this guy yet, but I'm going to try to see him tomorrow. I understand he worked with Lena, with some Indian tribe up in the western highlands. He's maybe in his mid thirties. A Guatemalan. Got his medical degree from Johns Hopkins, for Christ's sake. He's been back in Guatemala three years now. I hear his personal life is pretty interesting, very dedicated to his work. Not popular with the police here, because he calls a spade a spade. Considered a leftist, probably going to get himself killed.

"And before I forget . . ." Fossler gave Haydon his own address. "It's an old boarding house kind of thing, an old hotel."

"What about a telephone number?"

Fossler didn't respond immediately, and Haydon could hear the roar of trucks. It sounded like Fossler was in some kind of depot, maybe a bus station.

"No. You can't get me that way," Fossler said. "I mean there's a telephone there, but it's not good." He paused. "None of the telephones are good down here, understand? I'm calling you from a pay telephone, but . . . I'm still not sure it's good."

Haydon sat down slowly at his desk. "What's going on, Jim?"

"I've talked with the Muller girl twice," Fossler said. "The first time was Thursday afternoon. After I found out where she was living I just went there and asked for her."

"That was at Janet Pittner's?"

"Right. There was a kind of an awkward moment when Lena realized who I was. It seemed to me Janet Pittner didn't know about the trouble back in Houston. So Lena asks the woman to leave us alone for a few minutes. We had a pretty good talk, as a matter of fact. I told her that after she'd first disappeared it was thought she had been murdered and Baine was the suspect. She couldn't believe it, claimed she didn't have any idea. She asked a lot about her mother, how she was, seemed to regret having put her through all the worry, but she didn't give a shit about her dad. Didn't even care to talk about him. I told her about her mother's concern, that she wasn't going to tell her dad, that she wanted

20

to work it out with the girl, just between the two of them. She started crying. I didn't know what to think, whether she was afraid or relieved or depressed or what. Finally I got her calmed down. I told her to think it over, and that we ought to get together again the next morning— Friday—and talk it over. But she didn't want me to come back to Pittner's again, so we agreed to meet at a pastry shop.

"I didn't call Germaine Muller right away. I thought I'd meet with the girl one more time, get a better feel for how it was going to go. To tell you the truth, Stuart, I kind of liked the girl right off the bat. She seemed like a good kid. I didn't want to just leave it cold. Then the next morning I'm sitting in the shop by a window so I can see the street. She's twenty minutes late. I was about to give her up when she comes running into the shop, tells me to come with her, throws down some money, and we hurry out to the street where we jump into a car. Me in the front, her in the back. There's John Baine, driving. We ride around, and Baine begins grilling me, like he's checking me out, maybe I'm not who I say I am, and he's grilling me to get to the bottom of it. Lena keeps turning around and looking behind us, and Baine is always flicking his eyes at the rear-view mirror.

"Anyway, after a while they unwind a little. I tell them they're obviously in some kind of trouble and they ought to go to the American embassy. Baine starts swearing, and Lena says, no, no, that wouldn't be good at all. The embassy would be a mistake. Whatever I do, don't go there and mention them. Do not do this, she says. I said I didn't have any intention of doing that. I was suggesting *they* should do that. They're the ones with a problem, not me. No, they say. That wouldn't be good. We kept driving."

Though Fossler was talking in his usual deliberate manner, rather slowly, steadily, he was betraying himself. Jim Fossler was never loquacious. If anything, he tended toward the other extreme. More often than not you had to pull information out of him, a trait that was maddening if you were trying to work with him in a high-pressure case that needed to move quickly and relied on a rapid, free-flow of information among several cooperating teams. On the other hand, you never had to worry about him gossiping away more than you wanted other people to know. A loose-tongued detective was one of Haydon's pet peeves.

But Fossler always addressed the business at hand, if a little too slowly, and yet here he was saying more than he needed to, failing to edit himself. He could have summarized what he had said so far in four or

21

five sentences, but he was dragging it out inefficiently—slowly, to be sure —but dragging it out nonetheless. He was displaying an agitation Haydon had never witnessed in him before, and it made Haydon's stomach tighten.

"We drive around. More questioning," Fossler continued, "until they seemed to be satisfied I wasn't whoever the hell else they thought I might have been. But they didn't seem to want to turn loose of me. Baine asked me if I knew anybody at the embassy. I told him no, which was true. I didn't check in with the embassy when I got here because I didn't want to worry if maybe somebody was watching me. Baine said that was a good call, because the embassy sucked. Baine, he's maybe twenty-seven, twenty-eight, has been wandering around down here, all over Central America, six or seven years, so he's no kid. I didn't feel too bad about him.

"So after a while they dropped me off three or four blocks from where they'd picked me up. Lena said they'd get back in touch and let me know what to tell her mother, what she was going to do."

"So she knows where you're staying?" Haydon asked.

"Yeah, they know."

Fossler waited again for another surge of traffic to subside. Haydon still didn't know why Fossler had called him, except to inform him that the Muller girl was indeed alive. But there was more to it than that, Fossler just hadn't gotten around to it yet. He was about to.

"Something else," Fossler said. "There's a guy down here says he knows you. Taylor Cage."

Haydon sat forward in his chair. His memory of Taylor Cage was as sharp as if only a minute had passed instead of a decade. Haydon would never forget the hot, humid night he last had sight of him, his barrel chest thrust forward as he swaggered toward the rank hold of a cargo ship berthed in the Houston ship channel. Cage was alone, and even the jaundiced glow from the dock lights deserted him as he approached the pitch-black margin that marked the belly of the tanker and into which he disappeared without hesitation. Haydon had been sure he was watching a man stroll to his execution. He had never met another man who would have done it. But Cage had done it, and because of the nature of the operation, Haydon had had to live with the silence of the unknown denouement that followed. Then five weeks later, late at night, Haydon received a collect telephone call at home from a Father Guillen in Barranquilla, Colombia. Haydon didn't know anyone named Guillen, but when you dealt with the variety of people he dealt with, you never rejected a collect call simply because you didn't recognize a name. He accepted the call and immediately recognized Cage's voice: "It was a hell of an ugly trip, but I made it. I'll be in touch." That was it. Haydon never heard from him again, except as an item of gossip among the right kind of people, once every two or three years.

"You do know him, then?" Fossler asked.

"Yeah, barely. You spoke to him?"

"Oh, yeah."

"What's he got to do with any of this?" Haydon asked.

"Damned if I'm sure," Fossler said. "But he knows everybody I've mentioned. I only had a short meeting with him. Unexpectedly."

"Where did you find him?"

"He found me. Came to the place where I was staying. A different place. I've moved. Several times."

"What did he want?"

"This was before I found Lena, about five days ago," Fossler said. "I was sitting in my room, by an open window, trying to get some air—it's the dry season down here, summer, for Christ's sake—and there's a knock on the door. I get up and open it, and this guy just shoves his way in, you know, like a bulldozer, barrel chest first, and we're in the middle of the room before I know what's happening. Scared the shit out of me. This country, Stuart, it's full of things that'll scare the shit out of you. No rules down here. Everything's negotiable—or not. Anyway, I see right off he's American, and he starts shooting the questions. Some of them didn't make any sense to me, and I guess he saw this. So I explain myself, straight on—the truth. He looked at me. Do I know anybody at HPD? I tell him I used to be in homicide. No shit, he says. Do I know Stuart Haydon? Of course. So I tell him about you and this case."

A car, its horn blaring, faded in and out of the background sounds. Fossler continued.

"He asks a few questions about it, and I answer them. He seems satisfied. He gives me a couple of names and leaves, telling me to watch my ass and telling me to be sure and say hello to you. And that's how I came onto Lena. The names take me right to Janet Pittner."

"And you haven't seen him since."

"That's right."

"You said he was 'involved.' "

"My gut tells me he's got something to do with the reason the kids

23

are scared. It's just my gut, okay? And since he stumbled in on me I've picked up a tail. Maybe coincidence, but I don't think so. It's a woman, a girl. Guatemalan girl. She's good. In fact she may have been on me a long time. I wouldn't be surprised. I can't always spot her even now, but if I work at it I can find her. She's very good."

"You think Muller and Baine are trafficking?"

"No. I really don't. I don't think it's like that at all."

"Then, what?"

"I don't know. Look, I'm getting off this phone in twenty seconds. This conversation is not private, Stuart, remember that. Look, if you can't justify coming down here on this case, you know, coming down to verify the girl's alive so you can close the book on it, then take a day off. I'm asking for a favor here, Stuart. I'll owe you one. Come down here, give me twenty-four hours of your time. You've traveled around down here. You know how it is. I can't go into it anymore over the telephone, believe me."

This was extraordinary. Jim Fossler did not operate like this. The cloak-and-dagger business was alien to his nature. His investigative procedures were as down to earth as his steady diet of meat and potatoes, nothing fancy. He didn't see ghosts; he didn't let his imagination run away with him. And he didn't ask for favors.

"What do you say?"

"I'll talk to Dystal tomorrow."

"Look," Fossler said, "I've got to know before we get off this phone. Can you do it or not? There's one flight out of Houston every day. Continental. It'll get you here just after dark. I need to know now. It's important that I know now."

Listening to a man like Fossler, a self-controlled, unflappable veteran, forced by events to betray his nervousness, was an odd experience. It was like communicating in code. On the surface of things, Fossler never broke character, but his urgency was telegraphed in nuance and subtleties. He wasn't going to hit you over the head with it. When you communicated with Fossler, more than half the burden fell on the listener.

"Okay," Haydon said. "I'll be on tomorrow night's flight. You want me to get in touch with Mari, see if she has anything to send down?"

"No, no need for that. I talked to her just before I called you. I'll pick you up at the airport." He hesitated. "I appreciate this, Stuart. I've got to go."

In an instant, Haydon was listening to a dead line.

Chapter 4

"Get a little chilly?" Nina was walking into the library with the coffee service on a tray. Haydon was back in front of the fireplace, holding one foot up to the fire and then the other. Nina's feet were never cold. In fact, she was so warm natured that she seemed never to feel the effects of winter at all. She wore only cotton sweaters, and her big concessions to winter dress around the house were long pants—she rarely wore them otherwise—and socks without shoes. Usually she wore sandals or was barefooted.

After setting the service on a low rosewood table in front of the sofa, she poured each of them a cup. Taking hers, she settled back where she had been before, turning sideways and tucking her feet under the cushion again.

"Better get it while it's hot," she said.

Nina drank her coffee black and scalding, nothing complicated about it. Haydon, on the other hand, added one spoon of cream—not milk—and, when he could get it, a few shavings of bitter chocolate. As for the temperature, he liked it hot to very warm, not scalding.

He bent down and turned off the gas jet in the fireplace. The logs were burning on their own now, giving off a soft crackling sound and a sweet, spicy scent.

"Ramona's having a good semester," Nina said, watching him as he came over and sat on the edge of the sofa and pulled his coffee over in front of him. "I was afraid for a while that all the madness at home was going to distract her. She was getting a lot of letters from the family after her cousin was killed in Medellín. I don't know how she kept her mind on school with all that going on."

"She's lucky," Haydon said, taking the paring knife and the wedge of Lindt bitter chocolate off the tray and shaving fine curls of it into his coffee. "She could be trying to get through school in Bogotá."

"I guess," Nina said. "What a mess all of it is."

Haydon added cream to his cup and stirred the coffee, staring out the French doors to the deepening gray afternoon. He thought about Modesto Solis, who had made it possible for his niece to get out of Colombia. It was a mistake to believe the entire country was paralyzed by the narco wars. There were millions of people it seemed never to touch directly, though it was a growing menace and probably affected them in ways they never knew. But for the men and women like Modesto who were in law enforcement, it had been a nightmarish decade. It had changed their lives, changed the way they viewed the world, and even themselves. The good-natured Modesto that Haydon had known in the past had, in recent years, become a serious man, suspicious and distrusting. Modesto's own brother, Ramona's father, René, had been dead almost eight years. He also had been a Bogotá detective, one of the early casualties of the narco wars. It had been a long run, and there was no end in sight.

"Gabriela called while you were out this afternoon," Nina said. "She's going to stay another week."

Haydon nodded, still looking past the French doors. The ageing

Mexican housekeeper, who had been with Haydon's family since before he was born, was visiting her family in Mexico City. It was an annual trip that usually lasted several weeks.

"I'm going to go ahead and ask Lydia if she'd like to stay on full time," Nina added, musing to herself as much as to Haydon. "Ramona can't be expected to do much around here this semester. Not while she's taking eighteen hours."

As Gabriela had grown older, the large home, which she once had run with the discipline of a family doyenne, gradually had gotten to be too much for her. Nina and Ramona had taken up the slack when they could, and what they couldn't do was taken care of by another Mexican woman, Lydia Quiroa, who came in part time. Lydia, who was in her late forties and always wore her jet hair in a single long braid hanging down her back, had the disposition of an angel and had made herself indispensable. All of them, even the increasingly eccentric Gabriela, who had a critical eye for human foibles, had grown fond of her and considered her a member of the family.

"And I've got to start putting in more time at the studio, too," Nina continued. "The new commission in Careyes is getting increasingly demanding . . ."

One of the things that made a man like Fossler so valuable was his experience. Though he had taken an early retirement from the police department four years before, he had seen eight or nine years more mayhem than Haydon himself. A man who had seen that much didn't get too excited when he encountered something out of the ordinary. He had been through so much, seen so many things he had never seen before only to learn that he eventually would see them again, or see variations of them, that it was hard to get worked up about anything. Yet here was Fossler, calling from Guatemala City, acting against the grain of his own character, Fossler putting the pressure on Haydon to make a decision. And then, in the retrospect of the last few minutes, there was one thing that Fossler had done that bothered Haydon. He had not explained why he had given him the names and addresses. Surely it had not been necessary for Fossler to have taken the time to give them to Haydon if he was going to be seeing him the very next night.

"Hey," he heard Nina say. "I think your coffee's fine."

Haydon stopped, realizing he was still stirring his coffee. He looked around at Nina, who was studying him, and shrugged.

"Okay, what's on your mind?" she asked.

27

"Nothing, really," he said, and sat back on the small sofa, crossing his legs and holding the cup and saucer in his lap. He was only a few inches from Nina's legs, close enough to smell the sachet on her clothes.

"You've never had 'nothing' on your mind in your life," she said. "You can't do it."

He looked across the library to the cold landscape outside where the watery afternoon light was losing strength, giving way to the blue winter hours before evening.

"Bloody weather," he said.

"Who was that who called you after lunch?" Nina asked, leaning over and putting her coffee cup on the service tray. "Is that who you went to see?"

"Yeah," Haydon nodded. "I did."

"And then someone called you a while ago. I saw the light on the telephone in the kitchen." She ran one hand through the front of her hair to get it back away from her face. It was graying quite noticeably now, strands of pearl that streaked the rich chestnut and added a sphingine air to her beauty that he found unmistakeably sexy, which was fortunate, because the gray was there to stay. It would never occur to Nina to color her hair. It just wasn't in the realm of consideration.

"The call after lunch," Haydon said, "was Germaine Muller. Jim Fossler has found her daughter, living in Guatemala City."

"Oh, my God," Nina said. "She's all right?"

"Apparently she's fine. Then the call a few minutes ago was from Fossler. He thinks the girl's in some kind of trouble. Wants me to come down there, stay a couple of days. Help him look into it."

"You're going to do it?"

Haydon nodded, sipping his coffee. "I'll have to." He told her about both conversations, leaving out most of Fossler's puzzling behavior, making it sound as if he would only be going down to wrap up the formalities of closing Lena's case.

"But that's not necessary, is it?" Nina asked. "You could get the embassy down there to confirm she's alive, or whatever it takes, couldn't you?"

"I could, yes. But I'd rather do it myself. I'd like to meet the girl. It's something I'd want to do with or without it being an official trip."

"I didn't know you were that intrigued with the case."

"I am now. Fossler has come up with some interesting . . . information." He leaned forward and set his cup on a neat stack of art magazines on the floor beside him. He moved closer to Nina and put his left arm around her legs, leaning against the front of them, feeling them warm against his side. They sat that way a while as the blue winter light darkened and the logs burned to a slower, quieter flame.

Nina said nothing, but Haydon could feel her moving her feet under the cushion. He carefully turned his eyes to her, hoping to observe her unnoticed. She stared at the fire, her brow wrinkled, and her hair, its wiry gray strands now made even more apparent by being highlighted in the glow from the fireplace, falling down to frame her face again. It was a study in chiaroscuro, Italian baroque again. Now that night had closed around the house, the library's high walls of books were lighted only by the green-globe lamp by which Haydon had been reading at the refectory table and by a small Chinese lamp with a parchment shade that sat on the long mahogany table against the back of the sofa. These two pools of soft light and the gentle, wavering glow from the fireplace were all that held off the darkness and allowed an occasional glint to escape from the gilded spines of the books.

Haydon was acutely aware that with the discussion of Jim Fossler's situation in Guatemala an air of uneasiness had seeped into the warm library like a cold draft. It didn't have to be unsubtle for Nina to sense it, for her to know the smell of risk. Nor did she have to be told that, despite what Haydon had said, this was not in fact something he had to do. He did not know how she had decided to deal with this kind of situation anymore, only that she must have decided never again to make it a point of contention when he had made up his mind to do something she considered needlessly jeopardous. By the same token, he had never articulated that he would not give up, not even for her, a job that regularly placed him in the path of uncertainty. In a way, that she had chosen the course of keeping her own counsel—a tactic he could hardly object to since he himself always had favored it to deflect conflict—saddened him. In the past, the fact that she could be depended upon to speak her mind on this point was something of a comfort to him, her objection being invariably unswerving, straightforward. And it was not that she was now disingenuous about her feelings. She simply had resolved to be more reserved in this one thing only, and Haydon knew that any regret on his part reflected directly on his own implacable nature.

They stayed there, watching the fire together, until only the embers remained.

Chapter 5

Haydon's alarm rang at five-thirty. He took his arm from around Nina and reached back to the bedside table and turned the alarm off, then tucked his arms under the covers again. Nina had not stirred and wouldn't for two more hours. Since she didn't go to the studio until nine o'clock, and Haydon's shift started at seven, he had always let her sleep. It had been that way for years. He snuggled up to her for a few more minutes, grateful that she was warm blooded and slept in nothing but her panties. But he didn't close his eyes. Christ, it was black as midnight, another reason winter was a lousy season.

After a few moments, his thoughts drifted to Jim Fossler, a sure sign that he ought to go ahead and get up. Resignedly he slipped his arms from around Nina again and got out of bed. He thought he could hear the wind blowing, which made him cringe, but when he went to the window and looked out, he could see the bare trees against the dull glow of the overcast sky, and the black silhouettes of their bony branches were motionless. He turned and walked into the bathroom.

He took a hot shower, standing under the steaming water for a long time, until he felt warm all over. Nina told him his hot showers were extracting the natural oils from his skin, but he thought it was worth it if he could start the day warm. He got out of the shower and quickly dried off, combed his wet hair, wrapped the towel around his waist, and shaved, careful to work around his moustache. He dried his hair and combed it again, splashed a dash of cologne on his face, and walked into his closet to dress.

By five fifty-five he was descending the stone stairs and crossing the wide entry hall to the kitchen. He surveyed the jars of coffee beans, decided on a Sumatra roast, and then ground enough beans for four cups. Normally Gabriela would be in the kitchen in her dressing gown by the time the coffee had finished dripping, her thick, brindled hair combed out and hanging down her back in lengthy ripples. They would cook breakfast together, comfortable with each other's company and in a routine that had been established over many years, and then they would eat together, sitting at the enormous butcher's block in the center of the kitchen. When the weather wasn't cold, which was all but a couple of months out of the year, they ate in the adjacent sun-room.

But since Gabriela was in Mexico City, he was alone, thinking of 31 Germaine Muller while the coffee dripped and he cut thick slices of bacon and put them on the grill. While that was simmering, he went down a short hallway to the side porte cochere, braced himself against the anticipated cold, and stepped outside. Holding his breath, he hurried down the curving drive to the front gate where the paperboy tossed the newspapers through the wrought-iron bars. He slipped the plastic bags off the papers as he fast-walked back up the drive, then put the bags into a paper sack by the side entry as he came in. By the time he got back to the kitchen, the bacon was sizzling. He tossed the papers on the butcher's block and quickly grabbed a fork and moved the pieces of bacon around on the grill. He picked up the two eggs he already had gotten out of the refrigerator, broke them into a bowl, beat them rapidly with a whisk, and chopped two green onions into the bowl with them. He cut two thick slices of bread from the loaf on the counter and put them in the toaster, turned the bacon, and poured the eggs into a sauté pan. In a few minutes everything was ready, coming together at once like a piece of chamber music. He put everything on the butcher's block, reached for the newspapers, and sat down to eat and read. In the winter, the warm room and the mingling aromas of coffee and bacon and cooking onions made breakfast his favorite meal of the day.

At twenty to seven he was putting on his overcoat in the entrance hall, pulling the trilby firmly onto his head, pulling on his gloves, and stepping out to the cold, dark morning under the front porte cochere. He started the Jaguar and let it idle a few minutes, and then drove out into the open air, around the last half of the circular drive, pushing the remote control on the front gates and driving out between them to the street. It was a routine that didn't vary by five minutes the year around. And usually it was the last time for the remainder of the day that he could predict with any reasonable knowledge what was going to happen from one minute to the next.

As soon as Haydon stepped through the door of the homicide division, he went straight to Bob Dystal's office without even stopping to get a cup of homicide's notoriously bad coffee, a pot of which was always brewing. Dystal was already there, hunched over paperwork on his desk like an anthropomorphic buffalo in a white Western shirt with plastic mother-of-pearl snaps.

"Morning, Stu," Dystal said, looking up as Haydon walked through the door. He was sipping his own homemade coffee, black as crude oil, from the tin cap of his slightly rusty and dented Thermos, which sat on the corner of his desk. A well-worn chocolate brown suit coat sagged on a wire hanger off the side of the filing cabinet behind him, and above it, near the front edge, a little red plastic radio was softly playing country music, something with a lilting fiddle.

"Got a minute?" Haydon took off his trilby and hung it on a coat stand beside Dystal's door. He stuffed his gloves into his coat pocket and started unbuttoning the coat.

"You bet. Any damn excuse," Dystal groaned, dropping his ballpoint pen on the scattered papers. He straightened up, pulled back his beefy shoulders and twisted them this way and that as if he had been there all night. "I came in an hour early just to do this crap, and it feels like I been here all weekend." He reached out for his Thermos, uncorked it—Dystal was the only man Haydon knew who still owned a Thermos so old that it closed with a cork—and added a quick dollop of crude to the pewter-colored Thermos top that he used as a cup. "What's on your mind?"

"Lena Muller," Haydon said, slipping off his coat and hanging it beside his hat on the rack.

Dystal stopped his cup halfway to his mouth, "Uh-oh."

Haydon told Dystal everything that had happened the day before, the conversation with Germaine Muller and the later telephone conversation with Jim Fossler. As he talked, Dystal's broad, good-humored face clouded over and he stood slowly, holding his cup of coffee, and came around the desk. He stopped at the side of the empty chair beside Haydon, listening, staring out to the squad room, which was beginning to fill with the oncoming day shift. Listening, thinking as Haydon talked, he casually stepped over and closed his office door against the growing clamor outside and then came over and sat down in the chair beside Haydon as Haydon continued. He scooted the chair around a little so he was facing Haydon but still had a good view of the squad room through the plate-glass window. The enormous bulk of his body filled the much-abused wooden office chair, which creaked occasionally as Dystal shifted his weight. His stomach, always hefty, but formerly more firm than it was now, was easing a little more than it used to over his belt buckle, which was made from the rowel of an old Mexican spur backed in silver.

Haydon had known Dystal since they had been in the academy. At the beginning, they had been patrol officers together and, later, had gotten their first break in plainclothes on the same vice-squad special assignment. They had worked the same shift in homicide for years, though not always as partners. One of the first promotion opportunities that Haydon had passed up had gone to Dystal. They were as close as brothers, which meant they knew things about each other that nobody else knew, and they respected each other enough to keep it that way.

When Haydon finished, Dystal sat a moment without saying any-

33

thing, his log-sized legs stretched out in front of him, his 14E cowboy boots, polished but well worn, crossed at the ankles. He twisted his shoulders and neck from side to side again. The bulk and thick muscles that had won him college football glory and garnered a flood of offers from the pros were giving him hell in his late forties. Something masculine and mournful and barely audible was oozing from the radio on the filing cabinet.

"Guatemala," he said finally, shaking his head with a soft snort, still looking out to the squad room. He held the tin cup in the thick fingers of both hands, turning it slowly, idly. "Guate-goddamn-mala." He shifted in his chair, and the leather of his boots creaked. "Ol' Jim-bo tracked 'em down." He was thoughtful. "He doesn't even speak that good of Spanish." He raised his tin cup to his mouth, his eyes still on the squad room, and blew across the surface of the coffee. "Can't believe that son of a bitch Muller paid him for a three-week goose chase like that. Fossler, he would've gone to Bangkok for what Muller was paying him. But he shouldn't have. Man doesn't speak Spanish any better than ol' Jim-bo, he shouldn't go down into that damned country."

Dystal's broad, slick-shaven face showed a concerned irritation. To him, Central America was as alien and exotic as Bhutan, and therefore highly suspect and presumably dangerous. Besides that, he had absolutely no respect for George Muller or George Muller's way of doing things. Raising a thick finger, he scratched a well-trimmed sideburn. Dystal liked a close shave and a clean haircut, and now that he was nearer, Haydon could smell his Mennen's Skin Bracer. Haydon guessed Dystal hadn't changed shaving lotion brands since high school, certainly he hadn't as long as Haydon had known him.

"Shit," Dystal said. "The damn State Department sure can work with some squirrels, and they don't get any squirrelier than Cage, I guess. That's scary, dammit. Jee-sus." Dystal shook his head, thinking. "Fossler didn't believe the kids were trafficking, didn't think it was the police they were worried about?"

"He never referred to the police at all. Which, I suppose, you could figure is consistent with his hunch that it wasn't drugs. And he was definitely a little rattled."

"Not like him."

"No."

"Well, hell. I'd be rattled too, the second I stepped off the plane down there. He's got a right to be rattled. You don't go snooping around in a country that sends a death squad after you when they don't like the way you pick your nose. He found the kid, and that's what he went down there for. Fossler ought to come on home while he can still draw breath."

"I think he feels an obligation to find out a little more about the mess the girl may be involved in."

"Well, I guess I can see that," Dystal said, rolling his head toward Haydon. "What I don't see is why you think you need to help him."

"Come on, Bob, what was I going to do? Tell him I wasn't going to help him? Tell him he was on his own?"

"He's a grown man."

"He's in a bind."

"He shouldn't have jumped off in that kind of business. You cut yourself loose from the organization that goes along with law enforcement, you get out there on your own, you gotta expect to get into a bind."

Haydon didn't say anything.

"That whole Muller thing pisses me off," Dystal added.

Haydon knew that, of course. Dystal had been truly offended by George Muller's efforts to throw his weight around and manipulate the department. Dystal wasn't easily offended, but he found Muller particularly reprehensible.

"He's asking for a favor," Haydon said, referring to Fossler.

"Hell, that's a big favor, down to Guate-goddamn-mala." Dystal quickly held up his hand in concession. "I know, I know. You're doing the right thing." Then he squinted at Haydon. "But I'm not sure you're doing the smart thing. When you going?"

"The flight leaves at five-forty. I'll get there a little after nightfall."

"Department's not going to spring for this, you know. All you got to do to close this case is move the girl's file to the back of the drawer. You don't need a damn affidavit that says she's alive."

Haydon nodded. "I know it. Everything's in order here. I haven't got anything going that's urgent, nothing that can't wait a few days."

Haydon was working now without a partner, which he liked fine enough. After he had gotten back from Mexico City and before he had been assigned another partner to take Mooney's place, he immediately had been picked up for a couple of special assignments that required him to work independently. After that he had spent six months breaking in a rookie who eventually teamed up with someone else, and by then Captain Mercer had preoccupations elsewhere. Time passed, and Haydon simply continued to work alone.

"Okay, then you're looking at two days," Dystal said, pulling himself up out of the chair and walking around to his desk. He sat down, put his tin cup aside, and picked up a computer printout of officers' schedules. He got the ballpoint pen he had been writing with and, frowning, made a notation on the light green lines of the printout. He looked up. "Done. I hope to hell you know what you're doing."

Haydon went to his office cubicle on the far side of the squad room from Dystal's and made a call to his travel agent, who confirmed a seat on Continental's afternoon flight to Guatemala City. He made a few calls canceling appointments he had coming up in the next few days and checked his calendar to make sure he hadn't forgotten something that couldn't be postponed. When he was satisfied that everything was in order, that everything else could wait until he returned, he turned to his filing cabinet and took out his folder on Guatemala. Haydon had learned to be a copious note-taker whenever he worked a case that took him out of the country, which usually meant Latin America. He kept a file for each of these cases, complete with photographs and maps and the names of police agents with whom he had worked and names of informants he had used. Time didn't stand still, of course, and people and their circumstances changed with the passing years, but reestablishing contact with former acquaintances often was the quickest way to be brought up to the moment about the changes in the society in which these people had to function. But Haydon's contacts within the security forces in Latin America were more complex because of their endemic intrigues. There was a lot to take into account.

He flipped through his Guatemalan file, reviewed faces and names—enough for a start—closed the folder, grabbed his overcoat and trilby, and walked out of the homicide division without having spoken to any-one but Dystal.

Chapter 6

E ven though it was almost ten o'clock, the morning was dark with a charcoal gloom and a dirty fog hanging in the chilled air. The photosensitive sensors kept the streetlights on as though it was evening, and all the cars on the streets were using their headlights. It would have been easy to believe that dawn was still a few hours away. Haydon avoided the freeways and headed straight down Main. He had plenty of time, so he didn't fight the traffic, which gave him time to think. He hadn't bothered to make reservations at any of the hotels in Guatemala City, preferring to remain flexible. As it was, he was going empty-handed. Since this wasn't a trip for official inquiry, he left the slim files on Lena Muller back at the office, and he would have to leave his Beretta at home too, which made him more than a little uneasy.

He passed through midtown, past the Vietnamese shops and restaurants and clubs, and then under the Southwest Freeway, where the character of the street quickly changed as the ancient and giant water oaks loomed over the wet streets and formed a vast green canopy over the old wealthy neighborhoods of Broad Acres and Shadow Lawn and Southampton, and the Rice University campus. Just as he reached the Museum of Fine Arts, he turned right onto Bissonnet, into an area popular for its art galleries sprinkled among the fine homes in small streets lush with subtropical vegetation.

Turning into one of these lanes, he immediately pulled into a small gravel drive and stopped in front of the Galerie Deux Femmes, an old two-story home that had been renovated into large, open spaces for a gallery on the bottom floor. The top floor belonged entirely to Nina's architectural firm, which she had founded eleven years before with another woman architect, Margaret Lessing. Haydon & Lessing concentrated solely on residential designs and had decided from the beginning to keep the firm small, handling only one commission at a time in order to devote their full attention to each project. Their decision to concentrate on quality rather than quantity had paid off early on, and now their reputation was such that when they finished one commission there was always another one in line.

Haydon got out of his car and walked up the stone steps of the old house to the long veranda that ran its length. Inside the bright foyer of the first floor, he saw Denise Ronsard, one of the two inquisitive sisters who owned the gallery and the house. He returned her wave and smile, his breath billowing in plumes, and turned toward the stairs halfway down the veranda. In a moment he had rounded the first landing and was at the top of the stairs and walking across to the frosted-glass door that opened into the studio.

Even the ample distribution of skylights in the high ceiling did not allow much illumination from the day's gloomy sky, and the studio was lighted brightly with electricity, which wasn't often the case. Several large rooms opened off a spacious central space, with hardwood floors and white walls throughout. There was a conference room with a large oval cherry table directly across from the entry, and to Haydon's right he could see Margaret working in the model room from which issued the resinous odors of wood shavings and glue.

Margaret was a roan-haired woman with alabaster skin and blue eyes that almost closed when she smiled, which was often. She had a demurring manner that masked a hard-as-nails resolve and a distinctly ribald sense of humor. Just now as she worked over the model of the Careyes house, she had the hem of her long skirt tucked up into the thick leather belt cinched around her small waist, a makeshift style of convenience that resulted in the exposure of a considerable amount of one of her pale legs, while Pavarotti bellowed *"La donna è mobile"* from the speakers they kept in the model room. Bent over the table in a straight-legged stance, Margaret was looking into the model from an angle below grade. Without straightening up, she turned her head and saw him and smiled, not uncomfortable at being caught with her skirt up, her wavy hair floating around her head like a henna nimbus.

Haydon waved—there was no need to speak since Margaret wouldn't be able to hear him over Pavarotti—and turned to his left and went down the short hall to Nina's studio. He stopped at the doorway. Nina was at her drawing board, barefooted, half standing, half sitting on her stool, turned three-quarters away from him. Her hair was pulled back in a chignon, her tortoiseshell glasses planted firmly upon her nose as she concentrated over a drawing, a green drawing pencil clamped in her teeth as she measured some small dimension with a triangular scale.

"Can you hear Luciano all right?" Haydon asked, and Nina started and turned around.

"God," she grinned. "I didn't hear you come in."

"I could have come in shooting and you wouldn't have heard me," Haydon said, stepping in and almost closing the door behind him, muting the Italian tenor enough for them to hear each other without screaming. "Do the sisters Ronsard ever complain?"

"Never," Nina said. She took off her glasses and laid them on the board and put her pencil in the upward-turned crook of the earpieces. She stood. "But then Margaret doesn't usually have it that loud. She's getting frustrated with the model . . . the music goes up." She reached for her cup of coffee on a side table beside the drawing board. "What are you doing?"

"Going to Guatemala."

"Oh," she said, tilting her head to one side and half shrugging. She

39

walked over to a small sofa under the windows that looked out over the street and sat down. "Now?"

"Well, this afternoon. Five-forty. I'm on the way home to pack."

"How long will you be?"

"A couple of days. I don't think more than that."

"I was hoping Bob would make you behave," she tried to joke.

"I'll be home by Thursday. Down-and-back, just like that."

"I don't know. Latin America seems to be something of a time warp for you."

"It's a time warp for everyone," he said. "I think Jim Fossler is finding it a bit of a strain."

Nina nodded. She was sitting forward on the sofa, her legs together, her forearms resting on her knees, holding her coffee. Haydon was holding his hat, hadn't even taken off his coat. He ran his fingers through his dark hair. He needed a haircut, but it would have to wait.

"It's summer down there now," Nina reminded him, looking up. "Don't forget that. You'd be miserable in those wools."

"Yeah, Fossler said it was pretty warm."

"You said the flight was at five-forty. You want me to take you to the airport?"

He shook his head. "You'd just waste a lot of time on the expressway at that hour, and it'll be even worse with this weather. I'll leave the car in the long-term lot. That's easiest." He looked over at the drawing board. "How's it going?"

"Not too bad, now," she said, her voice picking up, glad to get off the subject of his departure. "The Spahns are coming by sometime within the next two weeks to look it over again. That should be about the last review. Then we'll all get to troop down to Mexico for the ground breaking." She stood, turning to the board. "What do you think?"

"I've told you," he said, stepping over near her. "The best one yet."

"Yeah, you know, I like it more all the time. It's a great site, overlooking the Pacific."

Haydon was a little behind her, looking over her shoulder. He tossed his hat on the sofa and stepped up and put both his arms around her from behind, encircling her waist, feeling her hips and then moving down her stomach and lower. He kissed her neck, kissed the slope of it as it came off her shoulders, kissed it where his lips could feel the strands of hair pulled taut in the chignon and felt the wisps of it that had worked free feathering his face. He inhaled the smell of her, kissed the lobe of her ear, feeling her warmth on his face, which was still cool from the chill morning air. He brought his hands up to her breasts as she tilted her head back, and he felt her catch her breath as his cool hand slipped inside her blouse, inside her bra. She turned her face to him, and his free hand unbuttoned her blouse.

Chapter 7

The flight to Guatemala City was forty-five minutes late in departing from the Houston Intercontinental Airport due to the bad weather. They sat on the taxiway in a queue of jetliners, like huge surprised beetles waiting out the gusts of sleet that shouldn't even have been happening. The cabin lights were dimmed, and Haydon sat alone in his row —the plane was less than half full—and stared out to the glistening tarmac and the huge space station-like terminal across a broad swath of frozen grass. Whatever the weather was like in Guatemala City, it couldn't offer a more unpleasant prospect than what Haydon was seeing out of his window at the moment. He was glad to leave this aberrant climate behind.

They were two hours and forty minutes in the air, and during that time Haydon declined the meal, drank several scotch and waters, and thought a lot about Jim Fossler and Lena Muller and Taylor Cage, and the last time he had been in Guatemala. The country didn't have much to recommend it. It was once known as the Land of Eternal Spring, but ever since the 1954 coup, initiated and backed by the CIA to overthrow a democratically elected president who was, nevertheless, too liberal in his thinking for U.S. interests, Guatemala had been wracked by a succession of ruling generals who gained their authority through coups and countercoups and established a tradition of political violence that became so entrenched as a way of life that the country would be forever stained by it. Military rule would prove cruel beyond imagining and would engender the concept of death squads, a phenomenon that would eventually spread to the rest of Latin America and become a trademark of twentieth-century Latin American politics.

Guatemala became and remained one enormous killing field. Death squads operated with impunity, and every day people were "disappeared" off the streets, never to be seen again, at the rate of fifty per month, while "extrajudicial killings"—that is, civilian assassinations—occurred at an average rate of fourteen per day for the last two decades. Regardless of who resided in the presidential residence, the army ruled. It was the most modern, best supplied, and most ruthless army in Latin America and, the modern world being what it was, it had plenty of help from foreign countries, all willing to sell their war matériel to an army that had no enemies but its own people. The generals were busy executioners who preferred to use a new blade every time they lopped off a head. And they wanted the latest in blade refinements, too, the ones with the brightest most technologically advanced edges. So the blade salesmen came from all over the world offering their wares, from the United States first, followed closely by the Israelis and the Germans, the South Africans, Italians, and Taiwanese. The executioner was busy, the blade salesmen were busy. There was a good living to be made in the killing business in Guatemala.

It had been in the killing business that Haydon had his first encounter with Taylor Cage. Late one August in the early 1980s, Haydon had caught three homicides in rapid succession, all in the vicinity of the

43

Houston ship channel. The investigations had been difficult for reasons that were only made clear when Haydon received a telephone call at home one night from Captain Mercer, head of the homicide division. He wanted to come to Haydon's home and bring "a gentleman" who could shed some light on the ship channel killings. It was the only time Mercer had been to his house, before or since. The man he brought with him introduced himself as being with the State Department and said he had information about each of the three cases Haydon was investigating. The stories took a long time to tell, but in essence, the reason Haydon had not been able to advance his investigations more quickly was because he was running into "American intelligence backstopping." Even so, he was pushing the cases to the limit of the cover division's files, and they had realized he was going to have to be brought into the operation to prevent him from damaging what was left of it.

The three killings were related to an elaborate scheme that, not surprisingly, had gone sour because of every operation's weakest link, the human factor. Human behavior is never as predictable, or controllable, as the human mind would like it to be, and the environment of covert operations was no exception. The story that unfolded involved the sale of Israeli military intelligence computer technology to the government of South Africa. For reasons that Haydon never understood, the hardware itself was being shipped from Tel Aviv, but the negotiations regarding the payment procedures were being conducted in Houston and involved the transmission of one commodity for another—cocaine was washing South African Krugerrands and Israeli shekels and Panamanian dollars in a complex laundering scheme that was meant to obscure the transaction and its terms beyond tracing. But it fell apart because of homosexual passions and universal greed, and Taylor Cage was brought in from some dark corner of the globe as a salvage expert. Haydon spent every second of seventy-two hours with him and found him to be a civilized human being by only the broadest of definitions. He was a habitual liar with the sexual appetite of a satyr; he was self-centered, incapable of empathy, without conscience, full of arrogance, devoid of malice, as calculating as a chess master, undeniably charming, and as possessing of true bravery as any man Haydon had ever met.

Their brief association had made an indelible impression on Haydon, and Taylor Cage entered Haydon's personal archive of fascinating, if often notorious, characters of acquaintance. It was only because Haydon knew so much that he was being co-opted at all. They let him play spy

44

for three days, humored him, and when it was over they made it clear to him that it would be best for them—and him—if he developed selective amnesia. He was magically provided with all the documentation he needed to properly close the three homicide cases. No one ever told him, of course, but he had always supposed that Cage was a CIA "outside officer," an officer in a foreign country who was located outside the embassy, who did not operate within traditional channels.

Considering this, Haydon had mixed emotions about meeting Cage again and was more than a little apprehensive at having learned that Cage seemed to have been in a position to lead Fossler right to Lena's door. If that was coincidence, it was certainly an extraordinary instance of it.

The plane touched down at the Aurora International Airport in Guatemala City at nine-fifteen, well after dark. As the plane's reversed engines roared in his ears and the airliner lurched and shuddered down to a bumpy taxiing speed toward the terminal, Haydon looked out his porthole at the miscellany of military and private hangars and aircraft and their attendant maintenance pools that shared the airport with the commercial airliners. Everything was dimly lighted, a trademark of Guatemalan nights, and Haydon could see the familiar and ubiquitous figures of armed soldiers lounging in the shadows, their Galils hanging over their shoulders as casually as the purses of prostitutes. It had been a couple of years since he had last been here, but just this first sight of the soldiers was enough to remind him of the sense of menace that was the chief characteristic of the Guatemalan Zeitgeist.

When the aircraft finally pulled into its slip and the engines were cut and its wheels blocked in place, there was no buzz of conversation, no scurrying to unload the overhead compartments, no jostling for position in the aisles. The scarcity of passengers and their disinterest in deplaning was indicative of the attitude of most people arriving in Guatemala. On the other hand, Haydon knew that all departing flights were always packed and hectic and lively. It was a country people much preferred to leave.

Haydon took his soft leather weekender bag from the overhead compartment and walked down the empty aisle to the door, past the smiling stewardesses—they were paid to smile and would be leaving the next morning anyway—and out into the sloping enclosed ramp that led to the terminal. He followed the few people in front of him down several turns of the long corridors until they came to a small desk in an alcove where

45

they obtained temporary visas and paid an entry fee. Having done that, he walked to the customs booths a short distance away where his passport and visa were stamped before he was allowed to go on into the bottom floor of the terminal where all passengers retrieved their luggage in one cavernous reception area that resembled nothing so much as a circus without a ringmaster.

This effect was enhanced by the curious fact that all arrivals were observed by an enthusiastic crowd who viewed the entire process from a balcony, or veranda, on the second floor above. This mezzanine was on the same floor as the gates to the departing planes, duty-free shops, shops selling native handicrafts and woven textiles, a post office, telephone and telegraph offices, a bank, a drugstore, and slot machines. Even with all these diversions, the main form of amusement for departing passengers awaiting their flights with friends and relatives, and for the people who had come to welcome new arrivals, was to lean on the balcony rails and watch the incoming passengers file into the baggage claim arena and wait for their luggage to be off-loaded. And then when they got their bags, there was the pleasure of watching them open their suitcases on long inspection tables for the customs officers and everyone else who was curious about what they were bringing in. While all this was happening, there were shouts back and forth from the balcony to the bottom floor as friends and families spotted each other or tried to get each other's attention.

It was a congenial chaos, a noisy, cacophonous scene, and one which disguised another, more sinister side. The balcony and the crowds that gathered there provided a perfect cover for the intelligence agents of the security forces who closely monitored, and often photographed and followed, new arrivals who were of special interest to them. It was easy to do. In 1983 when the Israelis installed the Aurora airport's radar system, they simultaneously "advised" the Guatemalan security forces in the use of computerized intelligence management systems. The Guatemalans had proved to be quick studies.

Haydon went straight to the customs-check tables, and while the agent was going through his bag, he turned and scanned the scattering of people standing behind the railings of the balcony on the second floor. A few were waving and smiling at the passengers getting their bags, some leaning over and shouting a word or two, their voices echoing off the tile and marble floors, some simply staring down, bored. But Haydon did not see Fossler, nor did he see anyone else who seemed to take any interest in him.

The customs officer zipped his bag shut and sent him on with a nod and a sideward jerk of his head. Grabbing the bag, Haydon walked out through one set of swinging doors, out into the long porte cochere where porters and taxi drivers were gathered in idle knots, gossiping and smoking away the slow evening. Immediately the warm, diesel-heavy air of urban Central America reset his psychic barometer. Everything he had ever learned or experienced about this beautiful and brutal country came back to him as if the years between had never existed. It was not an altogether comfortable feeling. Again Haydon scanned the faces, the isolated figure, for Fossler. Still he didn't see him. Thinking Fossler might be double-parked in the shadows just outside the lighted drive, Haydon walked to one end and then to the other and peered out into the darkness. No Fossler.

Knowing that in Guatemala nothing ever happened when it was supposed to, that schedules were considered to be only suggestions, not literal commitments, Haydon walked over to a concrete ledge near one of the car rental agencies and sat down, waving off overtures from cabdrivers. He would wait half an hour; he didn't want this to turn into a Laurel and Hardy routine of missed connections. But the half hour dragged by without Fossler's appearance, and Haydon signaled one of the taxis and headed into the city.

Chapter 8

The night was hot and the taxi windows were wide open as the driver clipped along the isolated airport boulevard lined with spindly, newly planted palms. Guatemala City's distinctive night air was already thick with the familiar smoky stench that settled over the urban landscape after the daytime breezes died down. Nearly encircled by mountains, the city sat on a shallow plateau that was severely eroded on all sides by deep ravines. As the army's thirty-year counterinsurgency war continued in vast areas of the countryside, preying on the rural population and disrupting an already backward economy, and as poverty became as perilous as the unchecked violence, the peasants fled to the capital city in the mistaken hope that life there would offer some refuge from fear and hunger. It didn't.

The city's population swelled to over two million, overwhelming municipal services and turning many of the *barrancas,* ravines, that surrounded the city into disease-ridden slums. Hundreds of thousands of squatters' shanties sprang up along their rims and spilled down their steep slopes together with the tons of garbage that the city dumped there and with what the slum dwellers themselves created. The poor scavenged along with the vultures for garbage to eat. In the rainy season, floods roared down the ravines and wiped out swaths of shanties, which were painfully rebuilt with a tenacity that only the despairing understand. In the dry season, the only moisture in the *barrancas* was runnels of raw sewage that drained down from the overcrowded city above. But regardless of the time of year, every evening the miasma from the perpetually smoldering dumps and shanty fires seeped up over the rims of the ravines and settled across the city like a bad dream. Wet or dry, every night the great populace of the dispossessed sent up a veil of bitter incense to cover the city, a constant reminder of misery's children.

Haydon always had seen a kind of egalitarian irony in the pervasive stench of these smoldering nights that discomfited the wealthy as well as the poor. Behind Guatemala's dismal record of human suffering was a small and very wealthy minority that controlled the fortunes of the country through an unflinching exploitation of the poor. Though these wealthy few might build their lavish homes in guarded enclaves and envelop themselves in the trappings of abundance in an effort to put the privations of the filthy masses out of their sight, and even though they might turn a blind eye to the ugliness of the poor who surrounded them in an effort to put their suffering out of mind, they would never, ever, succeed in getting them out of their nostrils. The offensive odors of misfortune did not defer to the priviledged.

They passed under the arches of the ancient stone aqueducts that still ran parallel to Bulevar Liberación and turned right, following the boulevard past the circle of the Clock of Flowers, past the Monument to the Indian, to the huge oval of Parque Independencia with its tall stone Obelisk commemorating Guatemala's independence from Spain. The taxi driver swung his car halfway around the circle and then shot off northward on Avenida La Reforma, one of the broadest and most attrac-

49

tive avenues in Central America, with towering cypresses that shaded both sides of the avenue. To Haydon's right was Zona 10 where the several-block area between 13 and 16 calles was known as Zona Viva, a sector of elegant shopping and dining and expensive hotels. They passed the ever-popular Camino Real hotel where Americans stayed who didn't want to leave the U.S. behind when they crossed the border, and a few blocks farther down was the American embassy. This section of the city was as good as the city got, and even then there wasn't much of it.

Looking through the dirty windshield of the taxi at the avenue, whose reputation for elegance outstripped its reality, Haydon felt the first twinges of eeriness that was the city's gift to any arriving traveler who knew anything about the country's history. The low-powered streetlamps gave a macabre glow to the smoke that hung among the towering cypresses of the boulevard like an infernal breath. Haydon could not avoid thinking of what the smog consisted of, for he had seen more than a few bodies dumped in the garbage of the ravines, most of them mutilated and swollen like sausages from the tropical heat. And often they smoldered like everything else in the dumps, adding their oily effluvia to the filthy air for the rest of the city to breathe. Here death was literally in the air, and everyone could taste it.

It was no surprise to Haydon that the taxi driver sped right through the city's nicest sectors on his way to the address of Fossler's hotel. Even with the exchange rate in his favor, Fossler was going third-class, which in Latin America could make for pretty bare accommodations. Posada Cofino was in Zona 1, the heart of the old central city where the streets were tight and narrow and poorly lighted, some of them only a block or two long. They were five or six blocks from the Plaza Mayor, where the National Palace and the Metropolitan Cathedral dominated the north and east boundaries respectively, when the driver pulled into a short street with a cobblestone surface and crept past six doorways before he found the *posada,* identifiable only by its name on a ceramic plaque set into the stone wall beside a grated stairwell. One weak light bulb burned inside the gate at the foot of the stairs.

Haydon got out and paid the driver, who put his car in reverse and backed out of the narrow street with his tires thrumming on the cobblestones and his motor whining all the way to the intersection of the avenida where they had turned in. Haydon stood on the sidewalk a moment and looked in either direction of the small dead-end street that was little more than a long courtyard. There was a stationer's across from him, a drugstore on the corner where they had come in, and a barbershop across from that, just down the sidewalk from Haydon. The rest of the doorways had no identifications that he could see, probably private residences or rooming houses or small business offices.

He turned to the gate in the wall behind him, expecting to find a button to press or a speaker box, but there was nothing. Nor was the gate locked. He pushed it open and saw that beside the stairwell there was a narrow passageway that led back to a courtyard. He was looking for room number 4, but no sign gave him a clue as to whether it could be found back in the courtyard, from which issued the vague, tinny transmission of a radio. Hoping to avoid having to climb the stairs, he walked down the short corridor that smelled of dank stone to the small courtyard that opened to his left, its center filled with plantains and a few scrubby palms that had grown high enough to obscure most of the opposite side. The sound of the radio was clearer here, coming from across palms. There was one door on each side of the enclosure. He stepped to the door closest to him, in the wall to his right, and saw a number 1 on the stone lintel. He turned back to the door on the other side of the passageway where he had entered and looked above the door. It was number 4.

Before knocking, he surveyed the courtyard once again. Mixed with the odor of musty stone was that of grilled onions and peppers and corn tortillas. Beside each door that opened onto the courtyard was a single window, and though numbers 1 and 4 were dark, 3 and 2, partially hidden by the vegetation, were lighted. Haydon eased along the wall a little way near number 3, and though the window was open to the night heat, he heard no sounds coming from the inside. Across the way, however, the radio voice, now identifiable as that of an evangelical minister, was coming from the other open and lighted window, and Haydon could hear, too, the clinking of dishes and someone coughing.

He went back around to Fossler's door, but the silence of the small courtyard made him hesitate to knock. If Fossler wasn't in, he didn't want to draw attention to his own presence. Fossler's room was dark, and Haydon doubted he was there. He reached down and tried the doorknob. It turned, and there was a soft click, a sound that made Haydon sweat. If Fossler had left, he would have locked the door. Haydon remembered Fossler saying that Lena and Baine knew where he was staying, and he remembered, too, that Fossler said he had moved several times. It seemed incredible to Haydon at this moment that he hadn't asked Fossler why he had done that.

He was holding the door knob, keeping the tension against the spring to keep it from clicking again as it moved back in place. He desperately missed his Beretta. Slowly rotating his wrist, he eased back the tension on the knob until the handle was in place. He stepped back against the wall and carefully, with outstretched arm pushed the door open into the room, while behind him, through the plantains, a chorus of tinny evangelical voices sang "Know, My Soul, Thy Full Salvation."

"Fossler," he said, not loud, but loud enough. "Fossler."

As the door drifted open, Haydon saw in the glow of a powder-blue light that came from another window that fronted the street that the room was exactly that, one room. He stepped across the doorway and looked into the room from the opposite angle. The door was open all the way, flat against the inside wall so that no one could have been hiding behind it. Haydon stepped into the doorway and surveyed the room as best he could in the half-light, the foot of the single bed facing him and above it the window, to the right a partition that was supposed to hide a toilet and shower, and then to the right of that a table and two chairs and a closet without a door. Something was hanging in the closet. Haydon picked up his bag and stepped inside and closed the door. He put one knee on the unmade bed and reached up over the headboard and pulled closed the simple curtain. The window that looked out onto the courtyard was closed. The room was hot and smelled of mildew. Haydon moved cautiously to the table, sliding his feet on the floor to avoid tripping, and flipped on the light.

The bulb must have been forty watts or less, but the jaundiced glow was bright enough to freeze Haydon to the spot. The room had been trashed. The bed covers were shoved up to the head of the bed in a dingy wad, one chair was turned over and the table askew. The shower curtain was ripped from most of its hooks, and for some reason the toilet tissue had been pulled from its roll and was strewn about the room in coiled, wormy strands that ended up in a pile at Haydon's feet. Even in the bad light he could clearly distinguish the deep rubiginous stains soaked into the soiled gob of paper. Instinctively his eyes went straight to the sink, the filthy, chipped enamel draped with slobbers of bloodied water, and above it, the mirror tracked with blood spatters that climbed right up the wall. He wheeled around to the closet where a shirt was half torn from a hanger, and on the window curtains beside the closet was a bloody smear, an imprint of grasping fingers. Haydon swallowed. Blood was everywhere, splashed, dribbled, spattered, smeared, cast off, and flung, but—

Haydon grasped at a thin reason to hope—none pooled. All of this had been shed in some kind of wild frenzy, but whoever had lost it had not stayed here long enough to make a puddle.

Suddenly Haydon heard the doorknob behind him click, and he spun around to watch the wooden door drift gracefully open just as slowly as it had drifted open for him. But the doorway was empty, and then a cat shot out of the passageway and into the plantains, and Taylor Cage stepped into the yellow haze, stuffing a huge handgun into the waistband of his trousers.

Chapter 9

"Hello, Haydon," Cage said. He hesitated a moment, almost as if he were giving Haydon the time to look him over, size him up, gather his nerves. He was about Haydon's height, but much more bulky, his familiar barrel chest now accompanied by some additional poundage, though he still carried himself in a solid, surefooted manner that indicated he was action-ready. His fair-to-pinkish skin was weather cured with a recent sunburn that was almost finished peeling on the humped bridge of his straight nose, his glaucous eyes were unchanged. He was wearing his kinky gray hair a little shorter now, but it was just as thick as it had been a decade earlier.

Keeping his eyes on Haydon, he came through the door and stopped just inside and pulled a pack of cigarettes from the chest pocket of his guayabera, which he wore with the tail out as was the fashion, and lighted one without offering any to Haydon.

"You knew I was here, didn't you?" he said, blowing the smoke away from them. He was perspiring, his forehead loaded with beads and a rivulet at his right temple.

" 'Here' outside, or 'here' in Guatemala?"

Cage looked at Haydon. "Christ, you haven't changed any, have you. Okay, let's see, let's try 'here' in Guatemala first."

"Yes."

"The street?"

"Of course not."

Cage turned slightly so that his back wasn't to the doorway but against the wall. He looked outside into the courtyard and then turned back. The handgun stuck in his waistband was clearly visible through the thin material of the guayabera.

"I don't know where your friend is," he said.

"Do you know what happened?" Haydon was having a hard time controlling the adrenaline. He didn't even want to think about what might have gone on here.

"No."

"You were here earlier?"

Cage pulled on his cigarette and nodded. Haydon had noticed that he was smoking a Guatemalan brand. Cage was a firm believer of when-in-Rome, even when Rome had pretty nasty cigarettes.

"I was here about half an hour ago." He looked around. "Shocked the shit out of me." He wiped a thick hand across his forehead, smeared the sweat, and wiped his hand on the tail of the guayabera.

"How did you know I was here?"

"When I got here, saw all this, I backed out, went down the street and made some telephone calls. On my way back, I heard a car coming down the street and ducked into a doorway." He nodded toward the other side of the street. "Saw you get out of the cab and go in the passageway here. When I saw the light come on I walked across."

"Why didn't you make your calls from here?"

"I wanted them to be private."

"His telephone was tapped, even here?"

Cage sighed. "This is a long story, Haydon. We need to get out of here. Come on. I've got a car around the corner."

Haydon was reluctant to leave. "You went through the place?"

"Sure. There's nothing. Cleaned out." If he wasn't lying, if he really had gone through the place, then Haydon could believe there was nothing to turn up. Cage knew how to go over a scene.

Cage turned and Haydon picked up his bag and followed him. At the door he stopped, turned around for one last look at the room, snapped off the light, and closed the door behind him. They returned down the dim passageway to the wrought-iron gate, the closing of which echoed out across the cobblestones and off the stucco walls on either side of the narrow street. The night was a little cooler here, away from the stuffy confines of Fossler's cramped compartment.

As they walked side by side along the gritty sidewalk, Haydon next to the buildings, Cage on the street side, their footsteps were the only sounds on the deserted street. Cage seemed preoccupied, and Haydon tried to remember back ten years whether this was his manner or if present circumstances were affecting him. He couldn't recall, one way or the other. Nor could he shake off the feeling that by walking away from Fossler's room he was walking away from Fossler, turning his back on him as surely as if he had turned on his heel and walked away from his friend's bleeding body. Haydon felt like he was leaving something behind in the stink of Fossler's ghastly little cell.

At the corner of the avenida, Cage hesitated but didn't stop, barreling on across the intersection, following the street down a slight decline toward the Plaza Mayor. They passed some storefronts and then ducked into a tiny drive that led to a dark walled courtyard where a few cars were parked along the walls and *ranchera* music came from a radio inside a lighted doorway. Cage went to one of the cars, a large-sized Japanese model, and unlocked it. Haydon threw his bag into the backseat as Cage started the car, and they eased out of the courtyard, into the narrow passage, and then out into the street, the tires thrumming on the cobblestones as Cage picked up speed.

"I get a different one of these about every ninety days," Cage said, shifting the car. "Mexican used-car dealer out on the Mixco highway. I trade them in, he gives me a decent deal, a little profit for himself—plus a little to keep his mouth shut—and I have a new car every few months. Makes it harder for them to keep up with me."

"Where are we going?" Haydon asked, thinking of the shirt half torn from the hanger in Fossler's closet. He thought of the bloody slobbers on the dirty enamel basin, the gore-soaked toilet tissue strewn crazily around the room. They were still in the tight streets of the old central city, but now there was traffic, a few people on the sidewalks, the traffic lights were working, a few sparsely populated cafés were open to the night.

"I'm hungry," Cage said. "We'll get something to eat, where we can talk."

They were on one of the calles crossing the avenidas heading east, the streets getting busier, and then Cage turned onto 6a avenida, and the narrow street was awash with neon signs that hung out over the street, advertisements for Jordache jeans, Panasonic stereos, Chinese restaurants, Wrangler jeans, Sony radios, Pepsi, shoe stores, beauty shops, Toshiba, Fuji, 7-Up —the first world, one street of it anyway—and then Cage turned again, and the commercial volume was reduced by half and then with each block it was reduced by half again until they turned for the last time. They were on 9a avenida, a gloomy street with a slower pace, dimmer lights, fewer people, and more shadows.

Martin Fierro's was an Argentine steak house with a front entry that opened off the corner of the building at 9a avenida and calle 15, its windows right on the sidewalk, thrown open to the night. It had a low-timbered ceiling shrouded in a haze of smoke from the cook fires, and simple wooden chairs and tables with oilcloth covers. It was in Zona 1, in the kind of location that Cage made it his business to know intimately in all the cities of Latin America. It wasn't the sort of place you went to accidentally.

Though the place was busy, they were able to grab a table from three men who were standing up to go. It was next to a window just inside the double front doors, but behind a railing that gave it some privacy. They sat down among the dirty dishes, and Haydon slipped his bag under the table, between the wall and his leg. Cage had said he ought to bring it; you should never leave anything in your car. The dishes were immediately cleared away by a young Indian girl with beautifully plaited hair who wore a traditional *corte* skirt and a *Die Harder* T-shirt through which her small breasts made little protrusions on either side of Bruce Willis' posturing heroics. When she had gone, the waiter came and they ordered Gallos, Guatemala's most popular beer. Cage also ordered *chur-rasco,* thin fillets of grilled beef. Haydon passed. The beer appeared immediately, its gold label sporting the bright red rooster trademark.

The table was snug up to the window, which opened right onto the sidewalk and street. Haydon rested his elbow on the windowsill and surveyed the sidewalks where prostitutes sauntered up and down, in and out of the pools of feeble light that fell from the old cast-iron streetlamps. Haydon's stomach was a mess of knots, but he was determined to let Cage do his lead-in. He tried to calm himself. He had to.

Cage upended his Gallo and drank nearly half the bottle before lowering it.

"What's going on here?" Haydon said.

Cage was still swallowing his last mouthful. He nodded. "Okay," he said. "How bad do you want to know what's going on here?"

"As of the minute I walked into Fossler's room," Haydon said, "everything changed. Before that I could have turned around and gone back home on the next flight without any problem. Now it would be a problem."

"Well, it'll be a problem if you stay too," Cage said. "It's one of those kind of things where if you get in, you get in up to your nostrils."

"I can't very well go home and tell Fossler's wife what I walked away from."

"Hell, don't tell her. You could report it to the consular office at the embassy and leave with a clean conscience."

"You could do that," Haydon said. Suddenly he was angry instead of numb. Logic, every impulse of common sense in him said he ought to go to the embassy and spill everything. He knew how important it was to move quickly after a homicide. Christ, was he making that assumption so easily? On the other hand, his gut was telling him something else. He had better listen to Cage first. He had better hear him out before his common sense got him into trouble in a country where there was a distinct lack of common sense and where the games were played according to a dynamic that he only faintly understood. As much as he disliked it, he was going to have to listen to Cage—for a while at least.

"I'm not going to let it go," Haydon said.

Cage shrugged. The perspiration was glistening on his forehead again as he reached into his pocket for his cigarettes. He lighted one and laid the pack and a red plastic Bic lighter on the table. The cigarette smoke hovered in the air, commingled with the haze of the cook fires, and then slowly drifted out the window into the darkness where it became part of the night breath, becoming one with the stench from the smoldering dumps and the shanty fires. Cage looked at Haydon.

"I've changed jobs," he said. "Not with the State Department, no perks, no advancement scale, no insurance policy, no hospitalization, no retirement program. I'm cut loose."

"When did that happen?"

"Almost two years ago."

"Your choice?"

"Absolutely. Got the idea from the Israelis, all those 'formers' who used to be with Mossad, Shin Bet, Aman. Shit, they were stationed all over the goddamn world. When the time comes, when they get fed up, they quit. Then they go back to where they were stationed and use their contacts to make fortunes in the arms trade. Big fortunes. Our guys do it too, but the Israelis are better at it."

He used the thumb of the hand holding the cigarette to squeegee the perspiration from across his forehead. A sip of the Gallo, a drag on the cigarette.

"But I'm not crazy to get myself blown away." Cage shook his head. "No, I stay clear of the arms trade. I stay clear of drugs. They go hand in hand and the money's . . . gigantic. But I can count a dozen men, big men, who should have been smart enough to quit when they could, smart enough to *be* smart, who aren't around any longer to spend their money. No, I'm looking at longevity. I watched those Israeli assholes, Mike Harari with old Noriega down in Panama, Pesakh Ben Or here in Guatemala, David Katz in Mexico, Sa'ada in Honduras. Where are they now? Well, shit, we don't know, do we, but there are rumors, and I don't like what I hear."

Cage looked out the window, thinking, maybe wondering if he ought to be saying what he was saying. Whatever he was going to come out with, Haydon could be sure it was calculated. Though Cage appeared to be an impulsive man, it was a credit to how well he could think on his feet that, even so, he never acted recklessly. If it wasn't to Cage's advantage to tell him, Haydon wouldn't hear it. Related to this, and of equal risk, was the probability that Cage could very easily be setting him up. If Cage didn't have something to gain by Haydon's presence, he never would have shown himself back at Fossler's room.

Cage held up an index finger as if to make and hold a point. "I more or less sell information," he said. "Marketing my skills, as it were. I've

59

been in Latin America my entire career, most of it in Central America. United States intelligence has piss-poor connections, I mean in human intelligence. Electronics, satellites, that's something else. But you can't do much good with just that, not in preemptive situations. You've got to have people on the ground. This is where the U.S. is screwed. The DEA, the CIA, they rely 95–98 percent on paid informants in the G-2, the Guatemalan military intelligence. Which is up to its ass in the drug trade, in death-squad operations, in the arms trade, in coup plots, you name it. And here we are paying some of them to please let us know about all this shit, please. The U.S. intelligence community is so completely locked out they've got to rely on crumbs from the G-2 officers who are simply lying to us and laughing at us while they take our money. Or they've got me.

"As for getting help from the army, shit, these generals, they take our 'foreign aid,' which is only State Department bribery, and then instead of the expected diplomatic reciprocation, which the generals in Honduras and El Salvador at least *pretend* to extend, these bastards just laugh in our faces and tell us to go screw ourselves. The U.S. hasn't accomplished anything here with its 'foreign aid.' I've never seen anything like it. We've got this thing about 'democracy' . . ." Cage stopped and shook his head. "Hell."

He smoked his cigarette a moment as if he were trying to calm himself. An Indian kid carrying a greasy-looking wooden tray with tiny bins from which he was selling colored plastic combs and colored plastic Bic lighters and colored plastic watchbands stopped at their window and looked at Cage. He said nothing. You saw what he had, either you wanted something or you didn't. Cage reached into his pocket and pulled out some quetzals and bought another red plastic Bic lighter and laid it on the table beside the one he already had, and the kid moved on.

60   "I sell information now," Cage said, picking up his story, "to the highest bidder. Not always to the U.S. This is a very dicey thing, but it pays like you wouldn't believe. I've got informants all over this crumby country . . . some at very significant levels. I've already put more money in a Swiss account than I could've put there in five lifetimes working for the government and saving every dime they paid me." He paused, his eyes on Haydon. "The point is, I'm independent here. That has ramifications for you. One: what few rules I used to abide by work-ing for State don't apply to me anymore. Two: there's certain shit I don't want to get mixed up in because it could threaten my business, and I have no intention of putting that in jeopardy. And three: I'm going to do

you a favor and then you're on your own and I don't want to see you the hell again. And keep this in mind: as good as you are, Haydon, and I credit you that, I hope you realize you're way out on the end of a rope here, and if you don't watch your ass you'll end up in the garbage of one of these ravines with your throat cut and your balls in your mouth."

Cage pulled down the sides of his mouth and gave Haydon a deadpan expression.

"What's the favor?" Haydon asked.

Cage shook his head and looked at Haydon as if he was a fool. And Haydon felt like one. He didn't like it, and it scared him, but there was no way he couldn't look into this. It was just bizarre to consider it. If something in fact had happened to Fossler, then, realistically, there probably wasn't much he could do about it except report him to the embassy as missing. But even then, he at least had to get in touch with Lena Muller.

"Information. I'll give you what I can."

"And what do you want from me?"

"We'll get to that," Cage said, putting out his cigarette.

"I need to talk to Lena Muller."

Cage took a drink of his Gallo. "You're a little late, my friend. She disappeared three days ago."

Chapter 10

T he *churrasco* came, with melodramatic timing, just as Cage uttered his
bombshell. While he waded into his grilled meat, liberally doused
with spoons of spicy *chirmol*, Cage filled Haydon in on what had happened since Jim Fossler had talked to Lena Muller on Friday. After
returning to Janet Pittner's, Lena had packed a small bag and told Janet
that she was taking an overnight trip to Panajachel, a small town on the
northern shore of Lake Atitlán, a popular vacation and tourist spot, with

John Baine. She said she would be back Saturday night. When she hadn't returned by Sunday afternoon, Janet Pittner called the hotel in Panajachel where Lena had said they would be staying, and the concierge told her that no one by that name had ever checked in. This precipitated a series of frantic telephone calls by Janet Pittner to other hotels in the resort area and then to everyone she could think of who might know where Lena was. No luck. Monday morning, this morning, she called Cage. All day Cage ran his own traps, also without luck, and then a few hours earlier, going through Lena's room, Cage found a scrap of paper with Fossler's address at the Posada Cofino. He went there, found the bloody room, and then Haydon arrived.

Cage finished his *churrasco* and pushed away his plate, and they ordered another beer each. Haydon couldn't believe what he had walked into. If this wasn't satisfactorily resolved the results would reverberate way beyond the infighting of Guatemalan politics. Three American citizens disappeared within thirty-six hours. If they turned up dead, Guatemala was going to find itself in a firestorm of American media hype. One of the reasons why the Guatemalan army and the right-wing death squads had gotten away with their massacres and assassinations as long as they had was because Guatemala itself had always avoided major international attention. But a rash of deaths of U.S. citizens could change all that.

"Fossler told me he thought Lena was in some kind of trouble, that Baine was involved too," Haydon said as Cage lighted another cigarette. "What about that?"

Cage nodded. "Yeah, I got some of that from Janet. She had noticed something was going on too, Lena acting spooky, secretive, all that. Janet didn't know what the hell was going on, didn't even attach much significance to it until Lena disappeared. Then, of course . . ." he shrugged.

"But she didn't know anything?"

Cage shook his head.

"What about Baine?"

"Baine. There's a little shit for you. Free-lance journalist. Been in Central America five or six years. 'Investigative' journalist, you know. Always wanting to 'expose' some terrible something, traipsing around Central America with a camera and tape recorder. Occasionally he'd come up with something for the wire services or hire out as a guide-in-the-know to salaried journalists with the big papers. These people usually are based in places with higher political profiles—El Salvador, Nicaragua, Panama—and pop in and out of Guatemala when the grapevine hints that something hot is stirring. Baine's a quick contact for them because he stays here and hears things and can bring them up to speed. But he never gets the 'big' story."

Cage wasn't impressed. No one in Cage's business would be. Men like Baine were their natural enemies.

"Do you know what he'd been working on? Did he have any particular interests? Military? Political squabbles? Anyone he wanted to do a job on?"

"All of the above. The guy was a scattershot, just ran around with his head in his butt looking for trouble."

Cage was holding out. Haydon realized they had been talking about Baine in the past tense. He looked at Cage.

"The kid was insignificant," Cage said. "If he had caught on fire . . . et cetera, et cetera."

"Did Lena have a job here?"

She worked with USAID, up in the highlands, Huehuetenango. She spent about half the time up there, the same area where she was stationed in the Peace Corps. She gathered crop production data for an agricultural program."

"How well did you know her?"

"Pretty well, and not too well," Cage said and looked out the window as if uninterested in the question. Haydon looked out too, in the opposite direction, and watched a man in a suit approach from down the block, saw him pass through the soft play of light from a streetlamp and, just at the edge of it, slow and stop. He was speaking to someone, just the flat of his back in the light. He moved a little more into the dark until Haydon wasn't sure if he was still there or not. Then slowly, as if they were engaged in a graceful sarabande, she came into the light, changing positions with him as though in a tandem turn of dance. She was smiling, tilting her head this way and that in beguiling conversation. But it wasn't to be. Haydon saw only the arm of the man's suit go briefly into the light with her, and then she turned and walked away in the opposite direction, looking back once at him in case he changed his mind. But the man had disappeared into the dark.

"I met Lena a couple of years ago," Cage said, turning back to Haydon. "Janet Pittner is one of those kinds of women who collect people. She knows everybody in the American community here. You come down here for a visit, Janet's going to know someone in your line of work, or she's going to know someone who has a compatible interest, or who knows just the sort of thing you're interested in, or who knows someone you know or used to know or want to know. She's divorced from an embassy man. She's lived in Guatemala most of her life. Twenty years ago her father was the director in charge of a large American coffee consortium whose fincas were located on the lower ranges of the Sierra Madre, on the Pacific slopes south of Guatemala City. He built a house in Zona 10, and as the years passed a lot of embassies built in the neighborhood, making the area a ritzy location. When he retired and went back to the States, Janet got the house.

"That's Janet. I don't remember exactly how she got to know Lena, but it was on one of those leaves the Peace Corps kids get from time to time. It was at an embassy party, I think. Anyway, Janet kind of adopted her. One time when I was going up in the highlands, up in the Cuchumatanes, Janet asked me to take some coffee to Lena who was with her Indians up there, the Chuj. So I did, found her up there in Huehuetenango, shit, thirty-six hundred kilometers up in the mountains in this remote little village called Ocante, up in the thinning pine and spruce forests where the mornings are frosty and foggy. Big vistas. She was a good-looking kid, brown as a berry from that clear, high-mountain sun. There were all these colorful Indian women in their bright *huipiles* and *cortes* and here was Lena wearing these damn filthy khakis. But . . ."— Cage was looking across the smoky room, not seeing, just remembering —". . . she had her long blond hair plaited in the Indian style, with an absolutely brilliant scarlet *cinta* interwoven in her braids."

Cage shrugged, but not before Haydon detected something more than a simple descriptive interest in his story.

"Anyway," he went on. "I stayed overnight because it was a full day's trip back down to the next *aldea* of any size. She turned out to be different than I expected. Entirely unselfconscious. She wasn't coy, didn't give a shit about her filthy khakis or stubby fingernails or having to piss behind a bush. And the Indians respected her, especially the women, who treated her with affection. I've visited these kids before, or other Americans out in the boonies, archaeologists, isolated missionaries, whatever, who after a few months would rather be *any*where else on the damn globe than where they were. Not her. The whole time I was there she

65

didn't ask a single question about life beyond the village. In fact, I was kind of a distraction for her. She was more concerned about where they were going to find the best grazing for the sheep they herded through those damn high, cold valleys, and preoccupied with the health of the cold-weather fruit trees they tended the year around. Shit."

Haydon was surprised to hear a hint of a grudging admiration in Cage's voice, and he watched as Cage took several swigs from his Gallo, and looked around the room while he got it down his throat. Haydon did the same. It seemed to him that Cage was making an effort to sound casual about this.

"Next time I saw her," Cage continued, "was several months later and under conditions that were a hell of a lot different. She had finished her tour of duty, and Janet was giving her a 'leaving-the-Corps' party before she flew home. Jesus, the American clothes and hairstyle transformed her, but it didn't change her personality any. She was still unpretentious, unassuming, but completely at ease in the swanky Trattoria, eating overpriced cuisine with all of Janet's privileged haute monde Guatemalan rich, the embassy crowd, the wealthy foreigners who live permanently in Guatemala. She was funny to watch, you know. Here are all these superficial party people and here's Lena, congenial, but not overly generous with herself. She was at ease, but not as though she endorsed all that shit. She wasn't uncomplicated. The kid was older than her age, but nobody seemed to notice that."

This last was an insightful observation from Cage, and one that Haydon wouldn't have expected of him. Not that he wasn't perceptive, Cage wouldn't have lived as long as he had in his line of business if he hadn't been perceptive about human behavior. It was the fact that Cage had allowed a crack in the monolithic façade he had constructed for himself. But the crack wasn't the kind that betrayed weakness; it was the kind that allowed you to glimpse something on the inside. Cage smoked the tail end of his last cigarette and ground out the butt.

"So she went home and in a month she was back down here. Janet's ex-husband got her this job with USAID. That was about three months ago, I guess. I haven't seen her but once or twice since she got back."

Cage abruptly took a small notebook from one of the pockets of his guayabera, ripped a sheet from the notebook, snapped the point out on a ballpoint pen, scribbled something on the paper, and shoved it across to Haydon.

"This is Janet Pittner's address," he said. "If you're thinking about going to the embassy with all this, think some more. Think about it for twelve hours. A lot can happen in twelve hours down here. And the embassy . . . I have my prejudices about the way the State Department handles its business in Central America."

This last was a huge understatement. Haydon said nothing.

"Think about it," Cage repeated. "It could save you some grief."

"What do you think has happened to her?"

"I haven't got a clue."

Haydon reached out and turned the piece of paper around without picking it up. He saw the address was the same Fossler had given him. He left it where it was. Cage looked at him.

"What's your relationship with—"

"Carnal knowledge," Cage said. "But we've got all that straightened out now, and it's a thing of the past. It was a delightful affair, but Janet's a much better friend than lover. Besides, it was a little incestuous, me working under her husband. I don't mind lying for business, but lying for pleasure too got confusing. I broke it off before he found out. And then Janet divorced him, which didn't make any sense, but then that's another thing about Janet: she doesn't usually make sense."

"You worked under Janet's husband?"

"Bennett Pittner, Chief of Station."

"Christ."

"Yeah, no kidding."

This was too much. Haydon finished the last of his Gallo to cover his surprise. He wondered if Jim Fossler had any inkling of what he had gotten himself into. And then Haydon realized that he probably had, which opened everything to a labyrinth of possibilities. "Fossler told me you visited him."

Cage nodded.

67

"He said you told him you had 'come across someone' asking about Lena."

Cage squeegeed his forehead with his thumb again. "That's right, I did. My people came across inquiries. Turned out to be Fossler."

"Fossler was the only one asking questions about her?"

"Only one I looked up."

"But not the *only* one."

Cage's hesitation was almost imperceptible. "Guatemalan security forces. Military intelligence. Department for Criminal Investigations—

they're Guatemala's equivalent of the Gestapo. Everybody you ever wanted to avoid was on her ass. Whatever she was doing, she was completely screwed. I couldn't believe it. I goddamned couldn't believe it."

Cage seemed angry more than anything else. Or at least Haydon thought it was anger.

Chapter 11

There was little to say after that, and in a few moments Cage said he had to go. He didn't offer to take Haydon to his hotel, in fact, he didn't even ask where Haydon was staying. He just said he had to go, stood, threw down some quetzals on the table for his meal and walked out.

Haydon sat at the window and watched him disappear down the dark street in the direction of where they had left the car. His thoughts went immediately to Jim Fossler. No wonder Fossler had been so peculiarly loquacious on the telephone. Like many unsuspecting travelers, he had found himself in thrall to Guatemala's strangeness and was hard pressed to come to grips with it. Fossler must have been mystified by everything he encountered here. He was the kind of man whose first impulse in any new situation was to sort things out, fit the pieces together, put things in order. After five or six weeks in Guatemala he must have come to the panicky realization that nothing was ever sorted out here, nothing was ever put in order.

Haydon looked at his watch. It was shortly after ten o'clock. He hadn't been with Cage that long after all. He paid his bill—in dollars, having not yet changed his money into quetzals—and the waiter was delighted to receive money that actually had value. Haydon gave him an additional tip and asked if he would call a cab. Within a few minutes the cab arrived, and the grateful waiter appeared instantly and accompanied Haydon to the door. The taxi turned out not to be a taxi at all, but a private car, probably a relative or friend of the waiter's. The middle-aged driver took Haydon's bag, put it in the front seat on the passenger's side, and opened the back door for Haydon. In an instant they were off.

By this time of night most of the Guatemala City's streets were empty, no matter that it was a city of well over two million inhabitants. At this hour you were safer inside, though if the death squads wanted you, they didn't care where you were or whether it was day or night. Still, human nature understood the menace of darkness.

The way things were done in Guatemala took a little getting used to. On the surface of things, the country paid a reasonable amount of respect to logic. Guatemala itself was divided into twenty-three regions, or states, called *departamentos,* and its cities were divided into gerrymandered sectors called *zonas.* The streets that had a roughly north/south orientation were called *avenidas,* and the cross streets were called streets, or *calles.* To locate an address you had to know the zona because the numbered calles and avenidas repeated themselves in each sector.

Beyond this point, nothing else in the entire country made sense. Reason was not a part of the national *Weltanschauung.* Nothing was reliable or dependable because no one paid any attention to the formalities that were necessary for an organized society. That is, rules. Here the rules were uniformly disobeyed or ignored or made exception to. None of which mattered anyway, since the rules themselves constantly were being changed by people who seemed to have an understanding about something of which no one else had been informed. What was important here was convention, knowing "the way things were done," and learning how things were done was largely a process of trial and error. The big surprise was that, in Guatemala, the errors could cost you your life.

Luckily Haydon's driver was content to travel in silence, and in no time at all they were back on the broad, central thoroughfare of the Avenida La Reforma. Haydon always stayed at the same small hotel in Guatemala City, the Residencial Reforma, which once had been a grand old private home belonging to one of the country's leading historical figures. Justo Rufino Barrios was a wealthy coffee grower who ruled the country as a dictator between 1873 to 1879 at which time he called a constitutional convention and magically became "president" (with a dictator's unlimited powers) and remained in absolute control of his country until 1885.

The taxi slowed on the avenida, made a U-turn at one of the cross-overs that periodically intersected the broad esplanade, came back a block or so and turned into the hotel drive. The home sat back from the avenida the distance of a deep circle drive, which was entered from the avenida between huge pillars supporting wrought-iron gates and flanked by a tall wrought-iron fence almost obscured by manicured shrubbery. The building itself was of an architectural style which could best be described as Moorish with Portuguese influences—two storied, white stucco, terra-cotta clay tile roof. The second floor was fronted by a deep veranda with abbreviated trefoil arches and marble pillars, and from which one had a wonderful view of the grand avenida. The center of the courtyard drive was occupied by a large fountain, its waters long-since silenced, its handsome basin now planted with cinnamon fern and blooming purple liriope, and from the center of which rose an alabaster statue of a naked angel with gloriously spread wings embracing a nude and swooning mortal.

The driver circled these two white souls frozen forever in stony pathos and stopped at the front door. He quickly hopped out of the car, came around to open Haydon's door and took his bag out of the front seat. Haydon paid him and asked if he would wait a moment and take him somewhere else.

In the small foyer, Haydon filled in the registration card, telling the clerk he wanted a room for two days. As a hotel, the old home had one overriding eccentricity. When it was divided for commercial use, there

71

was no effort made to turn the rooms into spaces of comparable size. The house was seemingly left as originally designed, except that a bath was added to every room. However, all of the rooms were the same price, whether you were put in what once had been a cell-sized servant's room with little or no circulation or whether you were put in a spacious upstairs suite with a wonderful cross breeze and a view of the city. Travelers who frequented this delightful hotel, affectionately known as "La Casa Grande," knew in advance to at least request certain rooms. If available, you could get a suite instead of a cell. Haydon asked for and got room 21, one of the largest rooms, with a sitting area and windows on two sides.

He let the eager houseboy take his small bag, and they stepped down into one of the parlors where a few guests slumped on sofas and comfortable armchairs, watching CNN on the television set that was seldom turned off, though always kept at a modest volume. They went up the circular marble stairs, turned right, and the boy let Haydon into his room and gave him the key and left. Haydon threw his bag on the bed and pushed open the glass of the two windows that overlooked the front courtyard. Even with its acrid stench, the cooling night air was preferable to the stuffy heat.

Without taking the time to unpack, Haydon returned downstairs. Giving his key to the concierge, he was told that the front gates closed at eleven, and if he wished to enter after that time he would have to push the button on the speaker box set into the front pillars and the gates would be opened electronically for him.

Janet Pittner's home was in Zona 10, the same area as Haydon's hotel. Things were expensive in Zona 10, and mostly they were safe as well. Like almost everything in the zona, Janet Pittner's home was protected from the tree-covered street by a high, solid wall, which, even in the gloam of the smoky darkness, Haydon could see was covered with *moneda* vine and garlanded along its top with boughs of bougainvillea. The driver stopped at the entrance, and Haydon got out of the car, leaving the door open, and pushed the button on the speaker box set into the pillar at the side of the wrought-iron gate. To his left, farther down the wall was another gate, which was the exit.

A maid answered in Spanish, and Haydon, talking slowly and deliberately, identified himself and mentioned Lena's name, thinking the maid would most likely garble the rest of it. There was a wait of a minute or two before the maid's voice came on the speaker. *"Pase adelante,"* she said, and the electronic latch on the small pedestrian gate beside the pillar sprung ajar. Haydon paid his driver again and walked through the gate, pulling it closed behind him.

By the time he walked across the drive to the front courtyard, a maid was coming out to meet him. *"Buenas,"* she said, smiling quickly, and he followed her through low, lush plantings illuminated by footlights placed among the foliage, to a second wrought-iron gate. Immediately inside this they stepped into a wide breezeway that led through into an inner courtyard surrounded by the loggia of the house. However, the maid turned left through a recessed doorway and led him into a living room that overlooked the courtyard outside, and where a worried-looking Janet Pittner was coming over to meet him.

"Mr. Haydon?" she was saying, extending her hand.

"Yes, Stuart Haydon, and I want to apologize immediately for coming so late and without an introduction."

"No, that's perfectly all right. I'm glad you did. Come on in," she said, bringing him into the room. "I'd like you to meet Bennett Pittner," she said, taking him toward a sofa where a man in his early fifties was already standing with a drink in his hand. They shook hands. "Uh, we . . . we were formerly married," she explained, alluding to their same last names.

Janet Pittner must have been ten years younger than her ex-husband. She was rather tall, with a thin frame that wore clothes to their advantage, in this case a sundress of pale lemon cotton. Her sienna hair was pulled back loosely and held in place with a clip, revealing silver pendant earrings. Her sundress had a scooped neck and snug waist, which allowed him to observe that though she was thin, she was not small busted. She was nervous, frowning at Haydon, her arms crossed.

Bennett Pittner, on the other hand, was quite calm. His suit, the coat of which was thrown over the back of the sofa next to where he had been sitting, was decidedly rumpled, and his tie and the collar of his white shirt were loosened. His ginger hair, shot through with gray, was worn rather more full than most State Department types. His mouth was smallish, and he tended to hold it slightly pursed. He held his drink in one hand, his other hand in his pocket, as he regarded Haydon from lazy-lidded eyes over a prominent hawk's-beak nose.

There was a moment of awkwardness, and then Janet blurted out that Haydon should have a seat, how about a drink. He declined the latter. He sat in an armchair and began to explain. He left out his observation of Jim Fossler's unusual behavior and said only that he had come

73

to interview Lena to satisfy the requirements for closing the case. He told Janet that Fossler had given him her name and that he had just arrived in the city. He left out his discovery of Fossler's bloody room and did not mention Taylor Cage or the fact that he knew Lena was, once again, missing.

"So," he said in conclusion, "If I could talk with her I would appreciate it. I could close the case and go home."

Pittner had returned to his place on the sofa, one leg crossed nonchalantly over the other, but Janet had not sat down and was standing a little ways from both men with folded arms, occasionally stroking her upper left arm with her right hand in a gesture of agitation. There was a brief silence during which Bennett Pittner simply looked at Haydon as though he expected him to continue.

But Haydon had said all he was going to say. He looked at both of them.

"Well," Janet said with a huge sigh, twitching her upper torso nervously and taking a few steps toward them. "I . . . really, it's not convenient for you to talk to Lena just now. Not tonight. Actually . . . it's, well, I'm not sure she'd want to talk to you."

"Really? Jim Fossler said he had talked to her twice and he didn't see that she would have any problem with it."

"It's not that easy," Janet said. She was flustered, and Bennett Pittner wasn't helping her, letting her sputter stupidly until she finally simply stopped and stared at her ex-husband.

He was looking at his drink, sensed she was transfixed on him in frustration, looked up at her in mild surprise, kind of shrugged with his eyebrows, and turned to Haydon.

"Actually," he said in a modulated tone. "Lena's gone missing."

74

The British phrasing was interesting. Pittner certainly wasn't British, of course, in fact Haydon had thought he had detected a slight Georgia drawl in his voice. But the British phrasing hung in the air politely, an embarrassed admission.

"Jesus H. Christ," Janet blurted, flinging her arms up in the air and pacing across to the windows that looked out into the courtyard. There were mellow lights in the shrubbery out in the courtyard, and Haydon could see a fountain burbling in its center and could hear it through the tall open windows. Janet came back to them.

"She's goddamned *disappeared*," Janet said to Pittner who regarded her with a mild expression of unexcited patience. She wheeled around to Haydon. "She's *gone,* Mr. Haydon," she said dramatically. Her hazel eyes were dancing with emotion. In a burst of staccato monologue she quickly told Haydon what Cage already had related, and when she had brought him up to the present, she turned abruptly and walked over to a small table covered with liquor bottles and poured herself a drink, without ice, straight.

Pittner had been sitting back on the sofa. Now he leaned forward, his forearms on his knees, his drink in his hands, and looked at Haydon.

"Janet thinks Lena has met with some misfortune," he said, without hurry. "The crime rate is bad here right now. People have to watch themselves."

"Oh, shit," Janet rolled her head and groaned. "The 'crime rate.' " She came over and fixed her eyes on Haydon. "You traveled down here before?"

Haydon nodded. "Some," he said.

Janet sat down on the sofa, at the opposite end from Pittner, closer to Haydon. "Then you know about the 'crime rate' down here. If you're aware at all, then you know that the 'crime rate' "—she said the two words as if they were an insult—"is institutional. It's the National Police's Department for Criminal Investigation, the DIC. It's the G-2, military intelligence. It's the Guardia de Hacienda, the border police. It's the goon squads that every political party keeps on its payroll so they can knock off their rivals à la mafia. All of these fall under the general rubric of 'death squads' . . . a.k.a., 'the crime rate.' "

She jerked her head around to Pittner. "Isn't that right, Pitt?" Back to Haydon. "Somebody gets killed down here, all these organizations blame it on the 'common criminal element,' but in reality everyone knows it's the work of the death squads, which everyone knows could be *any*body. The only way you know who did it is to know something about the victims. Who'd they piss off? Whose way were they in? Who would benefit from the victims' death? What were the victims' politics?" She looked around at Pittner again. " 'Common crime' my little American ass."

Pittner let his heavy-lidded eyes rest on her a moment while she took a strong hit of her straight drink. He turned to Haydon.

"I doubt if anything like that happened," he drawled. Pittner had the raw complexion of a heavy drinker. Haydon wondered if his slow-mo-

75

tion deportment was his manner or his condition. "It's rare—rare—that United States citizens fall victim to the 'death squad' kind of thing. That stuff . . . it's internal." He closed his eyes and slowly shook his head. "I just can't see it."

"That's for goddamned sure," Janet snapped.

Chapter 12

There was a silent moment while each of them turned to their drinks, as though the bell had rung and each had retreated to a neutral corner. Haydon glanced around the room. It was expensively appointed, a grand piano, dark antiques against the dun-colored stucco walls, a massive, well-used fireplace at one end of the room, over which hung an enormous oil painting of a Guatemalan landscape whose focal point was one of the country's numerous volcanoes. And there were books, a lot of them, scattered around and obviously read, a pile of them stacked on the floor at Janet's end of the creamy leather sofa. On a perch at the far end of the room was a majestic scarlet macaw, his scarlet and lemon and sapphire feathers as startlingly brilliant as if he had been made of richly dyed silk. He was as motionless as an artifact, but Haydon had seen him blink.

"What about John Baine?" Haydon asked, thinking he ought to break the silence, give them some relief.

"What about him?" Pittner asked.

"No one's heard from him either?"

"Oh, hell no," Janet said. Haydon couldn't tell whether her sarcasm was directed at her ex-husband's skeptical attitude or reflected her opinion of Baine.

Haydon looked at Pittner. "You don't think anything serious has happened to her?"

"Let's just say I really wouldn't expect to find her picture in the Gabinete de Identificación's book of unidentified bodies. We just don't have any reason to think like that." He regarded Haydon. "I mean, look at you. She disappeared on you, didn't she? That's why you're down here, isn't it? She seems to have this habit . . ." He gestured vaguely with his glass, which was empty, and the little bit of remaining ice zinged around in the bottom, attracting his attention to the fact that it was empty. He got up and went to the liquor table. Haydon noticed that he drank good American bourbon.

"What about it, Haydon?" Pittner asked, straightening up from the little table and turning around. "Why did she run away from up there?"

"She didn't talk any of that over with you?" Haydon asked, addressing Janet, not Pittner.

"No, she didn't," Janet said. "I didn't even know she was having trouble at home, if she was . . . whatever it was. Didn't have an idea until that investigator showed up here asking for her."

"When I talked to Jim Fossler on the telephone yesterday," Haydon continued, turning back to Pittner, "he told me that he thought Lena might be in some kind of trouble, and he thought Baine was involved too."

"Trouble?" Pittner was poker faced. He raised his eyebrows in innocent perplexity and looked at Janet.

"What?" she said.

"You hear her say anything about something like that?" Pittner asked.

"No. No, I didn't."

She had, of course. Her denial was as transparent as glass. Janet Pittner was incapable of hiding her emotions. She was the kind of woman who showed you her emotions first, right up front. There was a kind of honesty in it, and a kind of instability as well.

"You don't remember anything?" Haydon asked needlessly.

"No." Janet shook her head emphatically.

"Maybe she was pregnant," Pittner said helpfully.

"Oh, for Christ's sake, Pitt." Janet looked at him as if he was an imbecile.

"Fossler mentioned that she seemed frightened."

Janet's face reacted to this.

"Well, Mr. Fossler seems to have been particularly perceptive," Pittner said, walking back to the sofa and sitting down again. His drink was pure amber. A double. No water. He pursed his lips. "Have you already gone over this with him since you've arrived?"

Haydon looked at Pittner closely. "I haven't had time."

"But you must've come in on, what, that eight-forty flight?" He looked at his watch. "You've . . . well, I guess you've had things to do."

"What kind of work do you do at the embassy?" Haydon asked. If Pittner was going to be impertinent . . .

"Oh. Well, Political Section. Been doing Political Section for years. But not here always. Other Latin American countries too."

Janet was not listening. She had tucked one leg up under her on the sofa and was tapping her fingers on her glass, which she cradled in her lap. She was lost in thought. There was another moment of silence, and Pittner's eyes floated over to the scarlet macaw and then drifted back to Haydon.

"I'd like to know what happens now," Haydon said, straight to Pittner.

79

"Mmmmmmm," Pittner nodded. "I'm going to the Consular Section tomorrow and have them begin looking into it. I guess they'll poke around. I'm not sure how they'll do that. Anyway, I promised Janet I'd get something started."

"Are you planning to notify the girl's family?"

"Consular will tend to that," Pittner said. "And, of course, I'm sure they'll want to consult with the alert Mr. Fossler. And you. You could be helpful. You ought to check in with them tomorrow."

"What has Fossler said about this?"

"I guess he doesn't know," Janet said distractedly. She was massaging her right temple with the ends of her fingers. "We haven't seen him since . . ."

"Since Janet decided to get excited," Pittner said.

"You mentioned the Gabinete de Identificación," Haydon said to him. "Has anyone gone to the National Police Headquarters and checked the book?"

Haydon didn't know how long "the book of the dead," as it was commonly called, had been a part of modern Guatemalan life, but the eerie thing to him was that it had been around long enough for everyone to take it for granted, to act as if it was something that ought properly to exist in a civilized society. Most Guatemalans were so grateful not to be in it themselves, and so frightfully aware of how easily they could be, that they kept their mouths shut about it and didn't remark on its existence at all. With a few rash and desperate exceptions, the people of Guatemala were governed by fear. Fear had deafened them and blinded them and cauterized their hearts. It had created a suspicious and furtive society.

The grim book was kept in the National Police Headquarters, an old stone, fortresslike structure wedged into the narrow corridor of 6 avenida, Zona 1, on the northeast corner of Enrique Gómez Park. The book contained photographs, regularly collected from every morgue in the country, of unidentified bodies that had been discovered along road-sides, in garbage dumps, washed up on riverbanks and lakeshores and the shores of the Gulf of Honduras and the South Coast, found among the crushed cornstalks of small milpas, in the stagnant cisterns of old fincas, and against curbsides and in gutters, in *plazoletas* and in empty soccer fields. They were ubiquitous, these bodies. Fifty or sixty a month. Seventy. More in an election year, many more. And Guatemala had just been through a national election.

80

"No," Pittner said. "But Janet wants to. That's what we were talking about just before you came. But there have been some changes, with the book, I mean. It's not at the National Police Headquarters anymore. In fact, there's not just one book now. Some time back there were some administrative changes. Now each *departamento* keeps its own book in the police offices of the departmental seat of government. This way all those people don't have to trek to the capital if they want to look for a missing person. Saves them those damned long bus rides. Saves them money. Saves them the time off from work. Their own departmental police headquarters is so much closer."

"Oh, great, the beneficent Guatemalan democracy," Janet said, looking at Pittner. "Always think of the poor campesino." She shook her head and turned to Haydon. "He's giving you the official government line. Think of it. Twenty-three departments. Twenty-three books of the dead. When these death-squad goons pick up people, more often than not they drag them off to some clandestine prison, take them far away from where they kidnapped them, to do their jobs on them. Hell, they find these people's bodies hundreds of kilometers from where they were abducted. So if you're looking for someone who was disappeared, it's likely they were dragged off to another *departamento*. But which one, which direction? Now these poor people searching for missing family members, missing friends who have been disappeared, have their difficulties multiplied by twenty-two. Another grim triumph—through official decree—for the death squads."

Pittner was looking at her, his face emotionless, letting her have her say. When she finished, he kept his eyes on her and sipped his bourbon. He turned to Haydon.

"Janet has problems with the way the Guatemalan government conducts itself."

"Pardon *me?*" Janet said. "I have problems with reigns of terror," she clarified. She looked at Haydon. "The thing about embassy people is they have to be diplomatic. Even when they know they're dancing in shit they keep their eyes on the colored lights, never look down. What nice music, what nice lights, what a grand time. The State Department's great for looking at rhinestones and seeing diamonds. It's an unreal way to live. The ones who have scruples, it eats at them, this duplicity. But others"— she turned to Pittner—"they've sucked up so much they don't even smell the shit anymore."

"Anyway," Pittner drawled, unfazed, "I'm going to get the consular people on it."

Janet looked at Haydon and shook her head.

"Well, look," Haydon said, standing, "I'd better go. I apologize again for just walking in here like this, but I wanted to get on with it."

"What are you going to do now?" Janet asked, standing too. It was the first time her voice hadn't been charged with strong feeling since he had entered the room.

"I'm not sure. I'll think it over tonight."

"I'll get you a cab," she said, stepping over to a secretary near the windows that overlooked the courtyard and picking up the telephone.

"Where are you staying?" Pittner asked, remaining seated. It was an innocent question, a natural one, but to Haydon it seemed particularly sinister. But it was stupid not to tell him. He could know within half an hour.

"Residencial Reforma."

"Oh, close by," Pittner said mildly. "It's a good place."

Janet spoke briefly on the telephone and hung up.

"Well, look," she said, smoothing the front of her dress and setting down her glass, "why don't you check back tomorrow. Maybe she'll call in . . . or something. And if you find out anything, would you let me know? I'm . . . really . . . concerned about this."

"I'll be glad to." He stepped over to Pittner, who still hadn't gotten up, and shook hands, Pittner nodding once, closing his eyes as he did so, like a doll of a middle-aged man.

"See you," Pittner said.

"I'll walk out with you," Janet said.

They went out the living room door to the breezeway and then out through the first wrought-iron gate and through the front courtyard, where they stopped to wait.

"The cab was close by, down at the Camino Real. It'll only be a couple of minutes," she said, folding her arms again. "Honestly, get back to me, okay?"

"Sure, I will," Haydon said.

"Look," she said hesitantly, "I don't want to be an alarmist, but I really, really do think this is not good. Pitt disregards me. Fine. We had a shitty marriage. I wasn't diplomatic material. Too blunt. But anyway, I don't think I'm going to wait for his diplomatic shtick. I'm going to wade into this."

She was right, the taxi was there immediately. She reached out and touched his arm with the flat of her hand.

"I couldn't say everything in front of him," she said. "Call me."

The driver was impatient on the other side of the wrought-iron gate and beeped his horn.

Haydon looked at her. "Okay, tomorrow," he said, and she took away her hand and stood with her arms folded, watching him, as he walked out the gate and got into the car.

Chapter 13

On the way back to the hotel, Haydon stared out the window, the smoky haze and damp night air mingling in a ghostly way to make the avenidas sinister to the imagination. Bennett Pittner was everything an intelligence officer ought to be. He was bland, unexciting, and in a social setting he virtually would be invisible. Even his manner, which Haydon did not at all attribute solely to American bourbon, betrayed a man whose habit it was to assess everything thoroughly as it came to him. He did not find it necessary to act as quickly as he thought. Knowledge, not action, was power. Taylor Cage seemed to have learned that well enough from his former superior.

Janet Pittner was her ex-husband's emotional opposite, and Haydon guessed she was often underestimated because of it. He guessed, too, that they were the kind of couple who couldn't live with, or without, each other. Haydon's arrival seemed to have interrupted an already heated discussion about what action should be taken about Lena's disappearance, and from what Janet had just now said to Haydon at the gate, Pittner hadn't made too much progress with her. It was the story of their relationship.

The taxi pulled into the Residencial Reforma's drive and stopped immediately. True to their word, the management had locked the gates. Haydon paid the taxi driver, who drove away, and then turned to the button on the pillar. He pushed it, identified himself and gave his room number to the night clerk and shoved open the gates when he heard the electronic click.

As he closed the gates behind him and walked across the front drive, the swooning mortal and the ministering angel glowed palely in the fountain of purple liriope. The old house was dark. He got his key from the night clerk, a young man who was reading some kind of textbook, and stepped down into the small front parlor. A couple of American men were slumped in their armchairs in front of the television as if they were back home in Dayton, the brilliant flashes from apocalyptic explosions in the Arnold Schwarzenegger film illuminating their bored, pale faces like death masks. On the other side of a low wall the dining atrium was mostly dark, a pastel greenish light falling down into the long room from the skylight above the mezzanine.

Haydon went slowly up the stairs, realizing how tired he was, the whumps of muted explosions and the spitting of automatic weapons dying out behind him as he rounded the curving stairs to the second floor. At the head of the stairs he paused a moment to look down into the dining room again, long runners of ivy hanging down from the marble bannister, the room itself circumscribed by marble pillars that held up the mezzanine where he was standing and separated the room from the surrounding hallway. El Reformador knew how to build an elegant home.

He went to his room and undressed, hung his clothes in the large closet and washed his face. After putting on his pajama pants, he took the manila folder of Guatemalan contacts and got into bed and started going through the papers. The first man he would call would be Efran Borrayo, an agent in a branch of the security forces that was known as the Department for Technical Investigations, DIT, a branch of the National Police with a reputation for death-squad involvement. Haydon knew of the division's reputation, but Borrayo had played a key role in helping him and a Colombian homicide detective track down a man they twice had followed the length of Central America. Borrayo had been efficient and responsible. If he was around, Haydon could use his help again. He circled Borrayo's name, put the folder on the writing desk beside the bed, and turned out the light.

He lay in bed exhausted, the only light in the room a wan sapphire coming in over his head from the two small rose windows that overlooked the front courtyard and the Avenida La Reforma. He had pulled back the long curtains and draped them over the metal levers that held the glass open in an effort to let in as much of the still night air as possible. Every tiny sound carried on the thin air, an occasional taxi on the boulevard, fireworks spattering like gunshots somewhere—Guatemalans loved fireworks and shot them off at the slightest excuse for celebrating, or simply because they felt good—someone yelling their lungs out from a car passing on the deserted boulevard. Crickets.

He went to sleep and then woke, not knowing if it was almost morning or if only a few moments had passed. Crickets. He resisted the temptation to hold up his wrist and try to see the dial of his watch in the pale light. He tried not to think of Fossler's bloodied cell, or of Lena Muller, or even of Taylor Cage. Taylor Cage, sweating. Taylor Cage, remembering Lena. Taylor Cage, as pale as watery light.

He sat bolt upright fighting for breath, his mouth gulping for air like a fish's, his body cool to the air, drenched in perspiration, looking at Cage, green as an American Buddha, standing at the foot of his bed.

"Just . . . relax," Cage said, his voice low and calm. "Okay? It's just me, okay?"

Haydon managed to nod.

"Get up and get some clothes on," Cage demanded, having used up the full extent of his tenderness. "We've got to go."

Haydon threw back the covers. "What time is it?" He didn't know why it mattered.

"Almost two o'clock."

Cage sat down on a bench in front of the dresser across from Haydon's bed, while Haydon went across the large room to his closet and grabbed his trousers off the hanger, thinking instantly of the disarrayed shirt in Fossler's closet.

"What's going on?"

Cage was relaxed on the bench, watching Haydon without much interest.

"Well, it's payback time."

Haydon sat on a chair and pulled on his socks.

"While we were eating you asked me what I wanted from you for all this help I'm giving you," Cage said, sounding as if he had lavished information on Haydon, done his job for him. "Well, this is it."

"And what is 'this'?"

"Not a hell of a lot," Cage said.

"Fine." Okay. Haydon couldn't expect him to say much in the hotel room.

When Haydon was dressed, they eased out into the small mezzanine and followed the curving stairs down into the parlor where, at last, the television was silenced. At the desk the young clerk conveniently had his head turned as they went outside to the front steps where a small Ford van with darkened windows was waiting, motor running.

"Get in," Cage said as he walked around to the driver's side.

When Haydon opened the door he was surprised to see a young Indian girl sitting in the one seat behind them. For a moment he looked into the familiar face of hundreds of years of Mayan history. She couldn't have been more than eighteen. She didn't speak and neither did Haydon as he climbed in and sat down beside Cage, who was just closing the door and putting the van in gear.

86   Quickly they were out on the Reforma and headed north, breezing down the empty boulevard under the towering cypresses, their headlights burning into the haze of smoke and fog. Just before they reached the monument at the Plazuela Reina Barrios, Cage turned left and headed west, past the long Parque Centro América, and half a kilometer past that over the railroad tracks and into the western environs of Zona 8, a sector of narrow streets and poor buildings and hand-to-mouth lives. He continued into darker, bleaker streets until the van was slowed by cobblestones and then potholes, creeping along nearly at an idle. Haydon knew that the sound of the car motor was an ominous one for many of the

people who lived behind the walls of these deserted little streets. Many of them would waken and listen with their eyes open, holding their breath in the darkness until the van passed. Cage turned into a lane without streetlamps and downshifted the van as the lane began to climb. His headlights jarred on the rough stone and caught the coiled tail of a cur just as the dog topped the crest of the street above them.

At the top of the hill, Cage pulled to the side of the street, and the girl got up, slid back the side door of the van, and got out. There was no paving on the street at all here, and Haydon could even smell the dust along with the stench from the dumps. The girl climbed up on the sidewalk and went down two or three doors from where they sat and knocked softly on a door. Haydon noticed she wore modern clothes, not Indian ones, and she wore them well. The stucco buildings outside his window were chipped and derelict, the paint that once had covered the walls now faded, only faintly visible. Cage lighted a cigarette, the tiny flame from the red plastic Bic was phosphorous white, then gone. Haydon could hear the girl talking, a pleasing voice in the darkness. He remembered her face. Then she was coming back, down the steps, into the van, the door sliding shut, and they were on the move again.

Cage continued to wind his way through the wretched streets, but in a different direction, each street seeming remarkably like all the others, proving the monotony of poverty. They stopped again, and again the girl got out, whispered at a doorway, came back, and they were gone again. Now the neighborhoods changed, and Haydon recognized some of the landmarks and then he knew where they were, 4a avenida, Zona 3, one of the older, wider streets in the city that had been laid out during the tenure of El Reformador, who had grander plans for the capital city than ultimately came to pass. The buildings along the way were not great homes with echoes of neoclassical architecture as El Reformador might have imagined, like the grand homes around the cemeteries of Mexico City. Rufino Barrios' dreams proved to be only dreams. Instead, on this southern lateral approach to the Cementerio General, the city's oldest cemetery, there were mean, low-storied buildings of cement and stucco, with electrical wires draped across the way like torn, black spiders' webs against the smoky night sky.

Then to their left the powder-blue stucco wall of the cemetery rose to six meters in height and ran nearly a kilometer's distance to the far end of its façade, and behind it, a necropolis, a true city of the dead, with

87

wooded avenues and streets and alleys, paths, humble *hoyas,* pretentious crypts, and pompous mausoleums. The city of the dead was more organized, cleaner, more beautiful, and kinder to its residents than was the city of the living. And everyone there was mercifully relieved of the constant dread of becoming what they already had become.

Haydon was not aware of the police car they had picked up until Cage swore and began pulling over and the cherry splashes appeared on the windshield and back of Cage's head. Cage turned into the first side street, in front of a shuttered *marmolería,* its sign in the shape of a gravestone. The police car pulled around too, drove slowly past them, and then made a U-turn and parked on the other side of the street facing in the opposite direction. The police car's doors opened, and three men got out. The one on the passenger side of the front seat wore civilian clothes.

"DIC," Cage said. The man in civilian clothes and one of the officers stayed at the car, leaning on the fender, while the other officer began walking across the street toward them.

"Lita," Cage snapped. *"¡Ven aquá . . . tu camisa!* Haydon, put her on your lap, facing this way." The girl scrambled into the front seat with them, crawled onto Haydon's lap, frantically working at the buttons as Cage rolled down his darkened window halfway, opened the van door, and got out. The girl jerked open her blouse; she wore no bra.

Cage met the officer in the middle of the street, before he could get too close to the van, just as the officer's flashlight came up to shoulder height. Cage's body momentarily blocked the beam of light. The officer stopped.

"Muevese," he said, tilting his head warily and using the beam of the flashlight to motion Cage aside. *"¿Qué pasa?"*

The girl put her left arm around Haydon's neck, and he could smell the faint musky fragrance of her unperfumed skin and feel her breathing hard from her efforts. When Cage moved aside, the officer's flashlight beam caught Haydon's profile and the girl's laughing face and bare breasts just as she crossed her free arm to hide herself.

Cage laughed nervously, and the officer swore and grinned. There was a brief conversation in the middle of the street, Cage's voice lowering as Haydon heard him explain to the officer that "my boss" had been wanting "this little thing" for a long time. So Cage had arranged it, you know, everyone gets something out of it.

Haydon strained to hear, the girl's breasts still inches from his face, her body breathing with his, a wild combination of fear and eroticism.

"The two mans with the car no coming," she whispered to Haydon with a heavy accent. His face was close enough to hers that he felt her breath on his mouth and looked into the dark almond slant of her Mayan eyes as she fixed her attention on the charade in the street behind him. *"La mordida,"* she whispered again, referring to the inevitable bribe that Cage was proffering and which would be expected and accepted. Close enough to her eyes to see the moisture in them, Haydon was struck by the steely composure with which she was playing this out. Though he could feel the heavy breathing in her chest, he could tell it was only from the exertion of urgency, not from fear. The girl's face was as placid as a wooden altar angel's, though when the beam of the policeman's flashlight had hit her she had quickly laughed as lustily as a prostitute. Now her face was resolute again, waiting for her next cue. She was one of those people, truly rare individuals, who embraced a deadly serenity in a crisis.

Cage's voice was ingratiating, and the officer hissed and laughed again in macho admiration for what the man in the van was getting himself into. It was coming to a close. The girl quickly pulled Haydon's free hand to a breast, and almost at the same moment the bribed officer couldn't resist flashing the beam of his light one more time into the van, catching the side of the girl's smiling face as she turned away from the bright beam and pushed Haydon's hand away as if in coy protest and "accidentally" allowing the policeman to get a good look at her naked breasts.

It was over in a minute, and Cage was walking back to the van, opening the door, getting in, and rolling up the darkened window as the girl scrambled out of Haydon's lap and into the backseat.

"Holy shit," Cage said. From behind the darkened glass they watched the police car until it pulled away, went to the intersection, turned out onto 4a avenida, and disappeared. "I don't like *that* one damn bit." He was angry. He lighted a cigarette and sucked on it a couple of times, thinking. The girl was sitting behind them, buttoning her blouse, tucking it into the waist of her skirt, her head down so that her coarse black hair obscured her face.

" 'The DIC wants to talk to you,' the son of a bitch said." Cage pulled hard on the cigarette. "DIC. Shit. Those *micos,* the bigger the dog they have with them, the more they want you to pay them not to let him bite you. I don't like that one bit. I don't know *when* the last time was I got stopped. That whole thing smelled. I wish I could have gotten a look at the agent.

89

"Lita"—Cage raised his chin and looked at the girl in the rearview mirror—"did you see the guy?" She was straightening her blouse, her face in that moment still turned away from them. She only shook her head. "Well, I don't like it," Cage said again. Then he put the van in gear and made a U-turn.

Chapter 14

They were back on 4a avenida. They came to the grand neoclassical entrance to the Cementerio General on their left, looming dark and massive and deserted in the night, and passed by. At the end of the long powder-blue wall on the northern end of the cemetery, the height of the wall dropped to three meters, and the color changed to a smog-coated gray as they pulled off the pavement and onto a caliche strip in front of another set of gates. They had arrived at the Morgue Organismo Judicial. Looking up through the van's dirty windshield, Haydon saw a bare bulb under a dented reflective pan hanging from a goosenecked pipe on the span above the gates. The small bulb threw an improvised glow on the caliche. Just inside the gate's bars an equally jaundiced glow issued through the small window of the gatehouse and out through its open door. Everything in Guatemala City was poorly lighted, the bulbs were too weak, the power source overtaxed, the haze ever present.

Cage pulled the emergency brake on the van, left it idling, and got out. He walked around the front of the truck, approached the gates, and called through the bars to the gatehouse. There were shadows of movement inside the small building, and a frail, crooked-backed man who swung his arms in an alternating pumping motion made his way out to the gate and listened to Cage through the bars. The old man nodded deeply and then clacked the latch and swung open the gates as Cage came back to the van.

"Jesus, I've never known people who liked formalities so much," was all Cage said. As they drove through, Haydon heard a preacher of the evangelical *El Verbo* church railing on the radio in the hot little gatehouse.

The large rectangular compound of the morgue was empty except for a lone car parked under a eucalyptus tree in the median that ran the length of the courtyard to the far end where a two-storied building five or six rooms in width was wedged into the back corner of the compound against one of the high walls. The design of the building was spare, looking as though it had been built in the 1950s: a gap in the left side of the bottom floor was a foyer, now dimly lighted, to its right a long white wall with a single row of tiny windows just above head height all the way to the end of the building. Above that, the second floor was a single row of much larger windows where the offices were located, and a flat roof. That was all.

"You been here before?" Cage asked.

"Three years ago."

"Well, there's a new morgue under construction over here," Cage said, jerking his head to his left. Another low-slung building, same design. But the unfinished building was dark except for an empty and vacant foyer and two of the head-high windows from which issued a leprous fluorescent glow that quickly dissipated in the night.

"The new morgue will have refrigeration," Cage said, pulling up to the front of the old morgue. "But they're behind schedule on it. They tried to finish out the refrigerated lockers at least, so they could keep the bodies longer." He stopped the van and turned off the motor and leaned on the steering wheel. "Last month they thought they were ready and started putting bodies over there, half a dozen of them or so. They were so proud of those goddamned lockers that they let the autopsies pile up— you know, sort of to demonstrate there was no rush. 'Oh, we'll get to them in a few days' kind of attitude. 'Our new refrigerated lockers will keep them forever. No problem. Let's smoke a cigarette. Let's have a *cafecito.*' Well, days passed and then they finally went over to get the bodies to start in on the backlogged autopsies. But, holy shit, a surprise! They found they had had a Freon leak and the refrigeration had shut down. All eight of the bodies had gotten so hot closed up in those stain-less-steel locker drawers that they'd swelled up and exploded in there. Big mess." Cage stomped on the emergency brake. "Come on."

Haydon remembered every detail of the morgue. It wasn't a place you were likely to forget. It was, of course, like so many other buildings in Central America, of cinder-block construction. And stucco. Though the law provided that unidentified bodies could be held up to several weeks, pending identification, in actual practice the lack of refrigeration necessitated that bodies be autopsied as soon as possible and buried within twenty-four hours. Naturally, sometimes schedules could not be kept and bodies lay in the holding rooms until they began to smell. This happened so often, in fact, that there was a permanent smell of death about the place. In the rainy season it smelled so strongly of mildew and death you could actually detect the reek of the building before you got to it.

The three of them got out of the van, and the Indian girl, whom Cage still had not introduced, followed them into the morgue. There was only one attendant on duty, his feet propped on one of the two metal desks in the foyer, reading a sepia-toned comic book. When Cage pushed through the filthy glass doors, the man dropped his feet and looked as if he were going to bolt and run. Indeed, nothing had changed. The place was filthy, with overlooked spatters of blood turning a rusty black here and there on the floor or knee high along the unscrubbed walls. He did not want to be here, in these rooms where the sebaceous smell of death was inexpugnable, even by the candylike sweetness of the disinfectants they used in place of cleanliness and the ever-present charred odors of the smoldering garbage dumps that filled the Río La Barranca just beyond the long avenues of tombs on the other side of the walls. A soughing breeze moved up through the ravines and drifted in through the open windows and, like the invisible hand of an impatient angel, moved the swinging doors that led to the holding rooms with a lonely, softly lilting rhythm: flap-flap . . . flap-flap . . . flap-flap. Haydon looked toward the doors behind which the bodies lay in the ripening heat, and where, even now, he could see a glimpse of a waxy, bare foot.

Haydon had been only half listening to Cage's dialogue with the attendant, and now he realized that Cage was insisting on getting the papers known as Form 16 which was, in effect, the investigating judge's report and all the accompanying police reports that come with the discovery of the body of an unknown person, officially known as "XX." Finally Cage pulled out a wad of bills, and the man looked at them with an expression that betrayed a crumbling resolve and turned to the filing cabinet. He rifled through some files and pulled out a manila folder. He and Cage exchanged commodities, and Cage handed the papers to the Indian girl.

"Come on, Haydon," he said, and stalked to the swinging doors.

The room was small. Through poor planning, or more likely no planning, there were two small holding rooms instead of one large one, the second room accessible only by going through the first. Equally inexplicable was the fact that this first room was always filled with bodies before the second one, so that any additional corpses had to be bumped and maneuvered on gurneys through the crowded first room into the empty second one. It apparently never occurred to them to fill the one farthest back first. But only three bodies were in the first room now, not in body bags, but lying on gurneys and covered with thin sheets. The airtight plastic body bags would only have accelerated their deterioration in the stifling heat.

There were six feet showing. Cage paused, looked at them a moment and stepped to the last of the three gurneys and threw back the sheet. Her face was bloated and misshapen, and her blond hair was matted with blood and the debris of what appeared to be straw and twigs. Having seen Lena Muller only in photographs, Haydon did not believe he would have recognized her. She had already been autopsied, so there was the familiar Y-shaped incision, the upper branches of which traversed her chest just below her breasts, while the descending branch went straight down into her pubis. These incisions had been expertly done and neatly sewn. But there were other wounds too, ragged ones, wounds of deliberate cruelty and torture. Her handless forearms were crossed on her chest, and the hands themselves were stacked separately on her lower abdomen.

"Okay, Haydon. In Guatemala death is a hands-on kind of business. Let's get her in a bag."

The attendant was right behind them with a crackling plastic body bag, and they proceeded to wrestle her into it by putting a second gurney beside hers, opening the bag, and lifting her over into it. It wasn't easy, and the feel of her dead, gravity-bound body stirred a visceral anger in Haydon that he hadn't experienced in a long time and that surprised him by its intensity as it unexpectedly rushed up from his gorge like a sudden nausea.

They rolled her gurney out of the holding room through the swinging doors, which, when pushed open, allowed the soft swirl of the smoky breeze to stir the over-sweet smell of disinfectants that was so thick and heavy in the air that it seemed to Haydon it would leave a saccharine residue on his face, like soot. He waited with the Indian girl and the gurney while Cage backed the van up to the foyer, and the two of them put Lena into the back of the van and closed the doors. The worried and agitated attendant was glad to see them go. As the van approached the entrance of the compound, the little gatekeeper came out of his house, having seen their headlights, and pumped his way to the gates, unlatched them, and swung them open. He waved to Cage in a vague salute as they drove past, a model of discipline practiced in obscurity.

Cage was still not talking as he drove back along the way they had come, along the high wall until they reached the intersecting 20 calle, which dead-ended into the giant Roman-arch gatehouse of the Cementerio General on their right. But Cage turned left, and it was then that you could see that the cemetery was actually situated on a hill looking eastward. The street fell in a long, gradual slope, and Guatemala City lay spread out before them in a vast coppery glow.

Haydon rode down into the strangely lighted city in silence, trying not to be distracted by the pungent waft of formaldehyde that now filled the van. Guatemala has a way of bringing together disparate emotions in startling juxtaposition. You thought of things in ways you had never imagined them before, and sometimes you lived—and died—in ways you never had imagined. He wondered if Lena Muller had been surprised by the manner of her demise. He thought she might have been; he thought most people were. However, if she hadn't been, if she had had plenty of time to think about what was going to happen to her, if in fact it had happened to her so slowly that she had had the cruel leisure to contemplate its process, he wondered if she had faced it honestly. Now he wanted nothing more than to discover who had decided that Lena Muller should die and that she should die like this.

Chapter 15

In the daytime, where 20 calle drops more steeply toward Avenida Bolívar and the underpass bends sharply to Calle de Castillo, the street is a moil of commerce, its sidewalks almost impassable because of the booths and stalls of vendors who sold every imaginable ware, item, trinket, necessity, and folly—nothing too insignificant to be offered for sale in the hope that one meager need would meet another meager need to the mutual benefit of both buyer and seller. The street was congested, too, by buses and trucks and hand-pulled wagons and carts and people spilling out into the halting, murderous traffic, their dark Guatemalan faces darkened even more by layers of diesel soot and the soil of labor. However, the noisy, energetic activity did not reflect a profitable commerce at work, rather it was only a kind of desperate busyness in the face of a staggering economy. Commodities were exchanged for increasingly worthless quetzals; hard work only slowed one's irreversible slide toward the precipice. It was all done in a wild-eyed effort to forestall disaster, not for the sake of progress, which no one even bothered to talk about anymore.

But at half past two o'clock in the morning, 20 calle was silent. Exhaustion and fear had emptied it. Almost at the bottom of the long sloping street, and with Avenida Bolívar only a block or so away, Cage abruptly turned right into a darkened cramped lane, and Lena's slick plastic body bag slid to the left side of the corrugated metal floor of the van. Two, then three doorways down, Cage slowed almost to a stop and turned left into a covered drive over which hung a black sign with gold lettering that read: CAPILLA DE SANTA CLARA, and below these words the gold figure of a monk in a cowl, head bowed. The drive into the mortuary's courtyard had a slight upward slope, so that Cage had to gun the van, and again Lena's body slid, this time toward the back of the van. Immediately they came out into a small cobblestone courtyard within a quadrangle formed by the walls of stone and stucco buildings.

Cage pulled well into the courtyard, cut the motor, and set the brake.

"Wait a second," he said before Haydon could move to get out. They had had to roll down their windows during the short trip because the odor of formaldehyde had grown from faint to unbearable, and now they sat in silence as Cage seemed to be listening for something. In a moment he opened his door, stepped out of the van into the dark courtyard, and immediately a deep rumble of growling issued from the walls around them. Though the dogs were hidden in the darkness, the sound instantly reminded Haydon of the otherworldly growls of the heads of Cerberus.

"They're supposed to be chained," Cage said softly through the window. He moved away from the van into the gray light of the courtyard, and Haydon saw his light-colored guayabera moving first in one direction and then in another around the walls. As he approached each dog, it growled a little louder, but none of them ever barked or left the darkness. He came back to the van. "Come on," he said.

Haydon and Lita got out and followed Cage to a door in the side of the building directly across from the covered entrance through which they had just entered. The stone arch of the doorway was garlanded with bougainvilleas and furnished with a padlocked wrought-iron gate the exact size of the wooden door behind it, and which fitted flush with the stone facing. Cage reached through the bars and pushed a button set in the stone. At the distant ringing of the bell, one of the mongrels felt obligated to yowl, setting up a chain reaction of canine alerts in all the unseen courtyards up and down the narrow street outside.

A light came on in a small stairway window above their heads, and they waited for the next sign of life, the opening of the little window in the wooden door.

"¿Quién es?" An eye blinked at them through the opening.

"Macabeo, it's Cage."

"Cage. Ah. *Momentito.*" The little window snapped shut, keys and latches snicked and clicked on the other side of the heavy door, which soon swung open cautiously with the creaking sound effects of a B-grade horror film.

"¡Perro! ¡Callate!"

Macabeo rebuked the mongrel from behind the iron bars as he struggled with the padlock. The dog shut up as he was told, but the others nagged from the far-off courtyards, loath to forgo their birthright.

"Open the goddamned garage," Cage said, impatient with Macabeo's fumbling, and backed away from the bars. Immediately electric motors whirred behind an adjacent wall, and a corrugated metal garage door began peeling up from an alcove.

"I can't tolerate that little shit," Cage said to Haydon, not bothering to lower his voice. "To be a mortician is one thing. To be a mortician in Guatemala is another thing. To be a mortician in Guatemala with a thriving business in 'discreet' deaths, deaths with 'connections' is something else. Macabeo Micheo is nothing more than a well-paid maggot."

Cage walked away, and Haydon started to follow him, but he suddenly felt Lita's small hand on his arm.

"Espera," she said. Wait.

Haydon looked at her. She was still holding the folder Cage had given her at the morgue, and Haydon suspected that she would hang onto it until the end of time, unless Cage told her otherwise. He was beginning to think that she was more than an efficient apprentice, one of

Cage's strangely loyal band of free agents he had heard so much about over the years. He was beginning to think that she was extraordinary in ways he was yet to discover. As he looked at her, he thought he saw her smile faintly, though it was difficult to tell in the gray gloom of the courtyard.

After Cage backed the van around into the slip revealed by the raised garage door, he came back across the courtyard to them, and they opened the wrought-iron grille and pushed open the heavy wooden door. They entered a dim little parlor that smelled of old furniture and from which a curving staircase rose almost from the middle of the room. Lita closed the door behind them, and Cage stopped and turned to Haydon.

"I've already looked at the papers we got on Lena's case," he said, keeping his voice down. "And I'm going to give them to you. But you're going to find some surprises. The police report in there is written by the *subcomisario* in Huehuetenango." Cage paused. "I mean, the way it's set up now, she should be in the morgue in Huehue, right? In this report it says she was brought to Huehue morgue by some Indian women. It also says that a doctor—a Guatemalan doctor—brought her to Guatemala City."

"What's his name?"

"Uh, Gra . . . Grajeda, I think it was."

Haydon said nothing.

"Thing is, that was Sunday night, after midnight, way in the morning. Whoever got her, got her as soon as she and Baine arrived up there."

"Up there?"

"Well, the Indian women said they came from Yajaucú. That's about fifty-eight, sixty kilometers east of Huehue. Close to the Quiché border. There's a lot of shit going on here, Haydon. I'm not real comfortable with some of this." He sighed. "Okay, now what we've got to do is go in there and look at her. Take note of the wounds, remember what they are because we've got to leave her here."

Cage turned away and stepped into a small arched corridor that passed under the rising bend of the stone stairs. Haydon followed him through it into a musty, windowless little chamber that was Macabeo Micheo's place of business.

The close quarters were poorly lighted except for two white tile autopsy tables that dwarfed everything else in the small space. Each table had a lavage trough that went around its edges, and above each table a long, gable-shaped fluorescent lighting fixture cast its glare onto the white tiles. To their left, glinting in the oblique light, were four shiny stainless-steel lockers that had been installed into the stone walls, looking peculiarly anachronistic, like cryonic tubes in a medieval keep.

The first table was bare except for a plastic bottle of Shangrila mineral water. Lena was on the second table, her blanched skin almost shimmering in the white light, the lavage trough around her gurgling with circulating water that was being fed from a green lawn hose wired to the corner of the trough. The circulated water was sucking out through a drain at the foot of the table, and from there, probably out into the night gutters of the capital.

Macabeo and his assistant, a flat-faced and obviously simpleminded young Indian, stood at a kind of shambling attention at the head of the table, wearing rubber aprons and waiting expectantly.

"Buenas," Macabeo said. He was not exactly fat, but he was puffy, with a kind of jelly-textured body and large doelike eyes that were plagued by a crusty discharge. His coloring was peculiar, with slightly darker pigmentation around his eyes and mouth, which he tended to hold in a tight approximation of prim sobriety.

Cage half turned to Haydon, once again not bothering to lower his voice.

"The thing that's always given me the creeps about this guy," he said, jerking his head toward Macabeo, "is that he always handles the bodies as though his fingers are . . . fluttering over the final details of some kind of fancy cake decorations. It's an all too joyful mannerism for such appalling work, it seems to me." He looked at the two men and then back to Haydon. "The other one, the moronic Indian, is Nestor. Anything that requires some muscle power is done by him. He's the interesting one. That stupid face doesn't prepare you for what he does. He works fast and neat. He's a damned idiot savant about autopsies, has a precise, an uncanny knowledge of human anatomy." He shook his head. "These weirdos," he said, "get regular cash payments from the U.S. State Department. Through step-backs, of course. Untraceable."

Haydon needed to remember every single word. Cage was a man who never explained himself, so Haydon could only guess why he had been asked on this macabre errand. Whatever the reason, Haydon got the sense that it was "out of channels," that it was something that Cage normally would have done by himself, with Lita's help, of course. That was probably the reason he had gone to so much trouble to play out the charade with the policemen. Somewhere along the line Cage expected it

101

to make a difference that Haydon had seen all this, but as of right now Haydon couldn't understand why, nor did he understand why his face needed to be hidden from the DIC agent who had stopped them earlier, yet these two morgue rats did not seem to be a concern.

Cage stood looking at Lena a moment.

"Get out of the way," he said to Macabeo and Nestor, and they quickly scuttled back from the table and stood rigidly against the stainless-steel lockers as Cage and Haydon moved up to the body.

Lena's arms were again crossed on her chest, the nubs of her wrists already black with age. The severed hands themselves, apparently having been found near her body by the Indian women and having traveled all this way with her as "additional items," were again stacked on her lower abdomen. Cage walked around the table on the other side of Haydon, while Lita waited, away from the table.

The smell of Macabeo's chamber was so potent that Haydon could taste it, even, he thought, feel it on his face like an unctuous reek. He made a conscious effort to be analytic, to ignore his senses as he examined Lena's cadaver. Aside from the autopsy incisions, which Haydon noticed had been sutured with businesslike, regularly spaced stitches, he noticed the other wound, the one that had been business before the business of autopsy, the ragged, irregular line crossing from one side of Lena's abdomen to the other. It was a familiar wound, and seeing it he felt a wave of warmth wash over him like a jolt of fever that left his legs quivering and uncertain.

Her hands caught his attention again, dirt still caking the exposed ganglia, nails missing from half the fingers. There were wounds between her legs he wouldn't look at. But he did force his eyes to go to her face again. Her head was propped on a wooden block, and her long blond hair, still dirty, was draped over the trough and hung stiffly over the end of the slab. The punishment she had suffered had done gruesome things to her face. Now, as she lay pale and motionless on the slippery tile, there was hardly a feature familiar to him, though as he studied the anonymity of her face he wanted to believe that there was something in the whole of her distortions that recalled to him the beautiful young woman he had seen in so many pictures since her disappearance in Houston three months earlier. He thought of Germaine Muller.

"Don't do anything to her, Macabeo," Cage snapped. Haydon looked up. Cage's eyes were fixed on Lena's face too. "Don't wash her. Don't even by God touch her. Nothing!"

"Para servirle." The Guatemalan bowed quickly, orientally obedient and alert to the disturbed tone in Cage's voice.

"Bloody nothing!" Cage hissed, turning on Nestor. *¡Nada!*

Nestor blinked.

"Put her in the . . . goddamned locker and leave her the hell alone."

Nestor reached stiffly back into the shadows, his bewildered eyes locked on Cage as he turned off the water to the hose in a surreptitious movement meant to elude Cage's wrath. They all stood there and listened to the water in the lavage trough burble to the low end and suck down the drain with a loud, nasty gasp.

No one moved.

Suddenly Haydon turned around, and his eyes met Lita's gaze. She was studying him, dark eyes looking from the round face of a brown angel with a familiar, knowing intelligence. He moved around the end of the empty autopsy table and walked out of the dank little chamber, out of the muggy morgue-ish air, through the low, narrow corridor, through the musty parlor, and out into the courtyard, hating to leave Lena behind with death's monkeys, alone when the lights went out in a strange country, afraid for all he knew, even in death.

At the sound of Haydon's footsteps on the cobblestones, Cerberus moaned again from all his dark corners. Christ, what a surreal country. Haydon took several deep breaths as if to cleanse his lungs of all the death he had inhaled in the past hour. He looked up past the high walls of the courtyard, but the sky was starless, only a gray, drifting firmament.

He heard footsteps coming from the doorway behind him, light steps coming almost to him before stopping. Knowing who it was, he turned around. Lita reached out and handed him a pack of cigarettes and a red Bic lighter. He took a cigarette and lighted it and handed them back to her. The smoke was acrid, but chased the stench of the mortuary from his nostrils. He inhaled deeply several times, and the smoke hung reluctantly above his head, waiting in the still darkness. In Guatemala, vapors did not dissipate easily. They lingered, unconvinced that they had been genuinely severed from that which had brought them into being.

Lita stood with him in silence, holding the cigarettes and the manila folder. She looked at him a moment.

"This girl," she said, "is a friend, a good friend?"

Haydon shook his head. "No. I had never met her." He paused. "I know her mother."

103

"Ahhh," Lita said, probably misunderstanding the situation, Haydon thought.

"Cage," she said, pronouncing his name with a soft *g*. "I think he is very angry . . . of this thing. He has much pain of this thing," she said, the hand holding the cigarettes coming up to her heart. "This is the way of many peoples in Guatemala . . . a long time dying." She was silent a moment. *"Lo siento mucho,"* she said softly. I am very sorry.

Chapter 16

"I'll tell you some of what I understand and some of what I don't understand," Cage said, smoking and driving the van back through the gloomy calles and avenidas toward Haydon's hotel. "You know we had the national elections here not long ago. The U.S. government, which has tried to control this country one way or another since the 1950s, has made a big deal about this election being the first time in Guatemalan history that the power of government has been transferred from one elected civilian to another elected civilian. Democracy, right? Well, that's State Department rhetorical bullshit. Saying it's so doesn't make it so. But all the folks back in the States who want to believe that democracy is making progress in Latin America can settle back in their overstuffed chairs with a self-satisfied belch and watch the ball game without worrying about it . . . because the State Department says democracy's on a roll in Latin America."

Cage tossed his cigarette out the window of the van. "The facts on the ground are a hell of a lot different." He held up his thumb. "One: the army controls everything." He held up his forefinger. "Two: there's a tiny wealthy elite that holds most of the arable land and largely controls the economic fortunes of the country. Three: the military upholds this inequitable situation, and between the military and this mercantile elite there is an easy romance. But overall they complement each other and both want to see the status quo remain just that. Sometimes the military gets out of hand, but in general there's a kind of grisly checks-and-balances thing between money and repressive violence. Four: the big losers are 90 percent of the population. Five: none of this is about to change. The civilian "government" is a real farce. The minute they make noises like they're going to do something substantive, like demilitarization, agrarian reform, land redistribution, any move toward *real* civilian control of the country, bodies of legislators and politicians and judges and businessmen —or the bodies of their family members—start turning up like dead flies. Suddenly all the high-sounding words and idealism vanishes in an atmosphere of raw fear. 'Democratization' is still just a U.S. fantasy."

Cage had finally made his way back to the Avenida La Reforma, not far from Campo de Marte, the main military headquarters in the city, a fortress with parapets and high walls and armed guards. It was painted gray with white trim, as neat as a Disney film set.

106

"The Indians," Cage said, "they don't have shit. Nothing to lose. So you're seeing more and more organizing there, specially in some areas where they're refusing to participate in the civil-defense patrols, areas where they're trying to organize for labor reforms, for decent wages— just last month the wealthy landowners raised hell because the legislature was 'threatening' to raise the minimum wage of fieldworkers to two dollars a day. They said that would bankrupt them." He shook his head. "And people get killed over shit like this."

He drove a moment in silence, glancing up at his rearview mirror.

"I got this communication after I left you at the steak house tonight. 'Go to the Cementerio General . . . you will know which one to take to Macabeo's.' Shit. I had a feeling right then. So I went and found Lena. I read the report. But I didn't get her. Instead I went to get you. I wanted you to see all this, because I'm not sure how this is going to play from here."

The meaning wasn't altogether clear to Haydon, but Cage could make it clear—when he wanted to. And would—when he wanted to. Right now Haydon had to listen. He had to remember everything, because the time would come when he would have to make connections, and he had better be able to do it.

"In 1988 and 1989 there were three failed coup attempts to overthrow Vinicio Cerezo, the former presidential flimflam artist. Each attempt was initiated by a faction of the military made up of disgruntled hard-liners and was thwarted by a faction of the military loyal to the high command. After the third attempt, however, the high command and the president decided to give in to some of the hard-liners' demands, actually they gave in to *most* of them. Among these was increased military control of the police forces. So now you've got a national police force whose detectives —agents—are thoroughly infiltrated by military intelligence and who have become, in effect, an arm of the military. The major players in the police force are the agents of the Department for Criminal Investigations —the DIC. Within the military itself, the major players are the guys in military intelligence—G-2. A huge percentage of the death-squad work is done by these two groups."

Cage went into his guayabera for another cigarette, guiding the van with his elbows as he lighted it. He had slowed the van considerably to give himself time to tell his story. He blew a blue stream of smoke out the window and got his hands back on the steering wheel.

"Now in her work with USAID, Lena had been spending some time in a little town called Soloma, which is roughly in the middle of the *departamento* of Huehuetenango and not too far from a village called Yajaucú, which is right on the Huehue border with the *departamento* of El Quiché. Two things are directly across the border from Yajaucú in Quiché. One: a major 'area of conflict' known as the Ixil Triangle where for years the Guatemalan military has conducted a scorched-earth policy against the guerrillas. There are hundreds of military posts, military garrisons, military bases, airstrips, supply and ammunition depots.

107

Within this ravaged territory they also have set up bleak 'model villages' and 'reeducation centers' . . . that is, prison camps. A very grim situation with all the atrocities associated with this kind of thing where the native population is considered a lower form of animal life.

"The second thing that is in this area is a region of jungle known by the army as an 'area of refuge.' Basically that means an area that the army doesn't control, so they assume that the guerrillas take refuge there. Mostly it's occupied by a pitiful but plucky bunch of Indians from eight or nine different ethnic groups who have formed what they call 'communities in resistance.' Basically, these are people who simply refuse to give up everything and go live in the tin-roofed hovels of the model villages where they have to ask the army's permission to inhale or even piss on the weeds. These areas are periodically subjected to army sweeps, raids in which any village they find is destroyed. Usually these raids are preceded by strategic, quick-bombing raids by helicopters or Pilatus PC-7s, or A-37s. Those who aren't killed flee deeper into the jungle. When they return to their villages—if they return—there's nothing left but smoke and ashes.

"I have access to reports," he said. He had gone past the Residencial Reforma, which was across the broad esplanade on the other side of the boulevard, and was driving slowly toward the oval Parque Independencia, giving himself time to finish what he had to say. "I see things from a honeycomb of intelligence offices located in the National Palace and in its annex offices. One of them, the Presidential Intelligence Agency, works the G-2. They've been tracking Lena from the moment she arrived here from Houston three months ago. I don't know why, but they don't have to have much of a reason. They've developed quite a dossier. The thing is, I just came across this material a week or two before Jim Fossler showed up down here, and I only got the first two months of their reports. I don't know what's happened more recently.

"I started running some other traps. The DIC had stuff on her movements here in the capital. And the U.S. Defense Intelligence Agency had a flag on her. The Israeli advisors picked up on her. And others. The big zero was the CIA. They just gave me a big dumb look like they didn't know what the hell I was talking about.

"Then suddenly there was a change—and this is very unusual—I began to get frozen out on these inquiries. That's never happened to me before. This business is all about money. The CIA, the Defense Intelligence Agency, the Israelis, all of them pay for their information. All except the National Security Agency, which just listens in on everybody's business whenever they want to. But with all the rest it's money. You can just kiss off loyalties, high ideals, patriotism, stuff like that. It's money. You buy information, the more sensitive the product, the higher the price. It's not a complicated kind of a system."

They circled the Parque Independencia and headed back down the boulevard, Cage's van the only vehicle rounding the oval in the smoky light of the small morning hours.

"My contacts have always been excellent, my payout very high, my product superior. But they began to freeze me out on Lena. I couldn't get shit on her. It just shut off. All I know is that while she was working for AID up there in Huehue, she was taking time off and making trips across the Río Quisil, across the border into El Quiché into the area of refuge. These intelligence people could trace her in and then they had to stop, but they were never able to pick her up coming out. She'd just disappear and then show up in Huehuetenango or Santa Cruz Del Quiché or back here in Guatemala City or wherever and go on about her business. And when she was here in the capital the DIC had a hell of a time keeping up with her. She'd shake her surveillance more than half the time."

Cage paused to consult his own thoughts as they passed the Camino Real. On the other side of the avenue a single pair of headlights approached from far off, near the Plazuela Reina Barrios. Cage showed no interest in them.

"I have to tell you," he said, "I was surprised at what I was finding out, but I really admired her. The girl was good. Only thing is, I don't know what the hell she was doing. Whatever it was, she got killed for it."

They were now at the gates of Haydon's hotel, and Cage pulled off the street. Cage reached back to Lita and got the manila folder and handed it to Haydon.

"Better look at this," he said. "Don't tell anybody about tonight. It's all right if you mention to Janet that we've talked—it might even work to your advantage—but not about any of this. Keep it general. I'll be in touch."

It was a familiar phrase that hadn't proved to be highly reliable in the past, but Haydon was taking what he could get. Cage put the van in gear,

109

and Haydon looked back at Lita, who was staring at him with dark, unreadable eyes. He looked at Cage again, but instead of opening the van door to get out he said, "I thought you only sold information."

Cage had one hand on the van's gearshift, and they were looking at each other.

"I do what I have to do," Cage said. He didn't sound the least bit apologetic.

"Taking Lena's body to Macabeo's for Pittner was something you had to do."

"Damn right it was."

"Why?"

"Because Lena's beyond giving a shit, and I'm not. Because the reality is Pittner's still in control of a lot of history here."

"Why did he want you to do it? Why not one of his salaried people?"

"I didn't ask him."

"You don't know?"

"I don't want to know."

"Why did you want me along?"

"You'll know when it's time to know," Cage said. "You'd better get out."

As Cage drove away, Haydon once again pushed the button on the right side of the gates. When they opened, he pushed his way through and quickly walked across the silent courtyard. At the front desk the same night clerk already had Haydon's key pulled from its pigeonhole against the wall, and the blank expression in his eyes when they met Haydon's said he didn't want to be engaged in any kind of dialogue.

As soon as Haydon got to his room he removed his clothes and, even as late as it was, went straight to the shower. He bathed quickly, got out, put on his pajamas and got into bed with the manila folder.

110

The police report from Huehuetenango was several pages, but only because the police clerk had double-spaced it. The text itself was brief. A group of Ixil Indian women had brought Lena's body to the military commissioner in Soloma from Yajaucú, a small village on the Río Quisil, a tributary of the larger Río Ixcán, which roared into Guatemala from Mexico not many kilometers to the north. Because they came from so close to the Quiché border, near an area of refuge, the women had put their own lives in considerable danger by emerging from that country with a dead white woman whom, incidentally, they said they had found in their milpa where they had gone early that morning to work.

Though Soloma was only a dusty little town that lies in what once was probably the bed of a lake and surrounded by the Cuchumatanes, it was a designated *cabecera municipal,* a district headquarters. The men who were the local authorities there had obligations. An investigation was made into Lena's death by the local military commissioner—who neither slept nor dreamed without permission from the nearby garrison commandante—and it was determined that the guerrillas had killed her and "violated" her. If Lena had been an Indian, she would have been buried there, but no one wanted the responsibility of burying a white woman, so they "requisitioned" a place for her on a truck loaded with cassava and other vegetables destined for the departmental capital of Huehuetenango.

No doubt eager to be rid of the responsibility of this ghastly cargo foisted upon him, the truck driver drove at night over the dangerously crooked and precipitous dirt roads that crossed the Cuchumatanes to Huehuetenango. Still receiving special treatment, the "XX," as Lena and every other unidentified body was known, was taken to the main hospital, where an autopsy was performed by Dr. Aris Grajeda, a visiting physician from Guatemala City. He was told by the truck driver that the XX's mother wanted her in Guatemala. Dr. Grajeda agreed to see that she got to the capital. She was put into a heavy plastic bag along with several chunks of ice from the hospital commissary and loaded into Dr. Grajeda's van. End of report.

There was a separate document attached to the first, written by the precinct chief of the Gabinete de Identificación in Zona 6 in Guatemala City: The unidentified female was delivered to them "anonymously" on Sunday night, accompanied by the attached report, which was found in an envelope inside the plastic bag with her. She was photographed, and her picture was placed in the book of the dead. Her body was sent to the morgue at the Cementerio General that same night.

Chapter 17

Haydon slept until nine o'clock the next morning, when even his disconnected dreams about what he had seen and heard and smelled and felt since he had arrived in Guatemala City the night before could no longer ignore the roar of traffic that poured in through the two windows above his bed. Sometime during the still, quiet hours before daybreak a chill had crept into the old house, and he had groped around at the foot of the bed and pulled up the covers he had thrown off as he went to sleep. Now, as the morning began to warm again, he pushed back the covers once more and rolled over, his limbs feeling thick and heavy, his stiff neck making it difficult for him to find a comfortable position now that he was conscious. Even though he had showered the night before, he got up from the bed and pulled off his pajamas and stepped into the shower again. He felt as if he wouldn't be able to think straight if he didn't.

And he had to think straight. Lena Muller could no longer be the focus of Haydon's reason for being there. In the States he would be plunged headlong into a homicide investigation, here he could only walk away from it. At least that would be the conventional wisdom. Report her death and go home. It seemed an outrageous option, but he knew it was the only real one. But there was Fossler's disappearance. This was not so easily reconciled. There were options. He had no doubt that Cage had been right to walk away from Jim Fossler's place. If there was anything Haydon could do for Fossler—and he didn't have the remotest idea what it might be—he didn't think it would be through the embassy with its slow-moving front-door policies and its unknown back-door policies with their hidden agendas and unofficial status and deniable operations. Throughout the world U.S. ambassadors handled the CIA presence in their embassies in different ways; some tried to stay on top of CIA activities, tried to keep themselves at least halfway informed about the operations being conducted under the guise of the embassy's aegis, while others simply turned their backs, covered their ears, and shut their eyes. Deniability as a form of moral triage. Haydon didn't have the time to invest in trying to negotiate with the many faces of officialdom.

But there were other ways to look for Fossler, and he himself had given Haydon a lead or two. If Haydon could believe Janet Pittner, and he doubted he could, she didn't know anything about Jim Fossler. She was not going to be forthcoming, not just yet anyway. Cage had done his part. Baine was gone. And Lena was . . . gone. Of the names that Fossler had given him over the telephone that left only Dr. Aris Grajeda, who had already brought himself onstage again through the police report Haydon had read just a few hours earlier. Grajeda would be his next stop.

Haydon got out of the shower and dressed in his other change of clothes. He left the clothes he'd worn the day before in his room with a note to the maid to have them cleaned that day and went down to breakfast in the long atrium dining room.

The Residencial Reforma was usually comfortably full, and Haydon

113

had never stayed there when he didn't meet half a dozen Americans. With the embassy nearby, it was a popular place with people who had business there, from businessmen to student travelers. It was a quiet, comfortable place that was relatively inexpensive and had the kind of residential atmosphere—with its two parlors, American television channels, and friendly staff—that appealed to a more interesting kind of clientele than the Club Med trade.

He ate alone at a small corner table next to two of the marble pillars. Since the dining room opened at seven o'clock, the people who had business in the city had already eaten and were gone and the people there now were less likely to be on a strict schedule. He saw a couple of men who were dead ringers for "American advisors," of which there were scores circulating throughout Guatemala, a girl by herself who seemed to be a student, a young couple reading travel brochures on the Mayan pyramids, a middle-aged couple speaking German, and a young auburn-haired woman reading a French novel.

By nine-fifty Haydon was walking south on the Avenida La Reforma to the Camino Real, where he knew he could get a rental car. By ten-thirty he had rented a Japanese sedan and had spent ten minutes with a new map of the city.

There was no easy way to get to Mezquital. Even though it was not that far as the crow flies, it was on the other side of one of the major ravines that cut into the south side of the city and accommodated the Río Guadrón. Haydon had to drive northward on Diagonal 12 and then switch back southward at the *Trébol,* picking up Petapa, the main avenue to the University of San Carlos.

But where he was heading was far beyond San Carlos, the entrance to which he passed in only a few minutes. He continued along the increasingly industrialized thoroughfare past the Shell and Chevron storage facilities, past steelworks and a paraffin processing plant and a sack manufacturing company. There were few houses, all of them poor, and then even those became sparse, giving way to acres of weedy lots that surrounded the industries. He passed a glass factory on the left and then a tire manufacturing plant, on the right an industrial adhesives plant and a plastics manufactory, and then he crossed the railroad tracks. To his left even the industries gave way to broad parched spaces of scrub brush and weeds entangled with windblown trash, and then on the right a poor *colonia* sprang up like an afterthought. From there, nothing but the squatters' shacks and, in the distance, the majestic purple slopes and cloudy crowns of volcanos Pacaya and Agua southwest of the city.

Ahead of him a barefooted woman was walking toward him leading a scrawny, long-legged pig on a thin rope. As Haydon approached, he put his arm out the window and raised his hand as he slowed the car and stopped.

"*Perdoname, señora. Buscando para un doctor, un guatemalteco, que vive aquí.*"

The woman pulled the pig up short and smiled. Her teeth were bad, but she had beautiful jet hair braided up in the traditional Indian style with a brilliant green *cinta*. She wore the Indian *corte* wraparound skirt, but her *huipil* had been discarded for a man's baggy and transparent nylon shirt. She told Haydon she knew the doctor, a good man. She told him to go to the *pirul* tree and follow the path over the sandy embankment and down through the houses on the slope on the other side. Cross the railroad tracks. The *clínica* was to the left a little way.

Haydon thanked her.

"*Se va bien,*" she said, and turned away as Haydon put the car in gear.

He drove the short distance to the pepper tree and pulled off the road into its thin, lacy shade. He locked the car and looked up at the embankment that rose immediately from the roadside. Two boys were watching him from a hedge of dry weeds, like urchin bandits waiting for the advantage. He beckoned to them, and they came scrambling down the slope, their matted hair and rags and waving arms awash in a small cloud of dust. He gave each of them some money to guard the car and started up the shallow rut of the path. There was a remote chance they wouldn't strip the car before he returned. When he got to the top of the embankment the path branched out into a *colonia* of squatters' shacks perched on the slope that fell toward the railroad tracks fifty meters below. He chose one of the widest trails, packed hard by legions of bare feet, and followed it in a switchback pattern down the embankment past cardboard and tin shacks and an occasional better one of *lepa,* a cheap, hand-hewn lumber widely used throughout the city by squatters or anyone wanting to throw up a fast shelter.

He met a single file of women carrying plastic jugs of water on their heads and then on the switchback encountered two little boys squatting together as they defecated on the edge of the path, their dirty, sweaty

115

faces and large dark eyes looking out from under an umbrella of weeds. Their gazes followed Haydon with open curiosity and without embarrassment, as though he had been a large interloping crane that it was their happy pleasure to observe in passing.

At the railroad track at the bottom of the embankment, packs of children played along the rails that curved out of sight around a bend in both directions. He stopped a boy who had perched a runty and fly-pestered pup on a piece of wood that he was scooting along the hot, shiny rails and asked about the doctor. The little boy had no idea who he was talking about, but a girl, nine or ten years old, overheard his question and offered to take Haydon to him. She was well groomed and dressed in the bright woven clothes of one of Guatemala's many Indian groups, and though Haydon knew too little of their traditional costumes to know which one, he could tell that she was a newcomer from the countryside. She had not yet acquired the haunted look that the slums would inevitably give her, and her native dress had not yet given way to the inescapable filth of her surroundings or to the odd piece of nylon or polyester that would necessarily replace the worn-out *huipil* and *corte*.

Haydon followed her across the rails and into another maze of narrow trails and shanties, climbing gradually, the paths converging and veering off, the sounds of children crying and women's conversation and evangelical radio preachers issuing from the cracks in the shanties, the odors of wood smoke and corn tortillas, and of animal and human feces that dotted the edges of the paths and grew odoriferous in the increasing heat.

She walked at a steady pace, glancing back occasionally to see if he was still with her, her little bare feet working the uneven surface of the paths with a sure grip. As she walked she swung a frayed string with a red button on the end of it, around and around, making pink circles in the air. She was a gregarious, carefree child on friendly terms with her surroundings. Occasionally she would pause and quickly peek into a doorway or over a rickety fence and say *Buenas* to whoever was there and be on her way again before Haydon could even catch up with her. She paused to scratch a mongrel who lay in a hole he had dug next to a wall and paused again to touch a naked baby gnawing on a corncob in a doorway. But she never forgot her task, and before Haydon knew it they had reached an area where an occasional cinder-block building began to mark the ragged margin where the permanent slums merged with the squatters' hovels.

They came into an actual street, a narrow, unpaved one so gouged with holes that it was impassable by vehicle. The child automatically sought the thin ribbon of shade next to the cinder-block buildings, which she followed for three or four minutes before she suddenly turned in to a doorway, and Haydon found himself at the entrance of a dark room redolent of alcohol.

"El doctor," she announced proudly from the dark, and Haydon made out her figure across the room, standing in front of a glass cabinet next to the figure of Aris Grajeda half turned from the shelves where he had been working.

"Dr. Grajeda?" Haydon asked, and then understanding Grajeda's silence, he quickly added, "I'm Stuart Haydon."

"Yes," the Guatemalan said. He squared his shoulders to Haydon and put his arm around the child, who snuggled up to him. He was little more than a dim silhouette, but Haydon could see that he was several inches shorter than himself, the typical Guatemalan stature. His shoulders were neither broad nor narrow, but well proportioned, his weight neither light nor heavy. He waited calmly beside the child, who seemed to regard him with a comfortable intimacy. Haydon had the sense that the doctor was quickly but coolheadedly appraising him.

"Have you got a few minutes to talk to me?"

"An American?"

"Yes, I am. I'd like to ask you some questions about Lena Muller."

"Who?" Grajeda was taking no chances.

"The American woman you autopsied in Huehuetenango and brought back to the capital."

Grajeda looked at Haydon in silence, but because of the dim light in the room, Haydon could not see his expression.

"Are you attached to the American embassy?" Grajeda asked. His voice was rather soft and patient, even polite. He spoke excellent English and pronounced his words precisely. As he turned just right to the weak light coming in from the window just behind him, the surfaces of his eyeglasses threw two discal reflections from the shadows.

"No," Haydon said. "I'm not from the embassy." He explained briefly who he was and why he was there, and even took out his shield and handed it across to Grajeda, who examined it, holding it up to the light coming through the window behind him.

"Fossler is a friend?" he asked, handing back the shield.

Haydon nodded, wondering if he should tell him about Fossler's room.

"Then he did come by and talk to you yesterday morning?" Haydon asked.

"I like Fossler," Grajeda's voice lightened as he remembered his conversation with the American. "Why didn't he come with you?"

"I'm afraid that something might have happened to him," Haydon said. "He was supposed to have met me at the airport last night, but he wasn't there. I went to the address he gave me, to his room, and the place had been ransacked. There was blood everywhere, but Fossler was gone."

Grajeda listened to this without reaction, and there was a lengthy pause before he asked, "You didn't talk to him after he talked to me?"

"No."

Grajeda nodded and quietly stroked the child's hair.

Haydon's eyes were adjusting to the dim light now. They were standing in a kind of office. There was a desk by a window behind Grajeda and another doorway leading into another room where there was at least one table with a sheet over it. There were a few chairs lined along the wall to Haydon's left, and handwritten signs everywhere encouraging people not to defecate or urinate on the dirt floors of their houses—the Spanish was earthy: "shit" and "piss"—not to handle food after shitting or pissing until they had washed; not to walk without sandals (this admonition was accompanied by a huge, fierce drawing of a hookworm); not to have sexual intercourse without condoms, which *el doctor* would provide without charge; not to drink water until they had boiled it or put pills in it, which *el doctor* would give them without charge. All of these cautionary encouragements were accompanied by simple drawings with the condemned behavior crossed out.

"I talked to Jim Fossler on Sunday afternoon," Haydon said. "He told me then that you were a friend of Lena's, that you had worked with her in the western highlands."

118

Grajeda's face changed at this last remark. Though he was clearly a ladino—of European and Indian blood, rather than pure Indian—the doctor had retained the Mayan eyes of his ancestors, slightly Asian in their oblique relationship to his rather round face. His complexion was dusky and he had the coarse black hair of the Indian as well. He wore a neatly clipped moustache and goatee, and both his beard and his hair were prematurely streaked with gray.

"I am afraid Mr. Fossler has made a mistake," he said with a respectful smile.

"How's that?"

"I never knew this woman Muller. He said the same thing to me, that I knew her. I told him I didn't. Who told him that I knew her?"

"He didn't say."

"I'm sorry if both of you have come to see me believing that this is the situation, that I knew her."

"I don't know who told him," Haydon said, "but since I didn't get a chance to see him after he spoke to you, I don't know anything about your conversation."

Grajeda thought about this. "Well then, I suppose we should talk," he said. He looked down at the girl and then reached up on top of the cabinet and got down a crumpled paper bag that was clearly his lunch sack. Untwisting the top of the bag, he reached in and pulled out an orange and gave it to the little girl. He thanked her for her kindness in bringing this *gringo* to him, and told her to run along, his tone good-natured as if he were used to dealing with children. Turning back to the glass cabinet, he closed its doors, locked them, and put the key in the pocket of the short white laboratory coat he was wearing.

"*¡Siéntese!*" he said, and offered Haydon one of the rickety chairs against the plaster wall. He moved around behind his desk and sat down, the light coming in over his right shoulder from the screenless window. The day was heating up quickly, but a slight coolness remained within the thick walls. Haydon could hear chickens somewhere outside, and snatches of women's conversations as they passed by the open door of the clinic. Grajeda smiled again, a soft, almost bashful smile, the smile of Buddha.

"I didn't bring her back from Huehuetenango," he said with a huge sigh. "It was a tragedy. Fossler knew she was dead. I told him yesterday morning when he was out here."

119

Chapter 18

Dr. Aris Grajeda was in his early thirties. His thick Indian hair formed a rather low hairline on his forehead, and though it was neatly combed and barbered, a heavy wave of it hung in a romantic coil above his eyes. He had dark eyes that were at once compassionate and unflinching, and a straight nose with the pronounced nostrils of a Mayan. His mouth, however, was European, finely sculpted with a dimple in the center of his upper lip. His steel-rimmed glasses gave him the look of a man on the far edge of his youth. He sat in front of Haydon with his elbows on his desk, his hands clasped together as he leaned forward, and as he talked he sometimes stroked his handsome goatee in the manner of a thoughtful man. The sleeves of his lab coat were too long, and he had folded them back once to reveal the white cuff of a wrinkled shirt. His hands seemed to be the hands of a pianist, with long fingers and cleanly manicured nails.

"I was in Huehuetenango helping a surgeon friend of mine who works in the main hospital there," he said. "The one on 6a calle, if you are familiar with it, on the road to Guatemala City. He had lined up a number of surgeries, and I went up to assist him. On some of these things, you like to have doctors you know assisting. The man's an Italian, an ophthalmologist. He helps me here in Mezquital and at the Roosevelt Hospital, and I go up there. We are still cleaning up the human debris left behind by the measles epidemic." He regarded Haydon through his wire-framed lenses. "You know of the epidemic?"

Haydon nodded.

"You know how bad it was?"

"I read about it."

Grajeda sat back in his chair, took a ballpoint pen from his shirt pocket, popped out the point, and made a couple of doodling marks on a notepad.

"In the next *departamento* over, in Quiché, more than a thousand children died in one month of the epidemic," he said. "Just in one *departamento*. One thousand. Can you imagine one thousand little bodies lined up side by side in a road? Or one thousand tiny caskets? Rubella." He shrugged. "Just measles, that's all it was. A lot of charitable organizations from Europe and the United States had given money to the Cerezo government for the purchase of vaccine and to inoculate children through the Accelerated Immunization Project. A little vaccine was obtained, not nearly enough, and most of it went bad anyway. It wasn't properly refrigerated. It was in a warehouse here in the city. It never even reached the countryside. Not only that, two million dollars of the money disappeared. The Health Ministry blamed USAID; USAID blamed the Health Ministry. There is an investigation, of course. One thousand children. Just rubella, that's all it was. Very, very sad."

Though his story was a bitter one, Grajeda's manner did not reflect that attitude. As he doodled again with his pen, a serene smile remained

121

on his lips as if it were his belief that the corrupt men who had greatly contributed to this catastrophe were stupid children who could only be pitied for their horrible ignorance. He pushed back his chair and turned sideways to Haydon, his profile squarely in the center of the window behind him. He crossed his legs and looked at a colored poster of venereal disease sores on the wall opposite him and shook his head.

"Well, there were deaths in Huehuetenango too," he said. "Hundreds and hundreds. But there were also many cases, too many cases, in which the children survived . . . except for a lingering infection in the eyes. That's not so uncommon, but where you have modern medical facilities you can fight it. However, here . . . there is only one treatment." Grajeda looked out the window. "Either you let them keep their eyes and allow the infection to spread to the rest of their system and eventually kill them. Or you remove the source of the infection. Send these children back to their families in the countryside to continue living in poverty . . . blind. We spent days and nights taking out tiny eyes and throwing them away. 'Be of good cheer, Mama . . . we have saved the life of your child.' "

Grajeda watched something out of the window, the side of his face washed in an oblique white light. He reached up and ran a hand through the curl that hung over his forehead, pushing it back out of his eyes, and revealing a dark crescent of perspiration under the arm of his stained laboratory coat. He uncrossed his leg and let his foot drop to the gritty floor as he turned around to face Haydon again. He picked up a tiny, strangely shaped gourd and examined it. He held it up so Haydon could see it.

" '¡Un pescado!' Does this look like a fish to you?" He made it swim into the light and back, weaving it gently in the airy waters. Then he put it to one side on his desk again and rested his forearms in front of him and looked at it. "A child gave it to me," he said. "Of course, this child had never seen a fish . . . what did she know? Her mother had seen one once and told her about it."

He hung his head a moment, a gesture of weariness, then he looked up.

"So I was in Huehuetenango helping my friend, saving lives like Albert Schweitzer," Grajeda continued, a self-mocking remark with only a hint of cynicism. "It was ten o'clock at night, or ten-thirty. We had operated a long time, and my colleague had gotten sick and had to stop.

A stomach virus hit him quite suddenly. He had been down on the Río Buca. I think he got something there. Anyway, I was almost glad of the attack. I was exhausted, and if he had not been stricken with cramps and diarrhea I think I would have embarrassed myself by collapsing. They brought her into the hospital, these guys."

"The police?"

"Two were in National Police uniforms, two in plainclothes. I don't know if the two men in suits were G-2 or DIC agents. It doesn't really make any difference. They didn't bother to show me any identification. I was sleeping on one of the operating tables—it was the best place—and they just wheeled her in there and shook me awake. When I got up, they tossed her onto the table where I had been sleeping. Autopsy. ¡Ahorita!

"She was still wrapped in a *rebozo,* and she stank of rotten cassava. I called in a nurse and we started. She was so . . . pale. I had gotten used . . . to dark skin . . ."

Grajeda wiped a hand over his face and sighed. "It wasn't much of an autopsy. I was angry at them. I told them to get the hell out while I did my job, but the lieutenant insisted on all of them staying. They were nervous anyway, having the responsibility of a white woman like that. It was *muy importante* that they stay, he said, for official reasons. No. They were only voyeurs." He swallowed, tried to swallow again but couldn't. "I tried to do a real job of it, methodical, but they got impatient. I yelled at them to get the hell out of there and waved a scalpel at them. Instantly four Uzi's cocked and came up."

Grajeda raised his arms and positioned them close to his chest as if he were gripping the snub-nose Uzi and fixed the imaginary barrel and his eyes on Haydon. He held the pose a moment and then dropped his arms.

"Those guys, they're in love with those weapons. They love to swing them around and point them at people. They love to see your face when you suddenly realize there is just a small breath between the tension in their fingers and your death. Believe me, when you are in that situation it shows in your face. Forget *machismo.* It makes you want to shit your pants."

Grajeda stared at the top of his desk.

"While we were squared off like this, frozen, facing each other, one of them, one of the guys in street clothes, slowly reached out the barrel of his Uzi and put it under the hem of the nurse's dress. He put the barrel up under there, you know. She was petrified." He shook his head and smiled sadly. "All of these guys are cowards. I knew they could wait. Later the nurse would have to pay for my arrogant belligerence. And they would make sure I heard what they had done to her. That's the way they do it. My God." He waved languidly at a fly. "You slip into a kind of moral triage. Your friend was dead. The nurse had to go home to her husband and children. What the hell did it matter, really, if I didn't do the autopsy by the book? I had a live woman and a dead woman. What was I going to do? The nurse knew all this. She was terror-stricken that I was going to stand on principle or something.

"When I finished, they took the body of the girl away in a plastic bag with some ice from the commissary. That's all I know."

"What about the autopsy?"

Grajeda looked at Haydon. "What about it?"

"What happened to her?"

Grajeda was weary; he stroked his goatee. "Oh, she was tortured to death."

"How?"

Grajeda's eyes came back to him, and his face assumed an expression of mild curiosity. "Why do you want to know that?"

"I'm a policeman," Haydon said. "While I don't see torture as a general rule, I do see it. I have to report it in detail the same way a pathologist does. Unfortunately, it's necessary for me to know."

Grajeda's exotic eyes regarded Haydon through the lenses of his small round glasses. He was a striking figure, almost theatrical in his unusual mixture of features and his manner of seeming to understand and even accept with a kind of pained sorrow the horrors that were commonplace in his country.

"These are very bad things," Grajeda said. "These deaths."

124   Haydon waited.

"Here in Guatemala the cruelty is unimaginable," Grajeda mused. "They're trained, you know, these soldiers, to be inhuman. They do whatever they are told. So many of them are only ignorant kids, intimidated and brutalized. Indian kids the army has kidnapped off the streets of the little towns and villages all over this country. And then there are the sadists who get into this business. Every death is a message, a letter to the living. People are not just 'killed' by the death squads, by the G-2, by the DIC. Men are not just disemboweled, their genitalia are cut off and stuffed into their mouths. Women are not just raped, their uteruses are ripped out of their bodies and stretched over their faces. Children are not just killed, they are dragged over barbed wire until the flesh falls from their bones while their parents are forced to watch. Death is not 'just death' in my sad, unfortunate country."

For a moment his eyes seemed to lose contact, and Haydon believed that the young doctor's thoughts were far away from either of them.

"She didn't die quickly," Grajeda said finally. "That's all that really matters."

Neither of them spoke for a moment, and the sounds and the smells of the shanties and their attendant miseries accompanied them in their silence.

"Did you know that there's a report at the Gabinete de Identificación that says that you brought her to Guatemala City?" Haydon asked.

Grajeda sat back in his chair again and raised his eyebrows as though he were offering a mystery. "Let me tell you how it is in Guatemala," he said, "the true importance of the relationship between integrity and vocabulary. Words are nothing here . . . nothing . . . less than nothing. Here lying is pervasive; we discount language altogether. Because there are so many lies, because words are so cheap, they are considered little more than static in a system that has lost respect for language. People are judged by what they do, not by what they say. Belief in the integrity of language does not figure into the equation of everyday life. The lie has attacked my people like a disease and is destroying them as surely as if it were a pestilence. Sadly, it means nothing what the police say or what their reports say. The men who are entrusted with keeping the peace in my poor country are murderers and liars. This is horrible for me to say, but it is the truth."

"Then the last time you saw her was in the autopsy room?"

"The last time I saw her," Grajeda said kindly, "those four men were putting her into a plastic body bag and hauling her out to one of their vans with black windows, and the ice they had thrown in there with her was already melting and dripping out of the bag in little rosy driblets."

It was a cruel image, all the more shocking because of the soft voice with which it was spoken. Grajeda seemed surprisingly free of bitterness. It seemed to Haydon that perhaps the only way the young doctor could hold himself together in the squalor of Mezquital, amid the plastic bags of children's eyes, in the dirty autopsy rooms of the morgues, was to try to make some kind of philosophical peace with the easiness of human cruelty.

"How long have you been here?" Haydon asked, standing.

"The clinic?"

Haydon nodded.

"Three years," Grajeda smiled. "An eternity."

"How are you supported?"

At this question, the young doctor seemed to be uncomfortable. He stood too, facing Haydon across the desk. He seemed to be uncertain about his response for only a moment before he replied.

"I come from a very wealthy family, Mr. Haydon." He tilted his head a little awkwardly; another apologetic smile. "They were proud to have a doctor. My grandfather was a doctor, my father did very well in . . . business. But . . . they were not pleased at this kind of practice. Unfortunately, by insisting on this I caused something of a family disturbance. Now I am something of a black sheep, I'm afraid . . . but they allow me a small stipend. I use it here, and twice a year I go to the United States to raise funds."

Something caught his eye, and he looked past Haydon toward the door and stood up. *"Pase adelante,"* he said quickly.

Haydon turned and saw two soot-covered women in shabby Indian dress hovering outside the door, looking in with large skittish eyes. Their deeply lined faces had the blasted, greasy look of women who had trudged many kilometers along highways and roadsides and streets, grimacing against the hot, particulate thunder of diesel exhausts. They each had children, one with two, the other with three, each with one infant wrapped in a *rebozo.* Grajeda stepped around his desk and said something in his soft voice in an Indian dialect as he approached the doorway, trying to put the women at ease by seeming to speak of their children, three youngsters clinging to their mothers' stained *cortes,* their matted hair standing in shocks as if startled by their condition. Flies drank at the corners of their eyes and sought shade around their runny nostrils. The women shied away like wild, harried creatures, and Grajeda squatted down in the thin shadow a few steps away from his doorway and talked to them, smiling in his way, seeming almost as shy as the women themselves, who, despite the heat, were bundled up in the heavy garments of their people.

Haydon stepped out of the door behind Grajeda, who had completely forgotten him, and walked away. He knew that the Indian women were watching him, wondering if his presence would in some way mean trouble for them. It was best to be gone. He waited until he was about to turn in to one of the paths that went down among the shanties again before he looked back. Grajeda had managed to get one of the women to let him look into her *rebozo* at her infant, his shoulders hunched into a tender approach as he rose slightly from his crouch and looked into the crusty bundle of rags.

Chapter 19

He made his way back through the shanties, down the slope to the railroad right-of-way, across the tracks, and up the trails that wound through the shanties on the other side. The heat was stifling, and the rancid odors of poverty weighted the air as the cicadas sang in the wilting weeds. By the time he topped the embankment where the wispy *pirul* tree marked the position of his car, the dust had caked his shoes and stuck to his pants legs in dry rivulets where he had sweated through the material.

His car was still there, but the boys he had paid to protect it were gone as were his hubcaps and a long chrome strip that ran down either side of the car. He checked his windshield wipers. They were gone too. And the hood ornament. Considering himself lucky, he dusted off his pants legs, unlocked the car, and got in. Rolling down the windows to let out the pent-up heat, he started the engine, turned the car around, and drove back toward the city.

If Grajeda could be believed about the two men in civilian clothes, Haydon was guessing they were DIC agents. The G-2 probably would not have come in the company of two National Police officers, rather, they would have come in the company of soldiers or soldiers poorly disguised as civilians—an incredibly stupid charade that happened far too often. On the other hand, things had changed so dramatically in the last twenty months, the military and National Police had become so closely intertwined that Haydon doubted if anyone really knew their jurisdictions anymore, or even cared. Each agency and the departments within these agencies were little fiefdoms. Intrigue was their single shared characteristic, and turf wars were constant. It was impossible to guess who was in ascendancy or descendancy until the signs of change were so clear that it was too late to do anything but stand back and watch the slaughters that accompanied each shift of power.

That was all the more reason for Haydon to get in touch with Efran Borrayo. It had been Haydon's good fortune to have done Borrayo a big favor in return for his having helped in the apprehension of the run-amok Colombian. The favor turned out to have been a larger one than Haydon had in fact intended. He knew a Houston businessman who was opening a manufacturing plant in Guatemala City and recommended Efran Borrayo to him as someone who could set up an effective security operation for the company. Borrayo turned this one-shot assignment into a permanent second income, one that yielded much more than his captaincy in the DIT. This had continued for four years until the Houston businessman became involved in a political squabble with the government and closed his business. But Borrayo was eternally grateful to Haydon, and once when he had passed through Houston on his way to Virginia for a special antiterrorist course paid for by the State Department, he called a local liquor store and sent Haydon a case of Bordeaux. Even if Lena's story was way too delicate for Borrayo to become involved in, Haydon could at least expect some first-rate advice. And if the security forces had dealt with Fossler, Borrayo was likely to know about it.

129

The real puzzle of Lena's death, beyond the question of why she had been killed in the first place, was why she had found her way back to Guatemala City. Foreigners had disappeared before in the hinterlands of Guatemala, really disappeared. Why had the Indian women risked such a perilous journey, carrying a white woman's body out of their refuge? Or could that account even be believed? Why had the military commissioner of Soloma not buried her in the local cemetery rather than tossing her on a vegetable truck to Huehuetenango? Why had the report that accompanied her body to Guatemala City said that Dr. Grajeda was bringing her? Why had the Gabinete de Identificación in Zona 6 written an addendum pointing out the discrepancy between how the body had arrived at their offices and how the report said it had arrived? And once they (whoever they were) had gotten Lena back to Guatemala City as they wished, why had they left her in obscurity, put away in the morgue as an XX? And who had told Fossler that Grajeda was a personal friend of Lena's?

None of these questions seemed to issue from a common front. It was almost as if Lena's death had involved so many different factions that it would be impossible to say that it had resulted from any singular intent. Haydon could not believe that she had—in whatever way—made herself so threatening or bothersome to such a wide variety of factions that her death would have been welcome to all.

He looked at his watch. It had taken him longer to go out to Mezquital and back than he had anticipated. It was almost twelve noon, an awkward time to call on Janet Pittner. He turned off Diagonal 12 and went to the Los Cebollines in Zona 9 not far from the Plazuela España. He ate quickly, washing the food down with a couple of Gallos.

While he ate, he watched an old man on the opposite side of the street carrying an oversized load of new, terra-cotta *parrillas,* huge disk-shaped cooking griddles. The old man had them strapped to his back with a cheap but stout grass rope and a leather strap called a *mecapal* that went around his forehead and was attached to either side of the bundle on his back. His load and his age were so great that he was making torturously slow progress along a bare dirt path under the eucalyptus trees. During the time it took Haydon to eat, the old man managed to travel only a block and a half, even using a staff, his head bent and neck buckled against the *mecapal,* his eyes always on the dust at his feet. Drenched in perspiration, he stopped frequently, once even holding onto the trunk of a eucalyptus and going down on one knee to relieve the strain on his neck. But after a while he rose with a painful force of will and continued on.

His was the story of Guatemala. All over the country Haydon and anyone who bothered to notice saw these small people under enormous burdens, each single effort a metaphor for the history of their people. It was this figure, the solitary Indian struggling under grim burdens, that should have been on every piece of currency in the country, rather than the beautiful, emerald-tailed quetzal. Like the quetzal, which could only live and sing in freedom, the carefree peace that the bird symbolized was almost extinct. But *sufrimiento* was everywhere. Ugliness survived where beauty perished. The fact was that the land of eternal spring had vanished, and the land of eternal suffering had taken its place.

He left the restaurant and drove to Zona 10, pulling into the gates of Janet's drive shortly after one o'clock. Her gardener, another old man like the one Haydon had just seen, was cutting the grass beside the first courtyard with hand-held clippers, working on hands and knees, under a flamboyana. Haydon spoke to him as he entered, walked through the first courtyard, opened the wrought-iron gate and entered the breezeway. He rang the doorbell, and one of Janet's housemaids answered, recognized him from the night before, and let him into the *sala*. The room was cool and comfortable and was made to feel quite spacious by a pair of tall double doors that were thrown open to the well-kept courtyard and the shady veranda of the house that surrounded it. Haydon stepped out the doors where a slight, occasional breeze stirred the plants and wind chimes of brass butterflies. To his left, a little farther down the veranda, was a large jacaranda in which hung a dozen or so small wicker cages, each containing a confetti of tiny pastel parakeets whose reedy voices accompanied the brass chimes in an atmosphere of almost monastic peace.

131

Haydon walked over to the jacaranda to look at the birds and had not been at the cages a moment before he realized the tree was situated just outside what must have been Janet's bath. The next window beyond that and at a right angle to it, was the wide arched window of Janet's bedroom. Through the high open windows of the bath he could hear water splashing. This was not an unusual sound in Guatemala where the temperate weather made for casual living and windows that looked onto protected courtyards were most often screenless and open. Open courtyards, open doorways, open windows. Sounds carried, and odors and fragrances. Often one could see into houses, though not very well, for in Guatemala living in the shadows was an art form.

The water stopped in the shower, the high window of which was closest to him. Facing the cages, he adjusted his eyes to a different depth of focus and saw Janet come into the noontime shadows of her airy room, drying with a towel that she then tossed away. He saw her naked back and hips, the vague highlights of curved surfaces, glimpses made all the more erotic for their dusky inconclusiveness. A tall pedestal dressing mirror threw a glint of light, and he saw her move back and forth once or twice before he turned away from the cages and walked back to the open doors of the *sala* where he sat down on a leather-covered bench on the veranda.

It was not quite fifteen minutes by his watch before Janet came out of the *sala* doors in a simple eggshell-white dress of thin cotton, thin enough to see that she should have worn a slip. She apologized for making him wait, and he apologized for having once again come before calling. Her hair was freshly combed out, though still slightly damp. She wore no makeup, and he saw in the clear midday light that her pale skin did not require any.

"Have you eaten?" she asked, shaking her head slightly to loosen her hair. They were both standing.

He nodded. "I just had something."

"Then how about a drink?"

"A gin with lime would be good."

"Give me a second," she said and disappeared into the house. In a moment she was back with the drinks. "Go ahead and sit down," she said, and she sat in an armchair across from him, her back to the courtyard, an attractive portrait in white with the arches of the veranda behind her, and the verdant fronds of sago palms. The warming noontime air was filled with the fragrance of mock oranges, which grew thickly around the fountain. Haydon wondered what Cage had meant when he had said that Janet was a better friend than a lover. Coming from an old satyr like Cage, it was an interesting observation.

"I spent some time last night with Taylor Cage," Haydon said, and the pleasant, anticipatory expression on Janet's face abruptly faded.

"How the hell do you know him?" she asked, clearly stunned.

"I met him years ago, in Houston. I don't know him very well, just as much as you get to know someone over a couple of days' time. But Jim

Fossler had run into him here and put us in touch again when I came down."

"How did Fossler happen to meet him?"

"I don't know. That's part of my problem. Fossler seems to have dropped out of sight too."

Janet's eyes reacted with surprise. "I thought you were going to have some news of Lena," she said curtly, maybe a little warily, as if it were occurring to her that his motives for being there were suspect.

"I'm sorry, I don't. Last night you asked me to get back to you," he reminded her. He had other reasons, of course, but she was acting as if she had forgotten her invitation, and he wondered why.

"Oh. That's why you've come? Because I said that?"

"Yes."

She took a sip of her drink and looked at him.

"You said you couldn't talk in front of your ex-husband—"

"Don't call him that," she interrupted, and then caught herself and tried to cover her irritation by making light of the reference. "I'm sure he'd like to forget that," she smiled shakily.

"You said you thought something was terribly wrong with Lena's disappearance, that you weren't going to wait for Pittner's 'diplomatic shtick,' that you were going to 'wade into it' yourself. And you said for me to get back to you."

Haydon used her own words to pointedly jog her seeming loss of memory. He wasn't going to let her off the hook.

She nodded, a bit of an amused smile on her lips at his quoting her. "Yeah, I said that, didn't I. I guess I was really revved up." She seemed embarrassed now. "I'd been talking to Pitt. I'd gotten royally pissed at his . . . somnolent attitude. His damned foot-dragging. That's State Department SOP. You know, so damned cautious that nothing gets done."

"Then you were talking a little out of school."

"Not out of school," she said. "Out of control would be more like it."

Haydon wondered how much she knew about what Pitt really did. "How long were you married?"

"Eight . . . *eight* years," she said, as if it were far too long.

"What does he do at the embassy?"

"Political Section, like he said. I've read the job description, but that's all I know about it. I was not cut out for that kind of life. 'Harebrained' was the word Pitt most often used when referring to my lack of diplo-

133

matic savvy. But he loved me, poor devil. Still does," she added a little sheepishly. *"I divorced him."*

Haydon couldn't decide whether she was acting or whether she and Pittner really had lived such disconnected lives.

Janet looked at him a moment before she said, "What did Cage have to say?" She must have hoped it sounded like an offhand question.

"I'm not sure he was that helpful. What does he do, anyway?"

"You don't know?"

"I don't think I've ever heard him say." Haydon badly needed some perspective on who knew what about whom.

"He's 'independently' well off. I've never known what he does. I think he had a rich daddy. He used to pretend he worked in imports, Latin American antiques that he'd ship to dealers up north. But that was bullshit. Latin America is full of people like him, people permanently unattached. It's a culture that accommodates people in limbo, people who can't find themselves or don't want to find themselves, or who are running from responsibility. I know a lot of people who live down here in the fervent hope that they are far enough away from civilization that nothing will ever be required of them."

"How long have you known him?"

"Five years." She smiled slightly at him. "You having a hard time figuring out this bunch of us down here?"

Haydon didn't say anything.

"Were you at Cage's house?" she asked.

"No."

"Well, you missed something. Señor Cage has gone native on us," she said, and Haydon did not miss the slight note of sour grapes. "He lives with an Indian girl . . . a child, really. She can't be more than eighteen now."

Chapter 20

"**H**er name is Marielita," Janet said. "He calls her Lita. She's actually quite beautiful. He's had her with him almost two years, playing Henry Higgins, I think. And I can tell you it doesn't suit him. He's not all that sophisticated himself." She seemed to want to rein in her flippancy. "But the girl's got one hell of a story behind her, and whether or not you consider him a child molester depends on how you look at the grim choices life offers in a country like this."

Janet stirred her drink with a finger, picked up her lime and squeezed it, dropped it back into the gin, and dabbed her fingers on her napkin.

"Was she an orphan?"

"She was by the time Cage met her. Her 'story,' unfortunately, isn't all that rare in the highlands where the army is a fearsome presence." Janet took a sip of her gin and hesitated just a moment before continuing.

"She lived in a little village called Ojo de Agua, Eye of Water, in the northwestern *departamento* of El Quiché. Her father was just a little milpa farmer, like everybody else, just scratching out a living. When she was fifteen she and her parents were awakened in the middle of the night by a group of soldiers who grabbed the girl and forced her into a truck parked a few meters from their front door. When her father tried to stop them, the soldiers shot him in the heart, point-blank. Her mother's screams angered these guys, and they proceeded to bash in her face with their rifle butts and left her bleeding beside her dead husband. Marielita was taken to the nearby military garrison.

"But her mother wasn't dead. The old woman, bleeding profusely and crazy with fear for her daughter, managed to make her way through the night to the next tiny hamlet where Marielita's two brothers were also farming. The old woman told them what had happened. They left for the garrison within the hour, on foot, and arrived there about day-break. The garrison commandante said there was no such girl there. But, by the way, he said, didn't he recognize these two boys as guerrilla spies? So the two brothers were seized and taken into custody.

"The soldiers 'questioned' them using a method known as *el capucho,* the hood. The boys' arms were tied behind them, and they were made to kneel on the ground. Nylon hoods were slipped over their heads and pulled tight around their necks, and an insecticide was sprayed into the hood through a small hole in the top. It's strong stuff, commercial grade, and it scalded their faces, eyes, and lips on contact. And when they gasped for breath, it blistered their throats and lungs immediately. When they passed out, buckets of water were thrown on them until they re-vived. They were questioned. Wrong answers. *El capucho* again. This went on for a long time, I don't know how long, but I've heard that the soldiers are taught how to drag out the procedure to prolong the suffer-ing. The boys' faces swelled beyond recognition. They had convulsions, their lungs hemorrhaged and soaked their hoods and their clothes in bloody vomit. Just when it seemed they would not be able to endure another round of insecticide and water, they 'confessed.' They lied, of course, to save their lives. They made their marks on a piece of paper on which the commandante had helpfully written out their 'confessions.' Their tongues had swollen to fill their mouths; they couldn't talk.

" 'Just as I thought,' the commandante said, looking at the 'confessions,' and the soldiers took the boys out and cut off their heads with machetes because they were 'spies.' "

Janet stopped for a sip of gin. She looked away to one side, out to the courtyard for a moment and then turned back and continued.

"Marielita was kept by the soldiers for three days. When they were through with her, she couldn't walk out of the garrison. She couldn't even stand up. Without any fear or shame that anyone would see what they had done to her, the soldiers went into Ojo de Agua and brought back three widows with a litter. The frightened old women were taken into the garrison where they were made to put Marielita onto the litter and carry her back to the village.

"Marielita's mother died the day Marielita was brought back from the garrison. Wild with grief and anger, Marielita showed her pluck. Against the wishes of everyone in the village, she filed a formal *denuncio* with the village's chief commissioner, who was the civil patrol's liaison with the army. It was a hopeless, stupid gesture. It was her right under the law, of course, but people knew better than to accuse the army of atrocities. She was issuing her own death warrant.

"There was an 'investigation,' and it was determined that Marielita had lied. The 'facts' discovered were: that her father had died in an accident in his own cornfield; that the missing brothers' wives said the boys had left their families, like many other men, to work for the season on the coffee fincas along the Mexican border in San Marcos; and that, as for the rape charges against the soldiers, well, it was well known that Marielita would spread her thighs for anyone.

"The girl was stunned by these lies and was bitter that the villagers and even her widowed sisters-in-law had been too fearful to come to her defense or even to tell the truth. She withdrew into isolation. Cage came along at this point—he's always roaming around the countryside—heard her story, found her living alone, the sole remaining member of her family, an outcast in the village, and brought her to Guatemala City. I understand there was a long period of emotional rehabilitation. Time passed. He enrolled her in high school, and she got her degree. Then he enrolled her in the National University of San Carlos. She's studying there now."

137

In the course of telling Marielita's story, Janet's voice had lost its former impertinence. It was the kind of account that had its effect on its narrator as well as the listener. As with holy scriptures, you could not deal honestly with tales of moral outrage and remain unaffected.

"What goes on between them in the way of intimacy is the subject of rich gossip," she added, a piece of information from which she derived no pleasure.

"The girl didn't have any other family?"

"None. And the village was glad to get rid of her. She was a constant reminder to them, living alone like an aggrieved Hester Prynne, of their cowardice and cruelty."

Janet drank from her glass.

"There is one fascinating side story to all this that I would like to think is apocryphal but, actually, it has the ring of truth about it too. During the past two years, two of the soldiers who had broken into Marielita's home that night were discharged from the army. They'd served their time. One of them took up selling watches and Japanese radios from a vendor's stall in 6a calle, Zona 1; the other one went to work for his cousin in a parking lot only a few blocks away, near the Banco Metropolitano. Not long ago both of them were killed within two weeks of each other. There was a witness to the second killing. According to him, the assassins were a Guatemalan woman and a 'big' man. The witness told the newspaper reporter that the woman did the shooting. She walked right up to the victim and said something to him, and when he reacted in alarm, she shot the man in the face. After he fell, she bent down and shot him twice more. She tossed her gun to the 'big' man, and they disappeared in different directions. It was at night. The investigations never went anywhere, of course."

Haydon thought of Lita holding him to her naked breasts, thought of the way she felt and smelled; he thought of her standing timidly beside him in the courtyard outside Macabeo's medieval mortuary. *This is the way of many peoples in Guatemala . . . a long time dying. Lo siento mucho.*

"Some story, huh?" Janet said quietly.

Haydon nodded. He did not believe the story was apocryphal either. In Taylor Cage's world, it was entirely within the logic of the way he lived. Haydon thought a moment, trying to phrase the question without giving away more than he was learning.

138

"I understand Lena was working for AID."

Janet nodded. "Right. She was working on some data-gathering project having to do with crop diversification. You know, trying to get the Indians to grow something besides corn."

"Did she ever work with health service workers up there?"

Janet frowned at him.

"American or foreign volunteers working with the Indians, doctors, health specialists, dentists . . ."

Janet shook her head and crossed her legs at the knees, rearranging her skirt. "I don't know," she said. "She must have."

"Would you care if I looked at her rooms?"

"I guess not," she said. "But if you're going to be looking for something . . . I mean, I don't think you're going to find much."

"Oh?"

"No. The sleepy Mr. Pitt has beaten you to it."

"He's been through her things?"

"Not him, but some guys from the embassy. And they didn't go through her things. They took them. Practically everything. Cleaned the place out, boxes of stuff. It made me feel queer. I couldn't be in there when they did it. It was like she was dead, they were cleaning out 'personal effects.' I stayed over here in the *sala* and watched them gut the place over there," she said, looking across the courtyard to the other side of the fountain.

"Were Guatemalan police with them?"

"No. Just embassy guys."

"Were they from the consular offices?"

She shrugged, then said, "Well, I don't think so. I recognized one of the guys who'd been by here one time to pick up Pitt when we were still married. He had said at that time that he worked with Pitt, so I guess he was from the Political Section."

The Political Section.

"When was the last time you saw Jim Fossler?"

"Monday morning, yesterday. Lena was supposed to be home Saturday night. By Sunday evening I got worried and called the hotel in Panajachel where she was supposed to be staying, and then all those other calls. Couldn't turn up anything. I didn't sleep a wink that night, then Monday morning I broke down and called Pitt at the embassy. He said he'd come over. But before he got here, Fossler came by again. I was

139

really upset and spilled everything to him. I don't think he knew how to read what I was telling him, whether there really was something to be worried about or whether I was just a dingy woman. I was pretty agitated. I guess he had a right to think that."

"What did he say?"

"He said he was going to talk to a few people and would get back to me if he came onto something."

"Did you tell Pitt that Fossler had come by?"

"Yes."

"What did he think?"

Janet gave Haydon an exasperated look. "As far as I could tell, not much. Look," she said, daubing the sweat on her glass with her napkin, watching what she was doing as she thought. "Pitt . . . is uncommunicative. I may be 'harebrained' as he says, but I'm not a shrew. If Pitt had been halfway human there wouldn't have been any problem in the marriage that we couldn't have dealt with. I mean, I'm as flexible as the next woman. I can put up with normal human quirks. I'm not looking for perfection. But I do demand human qualities in a mate. Pitt . . . well, hell, he was a goddamned sphinx! If I'm going to be married to someone I want to be able to talk to him. I can *not* talk to somebody by myself; I don't need someone around for me *not* to talk to."

Janet stopped as if she had caught herself just before going off on a tirade of complaints that was all too familiar and had become boring and hateful even to her.

"What about Lena," Haydon asked, judiciously avoiding Janet's private life. "Did she date very much?"

"Actually, that was one area Lena was a little standoffish about. She wasn't chatty about it."

"What do you mean?"

"I mean, we were living together, and when you're close, when you know each other as well as we did, you talk about things like that, women do."

"But she wouldn't."

"Just enough to let me know it wasn't any of my business. She was like that, a very gracious person, really, but she set limits on familiarity. She drew lines and expected you to have enough sense not to cross them. But we were close and . . . well, I . . . that rather secretive side of her hurt me a little in the beginning. We were like sisters. Sisters share those sorts of things. Talk." Janet had begun massaging her crossed leg just behind the knee, at the hemline. "But after a while I knew it had to do with her nature, not any lack of rapport between us. It wasn't 'us.' It was her."

"But she did date a lot?"

"Not a lot."

"Did you meet any of the men she dated?"

"A couple."

"Were they Americans?"

"Yes. The two guys I met were people in her department at AID. I don't think she dated either of them more than twice."

"Did she ever date any Guatemalan men?"

"I don't know."

"Do you think it's unusual that she dated so little? She was a pretty woman."

Janet looked at him. "Was?"

"I'm sorry."

Janet didn't take her eyes off him immediately, trying to read the slip of tongue. Then, "Well, being a man, I suppose you do think it's unusual, but the fact is, men are not one of the major food groups. We can live healthy lives without you."

Haydon let it go. Men apparently were not a topic either Lena or Janet was fond of discussing. He drank the rest of his gin and put his glass on a rough wooden table in front of him.

"You've been patient and helpful," he said, standing.

Janet's face reflected surprise and more than a little disappointment. Either she expected a lengthier opportunity at verbal sparring, or she simply wanted the company. Despite her rather social reputation, Haydon found her to be a woman who skillfully disguised a loneliness that lay none too deeply beneath the surface.

She uncrossed her legs, leaned forward and put her glass beside his, and stood also. Her face was sober, and she looked at him without speaking for a moment, her arms crossed beneath her breasts.

"If you knew something . . . significant, you'd tell me, wouldn't you?"

"What do you mean?"

"I was talking rather bravely last night. I mean about going out on my own looking for Lena. Actually, I haven't the guts to do it alone. Not in this unstable political climate. Americans never know. Sometimes simply being American gives you automatic carte blanche to do just about anything. Other times it's the only reason needed to kill you on the spot. You never know when you're at risk and when you aren't. I've lived in this country a long time, but I've never seen it like this before. Nothing is what it used to be; I'm never sure anymore about what I'm getting into." She shook her hair to loosen it again. "I'm not going to learn anything from Pitt, not until it's all over."

Haydon looked at her. She had changed on him again. He hadn't expected her to turn off the bitchy business so quickly and so completely. She was looking at him squarely, her expression on the edge of showing fear.

"As soon as I understand what's happening here, I'll let you know," he said. "But I wouldn't hold my breath if I were you. I'm not likely to come up with anything on my own."

"Look . . ." she said, reaching out to him the way she had the night before. "If I can help you . . . I mean, I do know my way around . . . Let me help you."

Haydon did not doubt her sincerity, nor did he reject her suggestion out of hand. Unlike Bennett Pittner, Haydon did not discount Janet's assessments of what was happening around her. She had not become so jaded about life that she no longer recognized the macabre for what it was. In Guatemala, maintaining a sensitivity to madness was no small accomplishment.

"I appreciate your offer," he said. "I may need to take you up on it."

Chapter 21

Haydon drove back toward the Camino Real hotel thinking about Janet's offer to help him. In the right situation, she could, in fact, save him a lot of time. If something didn't break soon, he would get back to her without a second thought.

He parked outside the Camino Real, but rather than going inside to use their telephones, he walked a block away to a pay booth on the Reforma. If any hotel in the city was plugged into security forces listening posts, the Camino Real would be at the top of the list, since it was the overwhelming choice of most Americans staying in the city. He called the National Police and asked for the Department for Criminal Investigations, at which point he knew his call was being routed through military intelligence computers. It took a while before someone answered who confirmed they were the DIC, and Haydon asked for Efran Borrayo. He was put on hold. Like Fossler, he avoided the American embassy where he could have gotten the information within a few minutes.

After a while a wheezy male voice asked if he was talking to the man who wanted to locate Captain Borrayo. Haydon said yes, and the man said the captain was now the director of Pavón prison and was not directly connected with the DIC. Haydon thanked him and hung up. Director of Pavón prison? It seemed a long way from the cloak-and-dagger business and a curious career change. But Haydon knew that Grajeda had been right: words meant very little in Guatemala. Haydon would have to go to Pavón to see for himself. He walked back to his car and drove away in the direction from which he had just come, straight down the length of the quiet, shady street that ran dead into 18 calle, which shot off at an angle out of the residential neighborhood and into a more commercial thoroughfare.

In a few kilometers 18 calle became Carretera Roosevelt as it left the city and climbed into the hills east of the city where it became Inter-American Highway, CA-1, a serpentine highway that headed southward on a circuitous course to El Salvador where it crossed the border at San Cristóbal Frontera in the *departamento* of Jutiapa. Because of its border destination, this highway was known as the Salvador Road, and its shoulders and bar ditches were famous as a favorite dumping ground of the death squads. Victims of Guatemala's growing political violence turned up along this roadway with grim regularity, like so much human road kill.

144

Pavón was located twenty kilometers outside Guatemala City in a little municipality known as Fraijanes. As a prison farm it was sited in a sandy, semicleared pine forest, its perimeter clear-cut for security, though the forest picked up again not far beyond the guard towers. Pavón had become only recently a shadow of its former self, which was a blessing because its former self had been a hellhole. Originally the prison had been designed for four hundred inmates, but until late 1989 it had housed over two thousand men, with no separation according to offense. In Guatemala, where you were thrown into prison when you were arrested and were expected to work things out from there, that meant that traffic offenders were thrown into the same general population as sadists. Sixty percent of the inmates were awaiting trial and sentencing. There were not enough beds to accommodate two thousand men, not even enough shelter, so that those who were poor and could not afford to buy a dry corner or a shady eave were left out in the rain or crippling heat like animals. The state spent eleven cents per day per prisoner on food. There were only two things that could gain you improvement in your situation: either money, or the capacity to be meaner and crueler than the people who had what you wanted or could get you what you wanted. Life was cheap, drugs were expensive, prostitutes were easily obtainable, and male rape was routine.

But on Easter in 1989, the prison exploded. The wretched conditions had reached the point that some men thought that madness was the only sane response in an effort to change things once and for all. As it was, risking their lives wasn't risking all that much. The riot lasted a week, ultimately requiring the army to quell it. Fourteen men died, but the federal government grudgingly gave in to prison reforms, not so much out of a latent compassion for the miserable conditions of the prisoners as out of a desire to avoid that kind of negative publicity again. It was a messy kind of thing to have to deal with questions about it at ribbon cuttings.

Haydon guided his car up the sandy road off the main highway, past the little clutch of buildings known as El Centro de Orientación Femenino where women prisoners were housed, to a bare dirt parking area adjacent to a collection of cinder-block buildings outside the tall chain-link fence that surrounded the prison. He parked the car in front of a store that catered to the prison guards, some of whom were drinking fruit drinks in a concrete-floored breezeway between buildings, their straight-backed wooden chairs cocked back against the stucco wall. Two rangy black-and-white pigs rooted around in the rocks in front of the breezeway and fought over the orange and papaya peels the guards tossed out into the sun. The stench of manure wafted from the breezeway where the wandering pigs had left a few dollops of their droppings which the men hadn't bothered to kick away into the dirt.

Haydon locked the car, nodded to the men in the shadows, and started down the slight decline toward the gates. The heat from the sun in the nearly cloudless sky was radiating off the hard, pinkish clay under

145

Haydon's feet as if it were a griddle. The twelve-foot chain-link fence that formed the prison's outer perimeter was attached to cement posts and undulated in the heat waves as though it were melting in a sea of hot gases.

As Haydon approached the guardhouse on the other side of the battered pipe and chain-link gate, the odd strains of evangelical hymns replaced the sawing drone of cicadas. The ubiquitous presence of evangelicalism with its cheerless little Protestant buildings that had sprung up all over Guatemala in the last fifteen years, its un-Latinlike hymns that evoked images of prancing television preachers with coiffed hair and silk suits and million-dollar smiles, its spawning of Bible-toting Indians quoting Bible Belt proof texts, was a reality in Guatemala that Haydon could not get used to. It seemed to him to be another jarring intrusion into a largely Indian culture that was taking to a more trendy version of the ways of God with men as readily as it took to polyester clothes and plastic water jugs. It gave him the creeps. At least the polyester and plastic made their lives more tolerable on a moment-to-moment basis, even if a little trashier and culture destructive. But there was something jarringly discordant about the intrusion of Protestant evangelicalism, and something sad too. Whether it was better for the poor, desperate Indians in the long run, only the long run would tell. In the meantime, it was an ugly transition, and Haydon would have felt a lot better about it if he could have believed that God was a better God in a business suit than he was in a cassock.

"Buenas," Haydon said, stopping at the gate.

A corporal, senior in age and rank and shortest in stature of the six soldiers lounging under the portico, stepped up to the chain-link gate. He said nothing, but smiled and nodded, waiting for Haydon to explain himself.

"I'm here to see Director Borrayo," Haydon said. He pulled out his passport and shield and handed it through a hole in the wire. The corporal looked at the passport, his eyes moving over it appropriately though Haydon would have bet a hundred dollars that he didn't know what he was "reading." The shield was something else. The corporal knew this was *"policiá,"* though he probably didn't know Houston from Istanbul. Still, it was a "security force" identification and demanded a fearful respect. He nodded with a businesslike seriousness.

"Momentito, por favor," he said, forming a tiny space of time between his thumb and forefinger. He walked to a small cubicle in the portico and

picked up a telephone. Haydon looked at the other guards. A couple of them ignored him, one studied him with unblinking effrontery, and two others averted their eyes when he looked at them. All of them were armed. All of them probably were illiterate.

The corporal quickly came out of the cubicle, and one of the guards who had been close enough to overhear his conversation, jumped up from where he was sitting beside the evangelical broadcast and preceded him to the gate, unhooking the chain that ran through the gate from the fence post to which it was secured.

"Pase adelante," the corporal said. He handed Haydon's passport and shield to the surly-eyed man who sat at a small table with a book before him, and who laboriously recorded the numbers off of Haydon's passport and shield, both of which he then put into a cardboard cigar box for safekeeping until Haydon's return. He hammered a rubber stamp onto an ink pad and pressed it into the back of Haydon's hand, and then Haydon turned around and raised his arms to allow another guard to conduct a perfunctory frisking.

"Pase adelante," the corporal repeated, and Haydon walked out into the sun again and headed across the compound yard to the administration building.

Pavón looked almost deserted compared to the days when it was jammed with overcrowding. Haydon had interviewed the Colombian here, and the conditions had been so vile that even the guards were ashamed of it. Now the population had been so drastically reduced—that Haydon could tell even before entering behind the walls—that the teeming bazaar atmosphere was gone. There was no buzz of voices drifting out to the bare front yard. The place did not bristle with armed guards.

He stepped up onto the tile courtyard in front of the administration building, walked past the flagpole, and entered the one-story structure. The place was silent. There was no furniture in the foyer, only one clay pot with a single scrawny rubber plant with a few yellowing leaves. A receptionist's office to his left was empty, and a couple of minimum-security inmates were walking around pushing rag mops up and down the short halls that led to half a dozen offices. There were few signs, and he saw no one who appeared to be a member of the administrative staff.

But Haydon knew where he was going. He turned down a hallway to his right and followed the pale institutional green tile walls past doors thrown open to empty offices. There was no air-conditioning to speak of in Guatemala, and certainly not here where the screenless windows al-

147

lowed flies to wander the shady corridors as though it were an abandoned building. At the end of the hall there was a door on the left, half-closed.

"I hear you, Stuart Haydon," a voice said as Haydon approached. *"Pase adelante, mi amigo."*

Haydon walked in as Efran Borrayo uncrossed his legs from where they had been propped on the sill of the open window and stood up, taking a cigarette out of his mouth with his left hand and grinning broadly as he offered his right hand to shake.

"I appreciate your taking this time out of your busy schedule to see me, *Director*," Haydon said with mock formality.

The Guatemalan laughed. "No kidding, huh?" His laugh was slow and deep. He was a hefty man in his early fifties whose swarthy, handsome face, wavy gray hair, and easygoing manner belied a shrewd and vicious nature. "This place looks like something in the States, huh? Hell, it's no fun anymore. No shit going on here now. It's like the Boy Scouts."

"How long have you been here?" Haydon asked.

Borrayo pulled a long face. "Too damned long. Over a year."

"You don't like it?"

"Hell, no. Would you like it?" He shook his head. "Reform." He said the word like it was a venereal disease. "When that shit Cerezo was elected in 1986 he had to throw some little favors to some *políticos* and to the 'Americans,' huh."

Like many Latin Americans, Borrayo had a love-hate relationship with the United States. He simultaneously resented and envied the *gringos,* and one of his pet peeves was that they routinely referred to themselves as "Americans" as though they were the only "Americans" in the western hemisphere, as though the Latin Americans were not real "Americans."

Haydon nodded in commiseration, and Borrayo gestured for him to sit in the only chair in the room besides his own. It was directly in front of Borrayo's desk, on the edge of which the Guatemalan sat down facing Haydon, one foot on the floor. Haydon took a pack of Pall Malls out of his pocket. He had brought them along for just this purpose. Sharing your American-made cigarettes was a good thing to do with a man from whom you wanted a favor. He offered one to Borrayo, who eagerly took it. Haydon took one also and lighted them both. Borrayo blew the smoke into the still air of the bare room.

"Some of the boys in the DIT had gotten a bad reputation," he said offhandedly as if what had gotten them the bad reputation had not been reprehensible, as if their flagrant violence had not received the condemnation of international human rights organizations. "A few of us were asked to move to other branches of the security forces so they could say they had 'cleaned house.' I was moved several times, and then they put me here." He made a sour face. "I hate this shitty place," he said, like a true bureaucrat, and waved his hand. "So," he said, dragging on the cigarette, "what wonderful things have been happening to you?"

They caught up on each other's lives, talked about men Haydon remembered from before, rehashed the Colombian episode, and then Borrayo cursed the declining quetzal, inflation, the leftists, and talked about how the return of military rule (as if it weren't already a fact) was the country's only hope.

"Listen," Haydon said finally, mashing out his cigarette in the ashtray he had been holding in his lap, "I haven't seen the place since the 're-form.' You want to take a walk?"

Borrayo had been enjoying their little *charla,* but at the mention of a walk his enthusiasm faded. This was serious business, this taking a walk. No one in his right mind would rather have a conversation out in the hot sun than in the cool shade of a thick-walled building. But then, everyone knew that the hot sun did not have ears. If you wanted to walk in the sun, you had serious business and only the hot sun would do.

"Of course," Borrayo said, putting out what was left of his own cigarette and standing up from the edge of the desk. He ran his hands through his thick, gray waves and picked up his black-visored military-style hat. "These *chusma,* they like to see the *cacique* wear a hat, huh?"

He grinned and pulled the hat down firmly, low over his eyes.

Chapter 22

They retraced Haydon's steps down the pale green hallway, empty except for the flies floating like small propellered planes in the dead air heavy with the odor of industrial disinfectant. They passed the pathetically lonely rubber plant in the main entryway and turned right at the intersection and entered a short hallway at the end of which was a shady porch blocked by a chain-link fence and gate. They walked to the gate where guards and a few prisoners were hanging around chatting, most of the prisoners killing time as they waited for their turn at a pay telephone that was on a wall inside the chain-link fence. Each inmate had to reach an arm through a hole in the wire to put his centavo into the telephone and then hold the receiver against the wire, to which he pressed his ear and mouth to communicate. To the left of this porch was a short wing of half a dozen bungalows with an open-air corridor between them, *celdas* for conjugal visits, close enough to the popular porch for the sounds of intimacies to be shared with the loiterers. Beyond them was a long breezeway that led to the main prison yard with the various cellblocks beyond.

Borrayo turned right, however, entering a narrow, sunless passage between the stucco buildings which quickly opened into a small courtyard from which a dirt road emerged to follow a stretch of pine trees that bordered the outside wire fences of the prison. The sparsely forested countryside picked up several hundred meters beyond the three separate cordons of razor wire. To their left the rear walls of the cellblocks provided a huge slate for graffiti, the common obscenities of bored men, slogans of regional pride, and prejudicial hatreds.

"See," Borrayo said as each of them chose one of the two ruts of the dirt road. "Everything has changed. No guards follow us. I can go everywhere alone now. All is peace here. No problems."

Above them, in the tops of the pines, crows sent their caws across the coils of razor wire to echo in the shallow valley beyond.

"Where do you keep the *peligrosos* now, Efran?" Haydon asked.

"Ah, well, of course, the *peligrosos* are not in the general population."

Haydon reached down and picked up a pinecone and started snapping off the seeds as they walked. "You keep them chained in some pit?"

"Unfortunately, no," Borrayo said, missing the facetious tone of Haydon's question and thus the grim humor in his own reply. He put his hands into his pockets and looked out over the valley past the wire. "I would like to put them in the pit. If I had my way, I would hang them by their balls out in the sun. This damn government. They are always, you know, sucking up to you 'Americans.'" He stopped and turned to Haydon indignantly. "I have to go take human rights courses at the United Nations building now. Can you believe such madness? I choke on it. It is embarrassing to me."

Haydon looked at Borrayo. "Do you still have access to anyone in intelligence?" he asked bluntly.

151

Borrayo didn't change his expression. He had played games too many years to let an unexpected question appear to have come to him unexpectedly.

"Things have changed," he said philosophically. "Access? Well, you have to have a good reason for wanting to ask questions about intelligence. One question, one wrong one . . ." Borrayo shook his head.

Haydon could not expect Borrayo to do much without a full explanation, or something that sounded like a full explanation. No one ever gave the whole story on anything in Guatemala. You always held a little back, something in reserve that could give you an edge if you needed an edge in the event everything else had been leaked or discovered. Borrayo would have to hear Haydon's story.

They were walking again, approaching a little slope of the road and another sector of the prison, the small shacks and garden plots of the privileged prisoners. A few chickens pecked around outside the doorways and in between the neat rows of vegetables, and here and there a hibiscus burst into hopeful bloom.

Haydon told Borrayo his story without mentioning names or the discovery of Lena Muller's body and its removal from the Cementerio General. When it was necessary to mention anything that Cage was involved in, Haydon referred to him as "a friend"—perfectly acceptable discretion that Borrayo would understand.

"What I need to know," Haydon said, "is if any of them are alive— the girl or Baine or Jim Fossler."

They had come to a fork in the sloping road, the right branch of which went down to a soccer field, while the left one leveled off to a kind of compound about a block in length. On either side of an open area beaten bare of grass were rows of cement-block shops with hand-painted signs. SHOE HOSPITAL, PAVÓN. SHOP OF THE ARTISANS OF THE DIVINE MASTER —a metalworking shop that made lamp shades and rings that held pots for hanging plants. An Alcoholics Anonymous meeting room— BODYWORK AND PAINT OF THE SOUL. A laundry. A store. A shop where four men were making queer-looking teddy bears out of shaggy fuchsia and chartreuse material. All of these places were devoid of inmate customers, and most of the buildings surrounding the compound were simply empty.

Borrayo stopped again at the edge of the road, looking down to the soccer field where a game was in progress.

"We are in the last day of a three-day tournament," he said, his hat pulled down low over his eyes. "Sector 2 is the best team. I think they will win the tournament."

Two teams were on the bare, rocky field, running back and forth after the checkered ball in the hot sun. A few men lounged in the shade of small trees, watching the ball sail from one end of the field to the other, the teams wheeling here and there after it like a herd of stampeding wildebeests, veering and shunting in mass simultaneity.

"You are going to get your throat cut, my friend," Borrayo said, moving over to a *chilca* tree dotted with yellow blossoms and stepping into its shade. Haydon joined him, both of them squinting toward the soccer field. Occasionally shouts from the players broke through the constant throb of cicadas that filled the hot afternoon. "Do you know what is going on here?"

"I just need to know if they're alive."

Borrayo turned and looked at Haydon.

"You don't know, huh?"

"Not much."

Borrayo shook his head and pulled a yellow flower off the *chilca*. He plucked a petal off with his lips and folded it with his tongue, thinking, returning his gaze toward the soccer field.

"This is one you should look the other way, Haydon," Borrayo said. "This is very dangerous." His eyes squinted from under the black visor.

"You know something about it, then?"

"I've heard some things," Borrayo said, spitting out the little yellow pellet he had made of the petal. He lipped another one off the flower. "I heard about a *gringo* . . . that the DIC picked up."

"Baine?"

Borrayo shrugged and shook his head in ignorance. "A *gringo*." His eyes were on the soccer players.

"Where is he?"

"In one of the secret prisons," he said, his tongue working the yellow petal.

That wasn't great news for Baine. The clandestine prisons were used for interrogations, and where there were interrogations there was always torture.

"Where was he picked up?"

"Chichoque, Huehuetenango."

"What part of Huehuetenango is that?"

"What part? In the southeast."

"How far from the Ixil Triangle?"

Borrayo looked at Haydon. "What the hell is going on here?"

"I heard Lena Muller used to work just across the border from the Ixil Triangle. I wondered if it was close by."

"Not too far," Borrayo said, watching Haydon with a frown, his tongue working the yellow petal. He was thinking over his indebtedness to Haydon. A man full of *machismo* had to be given room to maneuver. Borrayo's own sense of honor demanded reciprocation for Haydon's help, which Borrayo had benefitted from for four years.

"Who is responsible for this, Efran? The military or the police? Who is worried about what this girl knows?"

Borrayo spit out another yellow pellet. "The army. G-2 were the ones who got this Baine."

Haydon was looking at Borrayo's profile obliquely. The prison director's strong brow was beginning to glisten in the heat, and Haydon saw a single bead of sweat sliding out of the gray hair at his temple and down the side of his jaw. Haydon guessed it wasn't only the afternoon heat that was wringing it out of him.

"And did they pick up the girl too?"

Borrayo took off his hat, pulled a handkerchief out of his hip pocket and wiped out the band of his hat. Next he wiped his forehead and put his hat on again. He turned to Haydon, and behind him one of the soccer teams burst into shouts and cheers.

"I know nothing about what is happening here, nothing," Borrayo said, his voice low even though they were isolated in the little spot of shade under the *chilca* tree. "But I will tell you that I have heard Victor Tablaya's name. Tablaya is an Argentine advisor to G-2. He is a friend, a very close friend of General Luis Azcona Contrera."

154

Haydon knew the general's name. A group of inmates slow-walked up the sloping road from the soccer field, leaning into the incline, not talking, passing a patch of hibiscus that grew in front of a little store that was dug into the side of the slope and which specialized in lukewarm, fruit-flavored drinks.

Borrayo eyed the men from under his visor and took a pack of cigarettes out of his shirt pocket. He offered one to Haydon, who didn't want it out in the heat like this, but took it anyway. Borrayo struck a match and lighted Haydon's cigarette first and then his own.

As the group of men passed, Borrayo and Haydon looked the other way as if they were waiting for someone, and then Borrayo turned and watched them until they were out of earshot.

"Listen to me, Haydon," he said, blowing his smoke out into the heat. "I'm not shitting you. I think this one is a very nasty woman, you know."

Haydon nodded. He did know, and he was beginning to think it could only get nastier. Borrayo had been in the business a long time, and he had a fine nose for trouble.

Haydon looked at the Guatemalan. Borrayo had turned his head again, avoiding Haydon's eyes. He simply glared out into the sun, out across the emptying soccer field.

"He's here, isn't he, Efran."

Borrayo's mind must have been stumbling over itself. Every man brought to every situation a secret index of possibilities. The way he behaved in each new circumstance depended as much on this concealed index as it did on the apparent elements. Borrayo was now reviewing his index, and Haydon knew that at the top of the Guatemalan's secret list of possibilities was a concern for self-preservation. Whatever he told Haydon, even if it appeared to be a favor requiring some risk, it would be in Borrayo's best interest. He was like Taylor Cage in that respect. The world they inhabited made pragmatists of them, simplified their lives by stripping away the crustaceous impediments of moral considerations. Life was reduced to only one major concern—survival. Everything else was secondary and was measured against this single criterion.

"There are a lot of empty cellblocks now, aren't there, Efran," Haydon said. "Places where no one goes anymore. It's handy, close in to the capital. Thick walls, entire wings of dark cellblocks."

Borrayo swallowed.

Haydon was right. Pavón was two prisons, an official one and an unofficial one. Borrayo had not been hung out to dry in some backwater assignment as he had wanted Haydon to believe. Instead he had been entrusted with a position of major responsibilities, one with close connections with army intelligence. Borrayo had become a key figure in one of the security forces' darkest secrets, the much-rumored—and angrily denied—network of clandestine prisons, the Latin gulag of the "disappeared."

Borrayo turned his sober face to Haydon.

"The boy is *un chivo expiatorio.*"

155

"A scapegoat."

Borrayo nodded again. "I think they are putting something together. When they have it, they will announce his arrest. I think it will be soon."

"How soon?"

"A few days, maybe," Borrayo shrugged. "They have to move fast. Covering up one *gringo's* death and then arresting another one in secret is a very risky trick, even for the generals, even for the DIC." So Borrayo knew Lena was dead too. "Everyone knows that 'Americans' believe their blood is *más mejor* than any stinking Guatemalan's. These people, they do not want to step in that shit."

"Then the American embassy doesn't know about his arrest?"

"No."

"What about Jim Fossler?"

"I know nothing about him."

"I need to talk to Baine," Haydon said.

Borrayo shook his head emphatically and looked down at his feet, blowing smoke at the hot ground. "They would kill me. I would have to have at least three men to cooperate in moving him to a cell where you could not be seen. I am not sure I can find three men who can be trusted with a modest bribe."

Still looking down, he grimaced and held his mouth in a tight, teeth-clenching manner that indicated they were facing a dicey situation.

"This is a crazy place," he said. "Certain people, they have *orejas* here, like a job. 'You go to Pavón for a year, live in Sector 4, and I will pay you well for everything you hear and see.' " He shrugged. "It is like a job in a bad place. You are not in prison; you have a job in a bad place, with hardships, but you are being paid very well. Stay a year and you will go home with a lot of money." Borrayo pulled down the sides of his mouth. "It's not like the old days when a quetzal here and there would buy you information." He dragged on the cigarette and flipped it out into the burning sand. *"Los ricos,"* he said, "and the generals, they run everything behind the scenes."

Borrayo was sweating, literally and figuratively. The loudspeaker came on, and from the tops of telephone poles all over the prison grounds an announcement was made that inmate so-and-so was being released that afternoon.

"I have to sign those goddamned papers," Borrayo said. Again he took off his hat and wiped his forehead and the hatband with his handkerchief before putting it back on and jerking the visor down over his eyes once more.

They left the sparse shade of the *chilca* and started back the way they had come, avoiding the main yards of the prison grounds. It was in the hottest part of the afternoon, but the pine trees were now on their left and were throwing a veil of shadows across the sandy road. They walked in the rutted road between the border of pines and the backs of the cellblocks in silence, the loudest sounds being the crunching of their footsteps on the road and the crows calling from the tops of the pines.

"What would it take for me to talk to him tonight?" Haydon asked.

Borrayo shook his head but said nothing for fifteen or twenty meters. Then, head down, hands in his pockets, he said, "I will try to get you some information. Be at your hotel at nine o'clock."

He did not ask where Haydon was staying, and Haydon had not told him.

Chapter 23

Haydon walked back across the barren prison yard to the front entrance where he retrieved his passport and shield and was let out through the huge chain-link gate. He labored up the slope to the little store where both of the black-and-white pigs had stretched out in the shade of his car, their heads up under it, just behind the front left tire, blocking the driver's-side door. Haydon kicked them awake, eliciting startled grunts, causing one of them to bang his head against the oil pan, but eventually getting them from under the door and out into the hot sun where they shook their heads, flapping their oversized ears to shake the dirt out of them.

He started the car and drove away from the bleak collection of buildings, down the road that took him past the women's unit to the highway and on his way back into the city. He had no idea whether Borrayo would help him or not, but if Borrayo had done nothing else, he at least had alerted Haydon to a very important name. General Luis Azcona was one of Guatemala's military hard-liners. He had been an ardent supporter of former general and dictator Efraín Ríos Montt, who had seized power in a coup in March of 1982. Ríos Montt was a born-again evangelical whose eye-for-an-eye brand of justice led to one of the worst periods of human rights abuses in the country's history. During his brief term of leadership—before he, too, was toppled by a coup—Guatemalans died and disappeared by the thousands. Azcona had been Montt's most aggressive general, his "sword of righteousness," always unsheathed and always bloody. He had played a key role in a period of brutal repression, a time that was remembered by the people who survived it as *la violencia*. Both Ríos Montt and Luis Azcona had been ardent supporters in the election campaign of the recently elected president. They were once again in favor.

Haydon did not notice the tail until he had left the few miles of flat, straight departmental highway and entered the larger Central American highway that quickly climbed and wound its way into the hills southeast of the city. It was a Jeep Cherokee with darkened windows, a favored security forces vehicle, one that had become so notorious that to use it in surveillance was itself a message. It was not likely that the tail was trying to be invisible. Intimidation was the first step in "civilian control." If the individual for whom the message was intended didn't take the hint, the message was reinforced, a sterner tone was employed. But the security forces were short on patience.

159

A few cars were between Haydon and the Cherokee as the highway grew increasingly crooked. Watching in his side mirror, Haydon saw the Cherokee continually pull out into the approaching lane as if it were about to pass, a maneuver which would not have been out of the ordinary since Guatemalans were outrageous drivers, impatient and foolhardy, and head-on collisions were common on the mountainous highways. But the Cherokee was not going to pass; it simply wanted to be sure that Haydon was aware of its existence.

Road repairs had closed one of the serpentine curves to a single lane, though the work crew was nowhere in sight nor was there a flagman to help the drivers decide which of the directions of traffic would have access to the single lane at any given time. This question of right-of-way was decided by the gutsiest drivers, and just as Haydon was nearing the single lane a truck claimed the right-of-way for the oncoming flow of traffic. The car ahead of Haydon yielded, and Haydon and all the cars behind him had to pull to the outside edge of the cliff just as they were approaching the long descent into the city, which was visible to his right. Just below him was a new housing development, the Refuge of the Beautiful View. And it was a beautiful view, or had been in former times. From here the city would be more beautiful at night, when the smoke and smog were transformed by darkness and their heavy, choking effluents hung low over the city and did not reach this high on the mountain road. But in the daytime you would have to stay in your walled garden to avoid this sight of a smothering city, and you would have to view the western volcanoes over the tops of your brilliant bougainvilleas climbing atop your walls. Nowadays only one's eyes and the tops of the volcanoes were capable of rising above the city's burgeoning decay.

Finally there was a break in the oncoming traffic and the driver ahead of Haydon gunned his engine and reclaimed the highway and Haydon and the others pulled back onto the pavement and joined the impatient traffic's headlong plunge into the valley. The Cherokee stayed with Haydon all the way into the city, always one or two cars behind him.

But when Haydon turned onto Avenida La Reforma at the Parque Independencia, the Cherokee roared up in the lane next to him and stayed beside him on the boulevard, as close as it could get without scraping him, slowing when he slowed, accelerating when he accelerated, its darkened windows making him feel oddly vulnerable. The intimidation infuriated him, but he held himself in check, looking now and then at the darkened windows as if he did not know that he was supposed to stare straight ahead as he had seen people do before, not daring to meet the beast face to face lest it be provoked to do something even worse than bullying.

Perhaps it was his adolescent refusal to be cowed, or perhaps it was the plan all along, but when they were well past the Camino Real hotel and approaching a traffic intersection where an opening in the median allowed cars to cross from the other side of the boulevard, the Cherokee suddenly swerved into Haydon's lane, cutting in front of him, raking its rear bumper across his front fender and driving him into the curb as he slammed on his brakes to avoid being bashed, and causing the two lanes of traffic to screech to a halt just as the intersecting traffic got the green light. The Cherokee sped through, narrowly missing the intersecting traffic that came only from its left, and disappeared down the boulevard out of sight.

Haydon's car had skidded halfway out into the intersection, partially blocking the merging traffic, his right front wheel up on the curb. It took him a moment to start his car again, to back it off the curb and out of the way of the merging traffic and back into his own lane where the other cars were also trying to straighten themselves after a near miss at a multicar collision. His heart pounding, Haydon glanced around at the motorists to his left side and behind him. Everyone was staring straight ahead, as though nothing had happened. They knew what they had seen, too, and they wanted nothing to do with the incident, not even to acknowledge having seen it.

The entrance to the Residencial Reforma was just beyond the light, and Haydon pulled into the courtyard and parked to one side, under a huge cypress. He got out and checked the fender, which was in worse condition than he had thought but not so bad that he couldn't continue to drive the car. He wouldn't bother to exchange the car for another one. Between this incident and the kids in Mezquital, he was going to have to pay a hefty fine when he turned it in to the rental agency. When he put the key in the door to lock the car, his hand was shaking.

He got his key from the concierge and walked through the front parlor and up the marble stairs. At the top he looked over the balcony and saw several people in the dining room, a couple of businessmen with loosened ties drinking beer, the young woman he had seen at breakfast having a fruit plate, a middle-aged couple. He turned away to his room on his right and let himself in. The windows overlooking the boulevard were still open as he had left them, and his room already had been cleaned. The sun was low enough that it was beginning to disappear behind the tall cypresses on the boulevard and came through the windows with the mellow tint of late afternoon. A slight breeze moved the curtains, and the sound of traffic on the boulevard was a steady muffled roar.

He took off his suit coat and tie and hung them in the closet where he noticed that his other clothes had been cleaned and returned. He unbuttoned the cuffs of his shirt sleeves and folded them back and

161

stepped into the bathroom and washed his face with soap and cold water. Painfully aware now of being tired, he dried his face and avoided looking at himself in the mirror. Coming out of the bathroom, he went to the edge of the bed and sat down. He untied his shoes and set them aside and lay back on the blue spread, looking up at the light on the high ceiling. He was exhausted. Lack of sleep and uncertainty and disappointment and tension had sapped his energy.

Laying the back of his wrist on his forehead, he thought of Taylor Cage taking him to see Lena's body. No explanation. He thought of what Borrayo had said about John Baine, that he was going to be used as a scapegoat. Haydon could understand that, one *gringo* kills another, a neat package of a crime. Only one thing bothered Haydon. If Baine knew anything significant about whatever it was Lena had gotten into, and if whatever she had gotten into did in fact involve General Luis Azcona, wasn't Azcona afraid that Baine would talk. Once they announced his arrest they could hardly deny him access to the embassy's Consular Section. Once they made the arrest public they would have to present at least the appearance of the due process of justice, in the course of which Baine would have an opportunity to talk to embassy officials and tell his story. Was Azcona really going to allow this?

And Jim Fossler. Haydon was going to quit kidding himself about Fossler. There was no reason he should be alive. He was a victim of bad timing, and he had been as expendable as a stray dog and probably had gotten little more consideration than that. What a country that these things could happen in absolute silence and Haydon could lie here in the changing light of late afternoon and think about them as if he had been remembering a movie.

He wasn't even aware of losing his train of thought as sleep overtook him. When the telephone rang and he woke in the bruised shades of dusk, he didn't remember anything that might have been a dream. He rolled over and picked up the telephone.

"This is Haydon."

"Mr. Haydon, this is Bennett Pittner. I was wondering if you had plans for dinner this evening."

"No," Haydon said. "I don't."

"Good, I'd like you to have dinner with me if that's convenient. I'll pick you up."

"That would be fine," Haydon said, trying to clear his mind and focus his eyes, looking across the room to the purple wall, at the mirror above the old dresser in which the cypresses of the boulevard behind him were reflected black against a lavender sky.

"Would half an hour give you enough time?"

"I'll be ready," Haydon said, and put down the receiver.

Chapter 24

To Haydon's surprise they had dinner at Pittner's home, an older house that was not large but, like Janet's, of a common quadrangle design and built of stone and stucco with the living quarters situated around a patio. Still in Zona 10, the house was in Colonia Berlín on a street where the houses sat a good way back from their walled entries and were secluded by the surrounding dense semitropical foliage. The house was sited on a bit of a promontory above a deep ravine that fed into the Río Negro. Across on the other side were the *colonias* of Vista

Hermosa where the real estate was more expensive and some of Guatemala City's wealthiest residents had built beautiful and well-guarded homes.

The house was comfortable and unpretentious, all tile and stone and mortar and timber and smelling faintly of the wood smoke of former fires in its fireplace. The table in the dining room was already set for them when they arrived, and as soon as Pittner made drinks for them they sat down. An Indian man and woman served them silently and efficiently, while Pittner made small talk about how much he enjoyed Guatemala, about how he had lived in this home ever since he had divorced Janet, a reference he made as if Haydon knew the entire story. He was wearing a dark gray tropical suit with a faint windowpane pattern in reddish brown and a white shirt with a collar that wanted to curl up at its points as if he had forgotten to put in the stays. His longish ginger hair was neatly combed, and Haydon noticed for the first time that he had a mole just to the right side of his nose. He lounged quite comfortably as he talked, and as the Indian couple served them as silently as ghosts. When everything was on the table, and with no signal from Pittner, they disappeared and were not seen again for the rest of the evening.

Pittner picked up his knife and fork and began eating, continuing to talk, asking Haydon about his own work, general questions to which Haydon gave general answers and which got them through the meal, each getting up once during the course to refresh his drink from a liquor table a step or two away. Even though Haydon sensed that Pittner was one of those men who preferred not to discuss serious business over a meal and that all was being held in abeyance until they had gotten the business of eating over, he found himself growing increasingly comfortable with Bennett Pittner. Haydon remembered Janet's description of Pittner's boorishness and was reminded once again of the inevitably tinted optics of the mind's eyes.

Finally, when they both had finished, Pittner pushed back his plate and got up and refilled his glass once more with bourbon, not offering to refill Haydon's, assuming Haydon would help himself if he wanted more. He came back to the table and turned his chair slightly to allow him to comfortably cross his legs. The dining room was in the end room of one of the U-shaped wings of the house. One wall of tall open windows looked out over the ravines and the Río Negro, on the other side of which the lights of the houses in the Vista Hermosa glittered in the haze

165

of the night fires that had made its nocturnal seepage out of the ravines and over the city. Another wall faced onto the courtyard from which the large open windows let in a loud thrumming of crickets.

"I took the trouble of inquiring about you," Pittner said, knitting his brow as if he were a school principal about to have a heart-to-heart talk with a recalcitrant student. He didn't seem to fear that Haydon would resent being checked on. "I don't think you're the kind of man I need to beat around the bush with. I understand that several years ago you met a man, an older man, who used to be my superior. Karl Heidrich."

Haydon remembered the name immediately, even though he had talked to the man less than half an hour. And he remembered the face as if it had been that afternoon. Like Pittner, Heidrich was also a ginger-haired man. He had been in his middle fifties and had a raw complexion that looked as if it had had too much of the sun.

"I didn't really know him, only met him," Haydon said.

"Los tecos, wasn't it?" Pittner said.

"Yes, out of Guadalajara. Heidrich cleared up a few things for me."

"That's what I understand. You lost a partner on that case too. Ed Mooney."

"Yeah, I did."

"Heidrich's retired now," Pittner said. "Lives in Virginia. Worked most of his life in Latin America and then went to live out the rest of it in Virginia. I've often wondered if he felt kind of out of place—in Virginia, I mean."

Haydon said nothing, looking at Pittner, waiting to see how he was going to handle this. By bringing up Heidrich he was letting Haydon know that he was aware that Haydon knew that he was with the CIA.

"But even before that, you spent some time with another man I used to work with. Taylor Cage."

"I spent three days with him."

Pittner nodded. "In his field report, Cage treated you quite well. Which is a compliment. Cage doesn't treat many people well."

"That was ten years ago," Haydon said.

"But you've seen him more recently, haven't you?"

"Well, if he works for you, you should know."

"Oh, he doesn't work for me anymore." Pittner shook his head as he sipped the bourbon. "No. A few years ago he went independent on us."

"How do you feel about that?"

Pittner looked at Haydon, holding a mouthful of bourbon a moment before swallowing it. He raised his eyebrows. "Oh, fine. It changed things, naturally. Some things are a bit more awkward, others . . . much easier." He shrugged and turned in his chair a little more toward Haydon and crossed his legs the other way, twisting his body slightly, an awkward posture with which he seemed quite comfortable, almost like a lounging adolescent.

"It's because of the way you handled yourself in both of these instances that I've asked you here to talk to you," Pittner said. "You seem to be a discreet man, understand the way State does things."

"I know the way they do things," Haydon said. "I'm not sure I understand it."

Pittner tilted his head in a languid shrugging acknowledgment of the point. "Whatever," he said. "Anyway, this thing about Lena Muller, well, it's involved . . . You seem to have a . . . knack for stumbling onto State Department things."

"There seem to be so many of them," Haydon said.

Pittner bounced his eyebrows and ran his tongue around in his jaw. "Yeah, well." He thought a moment. "The fact is, we were running Lena Muller."

Haydon stiffened inside.

"Ever since she returned to Guatemala three months ago," Pittner said, pursing his mouth. "Janet didn't know it, of course. I'd gotten Lena the job with USAID. I hadn't planned to run her from the beginning, it was just that after she went to work with AID they put her on a job that took her right back to where she had been stationed in the Peace Corps. In a very conflictive area.

"It was nothing major. The whole thing was informal. You know how it starts. After she'd gotten acclimated to her job, I just dropped in one day to take her to lunch, see how things were going. She was grateful that I'd helped and all that. Over the next few weeks I took her to lunch several times, talked about the job up there. By the way, did she ever hear any gossip about the so-called 'assassinations' of Indians by the army personnel up there? Oh, yeah, she did. She knew some of the widows. She told me stories. After I saw she was sympathetic to the Indians, it wasn't hard to ease her into it. Then I introduced her to the guy who would become her case officer. I didn't run her myself. She was very good. Very observant, sensitive to innuendo and nuance. Impressions."

Pittner paused, thought a moment, and straightened up in his chair, leaning on the table, facing Haydon. He looked tired, and the crow's-feet

167

at the corners of his eyes hinted at pain not too far removed from the surface.

"She was made to order," he continued. "It wasn't anything dangerous. I mean she wasn't anything special, just another set of eyes and ears. More of the same. Shit, all this stuff is always more of the same." He sipped the bourbon. "For months her schedule was two weeks in the field and one back here. Easy enough. She was always in the boonies, so she would bring in military things: what battalion was where, what village they'd raided and screwed up and blamed on the guerrillas. Or what villages the guerrillas had screwed up and blamed on the army. The milgroup here watches the troops, so she wasn't giving us anything we weren't already monitoring electronically. We knew where they were, but we didn't always know what they were doing. Up there near the Ixil and north, there's a lot going on. Aside from their regular messing with the civilian population, there are significant numbers of military personnel into poppies now. You can never get enough information about that sort of activity. And that's not just DEA jurisdiction now. State is into it . . . in a slightly different way.

"Lena was on the ground up there. She brought in stuff on the relationship between the army and the civil patrols, about the corruption: what military commissioner or patrol chief was in cahoots with what base commander to defraud a family of their land or take their daughters for sex or murder them to settle old scores; where and when the army had raided a village and 'recruited' a bunch of Indian kids, and how many. She kept us abreast of the disappearances and the assassinations in that area. She was a goddamned Tocqueville of abused Indians. The people trusted her. Told her all kinds of crap. She could speak a couple of dialects." Pittner swirled the ice in his glass. "That was it. Mostly hearsay, but that's all we expected from her. It gave us some additional perspective."

Haydon said nothing.

"We know you were at the morgue," Pittner said. "You saw her."

"I saw her at the Cementerio General," Haydon agreed. "But she doesn't seem to be there anymore." He wanted to see if Pittner knew he had been to Macabeo's mortuary. If Pittner knew he had been at the Cementerio General then he knew he had been with Cage, but he might not know he had also been to Macabeo's, and Haydon needed to protect that piece of information if he could.

"We don't have much of this figured out," Pittner said, not responding to the opportunity Haydon had given him.

"Was she involved with something she wasn't telling you about?"

"We have to think so."

"You don't have a clue?"

Pittner shook his head. "We don't."

Haydon didn't believe him. "But you don't think her death was 'criminal'?"

They both knew it could have been. The country was in its worst condition in decades, the economy was disintegrating, Cerezo had capitulated his authority to the army long ago and had spent his last two years in office scooping up loose cash anywhere he could find it, sometimes prying it loose himself, and the new president was expected to be as timid with the army as Cerezo had been. The army was deep into the burgeoning poppy trade. There was no real means of maintaining civil order, because the National Police was in shambles, pervaded with corruption. Vigilante groups flourished everywhere as right-wingers took "law and order" into their own hands. The previous weekend there had been forty-six murders in forty-eight hours. No one even pretended to keep up with the rapes. United States intelligence was flooded with data to analyze, and there was a real feeling everywhere that an entire society was unraveling. If Lena Muller had been a victim of common crime, neither of them would have been surprised.

"The point is," Pittner said, "we don't want her to become a headline. I know her disappearance was quite a high-profile case, that her father used his influence to stir things up, keep it in the media. That would be unacceptable down here, make us vulnerable on several fronts. Damn, the blowback would be enormous."

Haydon looked at Pittner. "How in the hell do you think you're going to keep quiet the fact that three U.S. citizens have disappeared in Guatemala in the last thirty-six hours?"

Pittner nodded. "We can't indefinitely. But we can for a while. We need time to get some explanations ourselves. We're caught with our britches down here."

"What about Baine? What about Jim Fossler?"

"We don't know where the hell they are."

"I don't believe that, of course."

"I didn't expect you would. That's why I'm asking you to give us a

169

leg up here. Let us get *on* the damned horse before you smack it on the rump. This is damage control here, pure and simple. This has gotten way out of hand."

"Out of your hand," Haydon said.

"Yeah, that's right."

Haydon looked away, out to the smoky haze and the winking lights. In the stillness he heard a peacock cry way off somewhere in the ravines, a shrill wail that echoed weirdly.

"I don't believe in 'larger considerations,' " Haydon said.

"I know that."

"I understand damage control. I don't understand cover-up."

Pittner nodded.

"You're telling me this is going to be different from what usually goes on down here?"

"We'd like to think so."

That weak-sister phrasing infuriated Haydon, but he kept himself in check. Pittner was, after all, warning him under the guise that he believed that the United States had ever had anything 'in hand' in Guatemala in the first place. If Haydon asked too many questions, it wouldn't be the U.S. State Department he would have to answer to, but one of the Guatemalan army's many death squads, the beasts behind the darkened windows of ominous vehicles who turned men to cold stone as surely as the face of Medusa.

"I'd like to think so too," Haydon said, "but I don't."

Pittner sat back in his chair. His hair somehow had become less well groomed, and his heavy eyelids had grown heavier from the bourbon. He regarded Haydon with an unenthusiastic thoughtfulness.

"So what do you plan to do?" he asked, the words lolling out of his mouth contumeliously. "Treat Guatemala City as if it were Houston? Carry on a legitimate investigation? That would be intelligent, then we'd have four missing Americans in forty-eight hours instead of three in thirty-six."

Haydon said nothing for a moment. "I've got to get back to my hotel," he said.

Pittner pondered him with his floating eyelids and then sat up in his chair, his hand bringing his glass to his mouth, his eyes remaining on Haydon as he finished off his drink.

"All right," he said, taking a deep breath and fishing in his pockets. "I'll drive you."

He finally found the keys on a table next to the front door, and they walked out into the smoky night to the car. On the way back to Avenida La Reforma, Pittner said very little. Haydon didn't know whether it was the bourbon, or the fact that his role had been played and he was reverting to a more real self, or whether he was pissed or simply exhausted. It was clear he hadn't been getting much sleep. As with all men who found themselves in positions that occasionally called for crisis management, the crisis was running his life now.

He pulled into the gates at the Residencial Reforma and rounded the statue of the naked angel and the naked mortal and stopped his government car in front of the door.

"Thanks for having me," Haydon said. "And I appreciate the advice."

Pittner was sitting behind the steering wheel stoop shouldered and rather limp.

"You know where to find me," he said. "You never know when you might want to reach out and touch someone you disdain." His grin was not altogether convincing.

Chapter 25

Haydon had managed to avoid looking at his watch the entire time he was with Pittner, but judged correctly that they were not overlong at dinner or in their discussion afterward. It was eight-forty when he let himself into his room.

He had left it dark, and he didn't bother to turn on the lights now since he could see rather well from the lights filtering through the cypresses on the boulevard. He hung his suit coat in the closet and removed his shoes. Pulling a comfortable armchair over, he propped his feet on the edge of the bed and leaned his head against the soft back of the chair. He had just started to think about his conversation with Pittner when the telephone rang and he grabbed it.

"Do you remember where that *pinche,* Berto, found God?" It was Borrayo.

"Yes."

"Be there in half an hour. The very same spot."

"Okay," Haydon said.

Berto Colones had been a vicious and corpulent officer in the Guardia de Hacienda, the Treasury Police, whom Haydon had gotten to know during his sallies up and down Central America chasing the notorious Colombian. He had agreed to sell Haydon and the DEA information about his superior officer, who was running a lucrative cocaine operation out of an isolated little port in Suchitepéquez called Chicago. Haydon's fugitive Colombian had been one of the superior's major suppliers, and the captain was supposed to know how to get in touch with him. It was a complicated operation, and Berto knew the details, which he was willing to tell a DEA agent for certain financial considerations. The agent insisted that Borrayo, who was then still with the Department of Technical Investigations and was working drug cases with the DEA, be at the meeting.

Berto had set up the meeting in the cinder-block hovel of a prostitute he knew in Colonia Santa Isabel, one of the most miserable slums in the city in Zona 3. The site, deep in the ravines of the Río La Barranca, was in an area he knew well, and he felt secure in using its dark labyrinth of paths and trails as an escape route if it became necessary. Haydon and Berto got there early and hid on a path well up the hillside and watched Borrayo and the DEA agent arrive and make their way down the switchbacks to the prostitute's hovel. They waited a few minutes to make sure they were not accompanied and then followed them down through the garbage on the slopes and the stench of sewage rising from the bottom of the ravine below. When they got to the hovel, Berto preceded Haydon into the single, dimly lighted room. Haydon paused only a second to scrape the mud from his shoes on a car bumper half hidden in the weeds outside the door.

Suddenly there was a shout, yelling, and then a boom of gunfire, and the hefty Berto came backing out of the door with Borrayo embracing him in a grim dance, Borrayo's 9mm automatic jammed into Berto's lardaceous girth, his other arm encircling Berto's fat neck, the muzzle

173

exploding again and again in muffled whumps, eating into the fat and blowing Berto's blood all over both of them. At the edge of the path outside the shanty door, Borrayo stopped and released his deadly embrace and fired one last time, blasting Berto over the edge and down into the ravine, his elephantine corpse crashing through the dark underbrush with a smashing commotion that set all the dogs in Santa Isabel barking.

The meeting was over.

The killing was a setback to the investigation, but as Borrayo said later, it had to be. It seemed that the moment Berto had walked through the door, Borrayo had recognized him as the man who had raped his niece three years before. It had been a bad thing. Through a strange set of circumstances, Borrayo had seen the man only moments after the crime but had not known who he was. It was only great good luck, according Borrayo, that Haydon had brought this bastard to his long-overdue destiny.

It was then that Borrayo started helping them with their investigation. Having deprived them of a major lead, he felt obligated to make it up to them.

Remembering this, Haydon had mixed emotions about Borrayo's choice of rendezvous locations. But he had no alternative. He quickly put on his shoes, grabbed his coat, and went downstairs. At the bottom of the stairs he surprised two of the hotel's dining room waiters, who, when things slowed down at night, spent a lot of their time lingering at the back of the darkened parlor, watching the American cable channels over the heads of the paying guests. He left his room key with the concierge and walked out into the dimly lighted courtyard to his car.

He unlocked it, got in, and rolled down his window as he put the key in the ignition and started it. Just as he was about to back out from under the dark cypress, someone reached through his window and held the steering wheel.

174

"Borrayo sent me," the man said, his breath heavy with tobacco. "Please to let me drive."

Haydon put the car in neutral and left it running as he slid across to the passenger side. The man opened the door and got in behind the steering wheel. He familiarized himself with the car a moment, adjusted the rearview mirror, put the car in gear, and they were off.

The driver did not talk. He was a Guatemalan a decade or so younger than Haydon, dressed in a sport coat and slacks, his hair richly oiled. By the time they passed the National Theater he was driving the car like it was his own, and occasionally, when he used both hands to make a sharp turn, Haydon caught a glimpse of the butt of a pistol stuck in his waistband. He drove carefully, his calm eyes constantly checking the rearview mirror. Sometimes he darted through a stoplight the second it turned red, and sometimes he careened across traffic, turning left or right from the opposite lane. Several times he doubled back on an opposite avenida, going back the way they had just come. He knew narrow, out-of-the-way streets that ran for blocks and blocks without intersections, and once Haydon was sure he signaled a man with a radio who stood on a dark corner just as they emerged from one of these narrow streets. This was more care than Haydon had anticipated. This was much more than simply being cautious.

The shantytown lay west of the tightly woven streets in the old central city, where scrawny fingers of heavily eroded land jutted out above the Río La Barranca and fell away into ravines that were steeply terraced with shanties and squatters' shacks. The river itself was a wandering scabrous wound that ran south below the Cementerio General to Colonia Landivar where the city's largest garbage dump sprawled in a stinking barren plain that resembled nothing so much as a bad dream of the end of time. To the north, the river ran under one of the city's most distinctive landmarks, El Incienso, the Incense Bridge, that stretched out across the wide basin of La Barranca on the Anillo Periférico, a west-side expressway that was under perpetual construction and suffered from the schizophrenic burden of most Guatemalan building projects, that of deteriorating almost as fast as it was being constructed.

There was no direct route to the internal environs of Santa Isabel, which was most easily approached by any of a number of dead-end calles and avenidas that halted abruptly at the serrated precipices of the several promontories encrusted with cinder-block buildings. It was through such streets that Haydon rode beside the silent man into the smoky neighborhoods north of the Cementerio General and entered an avenida that he knew would take them straight into a fold of the ravine's rim below which he remembered the prostitute's house to be located.

His driver stopped the car several blocks away from the dead end and parked along the street with several other cars. On either side of the street was a seamless stretch of stucco buildings with shuttered windows and darkened and bolted doorways behind which patios and dingy rooms sheltered families who had made themselves as secure as possible in a city of uncertain security.

175

The two of them got out of the car, locked their doors, and the driver tossed the keys to Haydon. Together they started walking toward the dead end two blocks away, but at the first calle the silent man hissed at Haydon, signaled to him, and they stepped into a darkened doorway. They waited a minute, watching the street, the smell of urine and moldy stucco seeping into their clothes. After a little while the silent man tapped Haydon on the shoulder, and they left the shadows and continued along the sidewalk toward the dead end.

As they walked the length of the next block, Haydon saw the contours of the shacks built on the ravine's rim where the stucco buildings stopped. The shacks were dark, and the ravine was dark where it fell away. Far off he could see the long strings of weak lights of El Incienso glimmering in the smoky distance. They stayed close to the buildings, the glow from the last streetlamp a block back growing so weak Haydon was practically in the shadows by the time they came to where the sidewalk ended and he had to step down into the rocky street. The buildings on the opposite side of the street extended half a block farther on, and they were almost to the encroaching margin of dried weeds that marked the head of the trails that branched off in zigzagging angles down into the ravine when Haydon again heard the familiar hissing.

"Ssssss—sssssst!"

Haydon looked toward the shell of the last building opposite, its gutted windows and doorways allowing imperfect glimpses of its crumbling interior. Borrayo stood at the corner, half in the darkness, half in the poor light. When he knew that Haydon had seen him, he did not move but simply waited for Haydon and the silent man to finish crossing the street.

"Buenas," Borrayo said in a low voice. They shook hands, and Haydon saw the dark panel truck tucked between the stone wall of the building and the undergrowth behind the first shacks. The silent man disappeared into the darkness.

"I've got someone for you to talk with," Borrayo said. His face was sober. "In there," and he jerked his head toward the truck.

"What about the *orejas?*"

"Oh, well one of them got a last-minute transfer to another sector. Another one had to go to the infirmary. The last one, he is in there too."

Haydon looked at him. Whatever the hell that meant. Neither of them mentioned the silent man nor the fact that the meeting was not taking place in the ravines as Borrayo had specified.

"Listen, Haydon," Borrayo said, backing farther into the shadows, Haydon following. They were at the back bumper of the truck now. He was wearing his sidearm, and Haydon could hear the leather creaking as he shifted his weight. "You have maybe only half an hour, and then I am going to drive off with this *maricón.*"

Haydon nodded.

"Okay," Borrayo said, and he stepped to the back of the panel truck, unlocked it, and pulled open the door.

In the low-wattage glow of the van's small ceiling light, Haydon saw John Baine lying on his stomach on the ribbed metal floor, his hands secured behind him, his legs tied together, his mouth taped shut, his eyes taped closed. Another man sat across from him, the *oreja,* a thin-as-a-string young man with a beautiful face and shabby, ill-fitting clothes who looked at Haydon with wary eyes as though he were trying to see in Haydon's face some hint of what was going to happen to him here.

"Get him over here," Borrayo said to the young man, who immediately grabbed Baine's arms and dragged him to the van door. He and Borrayo swung Baine around so that he sat at the back of the van, his legs hanging outside.

Borrayo got close to Baine's face. "I am going to remove the tape," Borrayo said in a low voice. "Do not yell. *¿Comprendes?*"

Baine nodded reluctantly.

"I will goddamn kill you," Borrayo said.

Baine nodded more vigorously.

"Okay," Borrayo said, satisfied. He tore off the tape from around Baine's mouth and neck with a ripping sound that made Haydon wince, and then did the same with the tape over Baine's eyes. Baine cocked his head sideways and looked up at Borrayo and Haydon, who were standing in front of him. His lips and eyes were puffy from beatings. His sandy hair was matted and stuck out all over his head, and his filthy clothes reeked of soured urine.

"It's not important for you to know my name," Haydon said. Baine jerked up his sagging head at the sound of an obviously American voice and looked in Haydon's direction, squinting even in the pale light of the alley. He must have had his eyes taped a long time. Haydon added, "But it's absolutely essential that you cooperate with me if you want any help out of this mess."

"Oh!" Pause. "Son-of-a-bitch! Oh, son-of-a- . . . ." He wilted. "Oh, God. I thought I was dea— I thought they were taking me out to shoot

177

me. What're . . . what . . . you an American? Huh? Man, get me out of this. Oh, shit, I'm not believing this. You from the embassy, or what?"

Baine was overwrought, his nerves strung way out to the thin ends of themselves. The kid had been through a very bad time. What he didn't know, mercifully, was that there was going to be more of it before it was over.

Chapter 26

"You want a cigarette?" Haydon asked, going into his pocket for the pack of Pall Malls.

Baine nodded. Haydon looked at Borrayo, who leaned over and uncuffed Baine's hands as Haydon lighted the cigarette and then handed it to Baine. He gave one to Borrayo, too, and lighted another for himself.

"I'm not from the embassy," Haydon said. "They don't know you've been arrested yet, but it won't be long before they do."

Baine sucked on the cigarette, which he held with a badly trembling right hand while his left elbow was tucked into his stomach in an apparent effort to alleviate an abdominal pain. His shoulders were hunched as if he were trying to hold himself together.

"When the people from the Consular Section come to interview you," Haydon said, "do not tell them about this interview. People risked their lives for this. They may be able to help you some more, but you've got to be savvy about it, know when you're doing yourself a favor by keeping your mouth shut."

Haydon paused a moment to let that soak into Baine's hammered brain. The young man was looking at him, but Haydon couldn't tell from his expression what was on his mind. Except that he was scared. Baine sucked on the cigarette. His mouth was so misshapen that even putting the cigarette to his lips looked painful.

"You didn't kill her, I guess," Haydon said.

Baine shook his head wearily. "Nooo, maaan. Jesus H. Christ! I didn't even know she was dead till they . . . the, shit, the G-2 picked me up last night in Masagua." He groaned, but Haydon couldn't tell if it had to do with pain or frustration or fear. "Kill her! Shit, man! This is bizarre! I didn't *kill* her!" Baine looked frantically at Borrayo and then back to Haydon. "No way!"

"Okay, look," Haydon said. "Just tell me what happened after you left Guatemala City with her. Just go through it."

Baine hung his head, tired, confused. He raised his hand.

"First. First, where'd they find her?"

"The police report said she was killed around Yajaucú, by the guerrillas."

Baine looked up, frowning. "When?"

"It must have been Saturday night sometime."

"Those sons of bitches," Baine grunted. "That's such bullshit."

"Who? What's bullshit?"

"The damn National Police. Guerrillas."

"You don't think it was guerrillas?"

Baine started to say something and then checked himself. "I just don't ever believe the police, that's all. It's a rule of thumb . . ." He shook his head.

"I need to know what happened," Haydon insisted.

Baine nodded, seeming to call on some inner reserve of strength. Even in these threatening circumstances, he was still showing considerable backbone.

"I asked her to go to Lake Atitlán with me for a couple of days," Baine began. "That was it." He shrugged. "I've asked her to travel with me several times, but she doesn't go that often. I was looking forward to it. We left about noon. It's an easy half-day drive to Atitlán, but she wanted to stop by Antigua first, to run up to Santa María de Jesus. You know, that little Indian village up on the side of the Agua volcano. I didn't much want to go. It's hot as hell up there, the dry season's burned everything up, the road's rough and powdery. Dust just fogs up. But she really wanted to go, so we took off. When we got up there she said she wanted to see some people she knows, Indians. She knows a lot of Indians everywhere. I didn't want to sit in one of those damned cinder-block ovens, so I hung around in the square. Got over in the shade of a building and watched the people. Ate some limes. She was gone a long time, longer than she said . . . longer than she said she'd be. By the time she got back and we got down off the mountain, it was getting on into the afternoon."

Baine dropped the butt of his cigarette between his feet in the dirt. "Could I have another one?"

Haydon gave it to him, and he and Borrayo lighted another as well.

"Right off, there was a disagreement. She wanted to go the lower route. I didn't, even though it's a little shorter. The army had just killed a bunch of people down in there—'guerrillas.' I didn't need that, not the damned army. That didn't seem to bother her in the least. But it was my car. We went my way, the high road, you know, Tecpán, Zaculeu, Los Encuentros, down to Sololá. In Sololá, Lena wanted to stop again. Same story, to visit some people. By this time it was getting dark, and I didn't want to do it. But she insisted. You know Sololá? Well, it's no place to be after dark. We negotiated these tiny cobblestone streets, her telling me where to turn. We finally found the place. She went in, and I waited in the car. She was gone about half an hour, and when she got back we headed down to Panajachel."

Baine stopped to smoke. Haydon looked at Borrayo, who was frowning, a little preoccupied, Haydon thought. He glanced at the young prisoner who was squatting on the floor of the truck and staring at Haydon with the look of a frightened animal. He didn't know what the hell was going on. His back was against the van's ribbed wall, and without a doubt he was nervous, looking like he was calculating his odds of bolting past Baine out the open door and over the cliff.

181

"We got to Panajachel about seven o'clock. I had reservations so . . ."

"You *did* have reservations?"

"Yeah."

"Where?"

"Sol Atitlán."

"And you stayed there?"

"Yeah. Why? What's the matter?"

"Go ahead," Haydon said.

Baine gave him a look and then went on. "We checked in. You know that place?" Haydon nodded, but Baine went on anyway. "Little bungalows about seventy-five, a hundred meters from the beach. Very nice in a kind of laid-back way. We checked in, threw our things in the bungalow, and headed for the bars. Atitlán was in good form. These neo-hippie kids all over the place as usual, the British and French and Germans—always a lot of German kids—and American kids from places like Boise and Long Beach and Houston and Raleigh. Everybody sunburned and looking like they hadn't washed their hair in a week and had been running around naked, which they had.

"We had a good time, talking to these *'jipis,'* hanging out. The bars at night, the beach in the day. Everything was going fine."

He paused for the cigarette again, and somebody came up out of the ravine, three people, talking, not even seeing them, going on down the street. Haydon moved farther into the shadow, and Baine lowered his voice.

"Next morning we got up fairly early—to be the first on the beach. Lena's like that—she's one of those people who doesn't need much sleep. We laid out our towels, stripped naked, and stretched out, letting the sun warm us as it came up." He shook his head, remembering it. "It was great. We dozed off and on, the beach got busier. We talked to a few people. About ten-thirty Lena got up, brushed off the sand, and said she was going up to the bungalow to get more suntan lotion. She slipped on this long shirt thing she wears—pulls it up over her breasts like a housedress or something—held it in the back so it wouldn't fall down, and took off. That," he said, taking another hit on the cigarette, "was the last time I saw her."

"Go on," Haydon said. Baine was taking too much time.

Baine nodded. "I laid there. After a while I wondered about her, but I dozed off. When I woke up and saw she was still gone, I got my watch out of my pants I was using for a pillow and saw she'd been gone forty-five minutes. I got my things together, and hers too—she'd left everything there—and walked up to the bungalow. She wasn't there. I thought maybe she'd run up to the store—there's a little *tienda* at the top of the . . . and I went on up there to look for her. But she wasn't at the store. I looked in a couple of bars nearby, nothing. Nobody had seen her. I went back to the bungalow and sat down with a beer to think about it. It was getting late by now. I finished the beer and walked back up to town and started around to all the bars. I went to all the places we'd been the night before and even to places we hadn't been. Nothing. Nobody had seen her. To tell you the truth, I got a little scared at this point. My imagination was really cooking now—what if this, what if that. At that point I walked back to the bungalow, trying to decide what next. When I got there the door was open. I'd locked it. I'm sure I'd locked it. Anyway, somebody had been there and all her things were gone."

Baine again dropped his cigarette butt between his feet, and he shook his head when offered another.

"Then I put two and two together. Or thought I had. The night before, we were at this bar, Popol. There was this good-looking German guy there, and he and Lena were flirting. She did that when she drank a lot. Very reserved . . . and then when she drank, her juices started squirting all over the place. I remembered that I hadn't seen him anywhere in any of the clubs I'd been to that night and immediately I *knew* she'd probably taken off with him. The more I thought about it, the more I was sure of it, and the madder I got. She had a key; she'd probably come back and gotten her clothes. I stayed the night, checked out in the morning, and drove back."

"You came back to Guatemala City?"

"Right."

"You didn't check with Janet Pittner to see if Lena had gotten back all right?"

"No, hell no. I wasn't going to go back after I thought she'd done that to me."

Baine started to stand up, but Borrayo shoved him back down, hard, so that Baine grunted sharply at the pain, held himself, gasping. The young prisoner, still squatting, shifted his weight and eyed Borrayo nervously.

"Was she in the habit of doing something like that?"

"I don't know," Baine grunted, his eyes avoiding Borrayo. "I just thought that's what she'd done, that's all. She could be pretty cold the way she used her sex."

"What do you mean 'used her sex'? I was under the impression she didn't date all that much?"

Baine looked at Haydon. "Who you been talking to?" he grunted again. "Lena was a big lay, for Christ's sake. You don't know that? Hey, sit around with embassy guys a while, the guys in the AID programs, wherever, you'll hear something about Lena. I mean, the doormen didn't get her, but she was had."

Haydon felt like an ass.

"But, listen," Baine said, "she was wicked about it. It wasn't for nothing. If you had something she wanted, she'd trade you. She wasn't easy. You had to qualify. Some of the guys at the embassy went out of their way to qualify. There was gossip about security breaches and all that."

"What kind of gossip?"

Baine was quick enough to realize his mouth had been ahead of his brain on that one, and he backed off.

"Just gossip," he said. "There's always 'security' gossip around embassies. Especially the places where there's a lot of State Department maneuvering with the host government, where there's a lot of interplay."

"How did you qualify?"

"What?"

"With Lena."

Baine winced and grunted as he leaned over to ease a sudden sharp pain in his stomach.

"They do this to me again, I'm dead." He looked at Haydon. "I'm really going back there?" he asked suddenly.

184   Haydon nodded.

"Christ Jesus, man! I'm out now!" He looked at Borrayo, then back to Haydon. "There's some deal here, right? What, I'm here just to talk to you? That's it? You got me out of that goddamned place just to *talk* to me . . . and then send me back?"

"I can't prevent that," Haydon said, hating himself. The kid really had thought Haydon had gotten him out, that he wasn't going back. "But you'll be all right." He had no reason to believe this was true. "Just gut it out," Haydon said. "When the consular people come in, maybe tomorrow, scream your head off. Get a lawyer."

"What the hell's going on here?" Baine said, indignant and petrified at the same time. "You son of a bitch, you got to tell me what's going on here."

"You're being framed . . ."

Baine gaped. "Framed? What . . . ? You mean Lena's death? Who's . . . ?"

"I don't know," Haydon said, talking quickly now. "I'm trying to find out."

"Oh, God Almighty . . ." Baine was holding himself, shaking his head in disbelief.

Haydon watched him a moment. There wasn't any way he was going to be able to help John Baine. Guatemala was the wrong place to get into trouble.

"You had a talk with Jim Fossler," Haydon said.

Baine's eyes shot up at Haydon. If the kid's face hadn't been so swollen from being punched Haydon thought he might have seen an expression of surprise.

"Is that what you are? Did Lena's old man send another private investigator?"

"No, I don't work for her father. You'd better answer me."

Baine only nodded. "Yeah, we talked with Fossler."

"Fossler said you and Lena were afraid of something, that he thought you were in some kind of trouble. Can you explain what that's all about?"

Baine shook his head. "He seemed to think we were Bonnie and Clyde or something. Lena didn't want to go back home. Actually, Fossler was sympathetic. He knew her mother wanted her back, but he knew her old man was a monster, too. Well, I guess he's got something to take home to Lena's folks now, doesn't he."

"I'm not sure he'll ever get to do that," Haydon said. "Fossler's disappeared, and the only thing I can find of him is some blood left in his room."

This time the shock was evident in Baine's eyes.

"You'd better tell me what's going on here," Haydon said. "There's a slim chance Fossler's still alive. I'm trying to find him, but I've got to know what he knew that put him in danger. If you hold out on me I'm not going to give much of a damn what happens to you."

Baine had hunched over farther, almost in a fetal position, grunting

185

in short bursts. Haydon was half afraid the G-2 had taken the beatings too far. The kid looked bad. Without a doubt he was bleeding internally. If Tablaya's men got to him again before the embassy did, Haydon didn't think Baine would make it.

Baine coughed up something and leaned over and let it run out of his mouth. He wiped his chin on his shirt sleeve, took a moment to catch his breath, and then turned his head away from Borrayo. "I was onto a story," he said hoarsely. He steadied himself against the back of the van.

"We've only got a few more minutes," Haydon said.

"I got onto this story about this general, actually his sister . . . selling orphans, kids out of the highlands."

"Orphans?"

Baine nodded. "In the highlands, over the years, since the late seventies there've been so many deaths, tens of thousands. There've been two hundred thousand kids orphaned up there. This country's full of homeless kids. It's a bad situation."

Suddenly Haydon was painfully aware of Borrayo's presence.

"Lena wanted information on this?"

"Wanted and had. She'd been working on that story a hell of a lot longer than I had. She'd been up there a long time. She saw a lot of shit happening; she knew stuff. I heard she had some documentation, and I'd come across some stuff too. Each of us had something the other wanted."

A radio crackled under the dashboard at the front of the van, and the driver answered, speaking in a low, fast voice. He turned around quickly and spoke through the dark van.

"Efran! ¡Vamos!"

"What documentation?"

Borrayo spoke to the young prisoner in the van. *"Maricón,* get out!"

186

The youth jumped out of the van and grabbed Baine's arm to help him get in, but he had misunderstood. "No, no," Borrayo said, and he stepped over to him.

"Do you know *which* general?" Haydon snapped. "What was his . . ."

There were two explosions, and Haydon reflexively fell back against the stone wall, reaching for his Beretta that wasn't there. Borrayo had his back to Haydon and was standing over the young prisoner, who had sat down hard in the dirt, stunned, weaving, dying. The driver started the van, and Borrayo turned to Haydon, his hands and his gun in the air with a placating gesture.

"It had to be," Borrayo explained, talking fast. "He was the only one I could not get away from. Look, friend," Borrayo said. "This had to be. This boy, he is a snake. Do you think Tablaya would learn of this meeting? Yes, of course he would. I want to help you, Haydon, but I don't want to die for you. Okay?" He raised his eyebrows in conclusion. "But this little *pinche,* he will have to die for you."

Haydon's heart was hitting his chest like a fist as Borrayo slowly turned back to the youth. The boy wasn't dying quickly, because Borrayo had shot him in the stomach. His eyes had stopped seeing, but he was making bleating noises, trying not to fall over in the dirt where there was death. Borrayo shot him in the face, which blew it away and knocked him backward as hard as if he had been hit by a cannonball. What was left of his head was in the shadows, the lower half of his body in the dim light that spilled out of the open back door of the van. Haydon saw how thin his ankles were, sticking out of his pants legs. He was wearing shoes without socks. Borrayo's shot had blown him out of one of his shoes.

Borrayo turned slowly to Haydon. "Okay?"

The gunshots were still ringing in Haydon's ears. What the hell was he going to say? That it wasn't okay?

"Now I have to go," Borrayo said, returning his gun to its shoulder holster under his jacket. He reached for Baine, who was stunned and glassy-eyed, leaning sideways on the back of the van. His muscles had failed him out of fear, and he couldn't hold himself up. His eyes walled in terror, and his swollen lips were peeled back in disbelief as Borrayo grabbed him, recuffed him, and rolled him back onto the ribbed floor of the van.

"You had better get the hell out of here," Borrayo said to Haydon, locking the back of the van.

"What about the driver?" Haydon asked, surprising himself that he was even thinking that logically.

"No problem," Borrayo said. "He is my brother-in-law." He slapped Haydon on the back. "Get out of here," he said again.

Haydon stood against the wall, hugging the darkness, as Borrayo got into the van, and his brother-in-law gunned the engine. The back wheels threw up gravel, and the van tore along the side of the building to the alley, then turned and disappeared.

Haydon thought about John Baine in the back, aching from his beatings and horrified. In the quiet night he could hear the van's engine revving through the deserted, distant streets. For the first time since he

187

had arrived at this steep ridge above the ravines, he was aware of the heavy, oily stench of the smoldering dumps. He looked one last time at the young prisoner's brain-spattered legs in the bloody weeds. In the dark, Haydon imagined he could hear the kid's blood draining out of the place that had been his face and into the sand.

Chapter 27

He took several deep breaths of the foul night air and held them, trying to bring his heart rate under control. Colonia Santa Isabel was quiet, holding its own collective breath after Borrayo's gunshots. Business was being conducted in the night streets, and no one wanted to know anything about it. Through the margin of brush that separated Haydon from the edge of the sharp banks of the ravine, he could see the lights of the Incense Bridge, wan and distant through the hazy space.

With difficulty he turned away from the dead boy and eased to the corner of the building, the rough stone and chipped stucco wall plucking at the shoulder of his suit coat. From the shadows he surveyed the street, the occasional lamp providing uneven blotches of sallow light. Two blocks away, his car was now alone by the curb.

He left the dark and ran across the street, keeping to the ragged margin where the first shanties teetered on the rim of the ravine and the paths started down into a maze of switchbacks. When he got to the other side and started toward the car, the first seventy-five meters were past a weedy stretch of land strewn with rubble and garbage and old car bodies with a backdrop of the city on the other side of the Río La Barranca. Hurrying to reach the buildings where he could quickly duck into a number of darkened doorways if he needed to, he jogged across the dusty stretch, dust that made him think of the kid with the skinny ankles and no face. It made him think of the unconcerned ease with which Borrayo had dispatched the boy's life, and it reminded him that if it hadn't been for him it wouldn't have happened at all, or at least it wouldn't have happened *because* of him. Borrayo was too damned accommodating in matters of death.

He came to the first building and the beginning of the sidewalk that climbed out of the caliche and hugged the buildings as it ran from block to block, at first two feet above the street and then growing closer as the grade grew shallower. He walked the last block to the car, past shuttered windows, past the uric doorway where he had stopped with his nameless driver, and through one of the pale blotches of light from a streetlamp. Haydon had first met Borrayo in the early eighties, during *la violencia*. One made assumptions about men's behavior in such extraordinary times, assumptions that often excused extremes, or at least pretended to understand them. He had heard that those times had returned, but he had not been prepared for this: Lena Muller, Fossler, Baine, and now this nameless boy . . .

He reached the corner, stepped down off the sidewalk and crossed the street to the opposite corner where his car was parked only a couple of meters from the first doorway. He was already reaching into his pocket for the keys, mentally unlocking the car door . . .

"Hay-don."

He flinched and wheeled toward the voice in the same instant that he recognized it, though his mind hadn't yet sorted out why it was out of context. With his last breath still caught in his diaphragm, he peered into the darkness where the corner of the opposite buildings blocked the weak

190

light from the streetlamp. She came along the wall, dressed in an Indian *huipil* and *corte,* her hair braided on her head in the customary
fashion. She was carrying a bundle in her arms, like a child wrapped in a
rebozo.

"Estoy Lita. ¡Anda listo! she said, and she hurried past him, her san-
daled feet slapping against the stones as she descended the steps into the
street. They reached the car together, and in a moment he was turning
the key in the ignition, flipping on the lights.

"Hurry!" she said, unwrapping the *rebozo.*

"What about Cage?"

"No, no is here . . . no!"

Christ! Haydon gunned the car into a U-turn, and the narrow streets
of Santa Isabel flashed by in the headlights, the buildings on either side
dividing to let them through, rushing past their windows like tunnel
walls. She gave him directions in a halting mixture of English and Spanish, until they emerged from the narrow streets onto the major Avenida
Elena and headed south on the commercial thoroughfare.

"Veinte cuadras más, más o menos," she said, and looked behind them
one more time before she turned around, reasonably relaxed, one hand
still inside her *rebozo.*

"How did you get there?" Haydon asked. "Where's Cage?" He
was both relieved to see her and furious that Cage had been following
him.

"I come with Cage."

"We weren't followed," he said.

She shook her head. "No. *Radio,*" she said, and outlined a box on the
dash with her small hand.

Cage had put a beeper on his car.

"And he left you there alone?"

She shook her head again and pulled a radio out of the *rebozo.* She
clicked it once and, as if to demonstrate, radioed their position. But it was
in code, Haydon recognized none of the coordinates. Hell no, she wasn't
alone; Cage had left her with a radio! Haydon wanted to ask her why he
had left her, but decided to save the question for Cage himself. Lita
continued to look straight ahead.

Avenida Elena ran parallel to the Cementerio General, and several
blocks east of it. They passed darkened furniture stores and cafés and the
ubiquitous auto-parts houses that littered every Central American city of
any size. The street grew narrower and began to climb slightly, and trees

191

sprang up on either side, tall ones, cedars and cypresses, dark and somber against the stucco walls of the buildings.

In the warm car Haydon could smell the cottony odors of Lita's *huipil*. Though the Indians' fabrics could be beautiful and brilliantly designed, they often were hot, being most commonly made of a tightly woven, thick cotton cloth intended for years of everyday use and meant to last through all seasons. In the rainy season nights their clothes kept them warm, but in the dry season they suffered the heavy material in stoic silence. There was no tradition of changing to lighter-weight garments to accommodate the seasons. Who had two complete sets of clothes? That was a notion for the wealthy.

"Despacio," Lita said, and Haydon slowed the car as they reached the top of a small rise. Following her single-word directions, Haydon turned left toward the central city and eased down a sloping side street. There were more trees, the lower few feet of their trunks painted white, a ghostly queue swallowed by the long throat of the narrow lane disappearing into a smoky darkness beyond their headlights. They drove past a car parked on the right side with two men in it, but Lita paid no attention though Haydon knew she had seen them, and then in a moment she raised her hand and pointed to their right, to a black door set in the high, uninterrupted wall behind the file of trees. Haydon pulled to the side and parked on the slope, turning his wheels to the curb and cutting the engine. He heard Lita signal a double-click on the radio in her *rebozo,* and then they got out of the car.

She waited for him under the cypresses as he came around the car to the sidewalk, and together they approached the narrow door, which Haydon now saw was actually a wrought-iron gate with a solid metal panel cut to its exact size and welded to its bars for privacy. A small window grate was set in the center of the solid gate. Haydon noticed that fifteen meters to their left, and farther down the sloping sidewalk, heavy wooden doors allowed cars to enter behind the wall from the street. The light was too poor for him to see whether or not a garage lay on the other side. Just beyond these doors another car was parked at the curb, and Haydon made out two more dark silhouettes. Behind them, on the other side of the street were more trees, another endless wall, more gates and doorways. He sensed that the courtyards behind these walls were large and that there were gardens in which the cicadas, of which he now became aware, were hiding and humming in the dark heat. A lamp was mounted in the wall beside the narrow gate, and Lita pushed the small amber button underneath it.

In the moment they had to wait, Haydon tried to see into the courtyard through the small grate, but it was too dark. He looked at Lita's profile against the little splash of dull light on the stucco wall. She was all business, quiet, stern, with the slightest hint of a frown between her dark eyes as she bent her head, waiting. She was remote—perhaps her dress contributed to her sense of inscrutability—and absent was any hint of the reserved tenderness she had shown the night before outside Macabeo's grisly mortuary. Haydon remembered her past. Perhaps that brief moment with her amid the groans of Macabeo's resentful curs had been an anomaly. It was, after all, only a "sense" of her that he had had. He didn't even know what it was, just a spark of communication, of unguarded sincerity that seemed like a flicker of revelative innocence in the context of the shadow world in which she lived.

An electric latch clicked, and the gate sprung ajar. Lita pushed it open without looking around at Haydon, and they entered a courtyard of cobblestones. There were buildings on three sides of the courtyard, a couple of large jacarandas growing almost in the center of it, which must have provided a delicate shade in the daytime. Plantains grew in the corners and along part of the front wall, which was now behind them. This was a more humble courtyard than Haydon had seen at Janet's or Bennett Pittner's. But it seemed to be much used, with several tables under the jacaranda and a few odd chairs scattered around. The three surrounding buildings were of differing stories, but of relatively the same height because of the sloping grade of the hillside. It was a compound of residences, with windows thrown open, a dim light behind curtains here, a glow of a television there, the smells of cooking food, and a whiff of cigarette smoke. There was an occasional voice, but none above a murmur.

Lita walked across the courtyard, veering to her right toward a lighted open doorway through which Haydon could see several men sitting in a large kitchen. One of the men was Cage. As they approached, Cage looked toward their footsteps, and Lita stepped through the doorway with Haydon following.

"Damn," Cage said to Haydon as they came in. "I thought for a little bit there that you were dead. Sit down."

Two Guatemalan men were at the large wooden table with Cage, and

193

an Indian woman was behind them, cleaning up the dishes from the meal that the men had apparently just finished. There was a modern gas stove, but the Indian woman obviously had cooked the meal at the wide-mouthed fireplace where several pots still sat simmering at the edge of the coals. There was a wide, seat-high hearth that went the full length of the room and where Lita sat down away from the heat of the fire, completely ignored by Cage. Haydon saw that as she unwrapped the radio and laid it on the *rebozo* on the hearth, she also unwrapped a large automatic handgun.

"You want something to eat?" Cage asked. Haydon shook his head. The Indian woman was already filling a plate of food for Lita, although they had not exchanged a word. Haydon sat down at the table at a right angle from Cage and across from the two Guatemalan men, who studied their beer bottles, avoiding Haydon's eyes. They were drinking Gallos, and Cage did not introduce them.

Nor did Cage explain why he had been following Haydon.

"When Lita heard the gunshots, she radioed that she thought you'd been shot," Cage said. "The last shot, the third one, she said was the coup de grace. She heard the car leave . . . or van, was it a van . . . ?" Haydon nodded. ". . . and she started in your direction. Then you came out from behind the damn building." Cage looked at him. "Want a Gallo?"

"Yeah," Haydon said, sure he wanted a Gallo.

Cage asked the Indian woman to bring a beer to Haydon. "What was going on?" Cage asked.

"I guess I shouldn't be surprised you were following me."

"Depends on how much you understand your situation here," Cage said, sipping from his own amber bottle. "If you don't understand, then you might have been surprised." He had pushed his chair away from the table and had stretched his legs out in front of him, crossed at the ankles. He wasn't all that goggle-eyed about the violence that had just taken place. His attitude was more that of one wanting to know how Haydon had found the company at the cocktail party he had just attended.

The Indian woman set Haydon's beer on the table in front of him, and he quickly took a long deep drink of it.

"Well, I am surprised," Haydon said. "You want to explain some of this to me?"

"Like what?"

194

"For a man who didn't want to get involved in my business here, putting a beeper on my car is a curious thing to do."

"I thought you might stumble onto something."

"If I did, do you think you'd know it?"

"It's the way I make my living, knowing shit like what you're doing. Knowing and getting involved are different sides of the coin."

"If I'd been shot back there in that alley, what would you have learned?"

"That you didn't know Borrayo as well as you thought you did. That Lena had been in some really deep shit."

Haydon didn't say anything. It was useless to try to unravel the ways in which Cage might have learned that Haydon knew Borrayo, or even that Cage knew it was Borrayo whom Haydon had gone to meet in Santa Isabel. Haydon wasn't going to kid himself. He couldn't operate here alone, and if there was even a remote chance of finding Fossler, he was going to have to cast his lot with either Pittner or Cage. Those were his two options, though Pittner really wasn't an option at all. He was sitting in front of the only man who could help him. But he had a hunch about Cage.

"I'll tell you something," Haydon said, and he took another long drink of the cold Gallo. "I think you're full of shit. Lita was in radio contact with you tonight, and you were telling her how to handle it. If you were only interested in information you would have been better off letting me go after the shooting. I would have driven off to stir up more trouble with the beeper firmly in place and still unknown to me. I wouldn't have known you were following me, either. But she didn't stay hidden. She stepped out, gave everything away, and then brought me here. And now I'm sitting here and you're waiting, these two guys are waiting, the four guys outside on the street are waiting. I've duly noted all this. You're showing me you've got all this capability, all these people. Why don't you just spit it out? I'm not the only one who wants something here, am I?"

When Haydon finished, he was looking squarely at Cage, but out of the corner of his eye he could see the two Guatemalans looking at him. Cage had the beginnings of a smirk on his face, and Haydon could tell that he was still formulating a response. As he looked Cage in the eye, he thought he saw the smirk change to an expression of satisfaction, as though Haydon had reacted as Cage thought he would or, perhaps, hoped he would. And then even that expression faded, and Cage grew sober. He abandoned his slouch and sat up in his chair, he put his forearms on the table and rotated his Gallo between his open hands, thinking. The Indian woman at the fireplace put a small root knot on the coals, and the smoldering chunk of wood filled the room with an aromatic waft that was pleasant even in the hot, still night. Now the two Guatemalans had locked their eyes firmly on Cage.

Cage looked at Haydon. "Lena's not dead," he said.

Chapter 28

There was nothing to say. Haydon simply sat there waiting for Cage to continue. He was aware of Lita watching him. The only sounds in the room were the root knot crackling in the fire and the soft kitchen sounds of the Indian woman as she moved about her business, careful to be quiet, invisible and silent. The two Guatemalan men were stone. There was a fleeting moment when Haydon wasn't sure what Cage was going to do, then Cage went on to play his part. It was what most men did in life, always. Behind Haydon, through the open window and the open door, the cicadas continued to complain of the heat of the dry season.

"Otro cerveza," Cage said, and drained the last of his bottle and set it aside. He turned a little aside in his chair once again, and crossed his legs, and pulled a pack of cigarettes out of his guayabera pocket. He took one, offered one to Haydon, but Haydon shook his head. Cage lighted his cigarette with his red plastic lighter and without looking at the two Guatemalans slid both the pack and the lighter down the table to them. It was the first time he had acknowledged their presence since Haydon had gotten there.

"I told you that I'd gotten a call from Pitt to go pick up a body at the morgue, that I'd know which one. I told you that I'd already seen the body before I came and got you." The Indian woman brought the beer, and Cage reached for it without thanking her or looking at what he was doing. "I thought it was her at first too, I really did. Guy threw the sheet back and . . . shit, I thought it was her. The girl was about the same size, close enough, and her face was beat to shit. I've noticed when they mess up the mouth it's harder to tell, on first look like that, especially if there's still swelling. But Lena had bigger tits, and that's what I noticed." He guzzled the beer, and sucked on the cigarette. "I looked at the hands. Lena had a small, whitish crescent scar behind the third knuckle of her right hand. It was just a little thing, and it's surprising I even remembered it. But the hands were bloody, muddy. I took the right one over to the sink there in the morgue and washed it. The scar wasn't there. Then I wondered if I'd remembered it wrong, and I took the left hand over to the sink and washed it. No scar."

Someone appeared at the open door, a woman, and said something in an Indian dialect. The two men at the table looked over at Lita, who got up from the hearth, picked up her *rebozo* and the radio, and walked out of the kitchen with the other woman, leaving the automatic behind.

"Smaller tits, no scar, wrong woman," Cage said. "I looked at her face, studied it. It was just too screwed up, but I was pretty sure it wasn't Lena. I photographed her, lots of photographs, because I had a hunch this girl could disappear on us."

"Pittner thought it was Lena?"

"I think he suspected it was Lena. It was probably an informant tip: 'Anglo in the morgue.' "

"But he didn't know."

Cage shook his head.

"What did you tell him?"

"I told him I couldn't tell. We'd have to wait for fingerprints, dental record confirmations. That's the sort of thing Macabeo does for them."

"Why'd you lie to him?"

Cage looked at him. "Jesus, Haydon." He shook his head and pulled on his cigarette. He took a drink of cold Gallo. He stared out the door into the courtyard. "I remember, after it got too crazy for me juggling screwing Janet and working for Pitt. I just cut it off. Janet went goofy about it. Almost blew the whole thing, showing up at my place at all kinds of hours. I don't know why he didn't find out. Finally I told her I'd kill her if she didn't stop. Make it look like an accident or something. That cleared her head. But then a month later they separated. And then a month after that, she told him she wanted a divorce.

"This last news had an interesting effect on Pitt. I was at my place one night, and Pitt called from somewhere and told me to stay put, he was coming over to see me. I could tell he'd been drinking. I thought, Oh shit he's found out about me and Janet. I figured she had gone all weasely and told him—she could be lunatic sometimes—and she had gotten hateful and wanted to twist the knife and told him. I expected Pitt was wanting to have this *mano a mano* confrontation sort of thing with me. When he showed up, he was in terrible shape. I don't even know how the hell he managed to make it. He had this bottle of his beloved bourbon with him, and he was in tears. Janet had told him that afternoon that she wanted a divorce.

"He'd started drinking at the embassy, a very risky thing to do, and one which showed how bad he'd been knocked back by the news. It was during the rainy season then, and we sat under the loggia at my place and smoked his American cigarettes and drank his honest-to-God bourbon, sat there in the dark and watched the rain dribble off the eaves like ink. It was a screwy scene. The bad news and the whiskey had plunged Pitt into this self-absorbed grief, and he proceeded to bare his soul to me. Shit. I hate that sort of thing. He told me all these intimate things— about him and Janet—like a goddamned college kid. He told me a hell of a lot more than I wanted to hear, but it was kind of funny too, him deciding to spill all that tortured erotica to me. Hell, I'd discovered more about Janet's buttons and juices in four months of adultery with her than Pitt had managed to uncover in eight years of marriage. But I got drunk with him and had a good time doing it. Did I have any qualms about deceiving him?" Cage pulled down the corners of his mouth and shook

199

his head. "I'd been lying to Pitt long before I started banging his wife. Pitt's the kind of man you have to lie to if you want to maintain any kind of integrity, any kind of self-respect."

The two Guatemalans had listened to this sordid story with stoic expressions, but Haydon had no way of knowing if they understood what they had heard, and if they had, what they might have thought about it. He wasn't even sure what he thought about it himself. What was the point of it? Cage seemed to have dug this unflattering memory out of the very blackest corners of his mind. Or maybe it had lurked there, staring at him from the dark, and he talked about it to relieve the mounting anxiety of its presence, the same way you periodically would lance a boil that swelled but refused to heal. Of course, that implied a moral quality to his telling of the story, and Haydon seriously doubted that was the case at all.

"He still doesn't know it's not Lena?" Haydon asked, choosing to ignore the narrative altogether. "Won't he have gone down and looked for himself?"

"No way," Cage said, and he raised his chin and blew a single smoke ring.

"Why did you take me to see her?"

"Ah," Cage rolled his head toward Haydon and pointed his index and middle finger at him, the cigarette smoldering between them. "When I realized she wasn't dead, I began to see some . . . possibilities. I started running my traps again. What was the scuttlebutt about this missing American? That sort of thing takes time. I wasn't sure what kind of options I ought to be prepared for. I knew you'd never met Lena, only seen photographs of her. I didn't know, but I thought maybe the occasion might arise when it would be necessary for me to have a 'witness' to the fact that Lena was dead. It could buy time, if nothing else, while the tests for a positive ID were being run. It would keep Pitt's dogs in the kennel another eighteen hours maybe, give me a head start. I wanted to find Lena before anybody else."

"What about that line you gave me about the Guatemalan security forces having dossiers on Lena?"

"True. All of it. Everything I told you was the truth except that that wasn't Lena's body."

"Where did the police report come from?"

"Just where it said it did. I had some people check on that."

"And the Indian women finding the body?"

Cage nodded.

Haydon stopped himself before he said it . . . what about Grajeda? How did his testimony hold up in light of all this?

Cage looked at him and then allowed a slow smile. "The good doctor? Well, I had somebody go check with the good doctor, but the good doctor was 'gone to the country.' Where in the country? *'No sé.'* Nobody knew."

Haydon wondered how much of what Grajeda had told him was an outright lie and how much of it was truth.

"And so you said you'd run your traps."

Cage nodded. "Yeah. Remember I told you last night that I was getting frozen out by my regular sources, that my inquiries about Lena were coming up craps? Well, this was different. All I wanted to know now was if an Anglo woman had been picked up by the security forces. I thought maybe they'd finally nailed her. That was a question that wouldn't cost anybody any pain. But nothing came in. Nobody was holding out, it was just that it hadn't happened. She hadn't been picked up."

"What about Fossler?" Haydon asked. "Did you hear anything about him?"

Cage shook his head.

"You asked?"

"Damn right I asked."

"I find it hard to believe that someone doesn't have something on that," Haydon said. He was reminded of Grajeda's remarks on the language of the lie, Guatemala's persistent plague of deception. It was easy to understand the fatalism that gripped a people trapped in a society of lies.

Cage flipped his cigarette butt out the open door and into the courtyard. He turned to the Guatemalans, and they slid the pack and lighter back down the table to him. He lighted another. The Indian woman finished pulling the pots away from the coals, finished the last of the dishes, dried her hands, and walked out of the room. There was only the four of them there.

"But I did learn," Cage said, blowing a chest full of smoke out into the air, "that John Baine had been picked up, in Masagua, Escuintla. But that's all I learned. I don't know where he's being held. They said it was G-2 that got him, so he could be anywhere; they've got these clandestine prisons all over the country. One source said that General Azcona Contrera himself had ordered the arrest. Not good for Baine."

"What's Azcona's situation now?" Haydon asked. "I know his background with Ríos Montt and all that, and I assume he's regained some of his old power since the elections?"

"Damn right he has. He's the head of military intelligence again. The G-2 is his baby now."

Baine knew this, of course, which was a large part of the reason he was so horrified at his situation. The very beast he had been trying to bell had woken up and snatched him.

"You knew that it was Borrayo that I met tonight," Haydon said. "What do you know about him?"

Cage shrugged. "Commandante at Pavón." He wasn't going to go for that kind of an open-ended opportunity.

"Do you know who else I met there?"

Cage shook his head slowly, his eyes on Haydon. He seemed like a tired giant sitting at the table with the two small Guatemalans. At this late hour his short, thick hair seemed more grizzled, the bridge of his sunburnt nose sharper, his glaucous eyes paler, his face heavier. He had always operated on very little sleep, and now the collection of years had begun to take their toll, and his addiction to adrenaline had begun to betray him. But none of this passage of time had tempered him. He was a long way from slowing down, or letting down his guard.

"I talked to Baine," Haydon said. "They've got him in Pavón."

Cage's eyes went flat with surprise. It was the only way his pride would let him react to being caught off guard, the cold lizard-stare of silence.

"To be honest," Haydon said, "I stumbled onto him. I had met Borrayo when I was on a case down here four or five years back. I thought he was still with the DIC. I was only checking in with him, to see if maybe he could bring me up to speed on a few things . . ."

Haydon told Cage about his visit to Pavón and about the conversation and events that had occurred on the upper rim of the ravine overlooking El Incienso just an hour before. He didn't hold anything back, and when he was through, Cage had finished his cigarette and was grinding it out in a clay ashtray on the table. He started shaking his head.

"Jesus H. Christ," he said, his eyes staying on the ashtray and the wisp of smoke that curled up from the dying cigarette. "That damned Azcona. Using Pavón as a clandestine prison . . . it makes sense. You can't keep up with them, those prisons. Course Pavón's a real prison, but mostly the clandestine things are just cellars or warehouses or private homes somewhere. They're always moving them. Guys like Azcona . . . he's a full-time freak, a functioning lunatic." Cage snorted. "And little Vera—Vera Beatriz Azcona de Sandoval—trades in babies. Jesus, what a family, huh?" He looked at Haydon. "What about Baine?"

Haydon finished his Gallo. "He was beaten badly. I think he's been seriously hurt."

Cage thought about that. "Borrayo. I wonder why he did that, brought Baine to you."

"I don't know. That bothers me a little."

"Yeah, it should. Consider his situation." Cage got up from the table, ran a hand through his thick hair, and stepped to the door, staring out into the courtyard. His frame filled the doorway, his posture—arms folded, barrel chest thrust out, feet slightly apart—made him a challenging figure. "His situation is that he's subordinate to Azcona, being directly in charge of the clandestine prison. He sucks up to Tablaya, who drags his prey in and out of there like some kind of grisly vampire. Borrayo covers for all kinds of shit, and he knows if the clandestine part of the prison is ever discovered it's his ass. But he'd never pass the buck on Azcona because Azcona would have him killed—eventually. So if it ever happened, he'd take the heat for that. It's a thankless position. Borrayo doesn't like it."

Cage turned around and walked back to the end of the table. He paused in thought, and his eyes found the automatic lying alone on the long hearth. He walked over to it and picked it up. He flipped the release and ejected the long clip, checked the action, put the clip in his trouser pocket and put the empty handgun on the table. A burst of static came from a handset that had been sitting out of sight in an empty chair by one of the Guatemalans. The Guatemalan picked it up and answered it, but not in Spanish, rather in one of the Indian dialects.

Cage waited while there was a brief exchange, though he paid no attention to it. He was thinking. The two Guatemalans had a few words between them, and then one of them got up and walked out of the kitchen, past Cage and out into the courtyard. Cage paid no attention.

Finally he looked up at Haydon. "I've got a proposal."

Haydon waited.

"You might find it a little dicey." Cage did not grin at this. "The only thing I want to do at this point is to find Lena, as fast as possible." He stuck out his foot and kicked his chair around and sat down. "You may be my best bet for doing that." He picked up his red plastic lighter and tapped the table with it. "I don't know why Borrayo brought Baine to you, but you can bet your white ass he did it for Borrayo, not you. He's got something going, and it's something significant, or he wouldn't have shot the kid. Efran doesn't do that for nothing anymore. He hasn't been in the killing business for a few years. But I'd wager a significant sum that he's already got his worms out looking for Lena. He knows how to do that sort of thing; he used to be the best at it."

Cage stopped talking, his thoughts running ahead of him. He tapped the red lighter on the tabletop, end over end, end over end, turning it and tapping it. Haydon looked at the remaining Guatemalan, who met his eyes with a look as impenetrable as if he had been sightless.

Cage slapped the lighter down hard. He said something in dialect to the Guatemalan, who immediately got up and left the room.

"He's going to tell them to let you go," Cage said, referring to the guards out on the street. "I've got to work things out on this before we can go into it. I'll get in touch with you tomorrow. You won't have any trouble getting back to your hotel. But don't ever come here again. All of these people will be gone after tonight. Only the Indian woman who made the meal lives here. It wouldn't do to attract attention to her."

Cage stood up, but Haydon didn't move; he was holding back a roiling anger. He knew he had no choice but to play the game by the rules on the ground, but he was chaffing at the necessity of leaving everything up to someone else. He didn't have any leverage, and he was feeling the emotional equivalent of weightlessness. This could be the last time Haydon would see Cage, and there wasn't anything he could do about it. Christ, what a futile situation.

Cage was reading his thoughts. "You'd better take what you can get, Haydon. That's always a smart choice down here. It can get out of hand real quick."

He reached out and picked up the automatic and put it in front of Haydon. He took the clip out of his pocket and laid it beside the gun.

"They've put a box of cartridges under the front seat of your car," he said.

Haydon stood, picked up the gun, picked up the clip and jammed it home. He put the gun in the waistband of his trousers. It was a hell of a deal. He knew how Fossler must have felt. He wondered if Fossler had had any warning before whatever had happened in the bloody room had happened.

204

Chapter 29

Haydon was grateful for the gun—which he had noticed was the latest Smith & Wesson 10mm—even though it was illegal for him to have it. But he had already seen enough to know that breaking Guatemala's gun control law—such as it was—was the least of his worries if he found himself in a situation where he had to use it. On the other hand he wondered what he would have done with it if he had had it when Borrayo shot the kid a few hours earlier. He might have made a terrible mistake. So maybe he had been lucky. But he had the queasy feeling that he still was going to have plenty of chances to make mistakes.

When he stepped out of the kitchen and into the courtyard he was on his own. The two Guatemalans were nowhere around. He crossed the cobblestones alone, and when he pushed open the wrought-iron gate and stepped outside, the men he had seen in the two cars at either end of the sloping street were gone. Considering that Cage had always been obsessively secretive about his security, Haydon was surprised that Lita had been told to bring him to this house. It wasn't a location he was likely to forget.

Getting in the car, he checked quickly with his hand to see if the 10mm cartridges were in fact under the seat. They were. He started the car and drove away, continuing down the hill until the street began to wind into the tighter streets of the central city. It took him a few minutes to find 7a avenida, and when he did he turned south, heading back to Zona 10 but avoiding the Avenida La Reforma. At 2a calle he passed under the Tower of the Reformer, a steel reproduction of the Eiffel Tower that spanned the avenue and was dedicated to Rufino Barrios. Another dictatorial folly of which Latin America had an abundance, and which said something about the odd, childlike gestures of whimsy in which "men of destiny" often indulged themselves.

Again, at the entry of the Residencial Reforma, he had to get out of the car and push the button on the pillar to open the gates. He drove through and found only one parking space open. The old courtyard was not that large, with places for only ten or so cars around the drive's perimeter and up against the walls that separated the hotel's property from its neighbors. He parked, turned off the engine, and heard the footsteps approaching his open window before he could even open his door.

"I've got to talk to you," Janet said, stooping down to the window. "I'll come around."

"No, wait," Haydon said. If Cage had the technology to track a beeper, he could bug it too. He got out of the car and locked it. "What's the matter?" he asked, turning around and leading her away.

"Let's go to my car," she said. She was talking fast, nervous, her hair was loose.

"Better not," Haydon said.

"What, your room then?"

"No, here's fine."

She frowned at him, but it didn't take half a beat for her to understand.

"Jesus Christ," she said.

Haydon took her by the arm and led her to the side of the drive to the grass where there were sago palms and another planted fountain, this one with a heavy-breasted water nymph as its centerpiece, her arms raised above her flowing hair.

When he stopped, Janet reached into her shoulder bag and pulled out a piece of paper that she unfolded and gave to him. Then she produced a small penlight and held the narrow beam on the paper.

The note appeared to be in a woman's handwriting:

I'm all right, but hiding. Will be in touch with you again, but only you. Do not show this to anyone but Haydon. I'm in danger. Be careful.

The note was unsigned but dated that day. The time was also recorded, two hours earlier.

"It's Lena's handwriting," Janet said. She was finding it difficult to control her agitation. "It was delivered to my house an hour ago. Mirtha, my maid, brought it in to me. She said a child, a little girl, came to the front gate and left it. She didn't see a car or anyone else."

"You're sure about the handwriting."

"Yes! Yes! It's her's. What in the hell is this? It's madness."

"You haven't told anyone else."

"No! Of course not . . . what do you think—?"

"Okay, okay. Did your maid read it?"

"Mirtha . . . I . . . she brought it to me folded. I don't know."

"Does she read English?"

"I don't think so, of course not. She hardly speaks it."

"Turn out the light," Haydon said.

"Oh." Janet turned off the penlight and put it back into her purse. "What do we do?"

Haydon refolded the paper. He had looked at his watch when Janet was holding the light. It wasn't yet eleven-thirty.

"When Fossler came to the house to talk to Lena that first time," Haydon said, putting the paper in his pocket, "did she talk to you about it after he left?"

"Yes, we talked. She told me what it was all about."

207

"Did she say if Fossler mentioned me?"

"No."

"Did you know that she and Baine met with him again the next day?"

"No, on Friday? The same day she left to go to Panajachel with Baine?"

"That's right. Jim Fossler called me from here on Sunday and asked me to come down. I flew down Monday night, and he was supposed to meet me at the airport but didn't show. I went to his room. There was blood all over the place. He's disappeared."

Janet stood in the pale greenish aura that came from the streetlamps reflected off the canopies of the cypresses on the median of the Avenida La Reforma, her face half jade, half obscured. The one eye he could see was fixed on him with the gravity that comes with uncertainty. At this hour, there was only an occasional car on the Reforma on the other side of the wrought-iron fence.

"The point is," Haydon said, "I don't think Fossler would have told her I was coming down two days before he had even talked to me and asked me to do it. And by that time, she had already disappeared."

"How do you know?"

"I'm sure of it."

She didn't respond immediately. They were looking at each other, their faces only a couple of feet apart, their voices lowered.

"In other words, how does she know about you?"

Haydon nodded.

"Christ! I *know* it's her handwriting."

"You couldn't be mistaken?"

She shook her head quickly. "No, that's it. I looked at it for that; I thought about that too."

208

Haydon wished he could see her face better. There would be another note, that was certain, and it would most likely contain instructions for Haydon to do something, go somewhere, a kind of treasure-hunt scenario, in preparation for a meeting. If it was genuine, the instructions probably would be complicated, a convoluted effort to avoid surveillance.

"What's the matter?" Janet asked.

"What do you think is going to happen now?"

"How the hell . . . I don't know. Another message, I guess. Something like that. Another note."

"What if it tells you to go somewhere, to do something?"

"I guess I'll do it."

"What if you're being set up for something?"

"Set up for what, for Christ's sake?"

"Don't you wonder why Lena is hiding, why she's in danger?"

"Of course I do. I think it's irrelevant to ask these questions now. We don't know what's happening, what's next."

"Why do you think she didn't want you to contact anyone but me? Why not Pitt? I'm not a legitimate authority down here. If Lena's in danger, you ought to be contacting the embassy."

"She said *not* to."

"Why?"

"I don't know," Janet raised her arms and combed back her hair with her fingers. She gave a sigh of exasperation. "I don't know." She looked around her, not because she thought anyone was watching them, but because she was impatient. She didn't want all these questions from him. She wanted him to give her some answers.

"What if she's involved in a criminal situation . . ."

"Criminal situation! Good God. In *this* country?"

"It doesn't matter what you think about a hypocritical government. They consider certain things 'criminal.' That's all that matters. The fact is, if you're going to live in Wonderland you've got to live by the Queen's rules."

"Look!" Janet snapped at him. "I thought you were going to be some help here. *Your* name is the one she mentions, not mine."

"But you're the one who's going to have to make a decision."

"You're not?"

"Of course, we're both going to have to decide something," Haydon said. "I'm only saying you'd better be ready to make a decision you might later regret. If you don't want to be involved beyond this point, be ready to tell me that when you get the next message."

"What about you?"

"I'm going to have to go on with it. For me it's more a question of 'how,' not 'if.' "

She looked at him. "Then I guess it depends on what we hear next. If it's okay with you," she said sarcastically, "I'll wait and make my decision then."

Haydon nodded. There was a moment when there was nothing else for them to say, a moment when Janet seemed to want something more from him, something more than uncertainty.

"One thing," Haydon added. "If you don't want to kill her, you'd better not have a change of heart about telling Pitt."

"What in God's name does that mean?"

"I mean if you have second thoughts, if you want a second opinion about what to do. If you do anything other than what she asked you to do, you'd better be prepared for the consequences. She trusted you. You'd better be good for it."

"I don't need any goddamned lectures from you, Haydon," Janet snapped indignantly. "Give me the note." She held out her hand.

"I'm going to keep it."

She started to protest.

"My name's in it, Janet. I'd feel safer."

She backed off. "Okay, sure, you're right. I'm sorry." She pushed back her hair again. "This . . . this is wild. I can't imagine what's happening with her; I really can't. Driving me crazy."

"Have you talked to Pitt again?"

"No. And I've waited. This is the first time I've left the house since you were over there. I kept thinking he'd call with bad news. I'd almost resigned myself to . . . something else, that she was dead. Now this . . . It's absolutely wild."

He thought about asking her if she wanted a drink. The bar in the Camino Real a few blocks away would still be open. But then he changed his mind. That would be a mistake. He didn't know how, exactly, but he was sure it would be.

"Look, you ought to get back," he said. "I'll check with you in the morning. If you hear anything, call me immediately. I won't go anywhere tomorrow without letting you know, and in the meantime you can get me here."

She nodded. Together they walked back to the stone drive, and he walked her to her car, a Land-Rover. A four-wheel-drive vehicle was a popular commodity in Guatemala where paved roads were at a minimum. Practically anyone who could afford one had one. She unlocked the Rover and got in and rolled down her window.

"Listen," she said, "you haven't seen Cage again, have you?"

Haydon shook his head. "No, I haven't."

She nodded again and started the Rover, and Haydon walked to the door of the old house and told the concierge to open the front gates. From the small foyer he watched her taillights wink cherry at the Reforma and then turn out of the drive, and she was gone.

He got his key—the concierge was a different young man from the night before—and went through the parlor, past the few people slouched in front of the television. He climbed the curving stairs, weary and worried. There was no way of knowing now what was happening. There wasn't a single person in the whole lot of them that he could trust. The only person who could qualify was Jim Fossler, and if the note was real, he was the only one now who had completely disappeared.

He let himself into his room and kicked off his shoes. The place was strange and lonely, and he wanted to talk to Nina, to hear her say something safe and predictable and reliable. He would call her in the morning. With stinging eyes, he took the gun from his waistband and put it on the small secretary by the bed, took off his suit coat and tossed it onto one of the armchairs, and then his shirt and his trousers and socks. He walked into the bathroom and washed his face with soap, brushed his teeth, and then went into the bedroom and fell onto the bed. Sleep was sudden and deep.

Chapter 30

W hat woke Haydon in the morning was the persistent, euphoric burbling of a bird in the large loquat tree outside his balcony window. It was what the Guatemalans called the *sinsonte de agua,* the water mockingbird, but it was the same familiar mockingbird that sang with joyful and prolonged abandon in Haydon's jacarandas and pyracantha and lime trees at home during the spring and early summer, which it was now in Central America. The morning light in the room was full but not bright, and Haydon noticed that the rumble of traffic on the boulevard was slight but building. He lay without moving, listening to the bird, a welcome celebration of simple happiness that was free of the complexities of human scheming and cruelty. He was glad the bird did not stop or leave, and only half aware of what he was doing, slipped back into a light, drifting sleep.

When he woke again the *sinsonte* was still self-indulgently exuberant, but the light on the walls had grown bright now, and the traffic outside had built to its full pitch, surging and roaring with the changing traffic signals. This time Haydon realized he must have fallen asleep the instant he hit the bed the night before. He was not wearing his pajamas, and he had forgotten to take off his watch, which he now squinted at and saw that it was eight-fifteen.

Rolling over on his side, he unbuckled the watch and laid it beside the automatic and then sat up on the side of the bed. Faintly he could hear the diners downstairs, the clinking of their cups of coffee and flatware echoing off the marble floors and stucco walls and up through the atrium to the mezzanine outside his door. Standing, he took off his underwear, threw it over on his wadded suit, and walked into the shower.

By the time he had shaved and dressed in the clean change of clothes, which was once again hanging in his closet, it was almost nine o'clock. He left another note for the maid to have his clothes cleaned and sat down in the chair at the secretary and called Nina. She was already at the office—Guatemala was in the same time zone as Houston and the only time there was a difference in hours was when the U.S. went on daylight savings time, which the Central Americans did not. As he knew she would, Nina brought him up to date on things: that Ramona had done extremely well on her tests the day before; that Margaret had gotten an emergency call from her sister in Vancouver, who said their mother was seriously ill in Tucson, and she had had to leave before she finished the model of the Spahn house which meant that the upcoming review with the Spahns would have to be postponed; that their accountant had called wanting some kind of clarification on something, and Nina had told her that Haydon was out of town for a few days; that the weather was still cold and messy and overcast.

For his part, Haydon lied to her glibly about how things were going for him and said that because business always moved slower down here than he remembered, he was going to have to be here another couple of days. He said he would call Dystal and let him know and arrange for

213

someone to cover for him a little longer. No news, really. Nina accepted this, which didn't mean she necessarily believed it. He knew she would make judgments about him more from his mood and the sound of his voice than from what he said. She wouldn't make much of his having little to say about the case because he never made more than simple references to his cases over the telephone.

He told her he loved her, and she said, "And I love you. Take care," and that was the end of their conversation. But it made Haydon feel infinitely better. There was, in fact, terra firma, and Nina was standing on it.

The next thing was to call Dystal, which he did with as little honesty as he had used with Nina. He gave generally the same reasons, and then used a vague reference to the "unreliability" of the telephones as an excuse for not going into more detail. Finally he asked Dystal if he could arrange for him to be covered for a couple more days. It was done. Haydon hung up the telephone and went downstairs to eat breakfast.

The bright dining room under the barrel-vaulted glass ceiling two floors above was a spacious setting for a home's grand *sala,* but it did not allow for many tables as the dining room of a small hotel. To the management's credit, they did not try to squeeze in more tables than were comfortable, and so the dining room accommodated ten tables, most of them for four people, but a few as well for only two. The tables and chairs were white wrought iron with linen tablecloths with a floral pattern that looked something like frangipani, and white linen napkins.

Haydon had never seen the dining room more than half-full, which was fortunate, because he had never seen more than one waiter. He was always the same young man, a pleasant, cherubic young Indian who dressed in black trousers and vest with a white shirt and bow tie. When more than five tables were occupied at any one time, he seemed actually to suffer real pain, which was demonstrated by an expression of genuine angst that would have done honor to even the greatest silent-film star. His name was Mateo, and his real talent was being pleasant. He relished welcoming you to your table and exchanging felicities for a few moments and practicing his English—which was wretched—before taking your order. Actually serving the food was a burden he had to bear, the downside of being a waiter.

The few tables for two were taken when Haydon entered the dining room, and so he chose one of the larger ones, the one most isolated from the other diners. From the cheerful Mateo, Haydon ordered coffee, eggs, toast, and a small bowl of *ensalada tropical*. He was sitting so that he could see into the front parlor and through a window near the small foyer and out into the courtyard. Though unable to distinguish any real detail, he could see the bright morning light on the white marble of the angel and the naked woman who swooned in his arms.

Waiting, his eyes vaguely attending to this scene, Haydon's thoughts turned to the few options open to him. Cage, Borrayo, Bennett Pittner. These were not appealing possibilities. Even less appealing was the appearance of Janet's message. He was uneasy about it. If the note was indeed from Lena, it seemed to him unusual that she would be contacting Janet in search of help to extricate herself from her troubles. And Haydon was more than a little worried that his name had been a part of the communication. He couldn't imagine why he should have entered into it at all. He wondered what Cage would think about such a turn of events. Without a doubt the message was a coveted piece of information, if it was authentic.

Mateo brought Haydon's breakfast, which Haydon ate without interruption. He had finished his eggs and toast and was eating the small bowl of fruit when a man came through the parlor and into the dining room. He hesitated at one of the marble pillars, quickly surveyed the few people in the dining room, and then headed straight for Haydon. In the moment it took him to walk the short distance, Haydon appraised him: he was in his late thirties, slight of build, not Latin American but dark, good-looking, well-groomed, at ease with himself.

When he reached Haydon's table he pulled out a chair and quickly sat down, smiling, leaning a little forward and speaking softly, "Pretend that you know me, please, and I will quickly explain. Okay?"

Haydon nodded. "Sure, go ahead."

The man smiled even more, genuinely this time. "Thank you. It's very kind of you." He leaned his forearms on the table. "I am Dr. Bindo Salviati, a friend of Dr. Grajeda's. You know Dr. Grajeda?"

Haydon nodded again.

"Good."

Mateo appeared, pleased to have another guest. Salviati quickly ordered coffee to get rid of him.

"I have come to you with a message from Dr. Grajeda. He would like to talk to you."

"I understand he's 'in the country.' "

"Oh, yes. He was."

"No longer."

Salviati shook his head. "He would like to meet with you this morning."

"Fine."

"He is concerned about the meeting being . . . completely private. You must not be followed."

"I understand."

"I am going to give you an address here in the city, okay? I am going to speak it, and you must not write it down."

The address was in Zona 1, the center of the old city, 18 calle between 6a and 7a avenidas. Haydon knew the street. It was one of the better known in the collection of narrow streets just around the corner from one of the city's largest markets.

"I understand you are an American detective," Salviati said. Mateo brought the coffee and poured a fresh cup for Haydon.

"Yes," Haydon said.

"Then you know how to avoid being followed."

"I believe so," Haydon said.

Salviati sipped his coffee and relaxed his smile for the first time. "This is very dangerous for my friend, very dangerous. If the security agents find him they will kill him."

Haydon was surprised Salviati said this so openly, perhaps he thought it was needed to emphasize how delicately the meeting had to be handled.

"At this address"—and he repeated the address he had already given Haydon—"is a shoe store. It is behind the booths that are along the sidewalk there. Go into the store and go to the back—you don't have to talk to anyone, just go to the back of the store. There is a door there that will lead out into a courtyard with a stairway. Turn left and go up the stairs to the balcony. A man there will know your name and help you."

"That's it?"

Salviati nodded and sipped his coffee.

"Are you the doctor who Grajeda sometimes helps in Huehuetenango?"

"Yes indeed."

"Can you tell me what this meeting is about?"

"He said you would know."

"Do you know?"

"Mr. Haydon, I sometimes help Aris, he sometimes helps me. He is a very good doctor. But . . . he is political. I help him because I am very fond of him, but I am never more than an errand boy. I won't refuse to do something for him if he asks me, but I am not a political person."

"It seems to me you take a lot of risk, considering you are not political."

Salviati shrugged, and this time the smile was his own, not part of the act. "It is almost impossible to be true to your heart in Guatemala without taking a risk." He glanced around the room. "The risk, you know, only seems to be important when certain people take it. The *indios* are risking their lives every day in the countryside, just to maintain a little human dignity. Nobody seems to notice that. What is it to me to deliver a message? So small a thing."

"Dr. Grajeda told you that we talked?"

"He did, yes."

"Just before I left him yesterday morning, in response to my question about how he supported his clinic, he mentioned his awkward relationship with his family. Do you know very much about that?"

"Something." Salviati hesitated. "I should tell you that Aris and I are boyhood friends. We grew up together. I am Italian, but a third-generation Italian here in Guatemala. My father and grandfather were doctors. I received my medical training in Britain and Aris went to the United States, to Johns Hopkins. Unlike many men who leave Guatemala for their educations and never come back, we vowed to return. So we, as you say, 'go back a long way.' "

"Then none of this . . . secrecy, the way things work here, is new to you."

Salviati closed his eyes wearily and shook his head. "It is a pity to say, but I have grown up with it." Then he looked at Haydon. "But Aris and I were on the other side of the fence when we were young. Our families were not poor. We saw Guatemala through the hazy lens of the romantic photographer. Over time that changed."

"What changed it for you?"

"I have asked myself that many times," Salviati said. He looked at his watch. "It's nine-thirty. Can you make it there in an hour? This has to be timed very closely. He has to know that you will be there when you say you will. If you need more time because you are not familiar with the city, if you are not sure where you can park—that is a very crowded area —then I can make it later."

"No, ten-thirty is all right."

217

Salviati reached across the table and offered his hand. Haydon shook it, and the doctor said, "I probably will not see you again. Thank you." He stood quickly before Haydon could say anything else and walked out of the dining room.

Haydon did not look around at the other diners. Salviati had come unobtrusively, visited briefly and quietly, and had left without any show of the goodbyes that often concluded a conversation with a meal. It would be up to Haydon to be equally inconspicuous.

He signed for his meal and walked through the parlor to the concierge at the front desk.

"Are there any automobile-tire stores near here?" he asked. The young man told him of several, gave him directions to them, at which Haydon nodded and then thanked him for the suggestions. He walked outside to the courtyard and looked at his car. He kicked the rear tire for the young man's benefit and bent down at the rear bumper to survey the treads. He did not see Cage's beeper anywhere inside the lip of the curving bumper. He went to the front of the car and did the same, his search hidden by a Jeep Wagoneer parked next to him. The beeper was not under the front bumper either, or in the wheel wells. Cage was no fool. He had probably had his people take it off while they were talking the night before. He knew better than to believe Haydon would allow the device to remain in place. Electronic surveillance could be expensive, and Cage wasn't about to waste a transmitter. Standing and walking out from between the two cars, he turned one more time and looked at the tires. He shook his head and walked back into the hotel.

Returning to his room, Haydon got the keys to his car, went back downstairs, left his room key with the concierge, and in a few moments was leaving through the Residencial's open gates. He turned right on the Reforma and left at the first opportunity and headed away from downtown until he came to Diagonal 12 where he turned right and immediately right again and pulled up near one of the few American-style convenience stores, just off the street. He parked and went to the pay telephone outside the store.

Janet was working on a caffeine high. No, she hadn't heard anything, no, she hadn't talked to Pitt. Haydon told her he would be out of touch for a couple of hours, and then he would call her again. If she heard from anyone, just sit on the message until he called her. To keep her in his camp, to keep her from getting impatient and doing something unpredictable, he told her he thought he had some information that would be significant and that would help them find Lena. She was immediately grateful, willing to help, willing to do anything. He had a couple of hours to think of something. He told her to try to relax, to stay close to the telephone. Then he went back to his car and headed downtown.

Chapter 31

S ix avenida was the only avenue on which one could travel from the south of the city north, directly into the old narrow streets of downtown without having to make a jog over in one direction or another to accommodate a park or a railway station or a public building or a larger major avenue merging on an oblique approach or a church or one of the city's many monuments. It ran straight as an arrow right down to the National Palace on the Parque Central.

However, in its undeviating course northward, 6a avenida makes one major change in its appearance. At 18 calle, the avenue drops down in size from a boulevard with a median to a narrow, old-world-style street, crowded, slow moving, and choked with the diesel exhausts of buses and cars, hemmed in by sidewalk vendors and pedestrians, and raucous with shouts and horns and gunning engines.

Eighteen calle itself was something of a crossroads. Only a few blocks from the country's central railroad station and its second largest produce market, it was known for its bazaar atmosphere. In one crowded section running for five or six blocks the street is divided by a median, with two lanes of traffic on one side going east and two lanes of traffic on the other side going west. Between 8a and 6a avenidas, the median was crowded with good-sized trees whose branches arched over the streets, providing a tunnel of welcome shade. The sidewalks were packed tightly with vendors' booths, stalls made of contrived frames of thin poles over which large cloths were draped leaving only the fronts open from which the vendors displayed and sold their wares. The backs of the booths were turned to the street to ward off the noise and unctuous exhausts of the traffic, making the sidewalks between the front of the booths and the front of the stores a pinched corridor of twilight shade. When the sidewalks became impassable, pedestrians spilled out into the streets, walking along with the traffic behind the booths, adding to the congestion and confusion.

Haydon parked in a side street not far from the railroad station and began his complicated journey toward the address that Dr. Bindo Salviati had given him. He had nearly three-quarters of an hour to make sure he wasn't being followed. He did not consider the extra precaution excessive. Aside from Cage's surveillance, it was a certainty that Pittner had put a tail on him too. There was the incident of the Jeep Cherokee, courtesy of the Guatemalan security forces; that is, Azcona. And finally there was Borrayo, the lynx of perpetual scheming. It seemed ludicrous to believe that all of those people were interested enough in what Haydon was doing to put a tail on him, but, on the other hand, it would have been naive to think otherwise.

From the side street where he had parked, he walked back to 18 calle not far from the railroad station, turned right and began a slow meander up the street. Eighteen calle was the major shopping section for much of Guatemala City's population who subsisted just above the poverty line. Soldiers and housemaids came here to buy domestic-made products and clothes and shoes made in Taiwan of plastics and synthetic fibers. Of such

221

a distinctive quality were the products sold here, that it was common to say of someone who was wearing cheap or tacky clothes that he had made his purchases in an "18 calle boutique."

Haydon stopped at every other booth, examined the products, talked to the vendors. He turned in the opposite direction and looked into the store windows, which were glazed with dirt and soot, most containing wares that seemed never to have moved from their shelves to be replaced with newer stock. Back and forth, back and forth, from booths to windows, he moved slowly up the slightly rising street, down the gloomy corridors of commerce with their smells of human sweat mingled with cheap perfume, cooking food, wafts of wood smoke and old garments, whiffs of souring fruit rinds and peels that had been tossed into the gutters to rot in the dry-season heat, and an occasional deposit of feces left behind by dogs or children. In the course of this rambling walk he was careful to note precisely the landmarks and the address where he was supposed to meet Dr. Grajeda. He found it and passed it by, continuing his leisurely movement up the street.

Every time Haydon turned from one side of the sidewalk to the other he scanned the crowds, hoping to notice a face he had noticed before, or a shirt or a dress or the back of any of these. He took particular notice of women. He remembered what Fossler had said about his tail, and he had seen enough of Lita to know that Cage employed an uncanny collection of surveillants. Evasion seemed a hopeless task. The culture was unfamiliar, which meant he could take nothing for granted, dismiss nothing as being unemployable by a surveillance team. He might be able to evade one tail, or one team, but he had to be very good to get away from the several he believed to be following him. For starters, he had to make them identify themselves. He had to narrow the playing field, eliminate as much of the crowd as possible and move into a setting that would make them more conspicuous, easier for him to identify.

222

He began looking for a church. It was an old standby he used for smoking out a tail who would not be satisfied with simply knowing that he had entered a church and waiting on the street for him to return. If the tail wanted to know who he was meeting there, then he had to follow Haydon inside. Haydon didn't have far to go. Above the trees in the median, he saw a bell tower to his left, on the other side of the street. He quickened his pace and headed straight for it. Crossing the street, he cut between the cars in the stalled traffic, stepped under the trees on the median, which itself was no wider than a sidewalk, and then crossed the other side of the street right in front of a line of buses that had just started up from a stop a block away. This in itself would delay a single tail, even eliminate him if Haydon got into the church fast enough. But some of them would be following him in a team, one on each side of the street in anticipation of his using the traffic as a shield. Eventually they would get together again, so it was important that he get to the church before the one he had left behind had caught up with the one who had picked him up when he crossed over. The few moments alone in the church were crucial. To give himself an edge, Haydon crossed the street just before he was parallel to the church.

The Santuario de la Sagrada Madre was large, but not of cathedral size, and was made of huge slabs and blocks of cut limestone, its gray surfaces mottled and stained from decades of rainy seasons and dry seasons, and pitted and sooty from the acidic toxins of the modern gasoline and diesel engine. The broad sidewalk in front of the church was scattered with the cloth-covered booths of vendors and with old women who had spread their shawls on the cracked cement to sell their candles and flowers under the hot sun, at the bottom of the tier of steps that ascended to the church doors. Haydon hurried through this crowd of pedestrians and vendors, past the old women, and up the steps and into the cool shade of the narthex, which lay just inside the heavy wooden doors thrown open to the city.

He had done this enough to know where the confessionals usually were situated and before his eyes could even become adjusted to the dim interior (another advantage to this simple maneuver) he hurried to the right side of the church and followed its wall toward the front. He found one of two booths, one on each of the side aisles, and approached it quickly. Two more strokes of luck: the priest was not hearing confessions and the confessional door was latticework. In an instant he was inside, the door closed, peering through the lattice. He quickly surveyed the nave. Two women, that was all, both of them in the back half of the church, no one at the front.

For a moment no one came in and the only sound Haydon could hear was the muffled echo of traffic outside and his own labored breathing against the wooden latticework. The building smelled of wax candles and stone and old wooden pews. A door closed far off in one of the transepts, echoing deep and hollow in the high environs of the church. An old woman came in, but he had seen her outside below the steps. She made a painful entrance carrying a load of candles in her shawl, which she proceeded to spread out to one side of the doors in the narthex. To sell her candles here was forbidden, but she knew it would be a while before a priest would discover her, and in the meantime she was out of the sun and close to the people who wanted her wares.

Then a man ran up into the entrance from the steps and stopped abruptly. He was Guatemalan, and he had a decision to make. He moved into the shadows to make it. The thing about churches was that they had several entrances. The front doors, of course, and then depending on their construction usually another two, one in either direction, in the aisle that crossed in front of the altar, and then often others that led into hallways on either side of the nave and which wound around and exited in courtyards or out onto the sidewalks at the rear of the church. The important thing was that there were always multiple exits.

If the tails were in teams, one or several of them would be diverted immediately to try to find these exits from the outside of the church, while the person who followed Haydon would wait in the narthex. At some point one of them would have to make a decision to either search the environs of the church, or to give it up, or to keep one man in the narthex while the others spread out onto the sidewalks.

An Indian woman carrying a child in a *rebozo* came into the church. She was not old. She was not Lita. She stopped and bought a candle from the old woman who had just arrived with her wares and then went to one of the banks of candles at the back of the church, not far from Haydon, where she lighted the candle she had just purchased. Then she moved to the pews toward the back of the nave and sat down. She knelt as if to pray, but her head was not bowed as much as those of the women already there.

Another man entered. He was also Guatemalan. Ignoring the old woman, he did not see the man waiting in the shadows of the narthex as he went to the far side of the nave and sat down in the last row of pews. He did not pretend to pray but simply sat and stared at the front of the church, his eyes scanning, waiting to adjust to the dark.

Haydon looked at his watch. He could get to the shoe store in less than a minute from the front of the church. He had thirty-five minutes for this to settle out. The only thing he was afraid of was that the man in the shadows of the front door would not be satisfied with Haydon's disappearance and would decide to look for him. A confessional was a lousy place for serious hiding. But he did not think they would do that. If they wanted to kill him, they would do it. But since they only wanted to discover who he was meeting, a search to discovery would be counter-productive. He bet himself they wouldn't, and then settled back in the confessional to see who would win the wager.

He had been waiting thirteen minutes without anyone moving when he heard footsteps coming down the side aisles from the direction of the altar. The footsteps were overlapping, two people, one walking along each side of the nave next to the walls. He could see the one on the opposite side from him, Guatemalan, wearing a suit without a tie, shirt open at the collar, his coat unbuttoned. He was moving relatively quickly since there was nothing much to see. The footsteps of the man on Haydon's side of the church grew louder as he lagged slightly behind his partner, who, when he passed the confessional on the opposite side ignored it completely. The man on Haydon's side, however, could not resist running his hand along the surface of the latticework, an idle, adolescent gesture, his fingers making a soft thrumming noise, passing within an inch of Haydon's face.

When the two men reached the back of the church, the man in the shadows of the narthex stepped out to talk to them. They held a discussion at the front door, a conversation that attracted the attention of the man in the back pew on the opposite side of the church. He looked toward them, then quickly turned his eyes back to the front. The conversation at the front doors was animated, the man from the shadows punching a forefinger into the chest of the man who had been on the opposite side of the nave. The man who had run his fingers past Haydon's face looked nervously outside to the bright sunlight, hoping to avoid being included in the chastisement. Their voices rose, a local curse word once, twice, and then the three men hurried from the narthex, their heads disappearing down behind the top row of stone steps outside the door of the church.

225

Haydon looked at the Indian woman. She did not move, but she had picked up on her competitor across the way. However, the man across the nave got up as soon as the other men were out of sight and hurried toward the altar. He left out of the transept aisle on the opposite side of the church, and after a few moments Haydon heard a door slam hollowly in the distance.

The Indian woman did not move for a moment, but then she permitted herself a look around. She seemed hesitant as to what to do. Then to Haydon's surprise, she again bowed her head slightly and waited. Haydon looked at his watch again. Another seven minutes had passed.

He had fifteen minutes to get to the shoe store. He wanted to give himself some extra time.

Fixing his eyes on the Indian woman, he opened the door of the confessional. At the click of the latch, she ducked her head as if in more fervent prayer, and he had no doubt that her eyes were straining at the top of their sockets as she tried to see the door of the confessional. He opened it and came out. He looked at her. She was stone. He closed the confessional door and walked to the rear of the church, around the pews and then came back up the center aisle until he was at the row behind the Indian woman. He entered it and sidestepped over until he was looking at the back of her head. Taking the automatic from his waistband, he leaned forward and put the barrel of it up beside the woman's shawl-covered head while his other hand steadied her shoulder.

¡Señora, ten cuidado!" He pressed the barrel to her temple. *"¿Sabe que es este?"* She nodded. Keeping his gun to her temple, he reached around her and carefully moved back the folds of the shawl to reveal the radio. *"Con permiso,"* he said, and he slowly pulled the radio out of the shawl. In Spanish he told her to stand up and go with him. They moved to the aisle, and then together they walked the considerable distance to the choir where they turned to their left and entered the transept aisle. In another five or ten meters they approached a door. Through the windows at the side of it, Haydon could see that it opened out into a courtyard with shrubbery and a small fountain and a wrought-iron gate that let out into 18 calle.

Haydon turned the woman around and looked at her. She was older than Lita, but still young, her oval Indian face looking up at him impassively, her dark eyes wide but not excited. He asked her if she had a watch. She nodded, and he reached down and pulled back the sleeve of her blouse. It was a black plastic Swatch. Cage. In Spanish he told her that he had come to the church by prearrangement. He said that he had people watching the exits and that after he was gone he wanted her to wait ten minutes before she left. He told her that she would be safe if she did what he said, implying that the alternative would be risky. Again she nodded.

Haydon took her by the arm and walked her to a bench against the corridor wall, facing the windows that looked out into the courtyard. He asked her where the people were who were working with her. She said there was a man in a car. Haydon asked her to describe it, which she did. She said he was around the corner on the side of the *mercado,* on the opposite side of the church from the courtyard gate. Who else? A man wearing a *Batman* T-shirt. He was carrying a leather jacket over his arm to hide his radio. Who else? That was all. Haydon reached down and picked up her wrist and moved her sleeve back with the barrel of the automatic. Ten minutes, he said. The girl nodded for the last time.

Haydon pushed open the door and walked out into the courtyard. That had taken four minutes. Eleven minutes remained. As he crossed the courtyard, he tucked the automatic into his waistband and hung the radio onto his belt by its metal clip, covering both of them with his suit coat.

He lingered a moment at the wrought-iron gate, watching the crowded sidewalk, first in one direction and then in the other. The traffic on this side of the median came from his left, and Haydon monitored its tempo, waiting until the traffic light a block away released a slug of cars and buses and trucks. Then he flung open the gate, burst out of the courtyard and across the sidewalk through surprised pedestrians and past vendors, and out into the street, just clearing the front of the first truck. He was out of the way even before the driver could use his horn. His heart pounding, he stood on the median only a moment before the traffic in the west-bound lanes jammed to a stop. Haydon moved quickly, cutting between the bumpers of the cars, swallowing mouthfuls of oily, acrid exhaust fumes, barely missing being hit by a motorcycle barreling between the booths and the traffic, before he ducked under the canvas side of a booth selling leather goods and plunged into the crowd streaming along in the dingy twilight of the sidewalk.

Quickly he headed toward the address Salviati had given him, saw it, approached it, passed it, and went into the store next to it. It was an appliance store, mostly televisions, five or six of them turned to the same channel, three clerks watching "The Price Is Right." One of them started toward him, but Haydon waved him off, moved behind a bank of sets still in their cardboard cartons and glued his eyes to the sidewalk. He was breathing as if he'd run a marathon. The three clerks looked at each other and then one of them, the biggest of them, who moved with his arms slightly out from his sides, started toward him with a frown. *"¡Eh! ¿Qué pasó?"* he said, and the other two followed. Haydon pulled out the radio, clicked it on for the static, and let them get a glimpse of the automatic stuck into his belt. He reached into his pocket and brought out his shield and held it out to them. They were not close enough to read it, but they knew what it was and they knew what it meant. They all

227

stopped at the same time, and Haydon fixed his eyes on the sidewalk again.

It seemed like an hour, but it was only six minutes. No one passed on the sidewalk wearing a *Batman* T-shirt. No one passed who looked like they were looking for someone. Haydon turned to the three clerks behind him, and six eyes stared back at him. They wanted nothing to do with him; they only wanted him to go away.

"Cinco minutos más," he said, gulping air.

The big man lifted his chin in a half nod, and then all of them pretended to be once again interested in "The Price Is Right," and Haydon turned his attention back to the street.

Chapter 32

He walked out of the appliance store with an all-or-nothing feeling, and in fifteen seconds he had entered the gloomy Monaco shoe store next door. The store was a bargain-basement establishment, with crudely made wooden tables piled with tangled heaps of shoes and sandals of every imaginable kind. The place had a high ceiling and no lights so that its only illumination was a pale reflected glow from the shady sidewalk outside. It smelled old and unused, but a few weary-looking people stood around here and there in its dusky, cheerless environs, raking through the tables of footwear.

There was a center aisle through the tables, and Haydon could see the door at the far end. He started toward it, leisurely, looking casually at the people about him. All of them ignored him, the few customers, the one or two employees, who were only distinguishable from the customers because they didn't look as tired. Haydon was invisible to all of them. He got to the back door, which was really only a grillwork gate, and pushed it open, letting himself out into a closed courtyard filled mostly with banana trees and damp beds of flowers and sago palms and a few old vine-strangled mimosas. A tiled path disappeared into the jungle of vegetation, and at the head of the path, just off the cement to his left, were three poles stuck into the earth, each with a bar across its top and a huge green parrot atop the bar. A rusty, horizontal disk jutted out from each bar and was littered with chunks of darkening fruit and a few nuts. The birds blinked at him, as bright and anomalous as emeralds. Immediately to his left, an exterior wooden stairway ascended to a balcony that encircled the courtyard on the second floor.

Suddenly he heard what he thought was the leather sole of a shoe on the gritty cement behind him. He turned as casually as he could manage and saw another set of stairs going up to the balcony on the opposite side of the courtyard. Under the stairs two Guatemalan men were turning to look at him, both of them wide-eyed and panting, frozen. One of the men, the older one, was standing up straight, just out from under the sloping angle of the ascending stairs, putting something into the waistband of his trousers, under his leather jacket. The other man, heavier, younger, was bent over, looking around at Haydon from under the stairs through the open risers. His legs were spread apart, and between his feet a third man lay facedown, blood from his head crawling out from under the lowest tread. Haydon could just see the black and and yellow Batman emblem across the back of the dying man's white T-shirt.

"Subes la escalera," the man wearing the jacket said, pointing to the stairs behind Haydon. He had trouble controlling his voice, which was tight with adrenaline. Haydon looked at him and nodded, looked once more at the man bleeding on the gritty cement, confirmed to himself that it was indeed a *Batman* T-shirt, and turned around and started up the wooden stairs. Behind him one of the parrots screeched, and Haydon flinched. Then he heard them dragging the body across the gritty cement on the other side of the courtyard.

230

The stairway long ago had given up its last coat of paint to the alternating seasons of sun and rain, and now Haydon's hand moved along a rail of wood that was split and gray. His gut told him he ought to have the automatic in his hand, but for some reason he didn't, as if something else told him that if he didn't give in, if he didn't commit to violence himself, there was still some hope of averting more of it.

When he reached the top of the stairs he stopped. The wooden balcony completely encircled the well of the courtyard. He resisted the impulse to look down to see where they had dragged the body, as if the drag marks in the grit could be seen from where he stood. He could go in either direction, either way he could walk completely around the balcony to where he had begun. Turning left, he started along the section over the doorway through which he had just entered.

Before he had taken a dozen steps, a man stepped out of a doorway ten meters in front of him. He was wearing dress pants and a white shirt without a tie, its long sleeves rolled up to his elbows. He held an Uzi in his right hand, which hung straight down by his side. Haydon heard another door open behind him, just at the head of the stairs, and he looked around to see a woman, also with an Uzi.

"You have a gun," the man said in heavily accented English. "Will you please to take it out of your belt and put it on the floor. And also the radio." He raised his Uzi at Haydon in anticipation.

Haydon moved slowly and did as he was told. He heard the woman walking up behind him as he crouched and put the gun on the floor, unhooked the radio and laid it beside it. As soon as he straightened up, she retrieved the gun and the radio.

"This way, please," the man said. He moved toward Haydon and opened a door that was about equal distance between the two of them on Haydon's right. He pushed the door open and then stepped back to let Haydon enter first.

Haydon walked into a single long room the length of the shoe store beneath it. At the far end were tall windows thrown open to the noise and polluted air of 18 calle. Haydon could see the tops of the trees in the median, and just a little to his right was the Santuario de la Sagrada Madre.

In front of the tall windows, isolated in the empty room were an old sofa, a low table, and several kinds of chairs. Against one wall was a kitchen stove, another table with wooden chairs, and "cabinets" made of

231

stacked wooden boxes. Three beds, mattresses lying on the wooden floor, were against another wall.

Dr. Aris Grajeda stood up from one of the chairs around the low table and sofa and approached from across the room. He was wearing a double-breasted suit without a tie, the coat hanging open. The suit was in need of cleaning and pressing.

"I understand you handled this very resourcefully," he said. "I am sorry I had to ask you to do it this way. Please, come over and sit down."

Haydon said nothing. He followed Grajeda over to where he had been sitting alone. The room smelled strongly of the deep resinous fragrance of coffee beans, as if the walls themselves had soaked up the oil from the harvested pods, and of the burlap sacks in which they had been stored. The bare wooden floor was worn shiny in places from decades of warehousemen's feet.

"I call them José and María," Grajeda said of the man and woman who had brought Haydon into the room and who now stood out of sight behind him. The doctor smiled at the obviously fictitious names. "They are not betrothed, however, and they are not particularly religious, though José used to be a Jesuit. Please, let's sit down and talk. Would you want a *cafecito,* Mr. Haydon?"

"I would, yes," Haydon said.

Grajeda went to the kitchen stove himself and took two coffee cups from the wooden boxes and poured coffee from a pot that sat on the stove.

"I don't think you were risking your life to come here to see us, Mr. Haydon," Grajeda said, as he picked up the cups and started back to Haydon. "But I can assure you that the rest of us have risked our lives to come here to see you." He held one of the cups out to Haydon. The cups were large, mismatched, each of them chipped and crazed. Haydon took the one being offered him and set it on the low wooden table.

Grajeda sat down in one of the straight-backed chairs opposite Haydon. He crossed his legs and balanced his cup on his knee, holding it with one hand while he stroked his beard once or twice with the other. He regarded Haydon a moment with an expression that portrayed ambivalence. His Indian eyes were almost oriental behind the flat lenses of his wire-rimmed glasses, his moustache and goatee cleanly trimmed, his black hair, streaked with strands of premature gray, was combed and looked rather elegant. He was actually a very handsome man.

"I apologize for lying to you yesterday morning," Grajeda said without preamble. "Surely you must understand that I had to be careful."

"I'm beginning to understand more all the time," Haydon said.

A flicker of uncertainty passed quickly over Grajeda's face. That was fine with Haydon. He was glad to have someone other than himself experience the slippery textures of ambiguity.

"I am guessing that you know that Lena Muller is not dead," Dr. Grajeda said.

"I'd very much like to know why you're making that assumption," Haydon said. "I seem to have met an inordinate number of people here who want to be clever with me."

"Who were the people following you?" Grajeda asked.

"I don't know."

Grajeda looked at Haydon as if he expected Haydon to start quizzing him. He seemed to want to know what Haydon was thinking without having to ask him. Haydon waited. He was in no position to gain anything by asking questions. Grajeda called the meeting, Grajeda could do the talking.

"Lena is in hiding," the doctor said. "And so am I, as of yesterday." Now he sipped his coffee for the first time. "I met Lena almost two years ago when she first began working with the Chuj in northern Huehuetenango. Dr. Salviati and I—you met Dr. Salviati." Grajeda smiled. "He is an old friend, a very good man with a personal philosophy that does not require him to think radically. I admire that. His approach to life, his philosophical attitude is already complete, and now all he has to do is live it, which he does, I should say, with integrity." Grajeda raised his shoulders, "Well, I am less mature intellectually. I can never settle whether I should strive to be a good Christian, loving my enemies and praying for those who persecute me; or whether I should be a good capitalist—there are several young doctors who want Bindo and me to start a new hospital, in Zona 15 of course—there's very good money to be made from first-class health care for the wealthy ladinos here in Guatemala; or whether I should be a good revolutionary—the opportunities for fulfillment there are limitless, this is the third world after all, and the masses suffer greatly, democracy is a sham, government is corrupt; or . . . Well, you see what I mean Up to this point, however, I have managed to be nothing more than a doctor doing some things that I believe are good, but which my government believes are unpatriotic and counterproductive

233

to their own goals." Dr. Grajeda smiled and tilted his head. "We have a genuine disagreement, this government and I, about my work."

Haydon was sitting with his back to the door of the long room, facing the windows. Though Grajeda tried to appear relaxed, he seemed to Haydon to be ill at ease, almost as if he were a guest here. Haydon did not have the impression that he slept on these beds or cooked on this stove or read the newspapers that were scattered on the table before them. Grajeda did not seem comfortable with the circumstances in the room or with the kind of life they implied—and which Haydon was still trying to assess—and neither did Haydon have the impression that he was part of this room's regular business. Haydon wondered how much Grajeda's hosts were telling him and if he knew what had happened just a few minutes earlier to the man in the *Batman* T-shirt. And he wondered, too, how Cage was going to feel about it.

Grajeda drank some of his coffee. It was good coffee, not the *café basura,* the trashy coffee that had grasses and twigs ground up with inferior beans, the only coffee the poor could afford. In Guatemala, most of the good coffee was exported. Grajeda seemed to savor it, as if it were a special pleasure.

"I met Lena in Huehuetenango," he said. "Bindo and I were working there, as I told you, and she accompanied one of the Chuj women down from San Mateo. I treated the woman and gave her some medicine that required several hours for a reaction, which I needed to monitor. The woman stayed in the hospital. Lena slept on one of the old sofas in the foyer. I was impressed with how—I hope this is not offensive—but how unlike an American she was. She was simply very comfortable with being where she was and doing what she was doing. I asked her if she would like to have dinner with me at one of the cafés not far from the hospital. We became good friends immediately. Sometimes when I came up to Huehuetenango from the capital I would take an extra day and drive up to San Mateo to see her before going back. It's about fifty-four kilometers from Huehue to San Mateo, but it's all dirt roads, so it takes a while. Usually I would stay overnight. We did a lot of talking on those trips, and then she began to come see me when she came into the capital. So we became good friends."

Another sip of coffee, and then Dr. Grajeda finished it and set it on the table in front of him. He never looked at Joseph and Mary, but gave all of his attention to Haydon. Outside the traffic had worked itself to a

234

significant pitch, diesel fumes rode the hot air up to the windows, and occasionally a blast of a car or truck horn was startlingly loud.

"About six months ago," Grajeda continued, stroking his beard thoughtfully with a small hand, "Lena very hesitatingly asked me if I had ever heard stories about people kidnapping children, small children, babies. I said, yes, unfortunately it was done from time to time, one heard stories. She said, no not an occasional kidnapping, but an organized situation, a group of people who stole babies and sold them to certain orphanages who are very lax in their adoption rules.

"Now the fact is, in 1988 and 1989 a very professional organization of kidnappers was broken up here in Guatemala. Several human rights organizations kept getting reports of babies being stolen from the Indians in the highlands. During *la violencia* in the early eighties, there were as many as two hundred thousand war orphans in the highlands, and many of those simply disappeared. During those years, many people in the United States and Israel and Europe adopted little Guatemalan babies under very suspicious circumstances. It was a very simple thing to do, almost like buying a Guatemalan parrot, only easier, because this 'animal' didn't have to be quarantined. As it turned out, it was discovered that some government officials colluded in these operations, generals in the army, even some women related to these generals. A very big scandal. When it was over, of course, nothing was done. It all melted out of the news, new scandals supplanted this one, people went on living their lives."

Grajeda had grown very sober and had lost his philosophical air. "After I left Johns Hopkins, I did my internship in a large hospital in Baltimore. It was my misfortune to be one of several doctors who formed a team that worked with a group of children who had been 'circulated' for almost a year by a ring of child molesters, you know, one of those kinds of organizations that kept in touch with each other on computer networks, and in whose homes were found boxes of despicable photographs and the names and numbers of people with whom they shared these things and these children."

Grajeda stopped and stared at the litter of newspapers on the little table before them. "Well," he said, his eyes immobile as he remembered. "You see, I had to make adjustments in my understanding of the nature of man. I had already done that, in a more or less continuous way, throughout my college years in order to try to justify the political and

235

moral system here in this country. You know, the nature of cruelty . . . the sort of things people wrestle with sometimes . . ."

Suddenly he looked up at Haydon as if something had caught his attention and he remembered where he was and the story he was telling.

"Excuse me," he said. He seemed as if he were about to apologize for his rambling, but then he smiled to himself, straightened up in his chair and touched his steel-rimmed glasses, an infinitesimal adjustment on the bridge of his nose. "As you may be aware, the violence has grown dramatically within the last eight or ten months, sometimes reminding people of *la violencia,* causing everyone to fear that those times could easily return once again. Disappearances and assassinations are on the increase, to everyone's dismay and trepidation, bad memories have come alive like nightmares that have stepped out of our dreams and taken on flesh and crawled into our beds with us in the dark.

"Well, into all of this hidden horror Lena came with perhaps some bad memories of her own, and suddenly this story of stolen babies became more important to her than anything else in the world. She listened to the stories of the sobbing mothers; she talked to the fathers, who, even with their heritage of *machismo,* could not stem the tears for a stolen child. For the first time in her life Lena came face to face with something that moved her to greater compassion, to greater indignation, maybe even greater love, than that which she felt for her own misfortunes.

"And then, of course, she did a very foolish thing. She investigated these rumors herself, came to Guatemala City, made inquiries, went to see people, asked questions. All of this, of course, violating one of the very first rules of the Peace Corps, that their people must stay clear of any kind of political or social turmoil. It was only after she had disturbed the nest and the wasps were buzzing about her head that she came to see me."

236

Chapter 33

As it had been in Cage's safe house, there were unexplained comings
and goings behind Haydon, whisperings at the door where he had
been brought in, the sound of feet—heavy ones, light ones, quick ones—
crossing the rough wooden floor of the warehouse, someone at the coffee-
pot on the stove, the rattle of latches on doors, the occasional muffled
clack of firearms being handled. Grajeda paid no attention to these
movements and sounds, and Haydon could not decide whether the doctor's concentration was such that it shut them out or whether he was

simply so naive about clandestine matters that he was not aware of their possible importance.

Haydon himself, however, tried to attend auditory detail. How many people were involved here? How many of them were women? Had the two men who killed Cage's man come upstairs and told the others? How temporary was this place, and how great a risk were these people taking by having Haydon come here? This last question had been answered partly by the death of the man in the *Batman* T-shirt.

"Actually, Lena was very circumspect about how she parceled out the information to me about her discoveries," Grajeda said. He was sitting now turned almost sideways in his chair, his legs crossed, one arm draped languidly over the back of the chair with its hand dangling at the wrist, his other hand resting on his thigh. He looked rather like a young philosophy professor relaxing with his graduate students, or perhaps a poet, chatting in a café about Yeats or García Lorca. He did not look like a man in hiding, or a man fully aware of the precariousness of his situation.

"I did not know that afternoon when Lena came to see me that she already had gone far beyond such simple inquiries," Grajeda continued, "and neither of us knew that by coming to my clinic she had inextricably involved me in her very dangerous campaign to 'do something' about what she recently had discovered.

"Of course I was already on the security forces' computers," Grajeda clarified. "It wasn't as though Lena had shined a spotlight on me. I have been very outspoken about the corruption in the government's public health programs. I have been an 'activist' in that regard, a 'provocateur.' I have 'Marxist' ideas about the responsibilities of a government to its people." The doctor smiled and raised the hand that had been resting on his thigh and held up two fingers toward Haydon as if he were blessing him. "You see, here in Central America, 'communist' is still a potent word. After four decades of having the United States pound into us the incomparable evils of 'communism,' of giving us foreign aid *only* if we say we will fight communism with it, of giving us military matériel *only* if we say we will fight communism with it . . . well, we know what a communist is now. We have had to learn in order to get along with Uncle Sam. It doesn't matter that the Great Red Threat is now in shambles, and its fearsome communist ideology is a routed ghost. Your legacy to us is that *we* still know a communist when we see one, and if we don't see one then we will invent one. Thank God for this wonderful democracy you have given us."

238

Grajeda's smile softened, and his hand dropped once again to his thigh. He looked away thoughtfully toward the tall windows where, just out of sight, Guatemala labored in the dust and heat of the *verano*. Grajeda kept his own counsel for a few moments and then turned to Haydon.

"In the nearly four decades that you have shared your kindness with your little brown Guatemalan brothers," he said softly, "you have not befriended the wisest of us and taught us how to build schools to educate our people; you have not embraced the kindest of us and taught us how to build hospitals to heal our sick." He shook his head. "Instead, you have schemed with the worst of us and taught us how to be suspicious and how to hate. You have very strange ideas of what it means to 'befriend' a people. I really don't think you understand what it means, or if you do understand, then you have been very perverse in your intentions. After four decades of your 'help' we have become numb with our own misery: we assassinate or 'disappear' more than one thousand of our fellow Guatemalan's annually; eighty-five percent of us live in poverty; eighty-two percent of our children under five years old are malnourished; eighty percent of us have no access to medicines; seventy percent of us are illiterate . . ."

Dr. Grajeda stopped abruptly. He looked at Haydon calmly and seemed suddenly, profoundly sad. "I apologize. I sincerely apologize. Blame is a very thin garment. The person who uses it to keep warm could easily freeze to death. The fact is, Lena had discovered that a woman named Vera Beatriz—"

"—Azcona de Sandoval . . ." Haydon said.

Dr. Grajeda looked at Haydon in shock.

"I assume," Haydon said, "that General Azcona is after Lena because she wanted to expose his sister's involvement in illegally procuring children for adoption, a process which is itself of dubious legal character here in Guatemala. I assume she enlisted John Baine's help in this, probably thinking that the best medicine for this kind of situation was to shed the bright light of the press on it, and that is why he's disappeared. I assume that Jim Fossler found out about much or all of this and has been killed in the cross fire. I assume that you were helping her more than you're leading me to believe; and I assume you need me to do something for you, which is why you've had me come here. I also assume you know where Lena is hiding."

Haydon said all of this with as much equanimity as he could muster, something he was finding increasingly difficult to do. He wasn't sure just how long he could hold at bay the craziness that was taking place all around him, following him like a pack of shantytown curs, waiting for him either to make a mistake or lead them to something tastier. Unlike Dr. Grajeda, he was not at all convinced that he had shaken all his surveillants. The man in the *Batman* T-shirt was just one of the unlucky ones. But there were others, and he did not believe that he and Dr. Grajeda were having this conversation unbeknownst to anyone but themselves and the people guarding them. Haydon had the distinct feeling that he was walking on the brink of a precipice and that the curs were shouldering in closer, right there, just at the edge of light, where the darkness begins.

"As far as I know," Dr. Grajeda said, considerably sobered, "most of your assumptions are correct. I honestly don't know about Mr. Fossler. But I fear the worst for him. And John Baine too, I—"

"Baine has been picked up by Azcona's DIC agents," Haydon interjected. "He's being held in a clandestine prison."

Dr. Grajeda looked at Haydon now with something like suspicion. He was obviously taken aback that Haydon had this kind of information.

"How do you know this?"

"Don't be too impressed," Haydon said. "Or unduly distrustful. I've come onto most of this through dumb luck. Understand, the only thing I want is to get Fossler out of here, if he's alive, and Lena too, if she wants to go." As Haydon said this, he felt a twinge of guilt. Nobody gave a shit about Baine. Later the American embassy would give a shit, but just barely, and only because they had to. Having to was weak motivation for an advocate.

"Only one of your assumptions is a miscalculation," Dr. Grajeda said. "I don't want anything from you." He shifted his eyes toward the door of the warehouse and then back to Haydon. "These people . . . are helping me." He lowered his voice. "It's a very . . . hard bargain. They will get me out of the city, help me escape Azcona's goons, but in turn I have to give them two years. I have to serve with their *compas,* who do not have a doctor. They have many cadres, some urban, some in the jungle. I will be a very busy doctor."

This time his smile was distinctly rueful, and he raised his hands in mock helplessness. "I have been drafted by the insurgency. The irony here is that I am only buying time, literally. They are saving my life now, but by the time I have spent two years with the guerrillas and am free to come back home, my life won't be worth a single cigarette. Even my father's influence—the reason, I am sure, that I have not been disappeared by the death squads already—will be of no help to me then."

"Couldn't you go into exile?"

"Oh, yes, there is always exile," Grajeda said, his expression ironic. "Yes, there's always that."

"Is this the only way you can escape Azcona?"

"The only *sure* way."

"You must have done something more than 'talk' with Lena to have incurred this kind of sentence from Azcona."

Dr. Grajeda nodded. "Well, of course, I did. But that is beside the point. Many people have been visited by the death squads for doing far less than I did to offend the General. There is not necessarily any relationship between 'offense' and sentence. The General may want someone disappeared because they have stolen national security secrets or because they cut him off in traffic that morning. It is all the same to him. He was offended by both gestures.

"But yes, you are right. In retrospect it was not so odd that Lena came to me with her suspicions of kidnapping in the highlands. After we became good friends and fell into the habit of talking late into the night about everything under the sun, one night I became rather animated— we were drinking too—about my feelings regarding the condition of the children in the highlands where I had been working. I started out on the subject of health care and then went on to the deplorable plight of the orphans all over Guatemala, but especially in the cities, and on and on. The point is, she knew about my concerns for Guatemalan children."

Dr. Grajeda sighed and looked away and seemed for the first time to have difficulty controlling his agitation.

"Thinking back on it, I wonder if I wasn't unconsciously luring her into this," he said, "though I can't imagine why, I mean, to what purpose. You see, I had already been compiling data on the disappearance of children, both in Guatemala City and in the highlands, actually anywhere I encountered it. I had names and dates and places . . . and with each instance I provided annotations—sometimes paragraphs, sometimes pages—of the 'rumors' of that child's disappearance. Now, being a doctor, I know that rumor, hearsay, is not a scientific way of doing something like this. On the other hand, if I were an anthropologist, a sociologist, it would only be appropriate to compile this kind of information. Nevertheless, by the time Lena came to me and asked me if I had ever

241

heard anything about kidnappings, I had already accumulated a considerable archive on the subject and had recorded hundreds of incidents . . . along with the rumors about what had happened to the child. So I had two kinds of archival information: statistical and anthropological."

Dr. Grajeda stopped and removed his glasses and rubbed the sides of the bridge of his nose, no longer pretending he wasn't tired. When he returned his glasses to his face and hooked the wire arms over his ears, he didn't look again at Haydon but at one of the warehouse walls where a chunk of plaster has fallen away from the stone.

"When she came to me she already had blundered terribly," he continued. "She was being followed by the DIC, and everyone she visited had their names added to the central computer file of 'subversives.' After she came to me and told me what she had been doing, I knew that I was marked. I already had been keeping two copies of my 'archive.' One here so I could work on it and one with Dr. Salviati. Now I went to a photocopy shop and made two more copies. I put one in my safety deposit box, and the other I took to my mother. I told her the bundle of papers was old medical-school papers that I didn't want to throw away, and I put them in the attic of her home."

"When was this?" Haydon asked.

Grajeda thought. "It must have been, yes, that was in April, nine months ago."

"Then within three months of mentioning this to you, Lena was discharged from the Peace Corps and had returned to Houston."

"That's right."

"But you talked about this again?"

"Only once more. Actually I had entered a time when I was helping Dr. Salviati quite a bit. I saw Lena only twice more before she flew back to Houston. Once, we discussed her preoccupation. The last time we did not."

"And were you visited by the DIC?"

"No. I suppose they thought it was over when she left Guatemala."

"But it wasn't, because she had told John Baine about it."

Dr. Grajeda nodded. "Yes, I am afraid she did."

"And he began snooping."

Grajeda nodded. "And then before I knew it, she had returned to Guatemala and had a job with USAID."

Yes, Haydon thought, and soon she was working for Bennett Pittner.

"Do you know if she continued looking into the story about stolen children after she returned?" he asked.

"Yes," Grajeda said. "She came to see me again. I almost had reached the point that I was wondering if I was paranoid. The DIC had not visited me. Perhaps I was being silly. Perhaps Lena had not inadvertently led them to me after all. And then one day she was back, and she came to see me at my clinic in Mezquital. She said she had this job with USAID, and she was going to be working again in the highlands. She was very excited about this. She told me she was going to expose Vera Beatriz, that she had the documentation to do it. Frankly I was skeptical of this. I cautioned her about what she was doing. I told her she could be killed for this. Yes, yes, of course, she said, but she now had very powerful protection." Grajeda shook his head. "I don't know what that meant, and, naturally, she didn't tell me."

"Do you believe that Lena actually had—has—good information?"

"I don't know," Grajeda sounded weary. "With her . . . do you know her?"

"No, I've never met her."

"Well, with her you never know. She can be surprisingly astute, intelligent, and then sometimes so childish. Is she from a wealthy family?"

It was an interesting question from Grajeda. If he didn't know, then Lena must never have told him, but still he surmised it. He was quite perceptive himself.

"Yes."

"I thought so," he nodded. "She never hinted that she was, but still, I thought as much."

Dr. Grajeda stood and stepped around behind his chair. He walked several paces, rather idly toward the high windows, and someone hissed from the end of the room behind Haydon. Dr. Grajeda turned around with a smile and held up his hand. "I know, I know. Don't go near the windows." He looked at Haydon and rolled his eyes slightly. "This is going to be a long two years with my cautious subversive friends, huh?" He wandered back toward Haydon. He came to the sofa and sat on the back of it, one foot on the floor.

"Actually, my two years with my brothers, here . . . well, one year is for me, and one year is for Lena. They are keeping her safe in Antigua."

243

Chapter 34

Antigua was a famously beautiful little colonial town about forty-five kilometers west of Guatemala City, practically in the shadows of the volcanoes, Agua, Fuego, and Acatenango. Haydon looked at Grajeda. The doctor was full of surprises, and Haydon suddenly realized that he had guessed another.

"You were the one responsible for the blond girl in the morgue."

"Let me tell you something," Grajeda said, fixing his eyes on Haydon. "We would not be sitting here right now if it hadn't been for that girl. If I live to be a hundred years old I will never encounter a more bizarre occurrence of serendipity, if that is not too light a word to use in conjunction with such a grisly murder. It happened just as I told you— even Dr. Salviati's illness. I was still fuzzy headed from exhaustion and sleep when they took the girl out of the body bag and rolled her onto the table and told me they wanted an autopsy. I almost went to my knees in shock. I literally had to grab the side of the operating table to keep from falling. Those stupid men looked at me, but they were too dense to realize that I thought I was looking at someone I knew."

Grajeda stood up from the back of the sofa, unable to talk about this sitting down. He put his hands in the side pockets of his suit coat.

"I started crying, but these men didn't see this. Her face was unrecognizable. My mind was an explosion of thoughts: how did this happen? Azcona? Where did they find her? Why have they brought her here? Is this some perverse game to see how I will react or just to toy with me before they take me away too? Above all . . . can I actually *do* this autopsy? How can I? And it was while I was staring at her that I slowly, haltingly realized that this was not Lena at all."

Dr. Grajeda took one hand from his pocket and wiped it over his goatee. "I knew some identifying marks on Lena's torso," he said softly. "And this . . . young woman . . . this girl's breasts were noticeably smaller than Lena's. And then upon closer examination . . . I knew. So. The rest of the story goes on as I told you when you came to my clinic. It happened just the way I said.

"However, I was not completely through with the autopsy when it occurred to me, this plan. Lena and I both knew that we were very close to being picked up by the DIC, and our 'window of opportunity' to evade this was very small. She was frightened and had called me at the hospital there in Huehuetenango several times. I had already talked to these people," Grajeda said, tilting his head toward the man and woman in the room, "and had made this arrangement, but I could not convince Lena to go along with it. Part of the agreement was that they would get her out of the country. You see, because of the computers now, it is impossible for anyone to leave Guatemala without elaborate escape plans. The airports, the bus stations, the highways, the security agents in all these places are linked by computer, all of them have lists, and it takes only a couple of taps on a keyboard and the security agents know about you all over the country at once." Grajeda looked at Haydon. "This kind of technology in a country that can not even feed its people."

245

He started toward the windows again and turned after a few steps and came back, glancing toward the man and woman at the door.

"I knew which morgue in Huehuetenango was used for the XXs. After confirming that she had been taken there, I got in touch with these people in Guatemala City. I told them to go to this lawyer and he would provide them with the papers they would need for a man and woman to go to Huehuetenango and claim the body of their friend and bring it back to Guatemala City where they would deliver it to the Gabinete de Identificación as an XX. I knew the DIC monitored the morgues there, and as soon as a body of this description showed up they would know it. After arranging this, I drove to Guatemala City to talk to Lena about my plan. This was on Friday, and it took me a while to find her because, as a matter of fact, she and John Baine had been meeting with your friend Jim Fossler."

"Why was Baine so frightened?" Haydon interrupted. "When I talked to Fossler on the following Sunday and he told me about this meeting, he described Baine as being as frightened as Lena."

"Yes, that's right. By this time Lena had given a lot of information to Fossler. The night before Fossler met with them, Baine's house was broken into and ransacked. The papers he had kept there were taken. And Lena had begun receiving anonymous telephone calls, warning her off the Azcona story." Grajeda removed his glasses and dug into a pocket for a handkerchief. He blew on the small lenses and wiped at them, doing this several times to each one as he talked.

"That's the way they do, you know, the DIC, the death squads. You get these damned calls. And then they might run you off the road while you are driving. Or you get a crudely written letter: if you do this or don't do this, we will cut out your tongue or disembowel you or whatever their sick, small minds can think of. They always warn you, sometimes there are a lot of warnings. Sometimes it goes on for months, and some people always think it won't happen to them, because of course, sometimes it doesn't happen. But then often it does. It's a great gamble once they start 'communicating' with you.

"Anyway, I finally found her and told her what I had in mind. She agreed immediately. I think Baine was really frightened, and having him in that condition made her think. So the two of us—Baine didn't know about it—put our heads together and came up with the plan that she would 'disappear' in Panajachel."

"Baine had already asked her to go there with him?"

"That's right. But to tell you the truth, I'm not sure what that was all about. If Baine was so frightened for his life I don't know why he wanted her to take a 'holiday' in Panajachel. It seemed a peculiar thing to me, but . . ." Grajeda shrugged.

"What about the report that accompanied the XX to the Gabinete de Identificación?" Haydon asked. "If your people had prepared bogus papers, why did the report say you had brought the body to the city?"

"I have no idea," Grajeda said. "I can only speculate that that was the working of the DIC. I imagine the entire report was retyped before the body was sent to the Cementerio General, and they put in it whatever they wanted."

Grajeda came around from behind the sofa and sat once again in the wooden chair opposite Haydon.

"You are seeing here the madness of Guatemala," he said. "Even I have succumbed to it, as much as I hate it. God knows who that girl was. Who knows where she came from or where she will end? I violated her identity, others did, probably even others will yet again before this ghastly charade is over. This is a mad society. We do things like this . . ." Grajeda let the words fade away, his eyes settling on the scattered newspapers. Then he looked up. "Do you read very much, Mr. Haydon? Fiction, I mean?"

"Some."

"Do you know the novels of Heinrich Böll?"

"I've read *Group Portrait with Lady* and *The Clown.*"

"Really?" Grajeda smiled hugely, surprised. He almost laughed. "How interesting. I am surprised. I mean . . ."

"I have a degree in literature," Haydon said, himself amused at Grajeda's reaction. "I didn't come out of the womb a policeman."

This time Grajeda did laugh. "This is a wonderful thing," he said. "What . . . Ah . . ."

"My father was a well-read man," Haydon said. "He had an excellent library, which I still have, and certain ideas about what an educated man should be. I got a degree in literature, which was fine with him, but it wasn't what he had wanted for me. He was a lawyer, and he wanted me to be a lawyer too. I entered law school and stayed two years. But I walked away from it. Then I joined the police force."

Grajeda listened to this brief biography with an expression of delight. "What a wonderful story," he said. "I am happy to hear it." He looked at Haydon, smiling, the surprise still in his eyes. Then he caught himself.

"So, good, you know the man, then, Heinrich Böll. Well, I once read an interview with Böll in which the interviewer asked him if he thought of written history as lies. He said, no, not lies perhaps, but it is more like a narrative of inaccuracies in as much as one can never precisely reconstruct it, and it therefore contains untruths. Böll said that, at bottom, truth was an 'assembled' thing. That it could not be found in one place, not in one book, one man's perspective, not in one man's testimony, or one government's history. These he implied, were only particles of truth. They had to be assembled, collated to get at the greater thing itself. I thought about that a lot after I read it. It is such an obvious thing, yet until someone says it right out like that one seems not to be cognizant of it. It seems to me that all too often we go through life holding only the particles in our hands, thinking all along that we possess the whole thing itself.

"Böll said that truth was so difficult to get at because the documents that we gather together in order to assemble the truth may not in themselves be truthful to begin with. He says that we know that governments and statesmen lie to each other and that these lies sometimes are recorded (as truth, of course) in documents which we then assemble (unaware of their deceit) like so many particles, and with the best of intentions, into a body of 'truth' that really is not the truth at all."

Grajeda looked at Haydon a moment. "And there you have it," he said. "The death and resurrection of Lena Muller, so intertwined with the death of XX that we may never know Böll's 'assembled truth.' It may not be possible to discover even in a thousand years. We, you and I, are principals in this story, a story that hasn't yet finished being told, and even we don't know the pieces of truth that fall within our own purview. As a matter of fact, you are here now, trying to decipher the lies that you have been told, in search of the truth. We have even contributed to the lies . . . or, forgive me, at least I have. It's a shameful thing, really, what habitual deceit can do to people, even a whole people, like Guatemalans . . . or Americans."

Haydon looked at Dr. Aris Grajeda. He was alone in this large empty warehouse in a way that Haydon was not, in a way that not even Mary and Joseph were alone, even though they had cast their lots outside the acceptable society, against their government, and lived as outcasts in the back streets and jungles and isolated *granjas*. He was not a sad figure, but a melancholy one, and Haydon believed that he understood the source of the doctor's rather wry gravity.

"Do you love her?" Haydon asked.

Grajeda didn't respond immediately, but his handsome features seemed to give up their pretense, and he regarded Haydon with defensive eyes.

"Does it show that much?"

"No, not much," Haydon said. "You do well. But I like to believe I have a faculty for seeing beyond the obvious in men."

Dr. Grajeda nodded. "You do well, also," he said. "Yes, my friend, I love her. The hard thing of it is, you see, I know the futility of experiencing an emotion that is more characteristic of a man half my age. I don't even have the innocence to be fooled by my own emotions."

"Does she know how you feel?"

"If she does, she has been cruelly reticent about acknowledging it."

"Cruelly?"

"What, did I say that, 'cruelly'?" Grajeda for the first time betrayed an awkwardness with himself. "I must've. Well, Freudian slips often are difficult to admit." He was pensive a moment before going on. "We had sexual intercourse, she and I, but I believe that is precisely what it was, sexual intercourse. Lena's sexuality is robust; she enjoys it totally with her senses the way one enjoys a delicious food or a pipe of opium. I could even say that she enjoys it with her mind, intellectually, even perhaps, like an ecstatic experience." He smiled wanly and shook his head. "But she does not put her *heart* into it. Not with me and—I say this with sadness and I hope without any dishonesty to compensate for the pain of my own disappointment—I doubt if she ever has with anyone."

Haydon said nothing. He was tempted to talk with this man about Lena Muller, what he himself knew and suspected about her life, but something made him hold back. It might have been his own uncertainty about what he really knew of her. After all, within just the past two days he had learned things he hadn't known before, and he suspected if he spent a year talking to people, or even to Lena herself, he would never get to the bottom of it. One never did. You could only talk about someone from your perspective at the present, at a given point in time, acknowledging your limitations, acknowledging that you could very well change your convictions tomorrow. But perhaps that was putting too fine a point on it, an excuse for cowardice. There was a very real possibility that Dr. Grajeda already knew Lena Muller better than Haydon did, even without knowing some of the more significant facts. If Haydon had

249

learned anything over the years, it was that facts often had very little to do with what people were really "about."

"These people have agreed to take Lena out of the country," Dr. Grajeda said, changing the subject. "I am telling you this because I know you have come down here to take her home."

"No," Haydon corrected him. "I came only to see that she was alive. Does she want to go home?"

"I only know that now she's trying to save her life. If you wish, these people can tell you where, at what border crossing they plan to deliver her, and you can pick her up there. I myself do not know the facts in this. It was difficult enough to arrange this meeting with you. These people stay alive by not taking chances. Any arrangement with them will have to be between you and them."

Haydon had no commission from Germaine Muller to bring her daughter back. He had no commission from the Houston Police Department to do anything. It was a matter of personal responsibility. As for Fossler, he was at a loss.

"Do these people know anything about Fossler?" Haydon asked.

"I've already inquired. Nothing."

It was as if Fossler had vaporized. It was the kind of "disappearance" that was always attributed to the death squads.

"What about the American embassy?" Haydon asked. "I don't understand why Lena hasn't gone to them in order to protect her life. I can see—maybe—why she didn't want to involve them in the Vera Beatriz affair. She wouldn't be the only American who was skeptical about what the U.S. State Department can and will do about such things. But I don't understand why she wouldn't call the embassy when she knew her life was in danger. Most people would do a lot of things to save their lives that they wouldn't do otherwise."

He was particularly interested in Dr. Grajeda's response to this. Haydon feared that the answer might lie in a circumstance that he knew should have been a secret, Lena's relatively recent recruitment by Pittner. If there was some other reason, Grajeda should know it. If there wasn't, Grajeda should be in the dark about it.

"I think you should ask the embassy about that," Dr. Grajeda said. "I don't know." He hesitated. "I presume you don't have to be cautioned . . ."

"No," Haydon said. "I don't."

"Then what do you want to do?"

"Does Lena want me to pick her up at a border designation?" Haydon asked. "Does she want to return to Houston? It would help if I could talk to her."

"I knew you would say that." Dr. Grajeda nodded. "I am trying to negotiate it. They are beginning to complain that I am asking more than we originally bargained for. Everything for them is a risk; they are always at risk. It is a nerve-wracking way of life, emotionally exhausting. I don't know. I'm trying to arrange it."

Haydon looked at Grajeda and lowered his voice. "The little girl who brought me to your clinic. Has she done any other errands for you . . . regarding this . . . regarding Lena?"

Dr. Grajeda's eyes stirred in alarm, but he remained calm. "No. Why? Have you seen her?"

"No, I haven't seen her," he said. "Can we stand up and talk. I've got to stretch my legs." He wanted to get away from the table, from the sofa and the chairs, which easily could be wired.

"Of course, of course," Grajeda said, and as he stood he spoke to the man and the woman telling them they only wanted to stand for a while, that they were tired of sitting.

They moved away from the small collection of furniture in the center of the cavernous room and walked over to one of the stone walls and then away from it, to a point roughly equidistant between the wall and the furniture, and stood together on the bare wooden floor.

"Janet Pittner received a message late last night at her home," Haydon said. He and Grajeda were side by side, facing the windows. "It was delivered by a child, a little girl." Haydon quoted the message verbatim.

"Jesus God," Grajeda said. "No. I can swear to you that these people would never have allowed Lena to do that. This did not come from her."

"Janet Pittner swears it was Lena's handwriting."

"I don't care what she swears," Grajeda said. "It did not come from Lena."

"I don't know why anyone else would want to do that," Haydon said. "I don't know who would want to lure me into anything. I'm no particular threat to anyone."

"This would be strictly prohibited by these people," Grajeda said. He had yet to name who "these people" were. Haydon could only surmise he

251

was working with one of the many guerrilla groups who persisted in Guatemala despite thirty years of the army's brutal counterinsurgency operations.

"Okay, fine," Haydon said. "I needed to know. I'll be careful with it."

Dr. Grajeda did not seem comforted by Haydon's acceptance of his convictions. Haydon had planted a seed of doubt in the doctor's mind, which he regretted, but which also told Haydon something of the doctor's circumstances. Perhaps he was not as sure of his guerrilla friends as he wanted Haydon to believe, or even as he wanted to believe himself. Haydon was slowly learning that no one could be sure of anything in Guatemala, not even of the workings of one's own mind.

Chapter 35

Leaving Dr. Grajeda was almost as complicated as meeting him in the first place. The woman who had taken Haydon's weapon and radio on the landing outside had changed clothes and was now wearing a honey-colored wig. Haydon guessed that she had changed clothes because she had been somewhere on the streets during the time he was working his way to the shoe store—another "faction" monitoring his approach—and did not wish to wear anything that might have been spotted earlier by the competitor surveillants. She looked good in the wig, and Haydon wondered if she had a blond one as well. Dr. Grajeda's story about how "they" had gone to the morgue in Huehuetenango to claim the body of a blond woman made Haydon wonder how they could have done that if they were clearly Guatemalans themselves. Surely, to claim an Anglo body from a Guatemalan morgue required something of a good story if the claimants were Guatemalans. Or perhaps Haydon was making assumptions, being too logical for a society where the vast majority of the people were so desperately poor that virtually everything was negotiable, virtually everyone was open to graft simply as a means of survival. In such an environment the word "graft" almost lost its meaning and took on an entirely different definition by virtue of its skewed context.

"We're going to take you out a different way than you came in," the woman said, tucking the last of her jet hair up under the honey wig. Haydon was surprised that she spoke to him in English and that she hadn't the slightest trace of an Hispanic accent despite the fact that she was obviously Guatemalan. "They know you're here somewhere, somewhere on 18 calle, and they're all over us."

"Who are 'they'?" Haydon asked.

"We're going to go down the stairs the way you came up," she said, ignoring his question. "And then we're going to leave by the back of the courtyard instead of through the shoe store." She was wearing 18 calle clothes, a skirt that fit her poorly, a dingy mauve blouse that hung loosely over her waist. She raised the blouse and unfastened a strap on a leather holster held with a tight elastic band stretched around her naked midriff.

They were standing by one of the beds on the floor of the warehouse, and she had dropped down on one knee on the mattress and was filling several clips, which she then put in a yellow plastic purse. Bullets and clips and silencer tubes and flashlight batteries and a couple of Uzi's were laid out neatly on the bed together with Haydon's automatic, which lay on a shred of blue towel. She picked it up as she stood.

"Do not be tempted to use this," she said, handing it to him. "We're going to keep the radio. Sorry, but they're hard to come by sometimes, and this is one of those times." She smiled a crooked and not unattractive smile. Her face was rather oblong, with a pretty mouth and a mole that was very much a beauty mark just to the right of her lips. "Okay?"

"That's fine," Haydon said needlessly. He was grateful, and surprised, to get the gun back. He turned up the butt, saw the clip, popped it and saw that it was full. "Thanks," he said, "I appreciate it."

"De nada," the girl said. "Let's go."

Haydon turned once again toward Dr. Aris Grajeda, who had not moved away from the collection of soiled furniture in the center of the warehouse. "Take care of yourself," Haydon said.

"Y su también," Grajeda said. He was standing with his arms crossed, one small hand toying with his salt-and-pepper goatee. *"Hasta la vista,"* he said, and he tilted his head in a gracious bow and smiled kindly. He looked like a man out of place, and yet at the same time philosophically at ease. Dr. Aris Grajeda was not a man who flinched at hard decisions, nor did he grieve for himself when it came time to live with the consequences.

The guerrillas had not survived for thirty years in Guatemala— though some would say only barely survived—without at least a modicum of expertise. Haydon did not doubt that the route they would be taking was lined with invisible *compas* with those hard-to-find radios who had already cleared the way as much as possible. They were operating in a very dicey territory, and Haydon wondered if they were truly risking all this solely for the benefit of having a doctor at their disposal for a couple of years. He wondered, too, how Dr. Grajeda had come to have such an easy relationship with these people. The man and the woman with Haydon were close to the doctor's age, and the woman at least, was well educated. It wasn't hard to imagine that the doctor's connections were old ones.

"What we want to do," the woman said, as the three of them walked out of the warehouse onto the veranda outside, "is to get you several blocks away from here before we let you 'surface.' We don't want to taint the neighborhood. The fact that you came to 18 calle to make your connection does not mean that the meeting itself actually took place here. The busy street life here makes it a favorite place for losing tails before going on to other locations. We gambled by setting the meeting here. We want to make sure we don't burn a nice touch, you know."

The man went down the stairs first, followed by Haydon and then the girl. They descended the same flight Haydon came up, setting foot in the courtyard near the three jade parrots. Haydon glanced at the foot of the stairs on the other side and saw that someone had scattered sand over the blood at the foot of the steps.

The girl saw Haydon glance at the steps.

"Did you know the guy?"

"No," Haydon said. "But I think I know who he worked for."

255

"Who?"

"Sorry," Haydon said.

"Okay. Look," the girl said as they stopped at the head of the damp path that led into the banana trees, "when we get to the door at the back of the courtyard, he's going to go first. I'll tell you when to go after him, and then you maintain that same distance, and I'll keep the same distance behind you. You just follow him, and then you'll know when you're on your own. Okay?"

"Okay."

They wound through the banana trees for fifteen or twenty meters before they came to a heavy wooden door in the high wall at the back of the courtyard. Above them, clinging precariously to the old stone and stucco building, the veranda ran gray and rickety, turning at the back of the courtyard and crossing above their heads at the back door. The man said something into his radio and got a response and then opened the door without hesitation and walked outside. The alley-like lane was one of those narrow corridors that ran between high walls and emerged onto a busy street that could be seen fifty meters farther ahead. Without saying anything to Haydon, the man stepped out into the lane, taking a long stretching step over a rivulet of sewage that dribbled down toward them from the main street above. The girl moved in front of Haydon and watched until it was time for Haydon to follow.

"Okay," she said. "He's on the street. When you get to the end of this lane, turn left. He'll be waiting for you at the newsstand. It'll be right in front of you. When he sees you come out and is sure you've spotted him, he'll move on. Keep that distance. Do what you know how to do."

Haydon did as he was instructed. The narrow alleyway smelled of soured fruit and urine, and he had to watch his step. Everything went like clockwork. The man in front of him did as the girl said he would do, Haydon did as he was told to do, and the girl behind him did as she said she would do. They went on like this for one block, turning a corner, playing catch-up, then another block and another block. Haydon watched the crowds as best he could, wondering if he could spot fellow *compas*. He never did, not that he knew anyway.

They turned another corner, went another block, and at the next turn Haydon suddenly realized he had lost his lead man. He quickened his pace, his eyes picking apart the people in the crowds. When he knew he'd lost him for good, he stopped to rake something off his foot on the curb and glanced back down the sidewalk to see if the girl was showing concern. She was gone. He hadn't lost anybody. They had cut him loose.

He had been so intent on keeping up with his guide that he had lost his orientation. Continuing to the next corner, he checked the calle and avenida. He was deeper into Zona 1 and about twice as far from his car as he had been when he entered La Santuario de la Sagrada Madre. And in the opposite direction.

He started back in the general direction of the car, imagining the crowd full of the other surveillants, imagining that he had already been picked up and was being followed by half a dozen persons of unknown loyalties. Then he stopped. If he had been "clean" five minutes ago, then he ought to be clean now. If the girl and her *compa* were as good as they seemed to be, and she knew her stuff as well as she seemed to, it was likely that the other surveillants had not stayed in 18 calle after they lost Haydon—with the exception, perhaps, of Cage's people, who had lost a man there and were probably frantically trying to find him.

He stopped where he was. Damn it, he wasn't thinking. It would be stupid for him to go back to the car. To get out of the stream of sidewalk traffic, he backed into a *tienda* to think. He would bet his life—in fact might be betting his life—that they were watching his car like buzzards over a carcass. It would be the one sure way of picking him up again. If he had indeed shaken his surveillants, he wanted to stay free of them as long as possible.

Turning in to the *tienda,* he found a less than clean little eatery with three small round and wobbly pedestal tables and four or five metal folding chairs. There were dozens of flies and four Vietnamese watching him from behind a high wooden counter: a ferret-eyed old woman, a slight young man in his twenties, and two women of the same age. Haydon guessed the latter were sisters, one of them perhaps the wife of the young man. The old woman, he decided, belonged to the girls. Haydon stepped to one of the tables, and the old woman's head zipped along the top of the counter, and she came around to him without ever taking her eyes off of him.

He ordered coffee in Spanish, and she literally jumped to oblige him as her family flew into a flurry of accommodation ludicrously inordinate to the task at hand. Magically, the coffee was suddenly on the unsteady round table, the old woman's eyes riveted to his to see if she could discern his pleasure or displeasure with what she had placed before him in a

257

small white demitasse cup, no saucer. Haydon thanked her and for several minutes sipped the stout coffee as he watched the morning shade on the sidewalk shrink in the face of the advancing sun.

Turning, he encountered eight Vietnamese eyes, six instantly turned away, and the head of the ferret-eyed old woman again zipped down the length of the wooden counter and was instantly at the edge of his table.

Haydon asked for another cup of coffee, and when she returned with it he asked her if this shop belonged to her family. Yes, yes, to her son and her daughter-in-law and her daughter-in-law's sister. Haydon asked if they had been in Guatemala long. Only eight years. The oriental perspective. They lived in Flores for a while, she said, chewing something haphazardly with fewer teeth than she once had had, but they were starving there so they went to Puerto Barrios. That was a goddamned bad town, she said, proving how well she had learned Spanish in eight years. Her daughter-in-law's sister got raped there. Her son got malaria. Her daughter-in-law had a miscarriage. It was hot there, hotter than Kuantan—that was in Malaya. Also a bad place. But Puerto Barrios was goddamned bad, and everybody there was a bandit. And there were diseases. She herself got hookworms. Once the guerrillas took over the entire neighborhood where they lived, and they had to feed the men for four days. And they didn't get any pay for it; all they got was not to be killed. They used up all their food and then the guerrillas just left. Just like the Vietcong. She hadn't seen any peace since she was a girl on a rubber plantation in the old French occupation. She didn't know what they would do. If this little *tienda* didn't make it, she was going to cut her throat and let the young ones worry about it. She was goddamned tired of worrying about it.

Haydon guessed the old woman had her share of opinions about most things and that she pretty well decided what the group of them did. Haydon said that he was an American. Yeah, yeah, she said. She knew that. What was her son's name, he asked. Phan. His father's name was Phan; and his grandfather's too. Could Phan drive, Haydon asked. The old woman looked at him, suddenly suspicious. Haydon gave her a bogus story that seemed to satisfy her. If Phan would drive his car to the hotel for him, Haydon would pay him and pay for his taxi ride back into Zona 1 from the hotel. All he had to do was park the car in the parking lot of the Residencial Reforma and give the keys to the concierge.

How much, the old woman asked, her eyes sliding away from him. Twenty dollars. American? Of course. The old woman brightened and broke into a gap-toothed grin. She would pull the car to his hotel with a rope for that kind of money, she said. Or the girls would, she added with a raspy laugh.

Good. Could Phan go now? The old woman called her son to the front and everything was explained to him. Phan listened politely, said he knew where the Residencial Reforma was. The old woman snapped something to him in Vietnamese, and the young man lowered his eyes and nodded, and then she seemed to scold him for something and he continued nodding and blinking.

Having settled the arrangement, Haydon gave Phan the twenty dollars, which the old woman immediately retrieved and then disappeared behind a curtain to a back room. The two girls came out from behind the high counter, looking worried as Phan seemed to explain to them his mission. One of the girls was pregnant, and she and Phan had a brief exchange of curt phrases during which she darted her eyes reproachfully at Haydon. Phan placated her concern with touches and soft words, which quieted her but in no way erased the anxiety from her face or that of her birdlike sister. Wearing expressions of almost frantic apprehension, the wife and sister were the epitome of concerned women who knew very well that the only thing that stood between them and destitution was this thin young man who was now about to walk away with a stranger to some sure folly of which they had only an instinctive fear. Phan seemed genuinely pained by the protests, but at the same time all too familiar with them, unhurriedly calming the women as though he were clucking to frightened geese. His eyes did not make contact with Haydon's as he abruptly turned away, and they walked outside into the bright morning light.

When they were only a block from the little *tienda,* Haydon thanked the young man and gave him the car keys and another five dollars, having noticed that the old woman hadn't given him any cab fare back downtown. He seemed like a mild person, a quiet man whose nature was ill suited for the hard life he must have lived in the past eight years, and probably for many years before that, if his mother was to be believed. He bore the becalmed demeanor of a man who had learned to live with being the last hope of three distressed women.

It was Haydon's good fortune that Phan moved slowly. His relaxed saunter made it easier for Haydon to keep Phan in sight and also gave him more time to watch for the others whom he knew would be waiting for him.

A couple of blocks from the car, Phan surprised Haydon by suddenly turning in to a side street. Haydon felt a momentary chill until he reminded himself that selecting Phan had been a random occurrence and the Vietnamese couldn't possibly be in the pay of anyone but Haydon himself. He followed Phan half a block into the side street until the young man entered a small shop. Haydon crossed to the opposite side and read the name: LIBROS DINH. A Vietnamese bookstore. The only one, surely, in Guatemala, if not in all of Central America.

Haydon stepped into a bakery, bought a wedge of cinnamon bread, and watched the bookstore. The most telling moment would be when Phan got into the car and drove away. It would be then that the people watching his car would have to make some quick decisions. More than likely they would follow the car. And how would they do it without giving themselves away to competing surveillants? It had the makings of a Keystone Kops skit. If Haydon were in the right position, he should be able to benefit from the spate of activity.

Phan surprised Haydon again. He emerged from the bookstore smoking a cigarette and in the company of a young Asian woman. They were smiling and talking, and Phan was slightly more animated than he had been before, using the cigarette to give himself a more self-assured and worldly manner. The young woman was rather dainty and once or twice touched Phan's arm when she spoke to him. It was a mutual flirtation.

Haydon followed them back to the main street where Phan dutifully headed for Haydon's car once again. Haydon followed them from the opposite side of the street, watching them through the throngs of people and over the tops of the bumper-to-bumper traffic, through the boiling haze of diesel fumes.

Phan and the girl made their way down the block. Haydon had parked on a busy section of the street with a pharmacy and photocopying store nearby. The signs of all the stores hanging over the sidewalks added to the crowded, bazaarlike atmosphere, and now five or six young men wanting to buy American dollars at an inflated exchange rate were openly and aggressively hawking their illegal bargains on the sidewalk, yelling out their rates to the bumper-to-bumper vehicles, sometimes stepping out into the street to shout into the windows of cars stalled in traffic. This sideshow ambience circulated around Haydon's car itself and was entirely ignored by Phan and the young woman.

Phan opened the passenger door with the key Haydon had given him and helped the young woman into the car, which was something of a tight squeeze because of the high sidewalks at that point in the street. After he got her inside, Phan went around the front of the car, pushed his way past a yelling money changer who was standing between the bumpers of the cars waving a fistful of quetzals. The girl leaned across and opened the door for him from the inside, and, pausing for a bus belching clouds of oily diesel smoke to pass, Phan swung open the door and quickly got in.

Haydon wondered what Phan had told the girl he was doing. He wondered what they were saying now and wondered if he was witnessing the stolen moments and tender pleasures of a man who had lived too few of them, fewer than most men were allowed by whatever or whomever it was that allocated such things in any man's life. He wondered what Phan was feeling.

The explosion was stunning.

The initial force of its shock killed everyone within twenty meters of the car who did not have the quirky luck to be protected from the direct blast, and knocked down people half a block away. The ball of fire that rolled up from Haydon's car engulfed the front of the closest stores and set afire people who had managed to survive the blast itself.

In the chaos of the aftermath, images of individual suffering remained with Haydon as though he had possessed them always, as though he had been born with the memory of them already planted in his psyche: the two teenaged girls standing next to him who had been knocked down by the ragged left half of one of the young money changers, the folded multicolored quetzals still in his fingers; the little street urchin draped over the horizontal arm of an old-fashioned streetlamp half a block away, one leg thrown backward over his head like a marionette's; the old woman who sold fruit slices from a two-wheeled cart, and whose small white skull had been completely and surgically skinned in an instant by the flying glass; the Indian child whose charred and flaming little body, arms and legs straight out, had cartwheeled and bounced across the hoods of cars like a macabre carnival effigy.

Even before the heat from the blast had begun to fade from his face like the passing of a foul, hot breath, it occurred to Haydon that Phan's sad little *amourette* would now remain a secret, the first bit of luck that the young man had had, perhaps, in all of his short, drab life.

261

Chapter 36

Haydon's instinct for survival took advantage of the chaos. If anyone
had spotted him in his approach, they were surely distracted by the
explosion and its Dantesque aftermath. Amid the screams and flames and
horns and sirens and shoving, panicked crowds surging away from—and
then back toward—the inferno and horror, Haydon had made his way
eastward through the narrow streets filled with streams of wide-eyed,
confused men and women going toward the explosion, drawn toward the

catastrophe by that inner magnet in human nature that lures the curious individual to the very bosom of calamity.

He stopped once, briefly, to vomit into the gutter and then moved on. It wasn't only the slaughter that made him weak-kneed. He could no longer believe himself to be an outsider to this endemic violence, no matter how he tried to view it or rationalize it. He had become an integral part of it, of this particular series of violent events, and if he suddenly were to cease to exist, he was sure it would be diminished in some proportional degree by his absence. The hell of Guatemala's violence stuck to you like napalm if you were foolish enough to let yourself be caught in the path of its fire. And he had done exactly that, with a degree of naïveté that was astonishing.

He thought of Fossler. If he was in fact dead, Haydon was certain he knew how Fossler had felt in his last moments. Both of them were veteran investigators, but it hadn't helped them avoid the surprise of being caught up in Guatemala's easy brutality. They were used to violence being in *opposition* to society, not in step with it. Here the lack of civil order provided no deterrent to spontaneous savagery. Haydon cursed his stupidity and cursed the nausea that came with having needlessly caused another person's death.

Turning to look back the way he had come, he saw a huge dark plume of smoke rolling up over the tops of the buildings. Sirens whined in the narrow, clogged streets. He turned away and continued on, the only person within blocks going in the opposite direction from the explosion.

Haydon started looking for a telephone. In the next block he spotted a parking lot with a little wooden shack for a ticket office at its entrance. He hurried to the office and found an old man listening to an evangelistic radio program. He held up a one dollar bill and asked if he could use the telephone. The old man snatched the bill, unhooked the telephone from the wall and handed the receiver to Haydon. *"¿Qué número?"* he asked, putting his finger up to whirl the circular dial. Haydon gave him the number of the American embassy.

He asked for Pittner, gave his name, and then waited on the hot cement skirt of the parking lot. The sun radiated off what was left of the asphalt in the parking lot and off the dusty cars jammed in tight little rows. The bad taste of vomit lingered in his mouth, and he spat out into the street, his head beginning to throb, his shoulders as tight as guy wires.

263

A secretary answered, and Haydon got through her to a man and then, soon, Pittner was on the telephone.

"I've got to talk to you," Haydon said.

"Okay," Pittner said. "You want to come over now? I'm . . ."

"No. I want to talk where we talked the other night."

"Okay," Pittner said. "When?"

"Right now."

"Okay." Pittner was not a colorful conversationalist. "It'll take me fifteen minutes," he said.

"I'll be there."

Haydon gave the telephone back to the old man and stepped out into the street. He had to wait only a few moments before waving down an aging Chevrolet with a broken plastic taxi sign on top. The car careened to Haydon's side of the street and shuddered to a stop.

Haydon paid little attention to what was happening outside the dust-glazed windows, noting only the big landmarks, the huge soccer stadium of Olympic City to their right just before crossing into Zona 10, then the medieval monstrosity of the Campo de Marte military complex, the military hospital, the Herrera Llerandi hospital on 6a avenida, where the Americans and wealthy ladinos could consult American-trained doctors, and then he lost track even of the landmarks, his mind's eye watching the two teenagers knocked over by the half body of the money changer, until the taxi began to slow at the address Haydon had given.

He got out on the busy avenida, paid the driver and then waited on the sidewalk under a jacaranda. He wondered if Pittner was ahead of him or behind him and finally decided he was ahead of him since Haydon had been twice as far away. When there was a break in traffic, he crossed the dusty street and headed into the smaller streets in the wooded neighborhoods above the Río Negro. He remembered precisely how to get to Pittner's. It wasn't much of a walk. The neighborhood was pleasant, even though most of the living took place behind the high walls covered in *moneda* vines. Still, the sidewalks under a gallery of *amate* trees wound gracefully and sloped gently providing pleasant glimpses of the Vista Hermosa districts across the ravine. The heat of the day was building steadily, making Haydon even more aware of his still queasy stomach.

Then he was across from Pittner's place; two unassuming stucco pillars flanked a gravel drive that disappeared around a curve of underbrush. Haydon looked at the gate from a distance. He saw no electronics, nothing obvious, anyway. If Pittner had an electronic security system, someone had gone to a lot of trouble to conceal it. There were no cars along the street, not even the obligatory pair of radio men. Pittner seemed sure enough of himself to manage to live without the high-tech spookery and personal security trappings that would have attracted attention. Or maybe there were other reasons no one else was there.

Haydon crossed the lane to Pittner's gate and entered the gravel drive, his feet crunching every step of the way to the front door. Pittner's car was already there. In the daylight, Haydon could see the house was considerably less grand than Janet's. It was, like Pittner, a little disheveled in a well-dressed sort of way. The stucco wall in front was crazed and mildew stained. There were flowers, but they had received no recent attention and were rather past their prime, hanging on because no one had bothered to clip them.

The weathered wooden door set into the front wall was standing open, and Haydon walked into a breezeway that went on through to the inner courtyard.

"Come on in," he heard Pittner say. Haydon turned in to a modest living room, and across the obliquely lighted space he saw Pittner in a kitchen adjacent to the dining room surrounded by windows where they had had dinner together. "I'm making a drink," Pittner said as Haydon approached him. "I'm drinking lunch." He looked up. "Want something?"

"A Coke or Pepsi, something like that."

"Okay." Pittner looked at Haydon. "You all right?"

Haydon nodded, loosening his tie and sitting down at the dining room table, facing the windows that overlooked the palms at the end of the property and the ravine beyond. In a moment Pittner came over to the table, put the soft drink in front of Haydon with a glass of ice, and sat down at the end of the table to Haydon's left. He was drinking his amber bourbon again, one ice cube. "What's the matter?"

"Who did it?" Haydon asked, pouring Coke into his glass.

Pittner said nothing, his heavy-lidded eyes, rather red rimmed today, regarding Haydon without giving anything away. He sipped his drink, swirled the single cube of ice, sipped the drink, obviously trying to decide how to handle this. Something told Haydon that Pittner was furious, but the man was sitting on it, which after all was part of his business, part of what he did for a living, swallowing his anger and frustration, keeping his own counsel. It was what was expected of him.

"We heard that John Baine has been picked up," Pittner said. "You don't know anything about that, do you?"

Haydon thought about the kid Borrayo had shot in the face. "Apparently it was the DIC," Haydon said. "He's in Pavón. Not in the regular part . . . Azcona's got clandestine cells there."

Pittner stared at Haydon. "How in God's name do you know that?"

Haydon explained about Borrayo. He explained about the meeting with Baine, about Borrayo killing the kid. About Vera Beatriz Azcona de Sandoval. About Lena's involvement. He didn't worry about Pittner burning him. Whatever they did about Baine, however they handled it, Haydon knew they would do it in such a way that they would keep him out of it.

"I think you've done a worse job with Lena than you'd led me to believe," Haydon said. He had taken several sips of his Coke, dampening the aftertaste of vomit. He wanted this out front immediately. "Either you recruited her without knowing about her interest in the kidnapping business, or you knew and used her in a situation that was way out of line with her experience. In either case it seems inept." He looked at Pittner. "But it only 'seems' inept, doesn't it."

Pittner had reassumed his mute role, his eyes seemed too tired even to react in a superficial way.

"Baine emphasized that she was insistent that they not go to the embassy with this kidnapping story," Haydon said with only partial honesty. "He said she would let the whole thing go if she had to go through the embassy. He didn't know, of course, that Lena was working for you. Did she in fact come to you with it? Did you know what she was doing?"

Pittner had made short work of most of his bourbon, and now it was only just covering the top of the ice cube. The two men were looking at each other, and Haydon thought how fatigued Pittner looked.

"You know," Pittner said, "your friend disappeared doing just what you've been doing. I don't know how the hell you missed the car deal just now."

Haydon told him. Pittner's face was emotionless. "You know who did it?" Haydon said.

"We don't know," Pittner shook his head. "We assume . . . Azcona, that whole operation."

"The whole operation?"

Pittner nodded once and took some more bourbon. "The DIC and the generals." Pittner sat back in his chair, his suit coat falling open to show the butt of the 10mm that had become the weapon of choice now among people in the know. He crossed his legs, his arm out, holding the glass of whiskey with which he was making damp interlocking circles on the wooden table, thinking.

"It's not just this seedy deal with the kids," Pittner said, weary of the whole subject. "The generals and their assorted relatives are into everything: smuggling pre-Colombian artifacts and mahogany out of the Petén; poppies in the northwestern highlands, fincas and food-processing operations in the Northern Transversal Strip where the Indians work for starvation wages on the same land the army took away from them in an ostensible effort to rid the highlands of guerrillas, arms trafficking, drug trafficking, influence peddling, things we haven't heard of or even imagined. All of these are sorry enterprises that involve every kind of human nastiness. It's organized in a way, and in a way it isn't. These people are bad about not sticking to a plan. If an organizational situation does develop, it's often disrupted by some lower-echelon individuals who toss their flimsy loyalties out the window like a banana peel as soon as they see a way to get an extra-big cut for themselves by screwing the screwers. It's endless, I mean absolutely endless.

"We try to keep up with all this as much as possible and use it to our advantage whenever we can and whenever we think it's necessary and to whatever design the State Department thinks is proper. No secret in that."

Pittner finished off his bourbon and set down the glass. For a minute he lightly tapped his fingernails on the empty glass, the sound thin and fragile and empty.

"It's a fluid situation," he continued. "Always. Right now Azcona's star is ascending in the army and in politics. Two elements that are not always in concert except when the army comes down hard and bullies the politicos into subjection." Pittner paused, seeming to want to put his words together carefully. He looked away to the windows overlooking the Río Negro. "We're co-opting Azcona . . . slowly. We think he's going to be around for a long time."

Enough said. Lena had developed a social conscience at the wrong time and in the wrong place.

"Azcona knows he's being courted by the powerful U.S. State Department," Haydon said. "He sees big possibilities."

"That's right," Pittner nodded. "You can imagine the rest of it too.

He doesn't want some *gringo* do-gooder screwing up his chances by stirring up bad press about his sister's kidnapping sideshow. They don't have to worry about the niceties of legal prohibitions down here. Of course Azcona is nowhere near the dirty work. If you pressed him about the death threats Lena had been receiving"—this was the first time Pittner had mentioned the death threats—"if you pressed him about the disappearance of Jim Fossler, about Baine's secret arrest, about the car bomb . . ." Pittner shrugged. "He would agree that many 'delinquent elements' in his country are out of control. The country needs a strong arm to keep the peace, the country needs . . . Yes, General Azcona, but what about these things in particular, we want them investigated. Of course, absolutely. Consider it done. We will begin an investigation immediately." Pittner shook his head and sighed wearily. "In Guatemala 'investigation' is a synonym for 'limbo.' Here it means the same thing as it does in the States when they say they're going to 'conduct a study' of a certain situation. Read: sweep it under the rug, hope people will forget about it, hope that something else sensational will come along in the meantime to distract the public interest. Of course here, if you're the army, you don't need the public to be distracted. You just tell them to piss off. And that's pretty well what they'll tell our State Department too."

None of this was new, and for an instant Haydon wondered why the State Department even bothered. But of course he knew why. For all its obvious poverty, Central America had an abundance of natural resources that were seldom discussed in the newspapers because they have to do with commerce and commerce for the most part was boring, even though it drove the politics that everyone found so exciting and controversial. The closest the American public ever got to understanding the relationship between commerce and politics was when it had to do with oil. While coffee and bananas and cotton and sugar may not be a glamorous target for the media, these interests drove Guatemalan politics, and because the United States consumed ever-increasing quantities of these commodities, they were billion-dollar businesses, and that kind of money was worth killing people for . . . other people.

Haydon looked at the tiny bubbles riding the ice cubes in his glass of Coke. Outside the midday sun was whitening the light that fell on the ravines of the Río Negro, washing the dark green of the palms in a laser brightness.

"I understand about the politics," Haydon said. "What I don't understand is why Lena didn't come to you about this."

Pittner nodded. "She probably knew I couldn't do anything about it."

"Or wouldn't."

Pittner closed his eyes as though shrugging. "It's six of one and half a dozen of the other. Vera Beatriz knew something was brewing. Her brother's DIC had picked up on Lena, knew what she was doing. To tell you the truth, they were satisfied with threatening her in various ways, messing with her, because they didn't think anyone would listen to her. Then she went to John Baine. Then she went home. That probably saved her life. But then she came back and Baine was onto her like a lamprey. He smelled 'big story.' And he was right."

"You mean you knew she was looking into the kidnapping story before she left the first time?"

"Oh, sure," Pittner said. "We knew." He stood and went into the kitchen to refill his glass. Haydon listened to him putting in the ice and then the bourbon. It was a comfortable sound. When he came back the tall glass was fuller than the first time, and he was stirring the ice with his finger. He sat down again and pursed his lips, looking at Haydon with lazy, exhausted eyes that were prepared not to be disturbed by anything.

"But you recruited her anyway."

Pittner nodded. "Yeah," he said. "I did."

Haydon looked at him. Pittner was savoring a mouthful of bourbon, not yet cold from the ice, his eyes on the table in front of him. He had made a decision and was about to commit himself.

Chapter 37

Pittner studied Haydon, his rumpled suit and baggy eyes providing a misleading image of a man whose mind, in fact, was as ordered as his appearance was discomposed.

"I'm going to have you expelled from Guatemala," Pittner said in such a tone and manner that if you didn't know the meaning of the words you would miss the impact of the message. Inflection and content had no relationship at all. "Interfering in internal politics, pissing in the boots of the generals, consorting with the guerrillas . . ."

They were only a couple of chairs apart, and Haydon was looking into Pittner's reddened eyes. He didn't know if their rawness had to do more with the lack of sleep or with the whiskey, but as far as Pittner's words were concerned, Haydon was pretty sure he was blowing smoke. The business about the guerrillas had to be a wild guess.

". . . interfering with State Department policies . . ."

Haydon said nothing.

". . . like 'operational climate' . . ."

"What is it you want?" Haydon asked in the same tone.

"Everything you've got."

"Regarding what?"

"Regarding everything you've done since you got here," Pittner said without enthusiasm.

"Then you'd better start processing the papers," Haydon said. "But when I get back to the States, I'm going to ask more questions than you're going to be comfortable with me asking. As I told you before, I don't believe in 'larger considerations.' I don't give a damn about State Department policies versus Jim Fossler's life or Lena Muller's life. It's been my experience over the years that the people who always want to talk about 'larger considerations' happen not to be the people whose lives are being disrupted so that those considerations can be realized. They make that kind of argument to justify why somebody *else* has lost their life or is going to lose their life—it's always somebody *else* doing the dying. I don't have any patience with that kind of brave language."

Pittner sat patiently a moment after Haydon stopped, his lazy eyes resting on Haydon with an inscrutable calm. Haydon had been careful to keep his voice as monotonously even as Pittner's. If Pittner's stomach was as tangled as his, Haydon thought, it was an odd display of twentieth-century dueling. Grown men doing what grown men have to do in the age of dispassion. Pittner decided to make another run at it.

"Cage is jerking you around," he said.

"And you're not?"

"He's just barely in control, if he is in control."

"You work with him."

"I have to."

"So do I. No one else has been so accommodating."

"Yeah, he's accommodating," Pittner said.

"Did you have someone following me this morning too?" Haydon asked bluntly.

271

Pittner nodded.

"What happened?"

"Apparently there was a surveillance traffic jam on 18 calle. Everybody spotted everybody else. Where'd you go?"

"When did you find out that the woman in the morgue wasn't Lena?" Haydon asked, deliberately disrupting continuity.

Pittner looked away, out toward the ravine past the palms. "If I had seen her I would have known," he said. "I didn't go to the morgue." Haydon studied Pittner's profile and realized that he looked older from this angle, almost like another man. "For one reason or another our ID people were tied up and didn't get by there as soon as we'd wanted . . . I found out last night."

He turned back and sipped at the bourbon. He was giving something a good deal of thought. Haydon couldn't have articulated what it was that he sensed had changed about Pittner, but something had changed even in the last few moments. He had lost his relish for doing what he did best.

"Everything has a life span, Haydon," Pittner said, and then slowly sipped from his glass, relishing the sweet whiskey in the precise, savoring manner in which men who loved their drink too much seemed to do. "Human lives, relationships, arrangements, grudges, obligations. Things run their course."

He set the glass down carefully in roughly the same place he had been putting it during their conversation. The sweat from the glass was making whitish rings on the polished surface of the wooden tabletop, but Pittner didn't put a napkin or a coaster under it. If you had mentioned it to him he wouldn't have known what you were talking about until you pointed it out. The finish on the furniture was a long way from anything that Bennett Pittner cared about.

272

"Years ago Cage and I were pretty close," Pittner continued. "He always was a bastard, but back then he was a likeable bastard. He had an undeniable joie de vivre, kind of a wholehearted screw-it-all way of treating the world that you had to admire. Not many people have the guts to do that, you know, just take all you can get, unabashedly self-serving." He thought a moment. "On the other hand, maybe it was only because I was young that I could tolerate him, that I thought that there was anything acceptable in him at all. But, of course, things changed. I changed, the business changed, the world changed. Everything changed except Cage. Actually, he changed too, only he didn't believe it. He didn't want to change, and he didn't understand that it was impossible not to. Eventually he was just a caricature of himself, himself in broad strokes."

Pittner stared at the glass of bourbon on the table.

"He and Janet had an affair," he said. "Quite a wild fling. They think I don't know anything about it. At least Janet thinks that; Cage probably doesn't give a damn one way or the other. I suppose it was inevitable. They're so much alike, their personalities. Spontaneous, headlong. But it was hard for me to handle it. It was like I was hyperventilating emotionally. I had to take long, deep breaths. I had to concentrate. It was hell."

He cleared his throat. "About Lena," he said. "I was sleeping with her."

Haydon shouldn't have been surprised, but he was. It occurred to him that he was losing his ability to anticipate. He was beginning to feel like an old fighter whose aging arms were no longer allowing him to keep his guard up. He was taking too many blows to the head. Haydon remembered the crickets that filled the air with their pulsing chirruping when he had been here the night before. Now it was the deeper rasping of cicadas.

"I'm not going to 'confess,' " Pittner said reassuringly. "I'm just telling you how it was. Nothing you haven't heard or seen before. Common stuff. That's why I had the guys go to Janet's and scoop up everything in her room and bring it to me. I'd never put anything in writing, but I didn't know if Lena kept a diary or what. I've been going through it myself. I haven't found anything." He stopped and took some bourbon. "Maybe there isn't anything." The thought seemed disappointing to him.

It was hard to tell about Pittner. He was forthrightly laying out his affair, candidly admitting it was a common middle-aged-man-and-younger-woman story. He wasn't going to pretend there was anything special about it simply because it had happened to him instead of one of the countless other middle-aged men they had seen it happen to during their years of snooping into people's often transparent and superficial lives. But Haydon guessed that Pittner's offhanded dismissal of his story gave the lie to the importance of it to him. After what Pittner had been through with Janet, it was understandable that he would have found Lena Muller a welcome refuge. The serious question was why Lena had done it. It was a depressing question, too, because the immediate implica-

273

tion was that she had not had the man for the sake of the man. Sadly, it was not believable that she would have. More than likely she had thought it would get her something. Pittner knew that.

"I came to my senses a little late," Pittner said. "I had night sweats over it. I don't know what she was after, but I'm reasonably sure she never got it. Even when I was wild after her, I never allowed a compromising circumstance. Never in my office. Never drunk with her. Never 'talked.' She never drew me out; I don't even remember her ever having tried."

He reached for the glass, picked it up from its puddle of condensation, drank, and returned it to the puddle.

"I asked myself about that later," Pittner mused, more to himself than to Haydon. "What the hell kind of a man would have an affair with a woman like her and never once be induced to abandon himself to his emotions, never once go crazy, step right up to the edge with her and jump. God. I watched my back every second, thinking: honey trap, honey trap, honey trap. I was so damned guarded about the whole affair that I'm surprised I ever managed to make it with her. But I did, and I kept on, night after night."

He was silent a moment. "I don't know why she did it. I'm honest enough with myself to be suspicious. But you know what haunts me? What if, goddamn it, what if . . . she just liked me? I've been in this miserable business so long I don't even know if I'd recognize an honest emotion if I encountered it. Lena Muller may have been a colossal mistake," he said, shaking his head at the whole mad affair, "but I'll be damned if I understand, even yet, just exactly what kind of a mistake she was."

He stopped and looked out the windows to Haydon's right, out to the courtyard. There was a dead fountain in its center, a common sign of dereliction in Guatemala, but unlike many others which had been converted to flower beds or wells for trees, Pittner's fountain was simply empty. The rainy seasons put water in it, and then the dry seasons caused the water to stagnate and then evaporate and eventually disappear, leaving behind blackened and scaling algae. The joints in the stones in the courtyard were punctuated with tufts of dried grass.

"This surprise you, Haydon?"

Haydon nodded. "Yes, it does."

"But . . . ?"

Haydon hesitated. "There were rumors about her . . . with a number of men."

"Ah." Pittner understood, his eyes lingering on the sunbaked courtyard. "You've covered a lot of ground. Well, I was aware of the rumors," he said, sighing. "I had them checked out. It was for personal reasons, mostly, but I justified it professionally, too, since I was running her. As best we could determine it was mostly rumor. She had a lot of guys panting after her. Some of them had overactive imaginations, locker-room wishful thinking. She had had a few relationships, but nothing that you would consider promiscuous."

Something wasn't meshing here, but Haydon left it alone. Janet said Lena was fairly discreet, didn't date much, didn't talk about it at all. Baine, hammered to shit and hurting, testified to a girl of a different nature. He even claimed to have experienced her body-for-hire techniques firsthand. Either Baine was rashly quoting trashy gossip for credible rumor with a grain of truth to consider, or he was seriously deluding himself about what he actually had experienced. And Dr. Grajeda had found her an elusive siren. A young woman, he hinted, who had a troubled soul. And then he had traded a year of his life for her. Lena Muller seemed to have inspired strong and conflicting emotions.

"Do you know where she is?" Pittner asked.

Haydon shook his head.

Pittner didn't believe him, but he didn't ask him again. He wasn't finished talking, wasn't finished coming straight from the gut, as though it were some kind of emotional self-flagellation; every time he mentioned her name or called up a mental image of her, it cut to the quick. But he would rather bleed than not think of her at all.

"She didn't know, of course, at first, that she was in danger," Pittner said. "I discovered it just about the time our affair began. Everything at once. That's the way it is, more often than not. I got everything I could on her, what the DIC knew, what the G-2 knew. After a while every breath I took was Lena Muller. I smelled her in my dreams."

He picked up the sweaty drink again and held it to his temple, ran the cold glass across his forehead, closing his eyes momentarily. Then he set it on the table once more where the growing puddle was spreading with every passing minute.

"When she returned from Houston, the G-2 started watching her the moment she landed at the airport," he continued. "And we picked up

275

their hit at the same time. That's why I recruited her. It was an excuse to keep close tabs on her. I don't know what I thought was going to be the upshot of all this. Actually I didn't give it any thought. That's how strung out on her I'd gotten. I was mainlining this girl.

"Keeping tabs on her turned out to be more than I'd bargained for. I had to do it by the book. I turned her over to one of the case officers, and before long she was bringing in her stuff. I told you the other night how it went. She was sharp, didn't take her long to learn to do it the right way." He shook his head. "But she didn't know enough. In no time at all the guy handling her picked up her affair with Cage. That hit me like an actual blow to the head and had the same effect. Sobering."

Haydon thought of his conversations with Cage. He had never hinted at this. For all his crass references to Janet and Pittner, even his perfunctory disregard for Lita, he had never said anything disrespectful about Lena. In fact, he had professed only admiration. Again, Haydon should have seen it coming.

"I told you earlier, I came to my senses a little late," Pittner continued. "I'd made the classic mistake. It could've been the end of my career. Still could be. You got here just as all of this was coming down. The point is, it's a mess. Different agendas, a multitude of subtexts."

Pittner turned in his chair, one elbow on the table as he crossed his legs.

"Unless you can make it a little clearer to me what in the hell it is you want," he said, his head bent a little, not looking at Haydon, "I'll get you booted out. Right now you're gasoline on the fire; I'm not going to sit here and watch you blow it all to hell."

"Fair enough," Haydon said. "I want to talk to Lena. I owe it to her mother. If she wants to go home, I'll arrange it. Otherwise, it's none of my business. But before I leave I want to find out what happened to Jim Fossler. He was a personal friend."

Haydon winced at his own use of the past tense.

"This country's full of personal friends who've disappeared," Pittner said wearily. "Jesus Christ." He was still sitting with his head bent, his eyes unfocused, his thoughts hidden behind a veil of alcohol and a learned suspicion that had shaped his life. "Regardless of my personal involvement with Lena," he said finally, "what I've got here is an agent in trouble. That's the way I've got to look at it. Now that's different from an officer in trouble. She's hired help. Technically. But I've known more than a few officers who have stuck their necks out for their agents.

Despite what the rule book says, a certain amount of emotional invest-
ment is inevitable when you're working human intelligence. That's the
definition. The point is, I'm obligated to get her out of trouble, for good
reasons other than the personal ones. If it turns out that she wrecks my
career when this is all over"—he shook his head—"well, hell, I won't be
surprised."

"You asked me a while ago if I knew where she is—you know, don't
you," Haydon said.

"We have an idea," Pittner looked up. "Listen," he said. "The only
way this is going to work is for you to cooperate with me. Otherwise,
you're out. That's the way it's got to be. I can't have you out there on
your own. It'd be stupid of me. I thought maybe it would work . . .
but . . ."

Haydon understood Pittner's position, and he knew Pittner could,
and would, do what he said.

"Okay," Haydon agreed. "But I want Fossler tied to this . . . as a
package."

Pittner studied Haydon and then nodded.

"It's a package?" Haydon insisted.

"Yeah," Pittner said. "Agreed."

They sat there for another hour and a half. Haydon finished his
Coke, but Pittner never touched another drop of bourbon. Haydon
started with Borrayo's departure from the alley in Colonia Santa Isabel.
He told Pittner about Lita picking him up and taking him to Cage's safe
house (he avoided identifying Avenida Elena), about Cage's plan to "use"
Haydon to find Lena but not telling Haydon the details of his plan, of
going home to find Janet waiting for him in the courtyard of the Residencial Reforma with the "message from Lena," about being approached the next morning by a messenger from Dr. Grajeda (he didn't
reveal Salviati's name or profession), about his trip to 18 calle and the
meeting with Grajeda (and about the death of Cage's man), and about his
subsequent use of the luckless and moonstruck Phan.

By the time Haydon had finished his story he had captured Pittner's
full attention, though Pittner lounged with his chin in his hand, his
elbow propped on the table as though he hadn't an ounce of strength left.
His eyes, which Haydon had come to realize were more indicative of his
mood than his languid posture, were unblinking, entirely absorbed.

Pittner stirred himself and sat up in his chair. "I've got to hand it to
you, Haydon, that's a lot of work. And a lot of dumb luck," he added. As

277

had happened at dinner the night before, Pittner seemed suddenly to have grown disheveled without having done anything to cause it. Haydon only now noticed the dingy condition of his shirt, the front displaying its wrinkles despite the suit coat and tie, the flabby collar showing a lumpy rib underneath it where the tie did not lie flat. Was it put on in a hurry, or inattentively? Pittner's eyes drifted away from Haydon and found another subject somewhere in the sunbaked court-yard beyond the windows.

"We didn't know," he said without moving his eyes from the court-yard, almost as if he were thinking out loud. "About the clandestine cells in Pavón. I'm not surprised by that; they move them all the time, have them everywhere. But it's good to know. We like to know." He sighed. "Cage," he said, his head shaking almost imperceptibly. "Damn, he's really pushing it. It's like when you get gangrene in your leg or some-where. How the hell do you get rid of it without destroying a part of your own body. He's going to make this hard for us . . . he wants her . . . but, you know, it looks like it's something we could cooperate on, doesn't it. I mean, why are we in competition on this? I don't see the sense in it."

He was ticking down the list of options.

"Janet . . . Janet's an interesting possibility. That note, it could have been from the G-2. You're learning too much too fast, and they see a real threat. The letter, the bomb, whatever it takes. Grajeda. The guerrillas. There's always one chronic problem with guerrillas—worldwide—and that's cooperation. They usually have one thing in common: hatred for the existing power structure . . . sometimes justified. But they're splin-tered . . . each little group is pissed off in a different way. Factionalism. Grajeda knows all this. He grew up on it. What he didn't tell you was that his little agreement was a gamble at best. He can't guarantee shit . . . maybe he can with this faction or that faction, but . . . it's just a goddamn mess."

"You think they're going to use her as a bargaining chip," Haydon said.

"They could, yeah. Azcona wants her; we want her. I don't know. Instability, unpredictability. We can be sure of that, and that's all." Pittner paused. "Look," he said, "I know I'm going to sound like Cage—which is not too surprising, I suppose—but I'm going to have to do some planning, check some things. Why don't you go back to the Residencial Reforma and stay there. It's . . . well, it's a 'known' location. You'll be

278

safe from Azcona there. But it's probably the only damn place you'll be safe. Understand?"

Haydon nodded.

Pittner stood. He seemed a little stiff, but only for a moment. "I'll take you back there," he said. "Stay there. Wait for me. I'm going to need you. If anything happens I ought to know about, call me." He gave Haydon a number. "That number will get straight to me. Come on, we'd better get going."

Chapter 38

He lay on the bed in his room and stared at the repoussé on the light fixture in the center of the high ceiling. After Pittner had dropped him off at the hotel he had gone straight to the dining room and forced himself to eat a large fruit salad. He hadn't wanted it, but he ate it because he knew he would regret it later if he didn't. Haydon was not one of those people who ate compulsively when they were stressed. In fact, it was just the opposite for him. All food lost its appeal, and he could skip two or three meals without any interest. However, several days of this would do strange things to his nerves, and he had learned he could stave off tension headaches with a steady diet of fruits.

So now he lay in the midafternoon heat, the heavy blue curtains once again pulled away from the windows and draped over the metal levers that held open the glass panes. His shoes and coat off, his tie loosened, Haydon surrendered to the scenes of the car bombing that he had been trying to avoid. Again and again he remembered that millisecond following the blast and before the obscuring debris and fire when he could see Phan and the girl sitting in the car like black manikins, still a millisecond away from realizing what had happened to them. Then, in the awful seconds afterward, the storm of fire and debris and cutting glass, the explosion flinging people, again, before they understood that they were victims. Those were the moments, dead moments in the psyche, when shock set in, nature's primitive defense against the too-horrible-to-live-with moments that were to follow. He thought of the mother and the wife and the sister-in-law and wondered how they would discover what had happened to their Phan. And he wondered who the girl was, and how her family or friends would learn of her obliteration.

Beginning with Jim Fossler's bloodied room, he reviewed the careless death he had witnessed within the last thirty-six hours. It was made all the more incredible when he reminded himself that it would make no difference whatsoever. In the past twenty years of Guatemala's history well over one hundred and fifty thousand people had been "disappeared" and assassinated and not one arrest and conviction had resulted. In a country of fewer than nine million people, the rate of assassination alone was roughly one thousand per year. In the United States, that rate would accumulate to over thirty thousand assassinations annually—for which no one ever would be arrested, year after year. This was a fact that could only be described as surreal. There were other descriptions for it, of course, all of them abominable and none of them mattering in the least, because there was no political will in Guatemala to stop the killing. It was a country whose last twenty years had been marked by a political depravity seldom matched in modern times.

Outside the traffic bolted in jerks and starts under the boulevard's towering cypresses and kept up a steady rumble that reverberated off the stucco walls of the room, and always, even in the stillness of the heat that seemed to squeeze the oxygen out of the air, he could smell the acrid effluent of gasoline engines.

Haydon turned over on his side. He thought of Nina and of the

281

sanity that framed her life. He wanted to be with her, to hold her in the still of the afternoon, to put his arms around her sane, reassuring body and pull her to him and feel her breathing steadily, reliably and smell her familiar fragrance that to his mind was as sweet as sachet. The temptation to turn over, pick up the telephone, and call her was almost irresistible; but he didn't do it. At this point, he simply didn't trust himself. The morning's horrors were on him like a dark pall, and he didn't want them to touch her.

Instead, he concentrated on the sounds outside. Could he hear anything besides the traffic? In the momentary lulls he could hear birds in the shrubs of the courtyard, and occasionally the conversational voices of people walking to their cars, and now and then the chink of flatware or dishes echoing up from the dining room. Footsteps on the marble steps, heels on the terrazzo floors . . . stopping outside his room. Haydon opened his eyes . . . he had closed them? He turned over on his back and looked at the door, his right arm reaching out toward the secretary beside the bed for the automatic.

There was a soft knock, a pause, another knock.

"Haydon. It's Janet." She sounded as if her face was pressed next to the door.

"Okay, just a second." He swung his legs over the side of the bed, bent over and stuck the gun between the mattresses. He stood and walked to the door and opened it.

Janet was standing there, her expression a mixture of expectant concern and conviction.

"Why didn't you call me?" She was wearing another sundress, sleeveless, powder blue with a long skirt. She smelled of something soft, a light and lingering fragrance, as though she had just stepped out of the shower. Janet was one of those women who seemed always fresh and clean.

"I was going to . . ."

He put his finger up to his lips. "Let me get this . . ." and he stepped over to the writing desk and got the room key and went back to and out the door, pulling it closed behind him. "Let's go out here," he said. They were only a few steps from a short corridor that led through an arched wrought-iron grille anchored to the stucco walls and out onto a veranda that overlooked the courtyard in front of the hotel. No one was there, and they went to one of the several sets of wicker furniture and sat down at a table with a tile top.

"I didn't call you because it didn't work out like I'd hoped," he began explaining. "There simply wasn't anything to tell you. There was nothing to say. I . . ."

"I've just had another visit from that child," Janet interrupted, reaching into a small, natural-leather clutch bag. She handed the note to Haydon without saying anything more, her eyes fixed on him. Haydon took it and unfolded the paper.

Janet . . . Get Haydon & meet me at the Cementerio General at 5:30 pm . . . follow the main avenue as far as it goes . . . turn right . . . follow the lane all the way to the back of the cemetery . . . wait. I'll find you . . . Important to trust only Haydon.

As with the first note there was no signature. Haydon looked at Janet. "Her handwriting?"

"Without a doubt."

Without a doubt. Haydon tried to think it through even as he spoke. "I've . . . I have reason to believe that she wouldn't contact you this way," Haydon said.

"You have reason to believe?"

"I do."

Janet nodded, only barely checking her anger.

"Someone's helping her," Haydon said. He hesitated and then went on. "They're helping her get out of the country."

Janet frowned.

"Helping her avoid the security forces. She . . . she and Baine have collected some incriminating evidence, documentation, about Azcona's involvement in a child-kidnapping operation. They wanted to go public with it, publish it. That's what brought all this down on them. Azcona found out. He wants the files; he wants them dead."

Janet was flabbergasted. *"General* Azcona?"

Haydon nodded. "Lena's been working on this a long time. You didn't know anything about it?"

Janet swallowed and shook her head, for once, speechless.

"I was contacted by the people helping her," Haydon went on. "At some point they want to turn her over to me, but they're holding her in strict security conditions. They claim she couldn't possibly have gotten the first note out without their knowledge. They're supposed to contact

283

me again, let me know when she'll be moved." He looked at the piece of paper he was holding. "But this isn't the way they would do it."

"How do you know?"

"I asked about the first note. They disavowed it."

"So that's where you went this morning, to see these people."

"Yes."

Janet's eyes searched Haydon's face. "She's all right?"

"They didn't mention anything otherwise."

"She has 'documents,' they say?"

Haydon nodded.

"With her?"

"I don't know."

"Are they going to see that the documents get published, these people?"

"I don't know."

Janet was pensive, turning her face away toward the boulevard, sitting on the edge of her cushioned chair, knees together, looking oddly prim and un-Janetlike. She was obviously discomfited, and as Haydon looked at her he felt the same way. He was uneasy with the fact that both notes expressed the demand that Janet trust only him. If Lena had indeed written the notes, where did she acquire this conviction that her trust should be vested solely in Haydon? If she hadn't written the notes, who had and why? The same people who wired the bomb to the ignition switch of his car? If someone was trying to lure him into a trap, why? He had nothing unless he had Lena, and all factions of this fiasco should know that.

"These people," Janet said. "You *know* you can trust them? Could you be wrong? Could they be wrong?"

284

Haydon slumped back in his chair and noticed that he had walked out of his room without his shoes. He thought of Grajeda. It was true, he believed him . . . he trusted him, but of course, he wanted to trust him. Grajeda was probably the only person in this whole mess with whom Haydon felt any real kinship. He felt immediately that he could understand Grajeda, the others he had to puzzle out. But could he trust him? Yes. The more important question was could Grajeda trust those in whom he had placed his trust? If Haydon believed Pittner's information, he doubted it.

"Well?"

Haydon looked at her. "Yes. I can trust my source, but I'm not sure he can trust his."

"Oh, Christ. Then—no—, the answer's no." She snatched the letter from Haydon's hands. "Goddamn it, I trust *my* source," she snapped, holding up the paper. "That child. This handwriting. Lena."

Haydon looked out from the balcony over the courtyard to the cypresses, taller than the surrounding villas, but challenged here and there by some of the more modern glass buildings that had sprung up along the boulevard like odd pieces of colored quartz that had fallen from the sky and were sticking upright out of the earth. A smudgy haze hung among the trees, discoloring the cobalt sky in the distance.

"You familiar with the cemetery?" he asked.

"Of course."

"You know what she's talking about, all the way to the end of the main avenue . . ."

"Yes."

Haydon looked at his watch. It was now two-fifteen. The note said to be at the cemetery at five-thirty. That was a good time, whether Lena had calculated it or not. The traffic on the way there would be at its worst, the best time to evade surveillants. Haydon was ticking off what he had to do . . . call Pittner . . . but he felt Janet's withering stare.

"You *are* going to go, aren't you?" she demanded abruptly. And then without waiting for an answer, "I'm going, by God."

Haydon had to hand it to Janet, as far as Lena was concerned she had been the only one with a straightforward desire to help her. It seemed that everyone else had ulterior motives: Lena, yes, but also . . . Janet had never expressed any interest in anything but helping Lena to safety. For all her craziness, she had the cleanest vision and the cleanest intentions: Lena was in trouble and needed Janet's help. That was it. Nothing to agonize over, nothing to calculate. She just wanted to do it.

285

Haydon nodded. "Yeah, I think we ought to go, but if you believe the note," he said, "then you ought to believe all of the note. You need to trust me and do it the way I think it ought to be done. You might not like it, but you need to do it."

Janet was listening. She looked cool in the shade of the balcony; she looked clean and far removed from the gritty realities of Guatemala. There was something about her that reminded Haydon of those crisp British colonists of another era for whom India and Africa were adventures that properly belonged to them. She had grown up in Guatemala, but she had not grown up Guatemalan. Despite her worldly knowledge of the country, there was no wisdom in it; she could assess the country and its people accurately, but without understanding; she could explain its history, but not its heart. There was a difference.

"I'm waiting," she said.

Haydon rubbed his face. The sun had moved well past the meridian, and the shade on the balcony had retreated to the edge of their feet and the stone balustrade had already gathered enough heat to begin throwing it off. The stultifying heat of Guatemala's *verano* had begun in earnest its daily worst.

"I want you to go alone," he said. "At the time designated in the note." He looked at his watch. "I'm going to go a couple of hours early."

"A couple of hours?"

"As soon as possible."

Her eyes searched his face again, and Haydon could almost see her mind working, catching up with him, anticipating him.

"Have you heard the news today . . . the car bombing?"

She nodded expectantly.

"That was my car." He explained briefly, cursorily, enough for her to understand the degree of complexity . . . and the seriousness of what she would be getting involved in. He wanted the gravity of the situation to dampen her enthusiasm and to sharpen her sixth sense. When he stopped, her eyes had lost their dancing impatience and her petulance had subsided. The more explanation she received, the more relaxed she became, as if the heart of her anger had been founded in what she believed was the patronizing attitude of Haydon and all the others who were keeping her in the dark.

286

"Assume your home is wired and any conversation there is being monitored," Haydon said. "Assume the same of the Land-Rover. Now that you've come here to meet me, you can also assume you're being followed. They want Lena; they want the documents. They think I'm going to lead them to her. That's what this is all about."

"I'm not sure I can do this," she said suddenly. She looked down at her hands in her lap where she was folding and unfolding the piece of paper. "It's . . . I'm not afraid," she said. "I'm really not. But I'm not sure I can avoid being followed. I'd never forgive myself for doing that, for leading them to her . . . I just . . ."

"You don't have to go," Haydon said. "If you don't show, I don't believe they'll be surprised."

She didn't say anything for a moment, then she jerked her head up. "Do you need me to do it?"

"You don't have to do it."

"I mean, will the goddamn thing go better if I help, or not?"

Haydon looked at her. "If you don't lose your nerve, it would be best if you came along. It could make it easier for me. But if you're not sure of that, if you're not sure of yourself and you get rattled and lose your head, it could end disastrously."

Janet rolled her eyes and started to put the note in her bag.

"Wait a minute," Haydon said. He reached out and took the note from her fingers. There was a book of matches inside an ashtray on the wicker table, and he tore out one of the matches and lighted the piece of paper and held it so that the ashes fell into the ashtray. The flames were almost invisible in the sunlight, and the paper seemed magically to turn brown and then quickly black.

"Okay," Janet said, watching the paper burn. "Just tell me what in the hell you want me to do."

Chapter 39

To get a taxi Haydon walked out onto the boulevard and went several blocks toward the center of town, near the Plazuela Reina Barrios where he stopped by a eucalyptus tree on a corner. There was a monument there and a triangular intersection where another avenue came in perpendicular to the boulevard. Taxis were everywhere, but he had to stop three before he found a driver who wanted his fare. As they zipped up to the curb and stopped, he told each of them the same thing: he was being followed and he wanted to get away from the people who were following him. There was no danger of gunfire. He would pay a month's wages for the ride.

The first driver swore and roared away into the traffic. The second driver said, "No-no-no-no," shook his head and raised both hands in a surrendering gesture and pulled away from the curb while Haydon was still talking. The third driver was young, which made a difference. Still he listened to every word Haydon said, the import of it registering on his face. When he heard the amount of money Haydon would pay, he checked his rearview mirror and jerked his head toward the backseat. Haydon crawled in.

They had to wait on the traffic before they could get into the stream of cars.

"I want to go to the Cementerio General," Haydon said as the young man watched the traffic in his mirror. "But I don't want anyone following me when I get there. I decide when it's okay. I don't care how long it takes."

The young man never said a word. The break in traffic came, but he still didn't move, watching his mirror. Haydon said nothing. When the next surge of traffic was bearing down on them, the young man gunned his engine and shot out in front, roared across to the next lane, straight into the approaching traffic that was merging into the angle of the triangle that would take them into the boulevard headed west. His breach into the oncoming traffic caused an accident immediately. Tires screamed, and Haydon heard the fenders crunching as the driver, elbows pumping like pistons as he fought the steering wheel, fought the cab into a whiplashing alignment with the traffic heading west. He pushed the car past traffic, staying to the outside lane until they were near the Parque Centro América, and then he shot across to the inside lane, again causing a long whining scream of tires as cars slid sideways and drivers fought their own steering wheels to avoid collisions. Then they were speeding down beside the park, going south in the inside lane, a last-minute suicidal switch to the outside lane and into the short, poor streets of Zona 8, where the driver pulled into a driveway with a high wall and an open heavy wooden gate. The turn into the drive was reckless, and the left rear fender of the car caught a tree near the curb, but the driver hardly noticed and didn't seem to care. Despite the mad ride his face never changed. Immediately he was out of the car, running back to the gates, and before the dust drifting into the windows had settled, the gates were closed and the young man was walking back to the car.

289

The driver's door was still open, and he sat down behind the wheel, his feet outside on the gravel, and pulled a pack of cigarettes out of his pocket. He lighted the cigarette and ran his fingers through his longish black hair. It was curly, unusual for a Guatemalan.

"Fifteen minutes," he said, blowing the smoke out into the heat. He looked over the seat back at Haydon. "This is my girlfriend's house. She works at Le Blé. You know Le Blé?"

Haydon nodded. "Yeah, it's a good bakery. Good coffee."

The kid grinned. "Yeah, good coffee." He smoked. "Where are you from in the States?"

"Texas."

"What city?"

"Houston."

"There are many Guatemalans in Houston." He smoked. "What do you do?"

Haydon would not say he was a policeman. In Central America you did not admit you were a policeman.

"I'm a lawyer."

"Abogado?"

"That's right."

The kid looked at him, put his cigarette in his mouth and reached over the back of the seat and extended his hand. "Dolfo," he said. He was a good-looking, very good-looking, young man and reminded Haydon of a young Hollywood actor who, one day after he became famous, would give interviews to magazines like *Vanity Fair* and tell how in his early years he supported himself driving cabs. He wore a fake Rolex and exuded the kind of confidence a young man acquired when he had to make his own way in a third world city that stayed alive by feeding on its own body.

290

"Where'd you learn to drive like that?" Haydon asked.

Dolfo was still looking at him. "I didn't 'learn' to drive like that." He smoked. "I just did it for the money." He smoked. "Who are these guys following you?"

Haydon shook his head. "We have a disagreement."

"Maybe I can help you."

"I don't think so."

"Who knows?"

"I don't think so," Haydon said. He looked at his watch. He hadn't heard a single car go by outside the gates, and they had been in the driveway ten minutes. The kid was right. Another five minutes ought to do it.

"This is my home," Dolfo said. "Guatemala City. I can help you. You will see how much I can help you."

"Where'd you learn English?"

The kid shrugged and tossed his cigarette out into the driveway. "I work two years in San Diego, Cali-fornia."

"What did you do?"

"I wash dishes in a Mexican café." He looked out into the driveway, at a cinder-block wall with cactus growing at the base of it. "The immigration, they come to that place." He waggled his hand with the dangling Rolex and moved it out the door. "Back to Mexico. This is three, no four times they find me, and one of those guys, he take me away to a corner and say if he see me another time he will cut balls. So I go to Mexico City for six months, but there is nothing there, and then I come here to my home." He looked back to Haydon again. "But I will go to the States again. Not to San Diego. I want to go to college at the University of Texas." He nodded seriously.

Haydon doubted college was what he had in mind, but the kid probably thought Haydon would find that admirable.

"Let's go," Haydon said.

Dolfo looked at his fake Rolex. "We wait some more."

"No, it's long enough," Haydon said.

"This is very important?" Dolfo asked.

"Very. We've got to be careful."

"If these people follow you when you get into my car, then they will be look for this taxi, huh?"

"That's right."

The kid thought a moment. "I have a friend, maybe he will give me his car. I will tell him he can have my taxi all day tomorrow and keep the money he makes if he will let me have his car today." He raised his eyebrows and looked at Haydon to see what he thought of this scheme. "Huh?"

"Sounds good to me."

"*Bueno.* Wait here. He is two houses that way," he said, pointing his flattened hand. "Five minutes, okay? You wait here. I will honk"—he made the motion with the heel of his hand—"two times. Okay?"

"Okay," Haydon said. "Five minutes."

The kid jumped out of the car and ran back to the gates and was gone. Haydon got out of the taxi. The courtyard was small, bare, a single *pirul* tree providing a wispy shade over the hard-packed dirt yard. The house was a cinder-block cube like all the others, and there were two chickens on the other side of the crumbling sidewalk that led to the front door. Now that he was out of the taxi, he could hear faint strains of *ranchera* music drifting through the open, screenless windows from the darkened interior of the house. Haydon had the feeling that there wasn't any girlfriend who worked at Le Blé, and if there was, this wasn't her house.

But he didn't have time to worry about it. A car honked twice outside in the street, and Haydon hurried to the gates, pulled one of them open enough to get outside. Dolfo was waving at Haydon from behind the wheel of a sun-bleached, red Japanese Starlet.

They headed toward town, through the tight streets of Zona 8, and then they hit the busy commercial thoroughfare of Avenida Bolívar where Dolfo drove only a few blocks before he exited north and got on 5a avenida, which ran straight to the cemetery and along its powder-blue façade. At 20 calle, which came up the hill from the city and ran straight into the cemetery's Greek revival entrance, Haydon had the kid pull over to the curb. He paid him as he had promised amid Dolfo's fervent insistence that he could be useful still further in many, many ways—the question of money never arising as he fired suggestions, examples of the kinds of services he could be relied upon to provide. Haydon said no, thank you very much, but finally had to accept the young man's telephone number, which the youth pressed on him with an entrepreneurial urgency that Haydon was too embarrassed to decline.

Finally the kid drove away leaving Haydon standing on the dusty curb of 5a avenida, facing the front of the Cementerio General. Across on the other side, the high walls of the cemetery were already providing a lengthening shade from the westward falling sun. The cemetery entrance was an architectural bastardization of Greek and Roman styles, having a tall Roman arch flanked by neo-classical pilasters and crowned with a staid Greek pediment. This romantic amalgam was bordered on either side for fifteen or twenty meters by the tall windows of the administrative offices. Beneath the windows was a wainscoting of dark paint. Along this wall groups of Indian women in their brilliant native *costumbres* sat at the base of the wall, their darkened and weathered faces peering out from behind mounds of fresh flowers, cerise azaleas, crimson and fleecy carnations, bloody and coral roses, snowy lilies and creamy gardenias, saffron marigolds and gold lantana, pink-bordered frangipani with peach centers, a rainbow of hibiscus, and the ivory and theatrical floripondio. A wealth of color offered by girls and women on the brink of starvation, flowers for the memory of the only people on earth who were more disadvantaged than themselves, the dead.

Haydon crossed the wide dusty street and entered the deep shadows of the long portico that soon opened into the cemetery grounds. The main avenue stretched out ahead of him, flanked by massive cypresses and cedars, their trunks painted white to form a bright colonnade beneath a dark canopy of green, and at the far end of the avenue, in front of a hazy sky, the cupola of a rich man's crypt. To either side other lanes branched off the main one, all of them lined with trees, mostly palms that reached nearly to the clouds before they burst into sprays of green fronds.

The main, more carefully tended, avenues and calles of the cemetery, the ones nearest the graceful arched entry, were dedicated in death, as in life, to the everlasting dwellings of rich men's bodies. Here the self-centered and arrogant wealthy ignored priestly wisdom and made every effort to bridge the gulf that separated what they had been in life from what they had become in eternity. Block after block of lavish mausoleums and tombs and crypts and vaults lined the shady lanes and avenues. Here was a mammoth mausoleum of stone that seemed to be an architectural blending of an Egyptian and Mayan pyramid, its doors of massive sheets of copper engraved with the images of an Egyptian king and queen surrounded by hieroglyphs and overspread with the embracing wings of a vulture. There was a miniature Tudor house of stone and wood, a miniature mosque with minarets, a miniature cathedral, a miniature Greek temple, many as large as actual houses. There were lesser crypts, too, of cottage size, and a vast array of motifs and styles—Swiss chalets, A-frames and dachas, modern and geometrically daring designs of glass and tile, bungalows, clumsy knockoffs of architectural themes reminiscent of every conceivable trendy modern design, kitsch run amok. All of these, odd little houses of the dead, many of them deteriorating as any house would if neglected. It was an altogether peculiar demonstration of how truly awkward the living felt in their inevitable confrontation with death.

And then there were the poor, the legions and legions of dead who claimed only the small space their bodies displaced. For these there were rows upon rows of low cement rectangular crypts, complexes ten meters high, a city block long, and of a depth that would allow two bodies to be

293

laid end to end, one pushed in from one side of the crypt and another from the opposite side of the building. These crypts were nothing more than coffin-sized cubicles stacked one upon the other, ten high. As each body was shoved into its space, a cement plate was fitted into the opening and plastered over. Sometimes the family paid extra to have the dead's name scratched into the cement plate, sometimes they couldn't afford it and painted it themselves. Sometimes they didn't. In any case, after several rainy seasons alternating with scorching *veranos,* the names were gone. But on the front of each plate, almost without exception, a little device of some sort was provided as a receptacle for flowers, and the long flat façade of these crypts was forever decorated with flowers, fresh and wilting and dead, and in all hues, bright and fading and dead. The plaster cracked and flaked off the fronts of the crypts, and some who treasured the maintenance of such things would repair them, while others who were too poor or too tired to maintain what housed only dusty bones and memories, did not. The broad sidewalks in front of the crypts were cracked and intruded with sacrilegious grasses, and the dead who were poor on earth rested in their plain, narrow eternities, quiet and unobjecting, while the dead who were rich on earth did the same, in a more lavish silence.

Chapter 40

According to his watch, Haydon was a little over two hours early for the meeting at five-thirty. He did not directly follow the route described in Lena's message, but rather walked to the first calle and turned into it in the opposite direction from the meeting site. The Cementerio General was, he recalled, the oldest burial ground in the city, and its narrow lanes were lined with old cypresses and stone pines and palms and cedars and *amates* and even wispy pepper trees. This lane was flanked by majestic palms, their high crowns a lush dark green against the hazy, glaucous sky. Large crypts faced each other from either side of the lane, structures of fine stones with statues in the romantic tradition portraying the deceased in the proud glory of his earthly form, or idealized personifications of his virtues.

Haydon followed this shady, shallow slope until he came to a cross lane which he took to his right, west, in the general direction of his ultimate destination. Here he saw the sides of crypts, *allées* of cypresses and pines, little paths behind the mausoleums where small sheds in which the caretakers kept their tools were tucked away out of sight. Occasionally he would see an old man moving through the cypresses, carrying a hoe or machete or pruning saw, sometimes two old men together, in sweaty shirts and ragged straw hats. They moved amid the rippling shadows of the tombs almost as if they themselves already had joined that other world, walking silently, always just out of shouting distance, now there, now gone, apparitions, the true dwellers of the necropolis.

Before he reached the next calle, he heard the faint piping trill of what sounded like a panpipe. He turned his head to hear it better, though he needn't have, for he and the music were approaching the same intersection. And then he realized it wasn't pipes at all, at least not the kind he imagined. What he heard was an incongruous mixture of melody and place and instrument. He stopped just short of the intersection, one row of tombs back from the black hearse that, covered in a film of summer dust, crept into the crossroads beneath the ancient cypresses and palms. An obese driver, seemingly wedged behind the wheel of the hearse, stared straight ahead, one arm hanging out the window, his job requiring no more concentration than was necessary for swatting flies.

The hearse entered into the intersection with its back door opened wide to reveal the casket inside. Close behind followed a loose rabble of a crowd, silent Guatemalans, all of them dressed in black, the women shawled and veiled despite the afternoon heat, the men in ill-fitting and dusty suits, their dingy, tieless shirts buttoned at the collar. They tramped along stoically in a swaying rhythmic shuffle, their dusty shoes—and bare feet—kicking up little puffs of powder, which, because the afternoon was as still as a held breath, rose no higher than their knees before it settled back to the earth only to be raised again by the people behind. These self-absorbed mourners, these new and unaccustomed city dwellers so recently from the countryside where their ancestors had buried their dead for thousands of years, had forfeited the keening of their forefathers to a tape recording, broadcast over a loudspeaker mounted behind the driver. The dirge was "Home on the Range," interpreted by the shrill up-and-down notes of a calliope's dolorous piping. This odd, melodious requiem rose up through the boughs of the cypresses and drifted out over the crypts with a morose gaiety, riding the dusty sunlight as it stole obliquely through the palms and struck the sides of the tombs as a post-meridian glow in the first moments of its softening.

Haydon stood transfixed as the grievers moved by through the rippling shadows, unwilling to move until the last mourner was well past and the notes of the calliope were fading among the tombs farther down the sloping lane. They were gone.

He was now parallel to the main avenue, monitoring his own progress as he reached each new lane. Just before he came to the end of the avenue where he had been instructed to turn right, he walked back toward the colonnade of white-trunked cypresses and crossed over to the other side into a warren of crypts, long alleys of flat-faced sepulchers on the one side, dead and dying flowers draped upon their chipped façades like the hanging gardens of Babylon in an age of drought and famine, and on the other side, lichen-covered stone vaults, rows and rows of them as far as he could see.

He turned back to his left, trying to stay within fifty meters of the narrow angling lane that diverged from the main avenue and headed down a shallow slope into an ever-poorer neighborhood of crypts. Here the walls of warehoused dead became the rule of burial, with sections of crypts interspersed. Gradually the lane he was following inched out onto a promontory, the cypress and eucalyptus trees crowding out the graves until across the lane the cemetery fell off into the vast ravines of the Río La Barranca. The lane itself became a rutted dirt road, the graves only on one side of it, and on the other, cypresses, and then the land fell away into the Gehenna of squatters' shacks and slums, their smoke and stench wafting up toward the cemetery on the late afternoon breeze.

Haydon came to the end of the road and to the end of the cemetery. A last cluster of tombs clung to the promontory, along with a mixture of cypresses and palms and eucalyptus, but on all sides the ravines dropped away into a smoky world of smoldering garbage, watched over, always, by the floating black cruciforms of *zopilotes* hanging in the opal sky.

A burble of conversation rose and died, sending a chill over his flesh before he reminded himself that no one he needed to fear would carry on a conversation at all. He moved away from the road toward the voices, heard the chink of tools, and walked between the crypts into a narrow corridor to the back side of the charnel houses. There on the edge of the ravines, behind a crypt on the margin of the cliff, an elderly woman and a girl who must have been sixteen or so were sitting on the edge of a hole they were digging, a glass jug of water between them as they rested. As Haydon rounded the corner of the crypt, they both looked at him as if he were a ghost, their sweaty faces frozen in his direction. Their hole was a ragged thing, crudely dug, and, as Haydon instantly realized as he looked at their startled faces, an illegal grave. They were probably from the terraces of shacks below in the ravines. Someone had died and needed burying, and they needed only a small piece of earth.

They looked at each other. The girl's eyes were as large as they could get and still remain in her head, and Haydon thought that if she hadn't been sitting with her legs dangling in the hole she would have bolted over the cliff. But the old woman regarded Haydon with benign resignation, the expression of a woman who had lived so long and seen so much that being kicked out of a grave in her closing years would not have surprised her.

"No tenga pena," Haydon said. Don't worry about it. Reaching into his pocket, he took out his pack of cigarettes as he walked over to the two women. He took one out and lighted it, and squatting down near them, held out the pack to the old woman. "Go ahead," he said. "Keep them."

Surprised, the girl didn't know what to do, but the old woman snatched the cigarettes from Haydon's extended hand and immediately shook one out for each of them, grasping the pack in her crooked and filthy fingers. She was too old to question opportunity.

Haydon looked into the hole they had scrabbled in the rocky soil. "Who died?" he asked.

298

"A child," the old woman said. "She likes this view. She likes the *zopilotes,"* she said, raising the gnarled hand with the cigarette and, pointing her middle finger to the sky, scribing circles in the air where the vultures wheeled in the distance.

"Did you find this spot yourself?" Haydon asked the girl, but she would not look at him. She only smoked and stared into the hole.

"Yes, herself," the old woman answered for her. "The poor girl is deaf," she explained. "We were going to dig only at night, to avoid the caretakers." She shrugged. "But it was taking too long; the child is smelling. So"—she looked at the hole in which their legs were hanging—"we finish it today. Tonight, we bring the child up in the dark."

Haydon nodded. Sweat was dripping from the girl's nose, her head was bowed, still avoiding Haydon's eyes.

"Is she a friend?" Haydon asked.

The old woman grinned. "No, no." She put an arm around the girl's shoulders. "She is my granddaughter," she said proudly.

Haydon tried to return the old woman's smile, but he felt the muscles around his mouth resist. Still he did smile, and the old woman saw that he understood her pride.

"You know the Roosevelt Hospital?" Haydon asked.

"I know where it is, yes."

Still squatting, Haydon took out his pen and a piece of paper from his wallet and wrote down the name of Dr. Bindo Salviati. He reached out and gave it to the old woman. "Take the girl there and have the doctor look at her ears. Maybe he can help."

The old woman took the piece of paper and nodded. She couldn't read, and she didn't have money for doctors, but she was being polite. Haydon told her the name and had the old woman repeat it. Then he reached into his wallet again and took out some money.

"This will cover the cost of your taxi to and from the hospital, and it will cover the cost of the doctor's examination. Dr. Salviati is a friend. He'll know what to do for her if anything can be done. Do you understand?"

The old woman nodded again and looked at Haydon, her face suddenly sober.

"Do this for the girl," Haydon said.

The old woman nodded, her eyes watering.

"For me," Haydon said. "If anyone comes asking you if you have seen me, tell them you haven't seen anyone."

"I will do it," the old woman said with resolve.

"I hope it goes well with you," Haydon said, standing.

"Se va bien," the old woman said, and Haydon walked away.

299

Chapter 41

He made his way back up the road away from the promontory, keeping away from the dirt track itself by cutting through the rows of crypts. At each alleyway he could see the dirt road fifty meters away and on the other side of it the fringe of eucalyptus trees. Through the breaks in the trees he could see the opal sky over the ravine of the Río La Barranca. The light through the trees continued to change as the afternoon sun fell toward the horizon, and now it was low enough to be directly in your eyes if you looked westward across the ravine.

When he was about halfway back to the main avenue he met two of the caretakers, one carrying a spade and the other a pair of pruning shears. They were carrying a large plastic water jug between them, each holding on to one of the handles, and were headed toward the promontory. Haydon called to them softly, barely above a normal voice, and they stopped and put down the water jug as he approached.

"Do you know the Capilla de San Rafael just off the main avenue?" he asked. He had seen it, a small Gothic mausoleum, near where he had stood watching the funeral procession.

One of the men nodded.

Haydon reached into his suit coat and produced his wallet once again. "If you will clean up around it now, before you go home for the day, I would appreciate it." He handed them more money than they could have made in two weeks. "Someone wants to be there tomorrow morning early, and I would like to have it clean for them."

"Con mucho gusto," one of the men said, and without further comment they turned around and picked up the water jug, with opposite hands this time, and headed back toward the entrance to the cemetery.

Haydon looked at his watch. There was a little more than an hour before the scheduled meeting. He turned his back to the sun and walked a few meters farther into the crypts, searching a little while for the proper nook to provide him cover as well as a good vantage point from which to see the road. He sat down on a marble bench in the shade. Reaching in his pocket for the cigarettes, he remembered he had given them away. But he was lucky, one had fallen out in his pocket. He took it out and lighted it.

He had been sitting there less than a minute when someone stepped between him and the sun. There wasn't even time to flinch.

"Well, well, an *American* smoking a cigarette."

Haydon recognized Borrayo's voice immediately. He looked up at the sun, Borrayo was no fool, and saw the Guatemalan's silhouette against it. It took all of his willpower, but he continued to smoke. Borrayo came a few steps closer.

"You are early, my friend," he said.

"Sit down, Efran," Haydon said. He squeezed his elbow to his side, making sure the gun stuck into his waistband was covered. "You might as well tell me what you're doing here."

"I guess you are right," Borrayo said, moving around so that he was opposite Haydon. He was holding the gun he had shot the kid with in

301

Colonia Santa Isabel. It wasn't pointed at Haydon, just in Borrayo's hand, which was hanging down at his side. He moved around behind a stela that sat at the front of the neighboring tomb and sat down in its shade. He rested his forearms on his knees, his hands dangling free, the gun carelessly held in the right one.

"This is my last cigarette," Haydon said.

"That's okay," Borrayo shook his head. He was not dressed in his prison director's uniform but in an old suit and a shirt with an open collar. His wavy gray hair was well coiffed, his handsome face, as he looked at Haydon, wore an amused if rather tense smile. "This is an awkward moment, huh?"

"I don't know," Haydon said. "That depends on your intentions. I don't feel awkward."

Borrayo laughed softly, appreciating Haydon's own brand of *machismo*. "Well, you ought to feel a little nervous, then. Guatemala can be a dangerous country for Americans . . . who travel alone."

"Not if you have friends," Haydon said. "Someone you can trust." His head was close to the stone, and he could feel the radiated heat. He could also smell the odors of old tombs.

Borrayo nodded, grinning. "You have these kinds of friends, huh?"

"I used to think so."

"Nothing ever stays the same, Haydon. It is a sad fact of life."

Haydon could not imagine how Borrayo knew to come here or why he had come. His casual handling of the gun didn't bode well for the meeting. Borrayo looked at his watch.

"It is not too long before we have to be very quiet," Borrayo said. "The fact is, I believe this Lena Muller is going to give you a collection of documents. I think General Azcona would love to have these documents. I would like to make him a gift of them." He shrugged. It was that simple.

"That's all."

"Of course."

"You need that gun to take the documents?"

Borrayo grinned. "I think it will make it easier."

"How did you know she was coming here?" Haydon dropped what remained of his cigarette and ground it out with his foot.

"When I was listening to your conversation with Baine," Borrayo said. "He mentioned this 'Janet.' After we got back to Pavón, I asked him a few questions about her. I had a couple of boys watch her house. I knew if her friend tried to get in touch with her it would have to be by messenger." He paused and looked around, then back to Haydon. "The child was a good idea. The boys missed her the first time. But the second time they knew something was fishy so they followed her when she left the house."

Haydon couldn't believe it. His heart began to pound though he knew they would not have harmed the little girl, because she couldn't have told them anything.

"A woman was waiting for her in a car a few blocks away. We questioned her, and she told us what was in the note."

When Borrayo "questioned" someone, the prospect of what might have happened at the interrogation was enough to make you weak in the knees.

"And you don't think the woman went straight to Lena Muller afterwards."

Borrayo shook his head. "I don't think so." And then he read Haydon's thoughts. "No, no, the woman was not harmed," Borrayo said. "She was hired for the job. It was only a job for her. She probably disappeared, knowing she would be in trouble for telling."

"Don't you imagine she was supposed to report back, to tell Muller the message had been delivered?"

"Perhaps. But I'm willing to bet she was afraid to go back."

"Then Muller would be suspicious if she didn't return." Haydon shook his head. "Nothing's going to happen here now."

Borrayo shrugged. "Do you think I would be here if I didn't believe she would come?"

Something wasn't making sense here. If Borrayo had actually "questioned" the woman, if she hadn't returned to Muller, or rather to the guerrillas who must have arranged it, then Haydon was right. The guerrillas weren't going to let Lena go anywhere. But Borrayo had shown up nevertheless. Haydon looked at the Guatemalan, who was watching him closely, watching to see if Haydon was going to come up with the right answer. It must have shown on his face. Borrayo slowly raised the automatic.

"Don't misunderstand what is happening here," Borrayo said. "We have to talk, and I am afraid you are not going to like the questions." Borrayo stood and slowly stepped over to Haydon. He released the safety on the automatic and pointed it at Haydon's face, just out of Haydon's reach. "Take the gun from your waist," he said. "Use your left hand."

303

Haydon's stomach rolled. He knew he could be dead in an instant.

"We are going to go to the back of the cemetery," Borrayo said, taking the gun. "General Azcona wants to have a short visit with you."

Haydon did not believe this. Azcona had nothing to say to Haydon. He only wanted him dead, the car bomb had not been an invitation to discuss anything. Borrayo wanted the gunshot to be a surprise, and he wanted Haydon close to the ravines so he could shove his body over the edge.

"Just turn around and go back the way you came," Borrayo said.

Haydon did as he was told, and they started back through the tombs and crypts. He was stunned. He felt light-headed and nauseated and disbelieving. He thought of the man who had raped Borrayo's niece and how Borrayo had embraced him as he fired point-blank again and again into his stomach until he went over the edge of the ravine in Santa Isabel. He thought of the young prisoner Borrayo had shot on the edge of the ravine in Santa Isabel, of how the blast had knocked him out of one of his shoes. When they got to the end of the promontory, in just a few moments, Haydon would be able to see the cliffs of Santa Isabel across the wide, deep scars of the ravine.

As they rounded a corner and began walking down the long flat façade of one of the multicrypt walls, Haydon felt as though he were wading through a surf, his legs became leaden, his muscles threatening to fail. He could hardly walk, and he was afraid his knees would buckle, something he very much wanted to avoid. Even if Borrayo actually killed him, he did not want his legs to buckle. He did not want Borrayo to see that. Even as this occurred to him, he thought how stupid such a prideful idea was at a moment like this. It was utterly lunatic.

They passed along a wall of vaults, dozens of meters of stone draped in dead flowers, reaching more than twice as high as Haydon's head, the falling sun dividing the wall into two distinct colors, its lower half blue with shadow, its upper half brassy in the changing light. It occurred to Haydon that he could think of nothing to do. He never dreamed it would be like this, and he felt as inept and helpless as an invalid. He couldn't even think of anything to say, and Borrayo's silence seemed insidious, as if he now had dropped all pretense that there was going to be any conversation at the end of the walk.

They came to the end of the wall of crypts and entered an alley of tombs. There was dead grass growing in tufts everywhere along the stone walls of the tombs, and he saw a lizard, a large scaly one, with his belly flattened on the cool stone in a doorway. Here the land dropped slightly toward the promontory, and the late-afternoon smoke from the slums and garbage dumps in the ravines was beginning to seep up through the lowest cypresses. It was not until the last moment that Haydon realized that he had led them right back to the grave where he had left the old woman and the girl. Suddenly his heart caught like a faltering engine at the absurd possibility that the old woman could save him. They were several tombs away, twenty meters. No, the old woman couldn't save him, but when they rounded the corner there would be a moment when Borrayo would be surprised that they had walked up on them . . . a split second when his eyes would have to go to them, reflexively, unavoidably. Haydon began to imagine his movements, began to imagine how in that millisecond he would dive for the cliff and anything that happened to him from there would be preferable to the damage that Borrayo's gun could do at close range.

Ten meters, and Haydon could smell the eucalyptus blended with the stench of burning garbage, and it was almost more than he could do to keep from bolting before it was time. They rounded the last crypt, and Haydon stood in front of the empty grave. The old woman and the girl were gone. He stopped and turned around.

"I can't believe you're going to kill me," he heard himself say. It was an entirely unremarkable statement, and having said it he began to feel extraordinarily strange, as if the molecules in his body were beginning to separate. At this same moment his head filled with a whirring sound, and Borrayo shrugged and started to protest—the Judas words that preceded the end. No, no, no, Haydon had it all wrong, Borrayo said, holding the gun straight out in Haydon's face. The General, he was going to come and talk to him. The General had questions. Haydon could not imagine why Borrayo was stalling. Haydon was suddenly sure that his legs were not going to buckle, and he judged the distance between himself and Borrayo, and between himself and the cliff. Borrayo was saying that Haydon would find that the General was a fair man . . . and Haydon observed the alignment of the barrel of the gun along Borrayo's arm . . . and he took in his breath as if he were about to go under water.

As Borrayo demurred in the moments before he pulled the trigger, with his back a couple of meters from the tomb behind him, Haydon saw the arc of something dull move forward above Borrayo's head.

The rusty point of the pickax struck Borrayo precisely and quite fortuitously in the hollow between his shoulder and his neck, just above

305

the clavicle. The location of the lucky blow made it instantly paralyzing, but beyond that, the force of the swing augmented by the heaviness of the head of the pickax was devastating, and Borrayo staggered, bending backward with the weight of the blow. But Borrayo's own weight threw him off balance, and he fell awkwardly toward the slope of the recently excavated earth, landing on his own gun, which went off with a muffled whump, blowing out the side of his neck.

Haydon gaped at the girl, who had swung the pickax, and at the old woman, who stood right behind her, her arm out as she reached to touch the girl's back. None of them said anything for a moment, and then Haydon's mind caught hold, and he scrambled across the mound of earth and rolled Borrayo over on his back. He pulled his own handgun out of Borrayo's waistband and retrieved Borrayo's automatic out of the mud of blood. He reached into the Guatemalan's suit coat and removed his wallet. It was fat with money, which he took out and held in his hand as he checked Borrayo's identification. There was nothing there Haydon could use. Standing, he flung the wallet as hard as he could down into the brush of the ravine, the papers flying out of it and scattering in the smoky dusk.

Haydon then grabbed Borrayo's arms and started dragging him the few meters to the edge of the cliff. The old woman and girl started to help, but Haydon waved them away. Somehow the thought of the two women dragging the gore-spattered body would transform the bizarre incident into a criminal complicity. As it stood now, it was an event of surrealism in a time and place that existed apart from a rational reality. In the space of time that bracketed Borrayo's death, there were no more corollaries. Haydon could accept that brief suspension of reality. It was one of those inexplicable things, it happened. But a conspiracy between himself and these destitute women crossed over into rationality. It allowed a flicker of light into the abyss, and right now Haydon did not want to accept the burden of trying to understand what the light revealed. It was better to leave the abyss in darkness.

Did that make sense? Sense? Could he ever employ the concept of "sense" in this context? He didn't know, didn't want to know, and then he was rolling Borrayo over the edge, and the bullish body of the Guatemalan who had committed so many cruelties fell like a millstone, crashing into the darkening underbrush high above the Río La Barranca.

Haydon turned and stepped over to the girl and looked at her, seeing for the first time that she had a face in transition. She was at once child and woman, and one had only to imagine a world for her and her face would assume the features to inhabit it. She was a changeling of necessity. Haydon wanted to embrace her, could almost feel the girl's thin, bony shoulders, but he didn't. He turned to the old woman and gave her the money from Borrayo's wallet.

"Tell the girl that I have no words strong enough or beautiful enough to thank her . . . and tell . . ." Haydon couldn't begin to express what he was feeling, the sense of rebirth at having been so astonishingly delivered from a certain death, the appalling bleakness he felt that the girl had done such a horrible thing on his behalf. And he didn't dare speculate why the girl (and the old woman) had done it.

"I understand," the old woman said, interrupting Haydon's mute and futile search for words. Her ancient face was turning gold from the light filtered through the cypresses. She looked at her granddaughter and then at the grave and her fistful of folded money. "It could not be helped."

Chapter 42

Haydon left the old woman and the girl once again and headed back toward the main avenue. This time, sure that Lena was not going to show for the meeting, he simply walked up the rutted road, not bothering to weave his way among the tombs for cover. His legs were rubbery, and he remembered how he had not wanted them to buckle before Borrayo shot him, but now it seemed an unavoidable embarrassment. He weaved off the side of the road and into the first row of tombs and dropped down in the shade of one of the stones. The muscles in his legs were as feeble as if he had been bedridden through a long illness. And he was drenched in a cold sweat. Suddenly he was vomiting, sitting on the flat surface stone of a grave, his head bent over the dried grass between his legs. For the second time that day he gave in to the revolt of his nerves, coughing up the fear that had curdled in his stomach.

When he finished, he moved away to another stone, to its shady side where he leaned his back against its cool face. He sat very still and thought of the peculiar sight of the arc of the head of the pickax as it rose and fell behind Borrayo. He thought of the expression on Borrayo's face, a grimace of pain that must have been so excruciating that it instantly became the center of Borrayo's existence, overriding even the surprise he must surely have felt for an infinitesimal flash. And then he fell on his own gun and shot himself as he had shot so many others, his own death his last execution. It was a queer kind of justice, though Haydon had to admit that by Guatemalan standards it was a symmetrical event.

Haydon's own salvation was another matter. The fact that he was sitting there in the shade of someone else's tombstone, alive enough to cough up his guts into the dried grass, made no kind of sense at all.

After a few minutes he managed to get to his feet. He leaned against the stone a moment and then went back to the dirt drive and started walking again. He was just about to the point where Borrayo had intercepted him when he saw Janet's Land-Rover emerge from around the only bend the lane made after it left the main avenue.

When she got to him, he could see her worried face through the windshield even before she stopped. He walked to the passenger door and got in.

"What's the matter?" she asked immediately. "You all right?"

"Do you think you were followed?" Haydon leaned his head back against the seat. His legs were suddenly incapacitated, and the muscles in his arms actually quivered.

"I've been driving, doing all kinds of crap, went into parking garages, private drives, the produce market downtown, everything. If anyone was following me they probably ran out of gas." She frowned at Haydon. "No one's here, are they?"

"No," he said. "And they won't be. Turn around, there, between those two tombs."

"I'll just go down to the end . . ."

309

"No. Here. Just do it."

"What the hell's going on . . . I don't think . . ."

"Just back around," Haydon said, and Janet threw the Land-Rover in reverse and backed in between the tombs and cut the engine.

"You tell me what the hell's going on."

They were facing the sunset, which hit the Land-Rover's windshield at just the right angle to create a screen of the dust and bugs plastered to the glass. He told her the whole story, how he had gotten there and what had happened. She listened, her face drawn at the craziness of it. When he finished, she leaned forward, resting her head on the steering wheel.

"Surely . . . you don't think . . . he did anything to the little girl, do you?"

"I don't, I really don't. Not because he wouldn't, but because he couldn't gain anything by it."

Janet sat there, staring at the dust on the dash through the steering wheel.

"You haven't heard from anyone else?" Haydon asked.

"No, nothing." She raised her head and looked at him. "You don't think this is the end of it, do you? She'll get in touch again, won't she?"

"I think she will." Haydon was so shaken, so tired he didn't even know what he could do to relax.

"This is too much," she said. "When this is over I'm leaving this goddamned country. Nobody wants to live like this. I don't have to. I don't need it." She was silent a moment and then she said, "This *girl* killed him with a *pickax?*"

Haydon had closed his eyes, and when he opened them the sun was striking the dusty windshield at such an angle that the glass was completely opaque with gold. He flinched and lowered his eyes. Janet had been driving with her skirt hiked up on her thighs because of the heat, and he looked at her long, bare legs.

He looked up at her, and she was staring straight into the gold, a gleaming molten ribbon of it running down her profile, outlining her forehead and nose and lips and chin . . . and on the other side of her, through the window and farther up the lane, he saw the glint from the front bumper of a car stopped just behind the white painted trunk of a cypress up on the main avenue.

"Come on," he said. "Let's get going."

Janet reached for the ignition, and suddenly Haydon stared at the keys. "Wait a minute," he said.

"What? You don't want to go?"

"Borrayo must've driven here. He wouldn't have walked in. Not very far, anyway."

"Okay."

"Up there, at the head of this lane," he said. "Someone's parked behind the cypresses."

Janet looked around. They were probably watching them with binoculars, and it was all right if they saw that she knew they were there.

"It doesn't matter now," Haydon said, "but I want to find Borrayo's transportation, and I'd rather do it without anyone seeing me. Let's just pull out and drive straight toward them. I'm guessing they don't want us to see who they are . . ."

"What if they're Azcona's—"

"Borrayo was Azcona's. I doubt if Borrayo wanted anyone with him. Just drive up there; they'll leave."

Janet pulled out on the lane, and immediately the parked car made a U-turn from behind the cypresses and disappeared. Haydon was secretly relieved. He had gotten to the point where he didn't know if his judgments were valid anymore or not.

"When you get to the avenue, start back toward the entrance," he said. "I'm going to look for the car, probably a Cherokee or something like that, or a van, parked alone. He probably dropped it off somewhere. Go slow and watch the lanes to your left. I'll cover the ones to the right."

In a moment they were back to the main avenue, and at the far end the deep portico with its high Roman arch was crowded with people leaving the cemetery before the official closing time, caretakers and tourists and visiting families and lovers who found the wooded lanes and isolated shady benches the perfect seclusion. Everyone, all of them, beginning a leisurely and general migration toward the cemetery's cool portico.

"There." Janet quickly took her foot off the accelerator but let the Rover idle along. She leaned her head back against the seat to allow Haydon to look across in front of her, and indeed, a red Cherokee was parked alone halfway down the lane.

"Go past," Haydon said. "Make a U-turn and come back, pull off just enough for me to open the door and get out using the cypresses for cover.

After I'm out, turn and go into the lanes on the other side of the avenue. Just drive around or stop or whatever you want to do. Give me ten minutes. Then come back and pick me up down there," he said, pointing two lanes down from Borrayo's Cherokee.

"Okay, I've got it," Janet said. And she did. She did exactly as Haydon had asked, the U-turn, coming back and pulling over as Haydon jumped out, and then crossing to the opposite lane, she kept driving.

Haydon ran along behind the tombs and in a few moments was coming up to the driver's door of the Cherokee. It was locked, of course. He picked up a piece of granite near one of the crypts and bashed in the side window, the sound dying quickly among the rows and rows of tombs. He reached in and unlocked the car. There was a radio and a small notebook on the front seat, which he immediately grabbed. Under the front seat he found a box of cartridges for the gun Borrayo had carried, which he slipped into his coat pocket along with the notebook. The Cherokee was trashy. Copies of the two dailies, *La Prensa Libre* and *El Gráfico,* littered the floor, along with empty Gallo beer bottles that clinked under the paper as Haydon hurriedly felt his way around in the grit. He found a Tupperware container with tortillas in it and a grease-stained grocery sack with the remnants of *pan dulce.*

In the rear seat Haydon lifted another copy of *El Gráfico* and uncovered an Uzi. It was well oiled with a full clip. He took it. Now that the Cherokee had been broken into, it would be irresponsible to leave the Uzi there, but it made him uncomfortable to have it.

Moving faster, he went back to the front seat and tried the glove compartment. It was locked. He got out and picked up the piece of granite again, crawled back in, and hammered on the lock until it popped open. Inside, bound with rubber bands, was a thick packet of identity cards of Guatemalans, men and women of every age who were, Haydon guessed, the occupants of obscure cells somewhere in Guatemala's gulag of clandestine prisons. Clearly Borrayo did not keep such evidence in his car at all times. He was, no doubt, about to make a delivery. Along with these cards was another notebook, smaller than the first one. Haydon pocketed all the ID cards and the notebook. There was nothing else in the compartment that was of immediately discernible value. He started to back out of the car and then at the last moment reached back into the glove compartment and picked up a couple of maps of Guatemala that lay on the bottom.

He scrambled out of the Cherokee and closed the door. The sun had dropped behind the horizon now, and the day was quickly reaching the hour when all colors were drained of intensity, softened and became pastels, just before everything gave way to shades of blue and slate and charcoal.

Running back toward the avenue, he was grateful for the painted trunks of the cypresses in the dying light. When he was within fifty meters of the avenue he turned right and worked his way through the tombs, one, two lanes west. Darkness was falling faster than he wanted, and then suddenly, to his left, he saw the taillights of Janet's Land-Rover. She was turning and coming back, driving slowly.

He stepped out quickly from the margin of cypresses until he heard the Rover speed up and he knew she had seen him, and then he stepped back so that he could not be seen from any distance except from directly across the way. Janet pulled the Rover to the side and stopped close to the trees as before, the door was flung open, and Haydon jumped inside with the Uzi.

"Damn, I was getting scared," she said, downshifting and turning back toward the entrance yet again. "They're closing the gates down there."

"It's okay," he said. "Don't worry about it."

"Christ, was that in there?" she asked, nodding at the Uzi.

"And other stuff," Haydon said. His pockets were loaded.

"Anything important? Anything we can use?"

"I don't know. I think so."

The dusk was thick beneath the cypresses, and Janet had to turn on the lights, her beams picking up the people filing out through the portico, the guards milling around, watching people leave. There was one other car ahead of them, a family, the small, busy heads of the children showing up like shadow games in the headlights. They crept through the portico in a tight cluster with the Guatemalans on foot, and for a few tense moments Haydon half expected the doors of the Land-Rover to be jerked open by gunmen. When they finally emerged out onto 5a avenida Haydon relaxed his hand on the Uzi.

"What now?" Janet asked.

Haydon was slumped against the door. He felt as if his body were five times its weight. He didn't think his system was capable of producing another single drop of adrenaline.

"I need a drink and a bath," he said. "I need to sit still for a few hours."

313

"What about Lena? What about the meeting?" Janet was frowning, leaning forward over the steering wheel.

"There's nothing more we can do until she contacts you again," Haydon said wearily. "There's simply nothing more you can do."

"Christ." Janet was flying down 20 calle.

"I don't want to go back to the Residencial Reforma," Haydon said. "I'd like to use one of your spare bedrooms. Just for tonight."

"Sure, of course," Janet said, surprised. "Fine with me. It would be better anyway, if someone comes from Lena."

"Your security system works?" he asked.

"Of course . . ."

"You haven't heard from Pitt?" He was holding the Uzi across his lap. "Or Cage?"

Janet shook her head. "No. I haven't heard from either of them."

"Did you see anyone back there, when you were waiting for me?"

"Anyone watching me? No. I looked for a car that might have been the one we saw, but I only saw three or four cars and none of them looked to me like they could have been surveillance."

"What does surveillance look like?"

"Okay, I don't know what 'surveillance' looks like, but I know I didn't see anybody I thought was watching me."

"Okay." Haydon's weariness was so great that he suddenly felt as if he had been drugged. He was absolutely sapped of strength. He couldn't get his mind off Borrayo, couldn't get his mind off the memory of himself standing on the edge of the ravine looking into the Guatemalan's handsome soulless eyes and knowing his intentions. There had been only a breath—less than that—between sitting in the car with Janet and lying in the brush of the ravine where Borrayo was now.

314

And he was furious with Pittner. Where the hell had he been? Before Haydon had left the Residencial Reforma he had called the number Pittner had assured him would ring on his desk. Someone else answered, and when Haydon had asked for him he was told Pittner was not there but that he could leave a message. That was hardly the kind of management he would have expected from a Chief of Station. Haydon hadn't had any choice. Either he was going to take advantage of the opportunity or he wasn't. Pittner's being conveniently out of the office made Haydon suspicious. Pittner had told Haydon not to leave the Residencial until Pittner got back to him. He had told Haydon that the hotel was a "known" location and would always be safe. Now it seemed that

Pittner's advice was a thinly disguised effort to keep him bound to one spot, out of trouble and out of the way. Haydon was a long way from having gotten a fix on Bennett Pittner.

And Cage, curiously, hadn't been heard from in almost twenty-four hours.

Chapter 43

Haydon got an old airline flight bag from Janet and put Borrayo's automatic and everything he had taken out of Borrayo's car into it and zipped it closed. He didn't take the time to look at any of it but followed Janet down the hallway past her own bedroom and around the corner to another bedroom, which, like hers, looked out onto the courtyard. The bedroom was large with a sitting area at one end and at the opposite end, the bathroom, also spacious, and also with windows looking out onto the courtyard.

Janet told him she would get something started in the kitchen and left him alone. He closed the door and locked it and turned off the light that Janet had flipped on when she led him into the room. With the lights off, he walked to the open windows and looked out. He could hear the fountain, and across the courtyard a soft topaz light illuminated the living room and farther to the right a slightly brighter light issued from the kitchen where he could see Janet and her maid moving about and could catch snatches of their conversation, a phrase here, a word there. The rest of the house, at least that part which faced the courtyard, was dark.

He turned away from the windows and walked over to the sitting area where there was a telephone to one side of an armchair. He dialed the number Pittner had given him. This time he wasn't given the brush-off; no one even answered.

He walked back to the bed and put the flight bag under it so that he could see just the edge of it from the bathroom door. He went to the bathroom and turned on the light and pulled the linen curtains over the windows. Returning to the bedroom, he took the Smith & Wesson out of his waistband and put it under the bed with the flight bag and began undressing in the half dark, shaking out his suit and shirt before he laid them out on the bed. He wished he had the clean change of clothes that was back at the Residencial Reforma.

He showered with the bathroom door open, concentrating hard on the sensations immediately at hand—the echo of the water off the tile walls, the spiky cold streams hitting his bare skin, the faint smell of the mock-orange flowers coming through the open windows from the court-yard—anything to keep the images of the long, violent day out of his mind.

Afterward he dried off with a towel, which he then wrapped around his waist, and started looking for a razor and shaving soap. He found them inside a little cabinet just to the right of the sink, laid out neatly on a white towel. There were three different kinds of cologne. Everything immaculate. Janet, he supposed, liked to be prepared for male companionship whenever it might happen her way. When he finished he combed his hair in front of the mirror and walked back into the bedroom.

He dressed, once again thinking of the clean clothes back at his hotel. As he was sitting on the foot of the bed tying his shoes, there was a knock at the door.

"Haydon," Janet said. "I've got a drink for you."

317

He walked to the door and opened it, and she stood there with two glasses. She held one out.

"Gin and tonic and lime," she said.

"Thanks," he said, and Janet stepped into the room.

"No lights?"

Haydon took his drink.

Janet closed the door and walked over to the sitting area and sat down in an armchair, putting her drink on the coffee table in front of her. She had changed clothes; she smelled faintly of bath oil.

"Earlier you cautioned me about listening devices," she said. "Sweeping a house like this is an expensive proposition. But I can afford one room. This is it."

"I don't believe that," Haydon said.

"Actually, it was Cage's idea, back when we were trysting. He put me in touch with a guy. I've kept in touch with him."

"Why not your bedroom?"

"Because it's *my* bedroom."

"Why are you telling me this?" Haydon asked, sipping gratefully from the tall glass of gin.

"Because I want to see what's in the flight bag," she said.

"I'm not sure that's a good idea," he said, walking over to her.

"I didn't ask you if it was a good idea," she said. "To tell you the truth, I think I'd be a fool to cooperate with you if you don't cooperate with me."

Haydon sipped the gin again. He had never met a larger collection of mercenaries in his life. He stepped over and put his drink down beside Janet's, went back to the bed, dragged out the flight bag and brought it around. Sitting down next to her in another armchair, he put the flight bag between his feet on the floor and unzipped it. Janet got up and closed the curtains and turned on a couple of lamps.

Haydon took out the Uzi and set it on the floor to his right. He took out Borrayo's gun, which he now noticed was also a Smith & Wesson 1006. It only proved how "plugged in" the Central American arms merchants were. The "new" FBI tests that recently had revolutionized thinking about the effectiveness of 9mm's and had caused the Bureau to change over to 10mm's had already made their impact in the hinterlands. The arms merchants had the new guns into the hands of the rabble in less than a year. This one was caked with the mud made from Borrayo's own blood. Haydon made a mental note to clean it. He laid it next to the Uzi along with the box of ammunition.

Then he pulled out the larger of the two notebooks, the packet of ID cards bound with rubber bands, the smaller notebook that had been with them in the glove compartment, and the two maps.

Janet leaned over slowly as though she could not believe her eyes and picked up the packet of identity cards.

"What in the hell are these," she said softly, realizing what she must be looking at even as she said it.

"There must be a couple of dozen there," Haydon said.

Janet removed the rubber band and counted. "Thirty-three," she said, looking at the collection of cards as if she had come upon the chronicles of a lost civilization, which, in a sense, she had.

"My God." She was almost whispering. "Those bastards. Some of these are driver's licenses, some of them are simple *cédulas.*"

Haydon picked up the smaller of the two notebooks and opened it to the first page. Borrayo was nothing if not efficient. It seemed that this was an accounting of the *desaparecidos,* the "disappeared", who had fallen under his jurisdiction during the time (nearly three years) that he had been the overseer of the clandestine prisons, not only at Pavón, but at six other sites as they had shifted locations over the thirty-two-month period. Borrayo had recorded the full name (and sex) of the person kidnapped, place and date of disappearance, and site of incarceration. Unfortunately the site was in code. Each of the six "prisons" had had lines drawn through the code and a new code penciled in, indicating the location of the prison had moved. The site with the least relocations was four, the one with the most was eight. Haydon guessed that a "prison" referred to a group of several interrogators (torturers) who, even though they were moved around, stayed together, constituting a unit.

When he realized what he had, Haydon quickly turned to the back of the book. The last week had yielded only three persons within Borrayo's jurisdiction . . . three persons and one asterisk.

As Haydon examined the notebook, he slowly began to realize that what he was looking at was in fact a rogue accounting. In the proper order of things, Borrayo apparently was supposed to turn the identity documents over to some other authority once he had collected them, but Borrayo's cunning could not allow that. For whatever reason, he was hedging his bets against the system. He was keeping his own files, think-

319

ing that some day in some way he might be able to exploit them. Borrayo knew that information was often the route to advancement, or at least, in a worst-case situation, it might well be a means of saving one's neck. Unfortunately, in this instance it hadn't paid off.

While he was examining the notebook, Haydon also kept an eye on Janet. She sat with her feet and legs together, leaning forward with the cards in her lap. She went through the stack methodically, picking them up one at a time, reading the name of each victim, reading the stark, bottom-line data available on each card, and then looking at the photograph. She tended to dwell on the photographs. When she finished, she put the rubber band around the pile of cards and returned it to the coffee table. She reached for her glass, took several swallows and looked at Haydon.

"What's in the notebook?" Her voice was flat.

He told her and made a mental note to himself that if the asterisk in the notebook represented Baine, then Borrayo must have kept his driver's license out of the collection or Janet would have discovered it. That meant that Baine's abduction was not even being registered within the clandestine system, further proof that General Azcona's quarrel with John Baine and Lena Muller was strictly a personal affair. Baine, at least, didn't even exist off the record. And Haydon saw no mention of Jim Fossler.

"These are people they've abducted," Janet said.

Haydon nodded. "I don't know what the time frame is here. Maybe a month or more. It's difficult to estimate with the recent escalation in disappearances. I'd have to read the notebook and compare it with the photographs."

"And they're in those goddamned hidden prisons," she said.

Haydon didn't respond.

"Alive," she said. "Or half alive. Soon to be dead." She jerked her head around to Haydon. "What are you going to do with this stuff?"

"I've got to think about it," he said.

"Think about it? Christ, don't *think* about it. Give it to the damn newspapers."

"You know better than that. Which newspaper do you think is going to stick its neck out?"

"Maybe they'd surprise you," she said. "Maybe . . . maybe someone would get some balls if they had solid evidence . . . like this."

"We've got to think about it," Haydon repeated. "If there's a way we can use this to help Lena we'd better make sure we've thought it through. We can't afford to screw it up."

Janet slumped back in her chair, and Haydon picked up the other notebook. This seemed to be just that, a notebook. It wasn't a calendar or an address book, though there were dates in it as well as addresses. It seemed quite a random collection of data that owed more to Borrayo's own peculiar psychology than to any conventional organization like the methodical list of *desaparecidos* in the other book. A few pages were torn out here and there, things scratched out, an abundance of doodling— mostly numerals drawn to appear three dimensional, thick numerals with shaded sides, sometimes evidencing a considerable ability at draftsmanship. There were notations about firearms, certain kinds of bullets with a list of various powder-grain loads. He came across a list of wholesale prices of truck tires, almost half a page filled with tiny numbers of tire sizes and the discounted prices for them in volume. On one page there were three columns of girls' names, one name after the other with no other notations at all except for a hodgepodge collection of the recurring three-dimensional numerals that surrounded the names. Addresses were scribbled on many pages and at every imaginable angle. And telephone numbers. Haydon couldn't make any sense of the book at all. If there was anything there for them to use he wouldn't be able to tease it out in time to help them.

Haydon tossed the book back onto the coffee table and picked up his drink.

There was a soft knock at the bedroom door. Janet looked at her watch. "That's Mirtha. She's been laying out something for us to eat before she goes home. You hungry?"

"Very," Haydon said. He bent and began putting the things back into the flight bag while Janet went to the door. He heard her talking to the maid, but it wasn't about dinner. Janet's voice changed, reflecting concern, the maid's voice an urgent stage whisper, repeating something, Janet's placating, telling her she was sorry, very sorry. She turned around.

"Haydon, I'll be back in a second," she said and walked out of the room with the maid, talking.

Haydon stood, stepped over to the lights and turned them off again, then went to the bathroom, turned on the light there and shut the door partway. He went to the windows, pulled back the curtains again and looked toward the kitchen windows where he saw Janet and the maid talking, the maid gesturing, Janet nodding, shaking her head, assuring.

After a moment the two women passed through the darkened dining room and into the topaz light of the living room, still talking, Janet's arm around the maid. They disappeared out into the breezeway, and after a moment Janet came back in alone and Haydon watched her return quickly through the house until she was at the bedroom door again.

She pushed open the door and came into the shadowy room where Haydon was waiting. Pausing, she closed the door behind her with one arm.

"What's the matter?" Haydon asked.

"Mirtha's husband drives a taxi," Janet said, her voice wooden. She came forward and stood in front of Haydon and folded her arms. "They live in Colonia La Reformita, Zona 12. Every evening at this time he comes and picks her up. Today, when he went by their house to check with the kids as he does routinely every afternoon to make sure they've gotten home from school all right, there were men at his house. Three men and a woman . . . a *gringa*. They were inside." Janet swallowed. "It was obviously Lena. She knew who he was, who Mirtha was, their routine. She wanted him to tell his wife to give me a message when he picked her up tonight. They made him repeat it several times. She just did that."

Haydon supposed the fate of the little girl and her mother had been a painful lesson to the guerrillas. This was a good solution, a smart one. This time the message would be delivered by someone who would not raise the suspicion of any stakeout.

"She wants us to meet her tomorrow night—'where I wanted to buy the amber candles' was what she said. She said this was the last chance. Be careful. She said, 'There is a *queez-ling*.' That's the way Mirtha pronounced it, *queez-ling*." Janet was puzzled.

Haydon was stumped for a moment, too, but only for a moment. "Quisling," he said. "A traitor."

"A traitor?"

"What about 'where I wanted to buy the amber candles'?"

"That's Cobán, a town up in Alta Verapaz. I remember that. Lena and I went there for a weekend one time and she found some huge amber candles there. They were for the altar of the church, I mean, that's what they were made for, altar candles. But she saw them, fell in love with them, wanted to buy them." She shrugged. "But the little store, the woman there had just made them for the priest and they were only hanging there until the priest came for them. Lena went on and on about them, they were huge . . . amber candles."

Haydon knew what was happening. "Why didn't she just say 'Cobán'?" he asked, wondering if Janet was going to see what Lena was getting at. "And why didn't she simply say 'traitor' instead of 'Quisling,' a word she must have had to teach Mirtha's husband to say?"

Janet simply stared at him and shook her head. Even in the night shadows he could see the puzzlement in her face.

"She didn't want the messenger to understand the message," he said. "Others besides Borrayo knew we were going to be at the cemetery. Maybe they also found out by other means than that used by Borrayo."

Janet's face did not change expression, she simply began shaking her head. "I don't believe that . . ."

"You can't blame her for being tempted," Haydon said. "Maybe she didn't even have a choice. She has a family to worry about. She obviously was frightened by Lena's visit to her house, her husband finding these people waiting there with their children when he came in. Who knows what kind of pressures were put on her to inform on you."

Janet turned away from him and walked to the windows and looked out to the courtyard. "I feel like a fool," she said. "Like a child. All this going on around me, and I blithely blundered on."

Haydon wasn't going to tell her who he thought Mirtha was informing for. He wasn't going to tell her that in his estimation Bennett Pittner had known everything that had gone on in Janet's house ever since he had moved out, and probably long before, too, which in all likelihood is how he knew about Janet's affair with Cage in the first place.

"What are we going to do?" she said. Janet sounded like a woman who had just had the wind knocked out of her. Perhaps she understood far more than Haydon believed, far more than Haydon could even know.

"If it worked," Haydon said, walking over to the bed and sitting down near her, "then we have a head start."

"To Cobán."

"That's right."

"But we'll be followed."

"That's right. But if we can lose them this time, if we do it right, we could make this last chance work."

"You know some magic tricks?" she asked.

"No magic," he said. "Just tricks."

Chapter 44

They drove to the nearby Zona Viva where the best restaurants in the city were scattered among high-dollar hotels and expensive shops and exclusive boutiques. They went to a Chinese restaurant, one wing of which was a huge renovated junk nestled into a stand of coconut palms and illuminated by emerald landscaping lights. The parking lot was full.

Haydon asked to be seated in the dining room with the largest windows, but at a table well away from them. They ordered drinks and appetizers, and while Janet watched the parking lot and the only entrance to the restaurant, Haydon went to the small anteroom outside the rest rooms. He took a notepad from the shelves underneath the telephones, wrote DESCOMPUESTO on a sheet of paper and wedged it into the frame of the telephone next to the one he was going to use.

He made several calls to Belize City before he reached the party he was seeking. He made inquiries, checked data, received confirmations, double-checked data, and hung up. His next series of calls were local. Again he had to make several calls before he reached the party he wanted. This conversation was briefer than the one to Belize City, but it required some explication. When he was satisfied, he hung up and looked at his watch. The calls had taken seventeen minutes in all. He made one more, but no one answered. He wouldn't call Pittner again. He took the sign off the neighboring telephone and walked back into the dining room.

"I was beginning to wonder," Janet said as he sat down.

"What's happened?" he asked, immediately filling his small plate with a variety of the appetizers. He was suddenly ravenous.

"I've seen only the one van," she said, nodding toward the parking lot. "The dark one straight across from the Rover. It came in while you were walking back to the phones. No one's gotten out or anything. It's just been sitting there."

"Who are the new diners since we've come in?" His gin was watery, sitting with the ice melting the whole time he was away.

"The young American-looking couple by the bar; the four tourists near the window; the Guatemalan man and Anglo woman just to my left, behind me; and the two Guatemalan businessmen over here," she said, picking up her glass and raising her index finger to her right.

As a safety precaution they weren't talking in the Land-Rover, so Haydon had to tell her the little he wanted her to know about what would happen next before they left the restaurant.

"I've decided not to go by the Residencial Reforma for the rest of my things," he said. "It will only raise questions, make it look like we're about to do something different, that there's a plan underway. It's best if they think we're waiting for instructions."

He paused for a few bites of shrimp and to review his own mental checklist. He didn't want to tell her even a syllable too much. She needed to know only enough for her to function within the plan. Besides, there

325

was still so much flexibility he himself couldn't predict much more than generalities at this point.

"When you go out of town," Haydon asked, "does Mirtha still come and open the house every day?"

"Yes, she does. But there's not much to do. I just want someone there every day, routinely."

"Okay, before we leave here I want you to call her and tell her you're leaving for a couple of days and that you'll probably leave before she arrives in the morning. Will she ask you where you're going?"

"Maybe. I usually tell her."

"Okay, just do whatever seems natural, but tell her you're going to Panajachel."

"If I want to make sure 'they' get the message, why don't I just call her from home?" Janet asked. "If the phones are tapped like you think, they'll pick it up."

"But that's not what you'd do if you suspected the phones were tapped and you didn't want them to know, is it?" Haydon ate another shrimp stuffed with crabmeat. "Don't worry. She'll pass it on."

They finished the appetizers and their drinks, and then, just before they left, he told Janet to make her call to Mirtha.

When she got up to go, he said, "I think I'll walk back there with you."

She gave him a strange look. "Sure, okay," she said.

The call was brief, and they returned to their table and paid and walked out into the smoky greenish glow, the hopeless result of landscape design in a city rapidly sinking under waves of impoverished immigrants. They got into the Land-Rover and made their way back to Janet's house, Haydon watching the progress of the dark van, which behaved as though the driver knew there was no urgency to their progress.

As they rounded the last corner on the approach to Janet's house, they saw a car parked in front of the wrought-iron gates. Taylor Cage was leaning against the fender.

Janet said nothing, but in the amber glow coming off the dials on her dash Haydon could see the flat expression of a woman steeling herself for what she clearly expected to be a stressful encounter. She pushed the remote control on the gates, and when they opened, pulled into the driveway of the walled courtyard.

Haydon got out of the Land-Rover carrying the flight bag and walked around the rear of the vehicle to where Cage was coming up the drive like a determined water buffalo. He was carrying a large manila folder, slapping it against his leg impatiently.

"Long time no see," he said to Haydon. He was wearing what must be his suit of business nowadays in the Central American heat, dress pants and a white guayabera, the tail out, doing a poor job of hiding his sidearm.

"I doubt that."

Cage snorted and turned to Janet, who was approaching, digging in her purse for the security-system key. She stopped. "Hello, Cage," she said.

Cage grinned at her and nodded. "Janet."

"What are you doing here?" she asked.

"Time to parlay." Cage slapped the envelope against his leg again.

Janet turned on him. "Parlay?" There was venom in her voice. It struck Haydon as she spoke that he didn't know anything about their relationship after their affair. Neither of them had ever mentioned it, an omission that suddenly alerted him.

"Janet, if you can just hold off on the bitch thing for right now I think we'd all get more out of this," Cage said. "Okay?"

She turned away and went to the courtyard gate and unlocked it, then went into the breezeway and turned off the alarm system.

"I appreciate your getting back to me," Haydon said, letting Janet go ahead without them.

"I don't understand why you're not deader than shit," Cage said, looking at Haydon.

"I could have used a little help," Haydon said. "I thought that was the idea, that you were going to give me a little help."

Cage held up the envelope. "Come on, let's go in. I've got something for you now."

When they got inside, Janet had already gone through to the kitchen, and they could hear her putting away the food that Mirtha had laid out for her and Haydon and that they had not eaten. There was as much nervous energy in what she was doing as practicality. Cage and Haydon stopped in the living room, and Cage walked over to the French doors and looked out into the courtyard. He took his time examining the view, slapped the envelope against his leg, and walked over to the parrot, who was busy eating cashew nuts. He stopped and stared at the bird, which ignored him, said, "Goddamned bird. I hate this bird," and then, still looking around the room, wandered over to the liquor caddy, tossed the envelope on the sofa and helped himself to a clean glass and a couple of generous splashes of Bennett Pittner's favorite bourbon. "Some of this?" he asked Haydon, holding up the bottle.

Haydon shook his head. He guessed it had been a while since Cage had been here.

"Make yourself at home, Taylor," Janet said, walking into the room. "What do you want?"

Cage sat down on the sofa next to the liquor caddy while Janet went over to one of the armchairs with its back to the courtyard, sat down, and crossed her legs. Haydon remained standing, though he had set the flight bag down beside a leather upholstered chair near the living room entrance.

Cage ignored Janet and directed his attention to Haydon.

"I suspect you met with the guerrillas this morning during that 18 calle fiasco, didn't you," he said straight out.

"Why do you think so?"

"Because my people found our man with his throat cut about an hour after the car bomb," Cage said. "The guerrillas always cut their throats because the stupid shits are so *guerrilla* oriented." He shook his head at the idea, as if there were less flamboyant, less juvenile ways to kill. "Them being in the city, though. That's new. The urban cells have been squashed quite a long time, but now here they are wheeling free on 18 calle. That's something new." He sat on the sofa like a minotaur, chesty with powerful shoulders and narrow hips.

"The General thinks it's the guerrillas helping her," he said. "And he's unleashing his bad boys. The bombing. He's yelling, *los guerrios* are turning our peace into war again. He's got the police scrambling, practically declaring a state of siege. There'll be articles about it in tomorrow's papers, about how the General is going to come down hard on this new resurgence of *terrorismo,* on the 'foreign subversives.' "

"Are you telling me to be careful?" Haydon asked. "You think I don't know who really put the bomb in the car?"

"Yeah, by God, I think you don't know, really, who put the bomb in the car. That's exactly what I think."

"Why?"

Cage slugged down a mouthful of bourbon, finishing the drink in short order and setting the glass on the edge of the liquor caddy.

"After you left me last night," Cage said, "I pulled out all the stops to find your friend Fossler. I did it the way you do here in Guatemala. The hospitals first, then the morgues. I started with my people in the western highlands, because that was the direction Baine and Lena were heading, and I guessed that was where Lena went after she left Baine. I thought maybe Fossler had gone after her."

He got up with the envelope and walked over to a chair not far from Janet and flipped on the lamp beside it. "Sit down," he said. Haydon did, and Cage gave him the envelope.

They were morgue shots, the kind of cheap theatrical photographs that morgue shots in color tend to be, like the promotional still photographs they used to put up along with the posters outside movie theaters when Technicolor was just coming into its own. Jim Fossler looked his worst, his lean naked body gaunt in death, the bruises painfully purple to a fault, the dried blood still with tinges of maroon, the burned away eyes not so terribly disgusting as one might imagine. But there were other wounds that boggled the mind.

Haydon went through all of the pictures, there were nine, and then he put them back in the envelope. Cage had walked back to the liquor caddy and had sloshed out some more whiskey.

"Those were taken in Chajul, El Quiché. That's where the guerrillas caught up with him," he said, turning around, putting one hand into his trousers, the other holding the drink as though he were at a cocktail party. "The same people you chummed up with this morning. That's who did Fossler." He looked at Haydon. "Dr. Aris Grajeda," he said. "He's disappeared. That who you went to see?"

Haydon felt like he was in some kind of creep show in which every episode, every new scene was just a little more grotesque than the previous one. The photographs of Jim Fossler seemed beyond the pale of decency, Cage carrying them around with ghoulish unconcern, slapping them against his leg in good-humored indifference.

"Grajeda is a sly one," Cage continued. "A little rich fart who's playing at this business of 'internal struggle.' By God, if I had a dollar for every one of those damned ideologues I've come across in all my years down here I could retire in Geneva tomorrow. And Grajeda's the worst kind. He *dabbles* at it." He gestured at the photographs with his glass as he paced back toward the French doors. "This kind of shit is what comes of it. Him and his bunch have taken Lena in because she is the best thing that's happened to their pissy little struggle in the thirty years it's been going on. She's being used and she hasn't got the foggiest idea of what the hell she's into. She's going to come through with this 'documentation' on Azcona, and the guerrillas are going to get publicity mileage out of her like you can't imagine. 'Black Market Babies: American Peace Corps Girl Reveals the Truth About Guatemala.' Hey, this is going to be big."

"What's your point here?" Haydon said. He was having a hard time even concentrating on what Cage was blowing hard about. He was thinking about Mari Fossler, and about Dystal's "Guate-goddamn-mala," and his "Fossler ought to get out of down there while he can still draw breath," a remark which, at the time, Haydon had discounted with a secret condescension as being an uninformed overreaction.

Cage continued pacing, gesturing with his drink, looking at Haydon, tossing his head to emphasize his words.

"My point is, Haydon, that I think she's getting the short end of the stick here, and you're going *way* out of your way to help her get it. My scenario: she's going to give you these files. They're potent stuff. Big story here because Azcona Contrera is our man in Guatemala. The usual shit will hit the fan with the righteous left . . . 'U.S. Right-wingers Giving Millions in Foreign Aid to Monster.' I think she's going to come out with this, and she's going to be hailed as a saint, a champion of poor people, a freedom fighter for moral causes, a child of new-age selflessness, the whole hoo-haa that only the American press can do up right, with lip-smacking photographs of this Madonna of Modern Goodness (not only *is* she good, she *looks* good), everybody getting worked up in misty-eyed admiration . . . and then somebody will lift up the curtain and look behind the medicine-show backdrop. The 'stuff' she's got on Azcona is going to be examined oh-so-closely by *serious* journalists, and they're going to find guerrilla black propaganda written all over it. The kid was put up. She was had. But it won't stop there. Some reporter's going to dig into her *personal* life. They're going to find out that she has screwed her way from one end of the Central American isthmus to the other, that she is cunning, conniving, and a user."

Cage was standing in the middle of the room with his empty glass, his hand in his pocket, his face a little red from reciting his "scenario," and the butt of his pistol making a bulge in the tail of his guayabera. "This has all the makings of a real piece of work, my friend. And you're right in the middle of it."

Haydon looked at Cage for a moment without saying anything. It seemed to him that Cage was curiously close to reversing himself on Lena. The irreverence with which he had just spoken of her conflicted seriously with his attitude about her before. Which of these two Cages was Haydon supposed to believe? And who was Cage trying to straighten out? Haydon or himself. The room was quiet except for the small crackling sounds of the parrot breaking open cashews.

Haydon picked up the envelope of photographs and held it up. "Who did this?"

Cage gaped at him as if he was incredulous that Haydon was missing the whole point of his exposition.

"Who did it? Jesus Christ, man, haven't you heard *anything* I've just said."

"I've heard all of it," Haydon said. "I just want to hear you say it."

"I told you, the guerrillas."

"Why?"

"Look," Cage gestured toward the manila envelope, "Fossler was good, Haydon, he'd done his legwork, he'd done his homework, he'd done a *lot* of work. He'd already snapped to the documents scam . . . I'm guessing here, okay, but I think he said something about it to Lena, she went straight to Grajeda, and Fossler was shut up. They were almost home with her, almost there. They weren't going to let something like Fossler's meddling screw it up at the last minute."

"Why haven't they just flown her out of the country?" Haydon asked. "It would be easy enough."

Cage shook his head. "No, when you've worked an operation this long, nothing is 'easy enough.' I have to admit this is sophisticated for these guys, a genuine advancement from what their nickel-and-dime struggle used to be, but it's because of guys like Grajeda. They're educated. In the past the guerrillas were Indians, homegrown and uneducated, just a lot of guts. Time passes, times change. Grajeda and some of the people around him are a new generation. They don't talk stupid Marxist crap. They've got more intelligent agendas, and they've got more intelligent ways of accomplishing them. They know all about disinformation; they know all about the futility of 'guerrilla' warfare as it used to be. They're slowly moving into the political realm. If they can't defeat the General Azconas of this army with firearms, they'll do it with words and ideas. The real wars lie ahead, and they're going to be fought not with arms but with brains. This is phase one. It's going to be interesting."

Haydon remembered the Guatemalan girl who had escorted him out of the warehouse where he had talked with Grajeda; he remembered her perfect, unaccented English. He remembered his discussion with Dr. Grajeda about Heinrich Böll's perspectives on truth. In retrospect,

331

Haydon could see that that discussion had been at the core of what this shell game with Lena was all about, and it might prove to offer the clearest understanding he would ever have of what had happened in these few hectic days.

Haydon sat in the pool of light the lamp was throwing over his shoulder and looked at Cage staring back at him from the middle of the room, a man who had lived and made his living completely outside society's acceptable codes of behavior. He operated in a moral free-fire zone, and in many ways he was only a more primitive version of Bennett Pittner.

"What the hell are you trying to do?" Cage challenged. "You think you can sit there and make *sense* out of all this? You think you're going to figure something out here?" He looked up at the ceiling and shook his head as if he couldn't believe what was happening. Then he let his head drop and pointed the empty glass at Haydon. "Remember what I said about Pittner being a man you had to lie to to keep your self-respect? About his self-absorbed grief over"—he jerked his head toward Janet without looking at her—"all kinds of shit? I'm beginning to wonder if you're not cut out of the same cloth. You can't get this Fossler thing out of your head, can you? Like you're mooning over some goddamned woman. Jesus."

Haydon lifted the envelope. "Where is he now?"

Cage gaped at him; he was seething. Haydon's stubbornness was clearly galling. "He's on his way down here, someone's driving him down."

"From Chajul?"

"From Chajul."

"Thanks," Haydon said, standing. "Thanks for coming by and bringing the photographs and for telling me."

332

Cage stood rooted to the middle of the room, the whole thing cut unexpectedly short, Haydon's courteous suggestion that it was time for him to leave was a worse insult by far than if Haydon had slugged him. He gave Haydon a smile that was no smile at all, really, but something to do with his face to keep his anger from getting the best of him.

"You're a silly goddamned fool, Haydon," he said in a tone of voice that was supposed to pass for calm, but which had the husky thickness that betrayed a throat strung tight. He looked at Janet, and in what was probably a moment of colossal self-restraint, managed not to say what he was thinking.

Chapter 45

Cage stormed out of the house, and neither Haydon nor Janet moved to follow him. Outside the fountain splashed almost too softly to hear, and one could easily be distracted from it by the small snicking sounds of the parrot eating cashews just a few feet away. Haydon looked at the manila envelope dangling from his hand and let it drop on the floor. He felt too numb and tried to ignore the crawling nausea in his stomach.

"I'm sorry . . ." Janet said. "I don't . . ." She stopped, it seemed, at the futility of being able to say anything meaningful. She didn't continue, but she reached up and turned off the lamp that Haydon had turned on between them, and they fell instantly into the softer topaz light of other lamps. Sighing, she laid her head back against her chair.

"The whole house is swept regularly, isn't it Janet," Haydon said. "Not just that one bedroom, but the whole place."

She said nothing, but sat as if wrapped in a dark silence of old and familiar disappointments, failures that no longer could be avoided with redirected enthusiasms and spirited denials, but which, ultimately, had to be confronted as the empty disillusionments of what finally had become the story of her life.

"I didn't understand . . . ," Haydon mused thoughtfully, "the extent to which your lives had become interdependent, the three of you, until Cage's remarks about Pittner just then. I realized Pittner wasn't wiring the house. Cage wouldn't have said those things . . ."

"But not out of respect."

"No, just because it would have been bad business."

"Apparently Cage has been talking," Janet said.

"Some."

Again there was a long while when there was only the sound of the fountain and the parrot cracking cashews.

"We've been unraveling for a long time," she said. "Each of us in his own peculiar way. We're just about at the end of it. It's been going on too long, the three of us. It's complex . . . hell, we don't understand it either."

Haydon didn't want to hear it. He didn't want to listen to anything confessional; he didn't want to know about it. He only wanted to concentrate on getting out of Guatemala with Lena Muller, if Lena Muller wanted to go.

334

"How long have you known Pittner was in intelligence work?"

"Years," she said. "From the beginning, Pitt shared a lot with me. Not actual intelligence, just realities about his job, the eccentricities about how he had to live. I think he did that because it was getting hard for him, the double life. He didn't want to make up half of what he was anymore. The house became a haven in that way. He made sure it was clean, still does."

"Why?"

"Because the divorce didn't really change anything that much. Between us, I mean. He was over here a lot."

"What about Cage and Pitt?"

"They were great friends, close friends . . . and enemies . . . long before I came into the story." She sat up in her chair. "I've got to have a drink. How about you?" Haydon nodded, and Janet stood and walked out of the room and into the kitchen. When she returned she had two glasses with ice and slices of lime in them. She went to the liquor caddy and mixed in gin and tonic. She walked over and handed one to Haydon and then went over to the parrot and stood by its perch and watched him, holding her drink.

"What's their relationship at this moment?" Haydon asked. "After all that's passed between them—among you—where do they stand?"

Janet continued looking at the bird, her back half turned from him. She sipped her drink and then reached out to the bird, which quickly leaned over and viciously nipped at her finger. Janet jerked back, her forefinger doubled up, blood already running down the back of her hand. She didn't say anything, only tucked her finger into her fist, trying to cover the laceration with her thumb. She turned and walked into the kitchen, and Haydon heard her running the water. A drawer opened and closed and then Janet walked back into the room with a damp paper towel wrapped around her finger. She came back to her chair, put her drink on the table between them, and began unwrapping a bandage.

"It was my fault," she said calmly. "I've done it before. I had another parrot, the one before this one, that would let you pet it. I'd had the bird a long time, this one's still young." She concentrated on wrapping the adhesive around her finger. "They're so pretty you want to touch them."

She finished with the bandage, and when she turned to pick up her drink again, Haydon noticed that she had tears in her eyes, a glistening trail on one cheek.

"I don't think they've seen each other in quite a while," she said. "I know I haven't seen them together in a long time."

"What's quite a while?" Haydon didn't think the tears had anything to do with the nip from the parrot.

"Five months, I guess. Tonight was the first time I'd seen Cage in . . . that long, at least."

Haydon quickly calculated that that was about the time Lena was discharged from the Peace Corps and left Guatemala.

"How much do you know about their working relationship?"

"I don't know anything about it at all," Janet said. "I really don't. I told you, I don't know detail kinds of things. Only that they're in the same business; they have some dealings with each other."

Haydon didn't believe her, but it didn't seem to matter. They were all lying. The best he could hope for was that at some point he would get a lucky break. His biggest concern was Pittner's silence.

"You seem to have a genuine affection for Lena," Haydon said.

"I do, yes."

"Why?"

Janet raised her glass to her lips and drank the gin. "That's a hell of a question."

"I don't think it's so unusual, certainly not as unusual as the relationship among the four of you. I thought you might find it a little awkward to have a close friend who was having simultaneous affairs with your ex-husband and your ex-lover."

Janet, slumped back in her chair, crossed her legs. "I would have bet my last dollar you would have to say that sooner or later," she said. "It's just too damn tempting." She daubed the bottom of her sweaty glass on her knee, making a dark splotch on her dress. "It rather conjures up images of dissolution, doesn't it."

She sat in silence a moment, and Haydon waited, his nostrils picking up the pungent fetor of the burned garbage with which the atmosphere seemed especially laden this evening.

"I kept looking for something that would make sense," she said. "In 'relationships,' I mean. And when I found it I was surprised that it was something . . . something more like friendship. It doesn't necessarily revolve around sex at all. It's less explosive than that, but somehow has more depth." She shook her head slowly. "I find that it doesn't matter to me—not when it comes right down to it—so much how it is between them and Lena. I can tell you this, though, whatever is going on . . . Pitt and Cage are kidding themselves. Men always go into these things like they're sleepwalking, with their eyes closed, their minds misreading dream and reality, and all their glands pumping overtime. They think they're awake, they act like they're awake, but their brains are asleep. I can promise you, Lena's the only one who knows what in the hell's going on here."

Haydon hesitated only a moment.

"You knew Pitt was having an affair with Lena?"

"I was reasonably sure."

"Did you have any idea what that was costing him?"

336

She looked over at Haydon. "Costing him?"

"It was a dangerous thing for him to do."

"Dangerous, you mean for his career?"

"Yes."

Janet smiled sourly and turned away again. She looked at the parrot, its round red eye, unblinking. "Pitt never runs that kind of a risk."

"He did this time."

"He told you this?"

"We talked about it."

Janet stared through the topaz light at the picture over the fireplace, the purple volcanoes looming over a lush landscape that Guatemala used to enjoy when it deserved to be called the Land of Eternal Spring.

"What did he say about her?"

Haydon hesitated.

"Did he say he loved her?"

"I'm not sure it was that. I can't say, really."

"Maybe it was a glandular thing," she said sarcastically. "Lena has that kind of effect on nearly every man who meets her. I've known a lot of pretty, even beautiful women who don't get that kind of reaction from men. It's something more than being physically attractive. It's like they think she's always in heat."

Haydon drank his lime and gin. Janet had mixed it so stout he could smell its resinous scent when he drank. His eye caught the manila envelope he had dropped on the floor. He felt queasy. He would have to go through the motions of reporting it to the Consular Section at the embassy, though they probably already knew. And he would send word to Pittner's office, though they probably already knew also. Still, he had to go through the motions. The motions would be very important when it came out in the newspapers.

"When we get to Cobán," she said, changing the subject, "how will we make contact with her?"

"We'll go to the place that was selling the candles," Haydon said. "They'll find us."

She looked at him. "You seem sure of that."

"You can count on it," he said. He looked at his watch. "We need to leave early in the morning, before daylight."

"It's only a three-hour trip, maybe three and a half."

"Yeah, I know. But we need to start before daylight."

She looked at him a moment and then nodded. "Okay."

337

"You've got an alarm, I guess."

Janet nodded again.

"I'd like to set it for five o'clock. We ought to go to bed now. It's almost eleven. That gives us five hours' sleep."

"Fine. I'll lock up, set the security system, and wake you at five."

Haydon leaned forward in his chair. "I think this is my last shot at this, Janet. I'd like to do this in a particular way."

"A particular way?"

"Yeah, come on. I'll help you lock up."

Haydon finished his drink and set the empty glass on the table. He followed Janet around the house, locking the front gates and setting the security system, and then the gates to the breezeway and inner courtyard and their security systems, which were connected to the house's windows and doors. It took a few minutes, but not long, and then they turned off the lights, leaving one on in the breezeway and front courtyard. Haydon picked up the flight bag and his empty glass as they turned out the lights in the living room and walked into the kitchen.

"I'm going to make another drink," Janet said. "You want one?"

"Yeah, that would be good." There wasn't going to be any sleep for a little while, he knew that.

Janet filled the glasses with ice from the refrigerator while Haydon cut more slices from the lime on the counter. He watched her while she filled the glasses from another collection of liquor bottles in the pantry. He put the lime slices in their glasses, and then they turned off the light in the kitchen and walked down the corridor to the first bedroom, which was Janet's.

"There's an alarm beside your bed, too," Janet said pausing at her doorway. "You might as well set it."

338   "I think we'd both better sleep in here," Haydon said. He had been in Janet's presence when she had received the message from Lena through Mirtha. If this was a setup there was nothing he could do about it, but if it wasn't, he wasn't about to let it get away from him.

"You're going to sleep in here?"

Haydon pushed open the door to her room, which, he saw, was much like his just around the corner. There was a sitting room to one side, with a fireplace and a couple of armchairs and sofas in front of it. The windows that looked out onto the courtyard were the ones through which he had seen her naked after her shower.

Once inside the room he turned, locked the door, and flipped off the lights. A bluish green glow came from the landscaping lights among the ferns and palms outside in the courtyard.

"Come on! I've got to shower, for Christ's sake," she said.

"There'll be enough light from the courtyard."

"What is this?"

"This is being careful," he said. He could tell she wasn't sure if there were any intentions in this other than being careful. That was her problem.

She made her way over to her bed and set her glass on the table beside it. There was easily enough light in the room to see how to get around, though it was muted and bluish, with pockets of shadows. Janet started undressing beside her bed. It wasn't much of a process. Her dress fell to the floor, and she peeled off her panties and that was it. She started into the bathroom.

"Leave the door open," Haydon said.

"I'm going to *pee,* for God's sake," she said.

"Fine, just leave it open."

She stood still in the bathroom doorway, and he knew that it was finally dawning on her what he was doing.

"You want to put a gag on me?" she said. "You want to handcuff me in the shower?"

"If you'll just leave the door open," he said, turning away from her and going over to the sofa. He picked up the cushions and took them over to the bedroom door and threw them down beside the flight bag. Putting his drink on the floor beside the cushions, he took the automatic from his waistband and laid it near the gin. As he began taking off his shoes, he could hear the fountain outside the open windows, and Janet going to the bathroom.

It was hot in the room, and the occasional waft of breeze that came through the windows from the courtyard was dense with a pungent smokiness. He stripped down to his shorts and folded his clothes beside him on the floor. Rearranging the cushions, he finally got them so that he thought he could sleep on them and leaned back in the bluish light, sipping his drink and listening to the splashing of the water in the shower.

After a while the water stopped, and he saw Janet's dark form step out into the pastel light, and he watched her dry off. She put the wet

339

towel over a hook near the shower and then moved to the vanity where she disappeared except for her buttocks and the back of her shoulders as she combed her hair.

When she finished she walked back into the bedroom naked, pausing briefly when she saw him on the cushions in front of the door. Then she turned and walked back into the bathroom. He heard a cabinet door open and close, and when she returned she was carrying a couple of folded sheets. "Here, you can do something with these," she said, tossing the sheets to him, and then got onto her bed, put some pillows against the headboard, and picked up her drink.

Haydon spread the sheets out across the cushions and on the floor and then tried to settle in. It was silent for a while as they stared across the blue haze at each other. Janet's hair was wet and stringy, hanging over her naked shoulders above her breasts.

"You have a wife?" she asked finally. She had one leg cocked over to the side.

"Yes."

"Children?"

"No."

Pause.

"What's her name?"

"Nina."

"How long have you been married?"

"Eighteen years."

Pause.

"What does she . . . ?"

"She's an architect."

Janet sipped her drink. "Eighteen years is a long time," she said.

"It seems like months."

Janet's naked body was a pale jade. He thought of the moon-shaped slices of lime he had put in her glass, jade and lime green; her hair and nipples and the small spot of hair between her legs were too dark to reflect color at all. He regretted being across the room from the windows. There was no breath of air against the wall. Occasionally a soft waft would move the curtains beside Janet's bed, but what little sigh of air had caused it died just inside the windows. His side of the room was darker and hotter. He took a sip of gin and ate a chunk of ice.

"Is she light or dark?" Janet asked.

"What?"

"Your wife. Is she blond or brunette, light or dark skinned?"

"Dark hair, olive skin."

"You like that?"

"Very much."

"Is she Anglo?"

"Mostly Italian. You haven't set the alarm," he said.

"Oh, sorry." She set her drink on the table and reached for the clock. It was a windup one, not electric. She sat on the side of the bed and held the face of the clock to the glow coming from the courtyard. "Okay," she said, and put it back on the table, got her drink and got back on the sheets.

Haydon stood and walked over to the bed and picked up the clock. He, too, turned the face to the light and checked the setting.

"You don't trust me?" Janet asked.

"I'm only double-checking," he said and took the clock back to the cushions with him and set it on the floor.

Nothing was said for a long while, and only the sound of the fountain and the occasional sound of ice in their glasses ruffled the silence. After a while Janet put her glass on the floor beside her bed and lay down, stretching out on the sheets. She said nothing. Haydon waited, sucking on the last piece of ice. It wasn't long before he heard the steady, measured breathing of her sleep.

Chapter 46

When the alarm rang at five o'clock, Haydon slapped his hand down on it and grabbed for the automatic as he sat up and peered into the greenish dark toward Janet's bed. She was there, still, unresponsive, her long naked body stretched out at an angle across the bed. He felt as if he had dozed only a few minutes. His arms and legs were heavy as lead, and his shoulders and neck felt as if they were fixed in cement.

He leaned back against the pillows. Nothing had changed. The heat had sucked all of the air out of the large bedroom, and the curtains hung limp and dampish. Haydon could taste the smoky night in his mouth and feel the thickness in his head from the two big glasses of gin. He felt a hundred years old.

He got to one knee and steadied himself and then stood, picked up the flight bag and the automatic and walked into the bathroom. He put the flight bag up under the tile vanity and laid the automatic on top of it. Taking off his shorts, he walked into the shower, which was simply a lower part of the room against a wall surrounded by curtains, pushed the curtain wide open so he could see Janet stretched across the bed on her stomach, and turned on the cold water. As he bathed under the gentle drizzle, he continued to keep his eyes on Janet, the water echoing off the tile walls of the bathroom as if he were in a small cavern. He washed his hair twice, soaped his body and rinsed until he was squeaky clean, and then turned off the water. As he reached for a towel, Janet stirred on the bed, rolled over on her back and pushed her hair out of her face. She stretched her long legs and her arms, lay still a moment, and then rolled over and looked at Haydon in the dark aqua light.

"Reveille?" she asked, staring at him.

"Yeah," he said. He finished drying, put on his shorts and combed his hair. He picked up the flight bag and gun and walked back into the bedroom where Janet was stepping into a clean pair of panties she had gotten out of the dresser. While he dressed, she went into the bathroom and washed up and then came back in and took a fresh sundress out of her closet. Haydon returned the cushions to the sofa, refolded the sheets and tossed them in one of the chairs.

"Do you want something to eat?" she asked, pulling her hair back. "I can make some eggs real quick, some toast."

"That'll be fine," he said, looking at his watch. "I'll help you. But first, if you want to take anything to Cobán, get it now and put it in a bag."

"Now?"

"Come on," Haydon said.

"Okay, okay." Janet went back to her closet and got a canvas tote bag with big looped handles and went to her dresser. She got hand lotion and tissues and opened a couple of drawers and got whatever sorts of things women carried on outings, a scarf, some cosmetics.

They went out, down the corridor to the kitchen, Haydon carrying the flight bag, which he set down near the kitchen table. Janet put her bag just inside the door to the dining room. While she started the coffee,

Haydon went to the refrigerator and took out the eggs, looked in the crisper for peppers and tomatoes and onions and began cutting them up on a small chopping block. In a few minutes they had everything ready and sat down together to eat. Neither of them had said a word the entire time.

After they had eaten a while and had had a couple of cups of coffee, Janet said, "You act like you've done this before."

Haydon nodded. "Every morning."

"No kidding?" She smiled.

"No kidding."

Janet looked at him as she sipped her coffee. She started to say something, but Haydon interrupted her.

"It's almost six o'clock. If you've got a Thermos, we could take some coffee with us. Okay?"

"Fine."

"But we've got to go outside a few minutes first."

Janet stiffened apprehensively.

Haydon shook his head, chewing his last bite of toast. "It's just some precautions I've taken. No big deal." He took another sip of coffee. "Come on."

Pushing away from the table, he picked up the flight bag, and they walked through the dining room and living room and out onto the breezeway. Janet unlocked the gate that separated the breezeway from the front drive courtyard and then turned off the alarm system from the control box just inside the gate.

"Go ahead and open the drive gates," Haydon said. Janet pushed the right buttons, and the gates at both ends of the courtyard drive slid back on tracks attached to the base of high stone walls.

344

Haydon stood with Janet inside the dark corridor of the breezeway, watching the street. "Just a few minutes," he said. The street beyond the gates was shiny with the nighttime humidity, and the smell of the garbage fires weighed heavily on the still air. The streets were empty, at least as far as traffic was concerned, but Haydon knew that somewhere out there somewhere, perhaps on an adjacent street nearby, someone had seen the courtyard gates pull open.

They heard the car before they saw it, and Haydon walked out to the courtyard just as the headlights hit the pillars at the gates and a taxi pulled slowly into the drive. Haydon waited as the driver got out and came around the back of the car.

"Dolfo, perfect timing," Haydon said, reaching out to shake the kid's hand.

"I tol' you. Whatever you want," Dolfo said, lighting a cigarette. He looked at Janet with an appraising eye. "Okay," he said to Haydon. He came around and opened the door to the backseat of the taxi and pulled a blanket off two people who were lying bent over in the seat, a man and a woman. They sat up and got out of the taxi.

Haydon looked at them, visually measuring their height, the woman's hairstyle. "Good, very good," he said. "What about the four-wheel-drive rental?"

"It is a Blazer. I have it in a parking lot in Zona 1," Dolfo said and gave Haydon the address. "The parking lot is behind walls, the other two people are waiting there."

"Okay," Haydon said. "Put the man in the front seat with you and the woman in the back."

"*Bueno.*"

"Give us a few minutes." Haydon walked back to Janet. "We've got to turn everything off in the house, just like we were leaving."

"We're not?"

"Not yet."

They went inside and closed everything up just as they had six hours before when they went to bed. After Janet got her bag and the Thermos of coffee, they turned off the lights in the kitchen last of all and made their way slowly through the dark house back out to the breezeway and the drive.

"Okay, Dolfo," Haydon said walking back to the kid, who was leaning against the back fender of his taxi. "Try to make it all the way to the border." He shook the young man's hand again. "Don't forget who you're dealing with here."

"No problem," Dolfo said, dropping his cigarette and grinding it out in the drive.

"*¡Buena suerte!*" Haydon said.

The man and the woman were already seated in the car and Dolfo went around to the driver's side. He started the car, flipped on the lights, and pulled around the curving drive and out into the street.

"Close the gates," Haydon said, and Janet reached up to the control box, and the gates slid silently into place. Haydon watched the taxi's taillights disappear.

"Okay, what in the hell is going on here?"

345

"You and I have just headed for the El Salvador border, Valle Nuevo," Haydon said. "It's one hundred twenty-two kilometers, about an hour-and-a-half's drive."

"You really think that's going to work?"

"Because of the dark, it can."

"Great. Now what?"

"We wait twenty minutes."

"Then?"

"Then you and I head for Panajachel."

"Not Cobán?"

"Come on," Haydon said, "let's double-check everything."

By the time they got back to the breezeway it was time to go. They put the bags in the Land-Rover, and Janet got behind the wheel. She pushed the remote control on the gates once again, and they drove out, and the gates closed behind them.

At Haydon's instructions she stayed on the back streets all the way downtown. The streets were virtually empty, which made it easier for him to pick up a tail if one drifted in behind them. He saw nothing. If there had been someone watching the house they had gone to Valle Nuevo with Dolfo. No one would know about Panajachel but Pitt's people, having learned it from Mirtha. They wouldn't be watching the house. Knowing Janet's Land-Rover, they would be waiting to pick her up along the Roosevelt highway or in Mixco, somewhere along the way before the possibility of various routes opened up. The nearer to the house, the safer. That was the reason for the second transfer.

They reached the address Dolfo had given them just as the sky began to lighten in the east, just as cars began to move in the narrow downtown streets. They pulled up to the gates of the walled parking lot, and a teenage girl wearing jeans and short-sleeved blouse appeared suddenly in Janet's headlights. Unlocking a chain that held the gates together, she pushed open the two wings and stood aside. Janet pulled the Land-Rover into the caliche lot, and Haydon directed her to park beside a Chevrolet Blazer sitting alone to one side, well out of the way of the gate. A man and a woman got out of the truck.

"Get your bag," Haydon said, grabbing the flight bag. "And leave the keys in the ignition."

He got out and shook hands with the man, a ladino, more European in appearance than Indian. His eyes were wary as they darted between

Janet and Haydon. The woman, also ladino, hung back by the rear of the Blazer. No one exchanged names.

"Dolfo has made everything clear to you?" Haydon asked, using the kid's name to reassure the man. "You have any questions?"

The man shook his head. "I understand everything."

Haydon looked at the woman. Her hair was fine, and she was wearing an American dress.

"Okay," Haydon said. "The keys are in the Rover."

"Hey," Janet said suddenly. "What in the hell are you doing?"

The man looked startled, glancing at Haydon and then at Janet.

"He's taking the Rover to Panajachel," Haydon said.

"Are you out of your mind?" Janet was incredulous. "I'll never see it again, for Christ's sake."

"It's the only chance we have of going where we're going alone," Haydon said. "This is it, and it's still a gamble. These people stand to make a lot of money if this works. I've arranged that. But in order to collect they've got to get the Rover back to you. They're running some risk too. I'll explain it to you, but we've *got* to get on the road. It's getting light."

Janet glared at him a second and then held up her hands as if relinquishing everything, the canvas bag hanging from her shoulders.

Haydon reached out and shook the man's hand. *"¡Buena suerte!"* he said.

The woman came from behind the Blazer, and the two couples crawled into their separate vehicles. Haydon got behind the wheel of the Blazer, which was new and smelled new. He didn't even start the motor, but waited for the other couple to back the Land-Rover around and drive out of the parking lot.

"It's about the same distance to Panajachel as it is to the El Salvador border," Haydon said quietly. "With luck we've got until eight o'clock or eight-thirty—somewhere in that range—before this little routine is discovered."

"This is goddamned extreme," Janet said. "I've got personal stuff scattered around in the Rover, for God's sake. You don't *know* how extreme this is. You don't just give your goddamned car away to people like this."

"After what I've been through, it doesn't seem extreme at all," Haydon said. He was staring at the crumbling stucco wall at the front bumper. A slogan, fading and partly obscured and just now coming into sight with the charcoal light, was scrawled in paint across the stucco and patches of exposed bricks: *UN PUEBLO CON HAMBRE ES UN PUEBLO SIN PAZ.* A country that is hungry is a country without peace. "Not extreme at all," he said.

He unzipped the flight bag and took out one of the maps he had gotten out of Borrayo's glove compartment. He laid it on top of the bag, which was sitting between him and Janet, and started the car. As he flipped on the lights and backed around, the teenage girl came out of the little darkened ticket office at the entrance of the lot and once again pulled open the gates. Haydon reached out and gave her several dollars, American, and steered the Blazer out into the almost empty predawn streets.

The city was not yet awake, but it was stirring as Haydon went a few streets over and turned left, which was north, on 7a avenida, which ran straight through the city without diversion on the north/south axis. Within moments they were entering the east side of the Parque Central, its broad spaces and islands of trees and fountains empty and forlorn in the graying dawn. To their right the Catedral Metropolitana sat like a brooding mountain against the growing light, its baroque-style towers and domes silent in the morning gloom. Its west-oriented façade would remain in the shadows until noon, after which it would offer to the post-meridian sun a glaring white face behind which the cavernous interior would provide a refuge of echoing and shadowy coolness from the swelling afternoon heat.

On the other side of the plaza, to their left, the Palacio Nacional glowered biliously, a three-story farrago of classic and colonial architectural motifs of light green stone whose beautiful and hidden inner courtyards and gardens were its only grace. Its soul was more accurately reflected in its exterior, a dishonest design for a mendacious government. The sight of it angered and frustrated and frightened hundreds of thousands, even millions of the people it was supposedly there to serve.

Janet sat curiously silent as Haydon pushed the Blazer through the long narrow street, a seamless corridor of stucco buildings that often reflected nothing of their business, the Hospital San Sebastián on the right, Hospital Santa Cleotilde on the left, farther on, the Association of Christian Mothers. Then abruptly, they arrived at the intersection of Calle Martí which would eventually become the Central American Highway Number 9, known to everyone as the Atlantic Highway.

Chapter 47

As the sun rose directly into their faces, the rather derelict boulevard was bathed in a reddish light. At first scorched palms grew out of the otherwise bare dirt median and then nothing at all, and the hard-packed earth was scattered with trash and bits of debris that blew across the asphalt. They made good time in the sparse traffic that was strung out along the commercial strip as it made its way to the outskirts of the city past the ubiquitous auto-parts stores and laundries and Wimpy's

Hamburguesas and billboards advertising Pepsi and pantyhose. The commerce thinned out and soon they were crossing the gorge of the Río Las Vacas on the long Belice Bridge, the shanties visible far down in the smoky ravines on either side.

On the other side of the bridge the highway began to climb steadily into the hills. The city gave way to industries, sawmills, brickworks, factories, and food-processing plants, set back off the highway in the *colonias* which themselves grew increasingly sparse and poor as the city melted away to a bare and desperate countryside burned by the *verano* sun and sheared of its forests by the hordes of immigrants who attached themselves to the edges of the city like rust and who needed the wood for their voracious little cook fires and for warmth in the rainy season.

The highway climbed and twisted into increasingly dry and parched hills, dropped into barren gorges and crossed long narrow bridges that spanned others, pushing deeper into a desert region that seemed entirely as if it belonged on another continent. Because CA-9 was the route to Guatemala's main port, Santo Tomás de Castilla outside of Puerto Barrios on the Gulf of Honduras, the highway was always thick with trucks and buses carrying produce and product and laborers. This morning as always the heat built early and the pace of the traffic kept abreast of the rapidly rising temperatures. All the buses and trucks seemed to be driven by sociopaths who flogged their often decrepit machines as though they were hell bound. They passed on downhill curves and uphill ones, honking and sweating and swearing, their faces sometimes blanching at the horrors of their own rashness as they forced mad passage between the traffic they were overtaking and the traffic that was approaching, often causing it to swerve onto precipitous caliche shoulders to avoid head-on collisions. But the drivers never slowed, barreling on in the heat, the canvas over their cargo flapping in the hot, tortured air like the capes on the bony backs of the Four Horsemen of the Apocalypse, men in reckless control of their destinies.

350

Soon locked in a hopeless conga line of overloaded buses and crippled trucks belching black acrid smoke as they labored on the climbing switchbacks, Haydon and Janet rolled down their windows. Janet gamely twisted her hair into a tight coil and pinned it up off her neck, hiked her skirt up high on her long thighs, put on her sunglasses and stared out to the embattled highway. Even though the hot wind coming off the dark stony hills beat against their faces as it whipped in through the open windows, Janet was unperturbed. She knew ahead of time what the trip would be like. But Haydon could tell she was still furious about the Land-Rover.

They continued in the heat through mountains with slate gray rocks that yielded nothing but cactus and scrub brush and occasionally a patch of withering corn on the steep slopes. Small whitewashed or dun-colored stucco houses sat isolated on far slopes or at the bottom of gorges, baking in the sun.

Haydon looked at his watch. "If this kind of traffic keeps up there's no way we'll make it in three hours."

Janet shook her head. "It won't. When we get to El Rancho we'll turn off north to Cobán. Most of this traffic, not all of it but most of it, will keep on going to the coast."

They came to another long climb, and the stream of traffic slowed to a crawl.

"Here, take the wheel," he said to Janet. "I've got to get this coat off." She reached over and held the wheel steady while he wrestled off his suit coat and threw it over into the backseat. He rolled back his cuffs and then took the wheel again. "Thanks," he said. "One more favor. Would you mind pouring me a cup of coffee?" His mouth felt oily from the constant blast of diesel smoke, and his eyes were burning from the hot wind and bright light as he squinted into the sun. He hadn't brought his sunglasses.

The traffic crept absurdly up the steep grades, picked up speed on the crests, and then plunged wildly into the downhill stretches, brakes screaming on the curves but not for long as each driver coped with as much speed as he dared in order to gain some momentum for the next long climb. Occasionally the cliffs beside the highway were recruited as political billboards on which the competing parties painted their initials and party logos, some of them very precisely rendered—a stylized brilliant orange sun, a blue flower, a white fist gripping a rose, a red rooster.

351

Janet handed him the cup of coffee and then poured one for herself, screwing the top on the Thermos as she gripped it between her knees.

"Have you been watching to see if we're being followed?" she asked, wedging the Thermos between the seats.

He nodded. "Yeah, but it's hard to tell. We've been lined up like this for so long. There are several cars and another Blazer, the rest in this string with us are trucks and buses." He sipped the coffee. "When we get to the right kind of place I'm going to check it out."

Janet looked at him, the black orbs of her sunglasses hiding what he needed to see, and then she turned back to watch the road.

The chance came ten hot miles later when the mountains jogged back southward and then again to the north and just in the kink of the bend a long suspension bridge spanned a gorge at the bottom of which was the unimpressive Río Plátanos and the glistening double rails of a railroad. On the other side of the gorge the highway rounded another bend, and just before it did, a dirt road cut off and meandered down into the gorge.

Haydon looked in the mirror and memorized the colors and makes of the cars and noted the color of the other Blazer. The vehicles steamed into the bend, meeting a straggling of traffic heading for the capital. They crossed the bridge high above the river at the bottom of the gorge and started around the other side. The traffic straightened out like a serpent rounding a corner, and Haydon kept his eye on the dirt road, which they were approaching at an angle that would obscure his exit to the traffic that was following the vehicles directly behind him.

"I'm going to turn off," he said quickly, and whipped off the highway, catching Janet by surprise and throwing her over onto him, her coffee flying, as they hit the caliche in a cloud of dust that boiled up and then settled around them as he turned into a grove of scrub oaks just off the highway.

"Dammit, Haydon," she yelled. "You could've said something . . ."

He hadn't anticipated the telltale cloud of dust, which, if it didn't settle quickly enough, would make the maneuver a foolish waste of time. The Blazer was facing the highway, and Haydon was out, the door open, watching the traffic. There had been two trucks and a bus behind him and all of them passed before the first two cars, wedged in between another bus and truck, then another car, the Blazer, a flatbed truck loaded with cinder blocks and another car. All of them went by, they had to. There was no way they could have anticipated the turnoff. Haydon had no way of knowing how far they would have to go if they wanted to turn around.

He looked around at Janet, who had unbuttoned the top of her sundress and was fanning the coffee stain on the front of it. But she, too, was watching the traffic.

"I don't know," he said, getting back behind the wheel. "Sorry," he added, looking at her dress. "We'll wait a while."

"Oh, great. This is a good place to wait," she said, holding the front of her dress out with one hand and wiping the perspiration from around her mouth with the other.

"You think you'd recognize any of those trucks or cars if you saw them again?" He wrapped his arms around the steering wheel and stared out the windshield. Another gathering of buses and trucks was already moving past in front of them.

"I might," she said.

"If someone was following us they'll wait up ahead." He reached for the map on the seat. "At Sanarate maybe. El Rancho for sure."

"Do you think there is someone?"

He tossed the map back on the seat and stretched his left leg out the open door. "I don't know," he said. "I guess we've reduced the odds some."

Looking to his left, he squinted in the glare out across the scrub brush where the mountain dropped down to the Río Plátanos. The traffic steamed and groaned on the highway, and when there was a break in the sound of diesel engines the cicadas whined and keened in the unrelenting heat.

"How long we going to sit here?" Janet played with the height of her dress on her bare thighs, her expression hidden behind the lenses of her sunglasses, her face slightly flushed from the heat.

"Not long," he said, looking at his watch. "Fifteen minutes."

They stayed in the Blazer because it was the only shade, and even though Janet opened her door to let through a cross breeze, the air was hot and biting. Haydon wished for some of the ice he had had in his gin the night before. Janet fanned her legs until it was time to go.

The rest of the trip to El Rancho was like what had gone before. They gulped hot, diesel-laden air, crept up the steep rising grades and hurtled down the falling ones. They saw a wreck that had occurred conveniently at a caliche pullover where the highway bottomed out in a ravine and began another ascent. A small green Japanese car had apparently pulled out in front of a flatbed truck carrying a load of clay pots headed into the capital. Everyone was sitting beside the road, doing nothing, looking exhausted and forlorn. Haydon could not imagine what they were waiting for.

Though the highway had taken them on an up-and-down course, they actually had been falling steadily in elevation ever since they had left the capital, crossing over a low, nameless range of mountains into the arid Motagua River valley that cut across the country from east to west, accommodating Guatemala's longest river.

At El Rancho, a dusty junction in the bottom of the valley, a film of sulfuric yellow dust coated everything including the stiff shocks of hair of the children who wandered along the caliche shoulders and lingered in the shade of the small food stands set up by locals hoping to take advantage of thirsty or hungry travelers slowing for the intersection. El Rancho itself was a couple of kilometers farther on, invisible beyond the undulating heat waves and dwarfed by a gigantic electric power station that rose stark and ominous like the ogre's castle on the outskirts of the junction.

Haydon turned left at the intersection and crossed over the Motagua River to the north bank and doubled back west. As Janet had predicted, most of the traffic was left behind at El Rancho. The terrain began to change. It was still desert, but this was true desert as opposed to what they had just been through, which simply had been a poor countryside burned up by the *verano* sun. Here the highway began to climb gently through a more picturesque setting, vegetation designed by nature for its environment, prickly pear and rangy cereus cacti, and thickets of thorny acacias. And, unlike the country south of the river, wildlife was visible here, orioles flashed like orange sparks in the dull reddish brush, and more than once Haydon saw brief flights of snub-nosed lime-green parrots, as exotic a thing as anyone would hope to see in the desert. And then there were the *zopilotes,* soaring, drifting, waiting, black crucifixes dangling like unimaginative mobiles from a glaucous sky.

354

The quickness with which the landscape changed in Guatemala was something that struck Haydon as marvelous the first time he visited there, and on subsequent trips it never failed to remind him of a theme park where every kind of terrain in "Guatemala" was represented in a short trip on a miniature train, here the desert, around this corner the cloud-crowned western highlands, here the northern jungles of the Petén, and now the volcanoes of the central highlands and the banana plantations of the east coast, and here the ever-rainy tropical cloud forests.

From an elevation of about fifteen hundred feet at El Rancho, the small two-lane highway rose steadily to three thousand feet and then to four thousand. The bare, pockmarked mountains of the desert gave way to hills with thicker vegetation, stands of pine suddenly appeared, and within ten miles the temperature dropped twenty degrees. Pockets of wispy fog began to appear here and there in the draws of converging hills, their vaporous tails sometimes reaching into the stands of pines. The air softened, and the moist fragrance of conifers wafted through the windows of the Blazer.

Then the road climbed sharply and they came to a village way station where they were supposed to stop, pay a fee, and have their car sprayed with an insecticide before progressing any farther up into the lush vegetation. The station, a cluster of half a dozen stucco buildings that looked distinctly European in style, sat off the highway on a thin isthmus of a ridge where the road turned and began a steep climb. The central building was vaguely triangular in shape, its two diverging sides forming two "streets" fifty meters in length before the hamlet ended where the ridge fell away abruptly into the valley on the other side. Haydon pulled off the turn in the highway and stopped the Blazer in front of the building. An Indian man and woman stood in the dooryard and looked at them silently, apparently unwilling to administer the insecticide and reluctant, or unconcerned, about coming out to collect the fee.

But one checkpoint's laziness was another checkpoint's offense. Haydon knew he had to have the receipt for passing the station, so he got out of the Blazer and went up to the doorway and paid. They gave him a receipt, and he went back to the truck, where Janet was buying candy from two little girls who were displaying their sticky, homemade confection on a dirty board.

Haydon got back in, Janet paid the girls, and Haydon slowly maneuvered the Blazer through a scattering of speckled chickens that were pecking all over the road as if it were a barnyard. That was the checkpoint.

From here on the land dropped again, back to four thousand feet, and they entered lush and cool pine forests cleared out here and there for *granjas,* small single-family farms with meager plots of corn or chickpeas, some with cinder-block houses with red tile roofs that glistened in the moisture-laden atmosphere, some with wattle-and-mud houses with rusty corrugated tin roofs, but each of the homesteads, the houses and their plots of corn and peas, was invariably partially hidden within a stand of limp and glistening banana trees.

They now were well into the *departamento* of Baja Verapaz, the

Lower True Peace, and the forests grew thicker, the highway climbed even higher, and suddenly, around a bend in the winding road, the Sierra de Chuacús threw up their muscular shoulders against a roiling, titanic bank of thick white clouds with depths of gray that churned and struggled against the summits but did not cross as the Chuacús grudgingly held back the life-giving rain from the parched Motagua desert valley below.

The light began to change, affected by the huge plumes of clouds that diffused the sun above them rather than blocking it out. They drove through a luminous land without a sun, without a sky, lighted only by a glowing canopy of tumbling clouds.

They climbed again to five thousand feet and crossed the invisible border into the misty regions of *la selva nublado,* the cloud forest, that exotic high-mountain tropical land of ferns and bromeliads and orchids, where the famous and mythical national bird, the quetzal, resided in sequestered and timorous resplendence as though it knew full well that it had retreated to its last refuge and was living through the waning days of its existence.

The pine forests were behind them now, and the light in this primeval region was brooding and embraced by a dense fog that rose and fell over black-green jungle-draped mountains like the breath of gods. This was the land of the *chipichipi,* the fine drizzle that fell unceasingly, touching everything lightly, intimately, penetratingly. There was no "dry season" in this region, though in January and February the drizzle was less heavy than during the rest of the year. It was not a land for people predisposed to melancholy or dark moods.

By the time they approached the Biotopo del Quetzal, almost three thousand acres of cloud forest set aside as a reserve and administered by the University of San Carlos, it was late morning and they were still an hour away from Cobán. They stopped at a small inn not far from the entrance to the reserve. It sat on the cliff side of the roadway overlooking a vast valley whose panoramic sweep could only be guessed at because it was veiled in floating clouds of mist and fog. Across the roadway a green wall of jungle-covered mountain rose up and disappeared into a gray eternity. They had fresh, strong coffee from overlarge cups and a small plate of fried plantains prepared by an Indian woman and her young daughter. Outside they stretched their legs a few minutes on the damp caliche shoulder, the huge silence of the cloud forest cushioning the sounds around them. Before they got back into the Blazer, Janet pulled a sweater from her bag, and Haydon put on his suit coat against the slight, but welcome, chill.

In a few kilometers they went through a village of scattered dwellings known as Pasmolon and shortly thereafter passed into the *departamento* of Alta Verapaz, the Upper True Peace.

Chapter 48

Cobán was a cloudy and mist-laden little town situated on the Cahabón River and surrounded by mountainous countryside veined with clear streams and pockets of meadows and small valleys that were kept lush and verdant by the constant gentle drizzle. In the late nineteenth century, President Barrios granted thousands of acres of this rich mountain country to German immigrants who were willing to plant the land in coffee. The coffee plantations flourished as did the German community until its members dominated the economy of the region, shipping their coffee harvests by rail and boat down through the Polochic River valley and thence to Puerto Barrios for export. The wealthy Germans reigned supreme in the high mountain valleys of Alta Verapaz, which in its richness and beauty was so much like their homeland, until the 1930s. Their open support of the Nazis back home, however, brought about their ruin when Guatemala entered the war on the side of the Allies, and the wealthy Germans who had retained their German citizenship were booted out of the country and their well-run and productive coffee fincas wcrc appropriated by the Guatemalan government. Today the German influence remained only in subtleties, in the occasional German surname or the Nordic architecture of an old home or in the blue-eyed Indian with unusually fair skin.

The central plaza of Cobán was small and triangular with its base facing east and anchored by the lichen-stained stone Catedral de Santo Domingo where a sixteenth-century wood carving of the Virgin Mary and Christ Child presided over the main altar. The other two sides of the plaza were fronted by the arcaded palace headquarters of the departmental government and the local army headquarters. Near the apex of the triangle, which pointed west, was the office of Guatel, the national telephone company.

It was here that Haydon wanted to go first, parking the Blazer at the curb of the cement sidewalk in front of the tiny La Providencia Hotel.

"Now what?" Janet asked. They had not talked much in the last hour since they had left the small inn near the Biotopo. The countryside had been beautiful, the weather cool, and the impending meeting with Lena very much on their minds.

"I've got to make a telephone call," Haydon said, cutting the engine and opening the door.

"I'll just wait here," Janet said.

Haydon looked at her, and she rolled her head and got out of the truck. Haydon got the flight bag out of the backseat, stuffed his 10mm into his waistband, and locked the doors. He gave three Indian boys a few quetzals to "watch" the Blazer, and they started across the apex of the plaza, up the slight incline to the Guatel office. The quietness of this small and isolated departmental capital was welcome after the madness of Guatemala City, but Haydon did not like the feeling of knowing he was being watched. In some ways it was even more eerie than knowing you were being tailed.

The Guatel office was a large gloomy room with the familiar apa-

359

thetic air of a governmental business. On the far side of the room behind a rail with swinging gates was a row of half a dozen wooden telephone booths, one or two of them occupied. In the middle of the room, with their backs to the railing, were two rows of wooden chairs. To his left was a wooden cage of the sort seen in old banks and post offices, behind which several women and a man worked in silence. The man was doing paperwork and the women were operating the antiquated telephone system.

Janet went over to the chairs and sat down, while Haydon walked to one of the grilled windows and gave the woman the number he wanted to call in Belize. She scribbled the number on a piece of paper, and then he went back and sat down beside Janet, who seemed preoccupied, staring out the open door to the gray street.

"Where was the place where she wanted to buy the candles?" he asked.

Janet made a vague gesture with her right arm. "Down that way, a little shop that sells coffee and cardamom and 'artifacts.' It's up some stairs, on the second floor. It's got a turquoise wainscoting on the outside, if I remember right."

"When was this?"

"Last year."

The telephone in one of the open telephone booths began ringing, and Haydon looked at the woman behind the cage, who tilted her head toward the ringing telephone and nodded at him. He got up and went through one of the swinging gates and went into the booth and closed the door, keeping his eye on Janet through the glass. The call was brief. Things were confirmed. Clarified. He hung up and went back through the gate to the grilled windows again, where the woman told him how long his call had been and what it cost. He paid; the woman gave him a receipt, and he and Janet walked back out onto the street.

"Let's buy some cardamom," he said. The street came off the northern angle of the plaza and headed down a slope toward the western end of town, fading away into the mist six or eight blocks in the distance. Cinder-block buildings formed a continuous face on both sides of the narrow street, none more than two stories, most of them only one. The long floppy leaves of plantains hung over head-high walls, and the façades of the buildings were a variety of familiar Central American colors—salmon and turquoise and blue and dun and ocher—sometimes the whole building had been painted and sometimes only a now-faded wainscoting.

Plastic prefabricated signs with lights inside them and announcing Pepsi and Coke battled for supremacy as they hung out in front of business establishments whose names appeared below or above the familiar colorful logo in small black letters: PEPSI: El Convite Café; COCA-COLA: Cafetería Rosita; COCA-COLA: Hotel La Providencia; COCA-COLA: Farmacia Cristiana; PEPSI: Restaurante El Sombrero Tejano. But Coca-Cola, which easily received first prize for the greatest contribution to the municipal tackiness, hit an advertising bonanza with the Hotel Cobán Imperial. This establishment, which sat on a corner, its façade running in two directions, devoted its entire color scheme to **Coca-Cola** red and white with blistering effect. Only the constant blanket of color-muting fog kept the building from igniting.

Stepping around a dog who had stopped on the sidewalk to lunch on a splatter of vomit, they crossed the street and went half a block farther to a turquoise building with two doorways. The first doorway was a wide-open sidewalk *comedor* where the rich savor of grilled meat wafted out into the fog, and the second doorway was a narrow opening above which a sign read, IMPORTACIÓNES TIKAL.

"Yeah, this is it," Janet said. "I remember the sign now."

Immediately inside the opening the wooden stairs ascended steeply to a landing where the stairs turned left into a frosted glass door. Again the words IMPORTACIÓNES TIKAL. Janet pushed the door, which had just enough room to swing open before another flight of stairs went straight up to a room. At the top of the stairs a hallway turned right, went ten or twelve meters, and opened onto an outside balcony that surrounded an open courtyard. Before reaching the balcony, however, they turned left through a doorway into a long narrow room with a wooden floor. In front of them, against the entire length of the wall, were rows of wooden shelves in front of which a glass display cabinet and counter also ran the length of the room. Opposite these, in the middle of the room, were double doors that opened out onto the balcony over the courtyard.

The room was full of sacks of coffee beans stacked against the walls and smaller sacks of a finer weave filled with cardamom piled on the shelves. The glass counter displayed candies and jellied fruits and regionally grown spices. Two Indian women were working among the sacks and cans and jars of produce, both of them wearing the traditional Indian

361

clothing of the region: lacy short *huipiles* decorated with bright embroi-dered flowers hanging loosely over pleated skirts that reached only to their calves. Each woman had her hair braided in a single long braid that hung past her waist.

While Janet talked with them, buying small sacks of coffee and car-damom and other spices, Haydon walked through the doors in the center of the room that opened onto the balcony. Half a dozen bright green parrots sat on the wooden railing of the balustrade that encircled the balcony, moving freely along the many meters of railing. Little tin trays of food were attached to some of the wooden pillars that held up the roof.

A wispy coil of smoke rose lazily from a fire in the courtyard where an elderly man and woman were cooking thin strips of meat and ears of corn over the grill of a brick oven. The courtyard was filled with orchids and bromeliads and plantains, among which little hard-packed dirt paths crossed at convenient angles from one side of the courtyard to the other. While Haydon leaned his forearms on the railing, a huge maroon-fronted parrot sidestepped toward him, thought better of it and then sidestepped away, just as the heavy fog turned to the region's famed *chipichipi* and the slow drizzle began thrumming on the tile roof of the building and slapping on the broad leaves of the plantains in the court-yard. The elderly couple, of course, was dry, their oven-grill well under the eaves. Soon the rain was running steadily off the eaves and falling past Haydon as though a shimmering veil had been dropped over the edge of the roof. It fell into a shallow stone trench built around the courtyard to carry the water away into the street. The smell of birds and rain and damp earth filled the air, and the drumming of the drizzle that fell straight down out of the gray was punctuated occasionally by a shriek from one or another of the parrots that waddled along the quadrangle of railings like grouchy old men.

362

A door opened halfway down the side of the balcony to Haydon's left, and a man and woman emerged, talking in low voices. Haydon scooted the flight bag closer to the railing with his foot and started to turn around to see what Janet was doing inside the shop when the couple approached and he recognized the woman, who was staring straight at him. She raised her finger to her lips, and the man stepped inside the doorway, blocking Janet's line of sight to Haydon, and took his time lighting a cigarette.

"You weren't followed into Cobán," the woman said in the same perfect English she had used in the empty warehouse above the shoe store. She spoke quickly. "But something has gone wrong. The local military intelligence has received a communication from the capital to look for you and to keep you under surveillance. They have discovered your car, and men in plainclothes are combing the area around the square. The old man and woman down there," she nodded to the courtyard below, "have a *comedor*. Eat there; don't leave. Don't tell the woman."

Her companion, whom Haydon now saw was not the same man she had been with in Guatemala City, shook out the match that he had used to light his cigarette, and the two of them continued around the corner and descended a flight of stairs that led from the balcony down into the courtyard.

Haydon picked up the flight bag and walked back into the shop. Janet was holding her hand out, receiving change for her purchases from one of the Indian women.

"There's a little *comedor* down in the courtyard," Haydon said. "Let's get something to eat."

"There are some good places to eat just off the square," Janet said, putting her money into her bag along with the paper sack of her purchases. "There's a good Chinese food place there, in fact."

"Downstairs looks good to me," Haydon said. "Besides, I don't want to walk back to the plaza."

"Why, what's the matter?"

"We ought to be careful until someone contacts us. They told us to come here, we did, now we ought to wait as discreetly as possible. If they're any good they'll pick us up. We don't have to parade around town."

"We're not going to 'parade.' The plaza's just four blocks away."

"Let's go downstairs," Haydon said. "Okay?"

She looked at him quizzically as if she suspected he knew something she didn't. "Okay," she said.

The rain had slackened and was only dribbling off the eaves of the tile roof as they rounded the corner and started down the wooden stairs into the courtyard.

The old couple's *comedor* opened off the far side of the courtyard and consisted of two adjacent rooms connected by a double-door opening from which the doors themselves had been removed. The rooms were fairly small, allowing for only four simple wooden tables with straight-backed chairs in each room. The outside walls of the two rooms were double French doors that opened onto two narrow balconies with wrought-iron railings and which, because the building was on a sloping hillside, overlooked the street below at about the level of the tops of the cars. The balcony doors were thrown open, letting in the sound of rain and washing the room in a luminous gray light that reflected dully off the time-burnished surfaces of the tables.

Three tables in the first room were occupied, so Haydon walked through the double-door opening into the second room where only one table was occupied—by the woman and man he had seen on the balcony. Haydon led Janet to a table away from them and near the balcony and sat down. As with the other room, the door that led out to the courtyard was open, and Haydon saw the old man and woman laboring at the open-air oven.

A young Indian man wearing a frayed dark green cowboy shirt, brown bell-bottom polyester trousers, and a wispy moustache came in from the courtyard and brought them bowls of onion soup with spoons and a plate of tortillas. Pieces of chicken were floating in the soup. Simply by walking in and sitting down they tacitly agreed to be served the meal of the day.

Janet looked at Haydon. "How long do you think we're going to have to wait?"

"I've got no idea," he said, picking up a spoon. He folded a tortilla and started eating. The soup was hot and good, the bits of chicken spicy.

There was no conversation coming from the couple a table away, but in the next room two couples sitting at one table conversed incessantly in a low murmur. As cars passed on the street outside, their tires swished on the rain-slick blacktop and, inexplicably, a rooster crowed somewhere down the hillside in the tiny streets blanketed in mist.

364

They finished their soup in silence, and the young man returned and took away their bowls. When he came back again he brought two plates, each with an ear of roasted corn, slices of lime, slices of avocado, strips of grilled pork, and a mound of black beans mashed to the consistency of pâté. And another plate of tortillas.

"Dos cafecitos?" he asked, and both Haydon and Janet nodded, and the young man quickly returned with two big cups of black coffee to which the sugar already had been added.

Haydon began to eat. He was so disconcerted by what the woman had told him on the balcony that he ignored Janet altogether. The G-2 had learned of their arrival in Cobán? How could that be? He went back over every step of his planning. The two diversionary couples. Janet hadn't been out of his sight. The woman had said they had arrived in Cobán alone. Everything had worked . . . but the G-2 knew he was in Cobán. Neither Dolfo nor the other decoy couple knew where he and Janet were going, so even if the G-2 had resorted to their infamously persuasive questioning techniques, they couldn't have given them away.

It hadn't been his planning . . . it had been his inability to understand the depth of the duplicity with which he was dealing. Thinking back, the only place where either he or Janet had mentioned Cobán was in her house. He looked at her as she squeezed lime juice over her avocado. It was odd about women like her, it didn't seem logical that such a woman was so constructed that one couldn't even decipher whether she were incredibly oblivious or incredibly clever. But such was the case. He didn't know whether Janet was being used or was herself designing. In either case, she was dangerous for him, and that had been abundantly emphasized only twenty minutes earlier when the woman on the balcony had warned him not to tell her of their communication.

Smoke from the cook fire outside in the courtyard seeped into the modest dining rooms, filling the still air with the tangy fragrance of oak. Outside the balcony windows the *chipichipi* was once again falling steadily, and a veil of fog drifted in with it, obscuring the red tile roofs along the streets below.

Haydon's brooding had the same effect on Janet that it had on Nina, she sensed it and decided to leave him alone. They finished their meal in silence, and when the young Indian came to take away their plates, Haydon asked for another cup of coffee. Janet started to protest and then thought better of it and nodded in agreement.

It was the first of three cups they were to order over the course of the next two hours. Eventually everyone in the two dining rooms left, even the man and woman from the balcony, but the young Indian never asked them to pay and never came in to bother them at all except when Haydon turned to signal him for more coffee. Haydon didn't know what he was supposed to expect, but he came to realize that this *comedor* was their safe house. They had to stay here until it was time . . . for whatever was going to happen.

At first Janet decided she was going to play Haydon's game. She sat with him in silence, sipping the earthy Cobán coffee with its raw cane

365

sugar and swinging her crossed leg impatiently, her eyes wandering about the two rooms, boredom quickly setting in. She lasted twenty minutes. She got up and started over to the balcony to look out, but Haydon stopped her. She knew why; she hadn't thought. Embarrassed, she went to the door that opened onto the courtyard and stood there looking into the lush, glistening vegetation. Haydon watched her and listened to the parrots shriek sporadically on the railings above. But waiting in silence was against Janet's nature, and she grew increasingly agitated. Finally she turned and stalked back to the table and picked up her purse, which was sitting in one of the chairs.

"This is bullshit," she snapped. "I'm getting out of here."

"Wait . . ." Haydon reached over and grabbed the strap of her purse.

Janet flared. *"What* in the hell do you think you're doing?" She jerked the bag, but Haydon held on, stood and gripped her by the arm.

"You're going to have to stay here, Janet," his voice was steady, low. "It's the only way I can be sure."

"Sure of what?"

"That we'll get in touch with Lena."

She stared at him. "You don't know that."

"What's your solution?"

"Get out there and let them know we're here. What are we hiding in here for?"

"They said to come here."

"They didn't say to *stay* here, for Christ's sake."

"Don't you think they'd let us know to do something else if that's what they wanted?"

Janet fixed her eyes on him. "I'm getting the hell out of here," she said, and an alarm bell went off in Haydon's head, something about the tone of her voice, as if she thought she had stretched her luck as far as it could go, as if something was overdue.

The footsteps were sudden and loud on the wooden floor, and Haydon turned reflexively to see the woman from the balcony enter the room with three men, all of them carrying the snub-nosed little Uzi's, their hair and clothes soaked by the *chipichipi.*

"They're getting signals from here," the woman said as she stalked across the room and snatched Janet's purse. "Get over there," she said to Janet, nodding toward the wall behind Haydon. Her companions stationed themselves at the doors, one of them moving over near Janet. The woman slung her Uzi over her shoulder and emptied Janet's purse onto the table. Working quickly, she went through everything, taking caps off lipstick, scraping out makeup from Janet's compact, disassembling a decorative key-chain holder, examining a flacon of perfume, anything large enough to have pieces came apart.

When she had gone through everything, she stood abruptly.

"Where is it?"

Janet was dumbstruck and simply stared at her.

"Where is it?" the woman snapped.

Janet stared.

"Take off your clothes," the woman said.

"Wait a minute," Haydon said. *"Who's* getting signals?"

The woman turned on him. "Cage is here."

"Cage? I thought you said they were G-2."

"They're both here."

Haydon was stunned. He turned to Janet. "What in the hell have you done?"

"We picked up his people shortly after I spoke to you on the balcony," the woman said. "Five or six of them—that's how many we've identified so far anyway, scattered around the plaza. And there's a van parked on the north side of the cathedral. We think the receiver is a powerful one, set up inside the van."

"You've seen Cage?" Haydon asked.

"No, not him," the woman said. "Half an hour ago, everyone, all of them started migrating toward Zona 1. That's here, and they've been working in this direction. We're leaving, but we've got to find the device first."

Haydon looked at Janet. "You carrying a transmitter?"

"Trans . . . transmitter?" Her face portrayed a calculating confusion. She was stalling, and it made Haydon's stomach knot.

The woman walked over to Janet and slapped her hard with the back of her hand, then three more times: whap-whap-whap, and before Janet could react, the woman grabbed the top of her sundress with both hands and ripped it wide open all the way down to her waist. The woman's left forearm shot up to Janet's throat and pinned her against the wall while her right hand thrust inside the dress searching for the device. Janet couldn't speak or breathe, and as her left hand came up reflexively in a futile motion of self-defense, the woman suddenly saw the oversized watch. She jerked her forearm off Janet's throat and grabbed her wrist,

367

unbuckling the watch as Janet slid to the floor. Walking back to the table, the woman used the butt of her Uzi to smash the watch face. Nothing. The woman turned on Janet again.

"Wait a minute," Haydon said. "It's not going to be anything small if it's going to have any range at all." He looked at the pieces of junk the woman had scattered on the table from Janet's purse. Janet's purse. He picked up the canvas bag and felt it. He tried to wad it, but it resisted, stiff on the sides. He turned the bag wrong-side out and saw that there was an inner lining. Finding a gap in the seam, he worked his finger under it and jerked hard, ripping out the lining and revealing a thin insert of material to which a complicated network of wafer thin transistors and batteries and antenna had been stitched. The entire purse was lined with a meshwork of sophisticated technology, making the bag a powerful one-piece transmitting device. This was not a simple toy.

He turned and looked at Janet, feeling stupid and confused and angry.

Janet ignored him, her eyes hidden behind her disarrayed hair as she sat against the wall trying to button the front of her dress and pulling her sweater together as she dabbed at her bloodied nose with the back of her wrist.

Haydon took out his handkerchief and stepped over to her and helped her up, giving her the handkerchief. She avoided his eyes. Haydon didn't know which disturbed him more: her betrayal or his own naïveté. They might as well be back in Guatemala City again. Everyone was here. Their guerrilla escorts were clearly feeling the pressure.

Chapter 49

T he woman stuffed the lining back into the purse and gave it to one of
the men, who opened his shirt and flattened the bag next to his body,
buttoned his shirt, and left through the adjoining dining room.

"What's in yours?" the woman asked Haydon, indicating the flight
bag.

"An Uzi, a handgun, some ammunition . . ."

"Give the Uzi and the handgun to him," she said, gesturing to another of her companions. Haydon unzipped the bag and did as he was told. "You still have your automatic?"

Haydon opened his coat and showed it to her, stuck in his waistband.

"Good," she said. "We can travel through three buildings without going outside, then we'll have to be very careful." She looked at Janet, who had gotten to her feet, wiping her nose with Haydon's handkerchief. "If you do *any*thing, he'll cut your throat," she said, tilting her head toward the third man, who had moved over close to Janet and who obviously was going to be in charge of her. "I am not going to risk my life—or theirs—for you. We don't risk anything unless it's worthwhile. Do you understand that?"

Janet nodded, accepting the pointed insult. But she shook her hair out of her face, her expression already reflecting a stubborn un-repentance.

Christ, Haydon thought. This had all the makings of a disaster.

The five of them left together, Haydon following the woman, Janet and her bodyguard behind him, and the second man covering their rear. They went out into the courtyard, turned left and entered a dark corridor with a stairway that doubled back above them. At the top landing they entered a door through a three-foot-thick wall that took them into the next building where they hurried to yet another balcony, fast-walking its length to enter another doorway. This time they traveled the length of a dim corridor that had doors on either side with numbers on them, a hotel or boarding house, Haydon guessed, and then down a double-back stairwell into a third corridor that led into a private home. The stucco-covered stone walls here smelled of old, mildewed plaster, and twice they had to go down two or three steps through narrow doorways since the house was built on a falling street. Once Haydon saw a dark face retreat around a door beyond the woman's shoulder, but when they passed by the face was gone and the door was closed.

They had stayed to the inner corridors as much as possible, but now they had to exit the buildings and enter another courtyard. It was small and bare, splotched with puddles of gray water, and patrolled by three or four ill-tempered geese, their breasts stained with mud. A wheel-less Toyota pickup that looked as if it had tumbled down the side of a mountain rested on its axles near the high wooden gates that gave access to the street. Another truck, with wooden side panels and a tarpaulin strapped down over its sideboards, sat with its nose against the gates.

They were hustled across the muddy compound and ushered through an open door into a small room that was empty except for a couple of crude wooden benches sitting against the walls and a corner fireplace with a smoldering fire.

"We'll be here a while," the woman said. "You might as well sit down and get comfortable."

Janet sat down immediately on one of the benches nearest the fireplace and wrapped her sweater tightly around her and folded her arms. Haydon sat opposite her so that he had a good view of the courtyard.

The woman and the other man disappeared through a doorway near Haydon, while Janet's bodyguard sat on a creaky chair, resting his Uzi on his lap. He lighted a cigarette and offered one to Janet, who refused, and then to Haydon, who gratefully accepted, letting the man light it for him. As he inhaled smoke from the bitter Guatemalan cigarette, Haydon heard radio static coming through the doorway from another room.

He looked at Janet as he smoked, but she kept her gaze on the floor. Finally, feeling him looking at her, she turned her eyes to him, and he saw something there that made him think of a lost soul, not a tortured one, not one grieving for past deeds and lost opportunities and abandoned dreams, but one who cursed the condemnation, defiant and begrudging to the end.

"You don't think I would understand if you explained it to me?" he asked.

"That's not the point," she said, turning her eyes to the fire. "I don't give a damn whether you 'understand' or not."

He smoked a moment, trying to see in her profile some hint of the complicated emotions she must be feeling.

"Do you love him that much?" he asked.

She said nothing. Haydon rested his head against the stucco wall and watched her. Her hair, already wiry from the humidity, was even more disheveled because of her encounter with the woman. Several of the buttons had been torn off her sundress, so she had to cover herself with the sweater, which also helped to ward off the damp chill. The sweater was smeared with pinkish stains from her nosebleed, and mud had splashed on the lower part of her sundress in their hurried flight through the buildings and across courtyards.

He finished his cigarette and ground it out on the floor as the bodyguard had done a few moments before him. Standing, he stepped over to Janet and reached out his hand.

"Give me the handkerchief," he said.

371

She had been holding it, wadded into a tight tiny ball, in her hands. She looked up and handed it to him, and he took it to the doorway and held it out under the dribbling eaves and washed out the blood, wrung it out and held it under the dribble again. Then he walked back to Janet and gave it back to her.

"You've got some dried blood . . ." he said, pointing to his own nose.

She took it, trying to maintain a dispassionate expression, but clearly grateful. He looked away while she dabbed at her nose, softening the dried blood. The geese were patrolling the puddles in the courtyard, straight backed and challenging. Without preamble the rain began falling heavily again, and the geese made their way over to the tarpaulin-covered truck and got under the rear end of its high bed for shelter. Through the open doorway, Haydon could hear the rain drumming on the tightly stretched tarpaulin.

He turned to Janet. "You want Lena's skin, is that it? Do you have any idea what will happen if Cage gets to her first?"

"Oh, Christ, nothing's going to *happen* to her."

"He assured you of that?"

She nodded. "Yeah, he did."

"What did he say?"

She held the handkerchief to her nose a moment, then took it away. "He said the bottom line was that Lena wasn't going to get out of Guatemala with the documents about Azcona. Period. He said he could at least save her life. If the G-2 got to her first, she was dead."

"But what about the way it was happening here? What about the way Lena wanted it? These people were giving us safe passage . . ."

Janet was already shaking her head. "You're goddamned kidding yourself about this, Haydon. Do you really believe Azcona is going to let this happen, that these people are going to outwit the G-2?" She lowered her voice to a hoarse whisper. "I don't know where or how, but Azcona's going to be all over these people. This ragtag operation was doomed from the beginning. This was never the way to have done it, Lena should have known that . . ." She paused. "You don't know what in the hell you're into here. You don't have a clue."

Something was wrong about this, very wrong. Haydon felt more trusting of the nameless woman in the next room than he did of Janet or Cage or Pittner or anyone else. He wondered if, perhaps, that could be precisely the conclusion Lena had come to as well. He wondered if she had decided finally just to cut through all the bullshit. Maybe she had decided that life really wasn't that complicated after all. The simple fact was that General Azcona was a brutal man who bred brutal ways, and if she wanted to drive a stake through his heart these were the only people who could help her do it and that was that. Maybe everybody else's cooperation—Cage's, Pittner's, Janet's—came washed in solutions of caveats. Everything they touched carried an implicit "yes, but . . . ," and ultimately those caveats simply watered down every noble intent to such thin soup that in the end nothing with any meaning at all survived. Maybe Lena, in her own youthful abandonment—even if she was being used as Cage alleged—was the only moral person in this entire collection of derelicts because she had the ability and good sense to simplify. Stealing children was wrong, and she wanted to stop the man who callously allowed such things to happen.

On the other hand, Haydon suspected that Dr. Grajeda's unlikely philosophical alliance with a deceased German novelist was closer to the mark as explanation. Truth was an assembled thing, unknown to a single person, nonexistent in a single ideology. It was more difficult to grasp than expired breath, more complex than the simple desire to possess it.

As the afternoon faded and the sky darkened, a fog rolled in so thick that it turned everything to a ghostly paleness and almost obscured the front gates of the courtyard. A distinctly chill air stirred the mist as the rain started and stopped, started and stopped. But the door to the room remained open, and the only concession to the chill was when the bodyguard got up and put another oak log on the dwindling fire. The simple wooden benches were uncomfortable, and after a while Janet swung her feet up off the floor, put them on the hearth next to the fireplace and covered them with her skirt. There was only the sound of the rain, the fire, and the scratchy static from the radio in the next room. Haydon heard no voices in the other room, no footsteps.

Then an Indian boy of nine or ten came carefully carrying three huge cups of coffee on a board, his eyes concentrating on the dark brew, of which he had spilled not a drop. He went straight to Janet, placing his crusty bare feet precisely on the gritty stones of the uneven floor, his head bent in concentration, and stopped in front of her. She smiled and thanked him and took a cup, and then he came to Haydon, who did the same, and then he turned to the bodyguard. This time the boy broke out

373

into a big grin as the man took his cup and reached out and patted the side of the boy's face.

"¿*Como le va, mi'jo*"? the man asked. Still smiling, the boy mumbled something and then tucked the board under his arm and hurried out of the room.

"Your son?" Haydon asked.

The man nodded. "Yes. He is a good boy. He has the face of his precious mother."

It was an oddly poetic statement, and it was the last thing anyone said for more than half an hour as they sat on the benches and nursed the hot, sweet drink that the cook had laced with a trace of cardamom.

Then Haydon heard heavy footsteps and the rattling of buckles against the metal bodies of the Uzi's. The woman who had brought them there came into the room with her companion. Both of them had changed out of their street clothes and were wearing olive green military fatigues. She wore an olive T-shirt under a long-sleeved khaki shirt, both tucked into her fatigues, and a pair of much-used lightweight army boots with nylon tops. Her dark hair was pulled back in an efficient single braid, which emphasized her high cheekbones and even the mole near her mouth. Each of them had an Uzi hanging from straps on their shoulders.

"Isauro led them north toward Sacanchaj. He left his radio on so we could hear everything. They got close enough to see who he was, and when they realized what was happening they chased him and caught him. They were thoughtful, too, and left his radio on so we could hear what happened."

"They questioned him?"

"He didn't die until just a few minutes ago."

"Cage's people?"

She nodded. "Cage has some ex-Kaibiles working for him. They are an army special forces branch trained in the jungles of the Petén. In the seventies your people came and taught them the philosophy of counterinsurgency, then the Israelis came and taught them. They learned fast, better than the devil, and improved on what they had been taught. Now your special forces come to the Kaibiles for training." She smiled sourly. "The Kaibiles call them 'pussies.' "

"I thought Cage's only interest was information."

The woman looked at him. "There are two ways to get information in Guatemala. Money and torture. One of them always works. And as you well know, money is hard to come by in this country." She paused. "We have to go. Isauro didn't tell them everything, but he told them too much. We can't stay here any longer."

"Wait a second," Haydon stood. "I don't see any use in keeping her with us," he said of Janet. "She's going to make it hard for me to do what I've got to do. She doesn't figure into it. Why don't you just keep her out of sight somewhere until it's over and let her go."

"If she doesn't figure into it, what's she doing here?" the woman asked with rhetorical sarcasm. "Look," she said, "we know who she is. She does figure into it. Very much."

The woman turned away and yelled something in an Indian dialect through the door into the back rooms, and there was an immediate flurry of activity. Haydon cut his eyes at Janet, who understood everything perfectly well.

Within moments a number of people, men and women—and the boy who had served them coffee—left through the rainy courtyard, some into each of the buildings on either side, and some through the gates. They were not in military fatigues as were the woman and her companions, but were common Cobaneros like the hundreds of others one saw on the street, like the ones Haydon had seen just that morning. Soon the rooms were silent, even the scratching of the shortwave radio had died, and Haydon and Janet were being hustled outside into the courtyard. They splashed through the muddy puddles as all the others had, and then the tailgate of the tarpaulin-covered truck was dropped open, and they were loaded into the back with piles of burlap sacks filled with coffee beans.

The truck had the name of a coffee finca painted on its door, but it was no ordinary flatbed. A long hole the width of the cab had been cut out of the cab next to the bed, and a low bench, its back attached to the back of the seat in the cab, had been installed. There was room for three people to sit, facing the rear of the truck and a full head lower than the driver and passengers in the cab. Janet and Haydon sat in this makeshift seat, and sacks of coffee were stacked around them until they were hidden. The woman and the two other armed guerrillas in fatigues were also hidden among the sacks. None of this was meant to fool anyone conducting more than a cursory cargo check. If they encountered a military checkpoint, Haydon did not believe the woman would surrender with a loaded Uzi.

A guerrilla in civilian clothes crawled into the cab with the driver, both of them armed, and after a few exchanges with a lookout on the

375

street, the gates swung open, the driver gunned the heavy-duty motor, scattering the geese, and the truck pulled out onto the street. From his backward-facing vantage point on the driver's side of the truck, Haydon could see along one of the sideboard railings, just under the flap of the tarpaulin. Behind them the narrow Cobán street receded in the drifting mist, the deep charcoal of evening coming early in this region of skyless light. They passed a dog and an Indian woman going in the opposite direction, the woman with one arm raised to steady a jug she was carrying on her head, both of them leaning into the slope of the street that the truck was now descending, downshifting gears in a tight whine. Haydon inhaled the pungent reek of oily exhausts and damp burlap bags and coffee beans and wondered if these were the last odors he would breathe.

Chapter 50

Night fell while they drove. It came disguised in its own cloak of fog, the darkest night Haydon had ever seen, so dense it was almost tactile. They drove for a while on what Haydon guessed was the major highway to Guatemala City, and then they veered off on a smaller roadway, still paved, but narrow. This course took them into country where the dripping forests closed in on them like the walls of a green-black dream. From his line of sight along the side of the truck, Haydon could see the draperies of the jungle flare darkroom red whenever the driver slowed and the brake lights illuminated the long scarlet corridor of the receding road. They reduced speed and negotiated curves and twice plowed through low-water crossings, the rushing of the water around the wheels of the truck almost drowning out the sound of the engine itself, the dampness of the streams smelling different from the dampness of the fog, as the wetness of the night smelled different from the wetness of the day. Sometimes he could actually smell the mildew of the decaying jungle floor, and sometimes he could smell the tangy spice of wood fires that drifted to the road from the dooryards of hovels hidden far off in the dark.

Haydon could not see his watch, so he had no idea how long they drove this way, but after a while he sensed a relief of tension among the guerrillas. They no longer crouched behind the sacks but stood spraddle-legged for balance, resting their Uzi's on top of the mounds of coffee. One of the woman's companions even lighted a cigarette, its acrid smoke whipping around briefly under the tarpaulin before the night air snatched it away.

Then the truck slowed differently from the way it had slowed before, and almost simultaneously Haydon sensed they were entering a community. Amber lights flickered here and there through the jungle and then more of them appeared closer to the road, and then the houses themselves became visible off to the side. Dogs barked as they passed, and the odor of cook fires became the predominant fragrance. They were among houses now, not just hovels but cinder-block houses, closer and closer together until they were at the edge of an *aldea,* the truck downshifting as they climbed, crawling, groaning, pitching up a street dying of potholes, to a small *plazoleta.* People walked along the street in dark knots—the town was too small, or too poor, for streetlights—and the truck rounded and stopped in front of a church.

The driver opened his door and got out as someone walked rapidly over to meet him. There was a conversation. The woman crawled over the coffee sacks and went to the back of the truck where she waited behind the tarpaulin, holding her Uzi down at her side. Haydon twisted beside Janet and was able to see the two men from their armpits down. The man talking to the driver was in uniform, military uniform. Haydon could only hope the man was being paid an adequate sum. The men shook hands, the officer walked away and the driver came to the back of the truck where he spoke to the woman. Their exchange was brief, and then the driver returned to the cab and got behind the wheel while the woman climbed over the sacks again.

They circled to the other side of the *plazoleta* and took a hard right, and immediately Haydon felt the nose of the truck pitch downward, turning left and traveling a moment or two before turning back the other way in a switchback. The street must have been cobblestones at first: it was rough but uniformly so, and then even the cobblestones played out. The truck straightened, but continued on a long sloping course, its progress reduced to a crawl as the driver time and again eased the wheels into an enormous chug hole or negotiated an eroded rut. The distinctive smell of pigs once or twice wafted up under the tarpaulin, and Haydon could see under the sideboards that they were in the outskirts, if that weren't too grand a word. The domiciles were hovels once more, with corrugated tin or thatched roofs. Finally the truck lurched to a standstill, and, after a moment's hesitation, the driver cut the motor.

"Okay, let's go," the woman said, and she and her companions began shoving aside the sacks of coffee so that Haydon and Janet could crawl out of their backbreaking sunken seat. As Janet stood to crawl out, the truck driver opened his door, and in the pale cabin light coming from behind him, Haydon raised his wrist and noted the time.

They waited at the rear of the truck with the bodyguard while the woman and the other guerrillas held a conversation at the front. Here at the diminishing edge of the settlement, they stood on the very margins of the universe. Behind them lay the orange lights of the known world, in front of them lay that peculiar dense darkness that might have been the outermost reaches of space, or the innermost folds of the mind.

"I have a bad feeling about this," Janet said. Her voice did not seem to come from her. He wouldn't have recognized it if he hadn't known.

"Maybe Lena will give you some reassurances," Haydon said.

"I doubt it. How in God's name can you be reassured in a place like this?"

She had a good point, but Haydon said nothing. It occurred to him then, standing at the back of the truck, which had come, literally, to the end of the road, that no one had ever once asked him how in the hell he expected to get Lena and her documents out of Guatemala.

The driver stayed with the truck, a solitary assignment Haydon did not envy him, and the rest of them—two in front of Haydon and Janet and two behind—set off down a rutted dirt road that ran perpendicular to the parked truck, and which Haydon was sure had not seen a vehicle

379

in years. There were a few shacks now and then on one side or the other, hovels tucked into the ubiquitous thickets of plantains. Soon there were not even hovels, and the two ruts gave way to a well-beaten path as the six of them traveled deeper into the black.

The path stayed in fairly good condition, though several times it led into streams, which, even before they approached, could be heard gurgling and rushing over the smooth stones like a soft warning. The streams were not deep, reaching only to about mid-calf on Haydon's legs, but having his lower legs and shoes thoroughly soaked by the crossing made for miserable walking from then on. The keening of the large Central American cicadas was nearly deafening, their throbbing tempo almost compelling one's heart to beat to the same indolent pulse until one felt possessed, or oppressed, by the din. The jungle converged from every side so that they were continually brushing through it, its seeping, dripping, weeping dampness soaking them as thoroughly as if they had been in a downpour. More than a few times Haydon felt Janet grab at the tail of his coat for balance as she slipped in the slick, gummy mud that sometimes came to the surface through the spongy jungle floor. Finally he told her to hook her hand inside the back of his pants, which she did without saying a word.

Again time was obliterated, his efforts to mark duration or distance by counting were ineffective because of the distractions of the terrain and his concern for Janet. Whatever the time, it seemed interminable. Twice during the ordeal the guerrillas stopped, squatted down on their heels and smoked cigarettes. They made no conversation with Haydon or Janet, but Haydon suspected that these three men and the woman did not have to stop to rest themselves but had done so in deference to them, knowing they were unprepared and ill equipped for so lengthy a trek in such arduous terrain. Though he could not see in the greenish darkness, Haydon could only imagine how Janet's thin sandals, designed for walking on city streets, must be faring. But she said nothing.

Haydon first knew they were approaching a community when he heard a dog barking, though he wasn't sure it was a dog at first. None of the four guerrillas took any notice of it, and Haydon suspected that their approach had been known even before the dog sensed it. Technology had outstripped nature, even in the depths of the jungle.

When they finally approached the small community, Haydon was surprised to see the permanence of some of the buildings. There must have been eight or nine buildings scattered on either side of a small

380

stream across which a sturdy footbridge had been built. Three of the buildings were constructed of cinder block and cement and had corrugated tin roofs, the rest were made of wattles and mud and had thatched roofs. Fires reflected off the sides of the buildings, and smoke hovered in the still air like pungent cloud.

There was no fanfare about their arrival. Outpost guards materialized out of the jungle perimeters and spoke casually to the guerrillas who were accompanying them, and the small troop of them entered the compound in a loose assemblage and crossed over the bridge to the only cinder-block house on the far side of the stream. The women and children who were milling around the compound's bare, hard earth as they arrived, quietly melted into the shadows or the doorways of their own houses where they watched the newcomers' arrival from the protection of familiar corners, out of sight.

As they approached the squatty house, Haydon saw from its screenless open windows that it had at least two rooms. The window at the front of the house was dimly lighted, and shadows of the persons inside crawled like dark giants across the walls. The window at the rear of the house was ablaze with light, a brilliant yellow glow that seemed to shimmer all of itself and which cast a golden splash on the bare jungle earth outside the window.

Haydon was curious about the light but had no time to speculate. They were taken straight to the front door, around which several boys and men with machetes sat on their heels and on chunks of logs, talking and smoking, their conversation falling into a lull as the group approached.

"Come on in," the woman said, and their escorts fell back as Haydon and Janet followed the woman into the room, which had a dirt floor with no threshold to separate it from the outside. It was a fairly large room, with three or four kerosene lanterns hanging from the exposed rafters, their greenish glow accompanied by a soft hiss issuing from their pressurized chambers. Haydon quickly checked his watch. The walk through the jungle had taken them a little over two hours.

There were three men and two women dressed in dirty military fatigues sitting on primitive benches around the walls and in two or three creaky chairs scattered around. In the far right corner a simple table sat at an angle. There was a man in a chair behind it. Papers and a handgun and several clips were scattered on the table, as well as a tin plate from which the man had been eating. Because of the poor light, Haydon could

381

not clearly see the man getting up from behind the table to greet them until he was reaching out his own hand to shake the one extended to him.

"Mr. Haydon," the man said, and Haydon stiffened, caught off guard just as their hands met.

"Dr. Grajeda," Haydon said. "This . . . this is where they've brought you?"

"This is where we came, yes," Dr. Grajeda said, smiling kindly, his moustache and goatee as neatly trimmed in the jungle as in the city. Haydon did not miss the slight difference in the way Dr. Grajeda framed his response, nor did he miss the use of the plural subject. "The forest can be a nasty place," he said, gesturing to Haydon's condition. "Especially if you're wearing a suit." He smiled wanly, tired; it was an effort. "Sorry." He turned to Janet. "My apologies to you as well, Mrs. Pittner."

Janet was not having any of his Guatemalan politeness and showed no curiosity that Grajeda knew her name.

"I just want to get off my feet," she said, and hobbled over to one of the benches where she sat down by a woman who was leaning on her rifle, her fatigue cap cocked back on her head. She looked down at Janet's feet, and Haydon followed her eyes. He was astonished to see that Janet was barefooted and that her muddy feet were cut and bleeding. The chic little sandals probably had been lost almost from the beginning.

The girl looked at Janet, who had lifted one foot and was massaging it, laid down her rifle on the bench, and called softly in an Indian dialect to a boy just outside the doorway who quickly disappeared. The woman tapped Janet's leg and got down on one knee in front of her, motioning for Janet to let her see her foot. Janet reflexively pulled back.

"She's going to clean your feet and put some medicine on them," Dr. Grajeda said. "There are a lot of parasites on the jungle floor, you can't stay like that. Let her do what she wants to do. I teach them to take very good care of their feet out here. She knows what she's doing."

Grajeda turned, taking Haydon by the arm, and the two of them walked over to the far side of the room where a rickety chair had been vacated at one end of a bench. They sat down together.

"You'll be going back tonight," Grajeda said. "But before you return we have a lot to talk over." He pulled a pack of cigarettes from his shirt pocket. Grajeda couldn't have been in the jungle for more than a day, a day and a half, but his fatigues, the sleeves rolled up just above his elbows, needed washing, and Grajeda himself looked as if he hadn't slept since Haydon had spoken to him in the empty room above the shoe store. He and Haydon lighted their cigarettes, and Grajeda gestured with his. "Not so great in the city, but in the jungle, they're just about as welcome as a good meal."

Chapter 51

"As you probably have guessed," Grajeda began with a sigh, one leg crossed over the other, and his forearms crossed on his knee as he leaned forward toward Haydon, "that business above the shoe store in Guatemala City was a bit of a ruse. The part about me, I mean. I'm a little more involved in this guerrilla business than I led you to believe. I can't really apologize for having deceived you though, because I would do it again. Caution before kindness. It has to be that way."

He looked over to Janet, who was leaning back against the wall with her eyes closed while the Indian woman washed her feet with soapy water that the little boy had brought in a pan.

He turned back to Haydon and lowered his voice. "I don't know whether she's a blessing or a curse," he said wearily. "My God, everything diverges. Nothing ever comes to an end."

"I suppose her value depends on what's going to happen here," Haydon said.

Grajeda nodded. "The documents are here, Lena's and mine both." He smoked and regarded Haydon soberly. "But that is a moot point now. It seems we've become the focus of attention."

"Here? They know this location?"

"No, no. Not this precise location. This region of Alta Verapaz is not an area of conflict. We have this place here as a kind of stopover, a clearing house. Our people come here on their way to other places, other business. The army knows about it, but only in a general way. You know: 'They say there are guerrillas in the Polochic valley.' For instance, they know you have been on the highway to the town above here, Calvario, but that town itself is an unpopular place for the military. Nothing much comes out of here, so they don't worry about us. If they had unlimited resources, then maybe, or if the generals weren't so busy running their mahogany smuggling businesses up in the Petén, then maybe. But this place is no threat . . . and they're not sure where it is, and it's not worth a large campaign to locate it. So . . ."

Grajeda smoked. "The point is, they know *you're* here."

"But we didn't see a single soldier all the way from Cobán—except one, above in Calvario."

"The fellow in town is ours," Grajeda shook his head. "But that's not the way it will be. In this instance 'Azcona's men' are not soldiers. They are the G-2, military intelligence. They will be men in street clothes like yourself, driving unmarked cars. These will be the death-squad men. You won't see any soldiers."

Haydon pulled on the cigarette. Grajeda was right, it was as welcome as a meal.

"They know what you're coming in here to get," Grajeda said. One of the hanging lanterns was reflecting in a single lens of his spectacles. He looked like a handsome and exotic Mephistopheles, the devil with a golden eye patch. "And they know that you're coming out with it. They're just waiting for the return trip. This waiting is Pittner's doing. Azcona would have sent in helicopter gunships, he would have had

385

columns of troops up and down the Polochic valley, torturing local farmers for information, burning milpas, rounding up the men and calling
them guerrillas so he could 'question' them. The CIA is desperately
trying to keep him under control. They have a lot invested in this brutal
man. It takes a long time and a lot of money to cultivate someone the
way they have cultivated General Luis Azcona. He's 'their' man. Pittner
has had his hands full, and he had been successful up to now."

They both smoked a moment. To Haydon's left, on the other side of
the room, pieces of burlap had been sewn together to create a curtain
over the doorway between the two rooms. Beneath the burlap he could
see the bright margin from the curiously illuminated room.

"I understand Cage did some work in Cobán," Grajeda said. His eyes
were settled on a place on the dirt floor, thoughtful and heavy with
exhaustion. "He is our real problem. He could do something crazy."

Haydon suddenly detected something in Grajeda's mood that conflicted with what he had believed was going to be happening here in this
moldy jungle compound. His stomach twisted inside as he sensed a
change in the agenda.

"What do you mean, our 'real' problem?" Haydon asked. "It seems
to me all of the problems are real."

Grajeda nodded thoughtfully, his manner grimly concessionary. "Tell
me," he said, raising his face to Haydon. "How is it that you planned to
get the documents out of Guatemala?"

Haydon saw no reason not to explain. As Grajeda himself had said a
few moments earlier, it was a moot point now. It wasn't going to happen.

"First of all," Haydon said, smoking the last of his cigarette and
grinding it out under his shoe, "I'd hoped to get to Cobán alone. It seems
absurd now, but at the time I thought it was possible. I planned for it."
He stopped.

Dr. Grajeda was nodding, waiting for the rest of it. Even though
Haydon knew in his heart that the whole intrigue was fouled, he was
hesitant to part with the last piece of information that he had kept only to
himself. But it was over.

"I have friends in Belize." He looked at his watch. "They should
already have flown in to the Cobán airstrip. They'll wait there for me
until daylight."

Dr. Grajeda nodded thoughtfully. "I hope they have very good
equipment on their plane. Cobán's rain and fog require good equipment."

"They live in Belize. They're used to flying into Guatemala," Haydon said.

"And you will be flying out to . . . ?"

"Belize."

Dr. Grajeda nodded again but did not respond immediately. He sat in his chair, his shoulders slumped, his whole demeanor that of exhaustion and dashed hopes. Janet was looking at the two men from across the room. The woman who had cleaned Janet's feet had finished and was now the only person in the room besides the two of them and Dr. Grajeda. She was sitting alone near the doorway, her rifle lying across her lap. Janet's feet had been bandaged, and she wore a new pair of sturdy Indian sandals and an expression of dazed resignation. She still kept her filthy and soggy sweater wrapped tightly around her, holding it in place with her folded arms.

"Then it's all over?" Haydon asked.

"You will be stopped twice, at least," Dr. Grajeda said, rousing himself from wandering thoughts, straightening up in his chair with a sigh. "By Cage's people and by army intelligence directed by Pittner. Azcona will never show his face in this operation. He is probably making himself very visible somewhere far away. The searches will be thorough. You couldn't sneak a toothbrush out." Dr. Grajeda shook his head. "It was a good try."

"What about Lena?" Haydon asked. "Is she going to leave with me?"

"Yes, my friend. After all of this, she is going with you."

"I actually thought she might stay."

"No one is staying. Once you leave, once Azcona learns he has not recovered the documents, he will throw a tantrum. What Pittner has managed to keep him from doing up to now, Pittner will no longer be able to prevent. Azcona is going to come. The people in this compound will leave when you leave tonight, but we will go north, into the Petén. Azcona will find only these few empty buildings on which to vent his fury." He looked at Haydon. "Our little piece of the truth will have to wait to be assembled at some finer day in the future. We did our best."

He stood up and dropped his own cigarette, which had long ago died in his fingers, onto the dirt floor. He turned to Janet.

"Mrs. Pittner," he said. "If you want to talk to Lena . . ." He turned sideways and held his arm out toward the covered doorway.

Janet, surprised, looked at him with anticipation. She stood, a little stiffly, and she and Haydon followed Dr. Grajeda, who threw aside the burlap curtain. Within four steps they had entered the brilliantly lighted room.

Lena's body lay on two *lepa* boards that had been placed across the seats of two wooden chairs set facing each other, and which themselves had been placed on cinder blocks, raising her body to just a little above waist high, the backs of the chairs forming bierlike brackets at her feet and head. Her hair had been combed out, clean and shiny, unlike the twig-tangled hair of that other Lena whom Haydon had seen so long ago in the morgue of the Cementerio General. She was wrapped in a white, gauzelike material, the kind the guerrillas must have bought by the dozens of yards for bandages, and which was pulled up under her chin as though she were wrapped tightly against the everlasting chill of death. White wads of the same material had been wedged into her nostrils and ears to keep out the insects. The room glittered with candles placed on every available surface, in every nook, on every small ledge, on sticks that had been wedged into the countless cracks of the cinder-block walls. The room was heavy with the odor of melting wax.

Janet staggered, and Haydon reached out and held her. Dr. Grajeda walked around to the other side of Lena's crude bier and bent down and kissed her forehead. He straightened up and looked across at them.

"Go ahead and talk to her," he said calmly. He seemed oddly serene, the way a man is serene about a tragedy after he has had time to give it much thought, to assimilate the shock of it into his theory of the universe and insulate himself from its hard truth with a myth of philosophy to make it bearable.

Haydon stood in the crude jungle shrine to Lena Muller, holding Janet's shirking body and wondering if he ought to believe his eyes. This gray corpse could be a phantasm, a specter in the shimmering light of a hundred candles, which, if all the candles were extinguished in an instant by some eerie jungle gust, would vanish on the spiraling curls of smoke from a hundred wicks. He would stand in the dark heat and only imagine her; she would be elsewhere as she had been elsewhere from the first moment he had heard her name and seen her photograph and imagined her, no closer to her reality now than then.

This time Haydon had no problem identifying her. Her face was unblemished; there were no distorting wounds to interpret, no discolorations to decipher. Lena Muller was dead at last.

388

He was suddenly profoundly sad, even, irrationally, nostalgic for an irrevocable time that never had been. He wanted to talk to her, felt almost desperate to do so, and fought a swelling frustration at having been cheated of what he had anticipated for so long. By virtue of time's trickery, the search for Lena Muller seemed to have taken a good portion of Haydon's life. He would have felt no more deprived if he had known her a lifetime, so compressed by unreality had been his days and nights in Guatemala, so imbued with imagination had been his knowledge of this girl who always had existed just beyond his reach like a rumor of angels.

"I can assure you she will respond," Grajeda said rationally. "She will speak in the most eloquent of all languages—silence—the silence of a life lost for reasons that only people who have something to lose will perceive as futile." He looked at Haydon. "You may think me cruel, maybe cynical? Not so. You see, I envy her because her peculiar language possesses an integrity that ours can never achieve. That's the way it is with such things. The only real moral integrity is living selflessly . . . only . . . we find it so painfully difficult to do . . . and, of course, it often comes to this."

Dr. Grajeda looked down at her again. "And the rest of us? Well, the rest of us are left to go on compromising, to go on accommodating, to go on negotiating and 'settling,' until we finally hear ourselves speaking a language so different from hers, and from what our own ideals once had been, that we hardly can recognize our own voices. The way we eventually end up living our lives becomes so distorted from our dreams that we no longer speak the same language that we once imagined, and one day we wake up to find that we have become aliens to our own hearts."

Dr. Grajeda's eyes were dry as he stood beside Lena's body and looked down at her.

389

"What happened?" Haydon asked.

Looking up, Dr. Grajeda fixed his eyes squarely on Haydon, and he shook his head in disbelief. "It was a banal death. An absurdity," he said. "She died in a car crash, up there in Calvario, not five hours ago."

"Oh, Christ!" Janet said. She pulled away from Haydon and stepped over to Lena as Dr. Grajeda moved back out of her way. She stood with her arms folded a moment, looking at Lena as though she were trying to remember, and then she reached down and put a hand on Lena's forehead as if she were feeling for a fever. "She's dead," Janet said. "My God."

Taking off his wire-rimmed glasses, Dr. Grajeda rubbed the bridge of his nose, and then he put them on again. He ran his hand through his thick, graying hair. When Janet started crying, quietly at first, then sobbing, standing beside Lena with her hands on the dead girl's arm, Dr. Grajeda looked across Lena's body and caught Haydon's eye and tilted his head toward the door. Haydon followed him through.

"We have to talk about what happens now," Grajeda said, pulling the burlap across the opening once again and moving away from the doorway. "For you, this is still an extremely critical situation." He stroked his beard as he walked toward the center of the room. The woman with the rifle still sat alone near the door that led outside, and the gas lanterns still hissed overhead in the rafters. "Is the plane large enough to take her to Belize?"

"Yeah," Haydon nodded. "It is." He was irritated by the question. It was too soon for the prosaic and the ordinary. Lena was still there in his mind, floating in a night sky of candles.

"Good. Now, we have made a simple coffin of *lepa,* and I have four men who have volunteered to carry her back through the jungle. Even that is risky for them, because Cage, or even the G-2, may have changed their minds and followed you into Calvario. They could be at the truck. In any case, these men will load the body into the truck for you, wedge the coffin among the coffee sacks so that it will be secure. But you will have to drive the truck back to Cobán alone."

"Christ, Grajeda. I was in the back of the truck the whole trip," Haydon protested. "I don't have the remotest idea where I am."

Dr. Grajeda was shaking his head. "No, it's not a problem. From Calvario there is only one paved road to the Cobán highway, the same highway that you drove on from Guatemala City. Anyone in Cobán can give you directions to the airstrip."

Haydon looked at him. It didn't matter. This was all madness, all of it. One more impossibility couldn't make it any more insane than it already was.

"I am sorry," Dr. Grajeda read Haydon's face. "But none of my people would survive a roadblock."

"No, it's okay. I understand," Haydon said. "But one thing, earlier you remarked that you thought Cage was our only 'real' problem. Maybe there's something else I need to know."

"Evera," Grajeda said, ticking his head toward the back room. The girl stood and moved to its burlap-covered doorway as Grajeda and Haydon walked out into the compound. Fires were burning all around in the darkness, orange glimmers here and there around which small clutches of people lingered in the smoky haze. "There's always a lot of cooking at night," Grajeda said. "Because the last fires have to be out by four-thirty so the smoke will dissipate before daylight. The helicopters can see the smoke in the trees."

They walked over to one fire and Grajeda asked for *"Dos cafecitos, por favor,"* and in a moment they were sipping a sweetened brew that didn't taste exactly like coffee.

"It's only half coffee," Dr. Grajeda explained. "The rest is ground corn with a sprinkling of cardamom. Ironically, here in the coffee regions, the indigenous people cannot afford pure coffee. It's too expensive. And then what they do get is of an inferior quality. The good beans are saved for the stores where only the wealthy can afford to shop, or it is exported."

He motioned for Haydon to sit on one of several logs that were cut knee high and sat on their ends around the fire.

"About Cage," Grajeda said. "I know nothing specific, nothing to tell you to fear, but this Mrs. Pittner has gone to some risk to make sure he has made it to Cobán. Something is not right about this. Cage, as you know, is a man with no conscience. This has helped to keep him alive, of course. But it also has earned him many enemies." Grajeda looked into his cup, trying to choose his words carefully. "The problem is, I am not so sure that Cage can distinguish anymore between his friends and his enemies. He is like a stick of dynamite that has been hidden in the jungle and allowed to deteriorate: the nitroglycerin has begun to separate, which makes it very unstable."

Haydon and Dr. Grajeda sat a little apart from the others at the fire. The few Indians who had been around the fire where Dr. Grajeda had made himself at home seemed comfortable that the two men had joined them. They neither moved away in deference nor ceased their conversation, but continued talking softly among themselves, their lilting voices gliding through the strange syllables of their dialect. Haydon turned his feet a little to the fire, surprising himself that he was finding it pleasurable, that he was even enjoying the tangy ropes of smoke that whorled up from the small flames.

"You will have to leave within the hour," Dr. Grajeda said, breaking

391

the silence that both men would have preferred to continue a little longer. "You will have to make good time to reach the airstrip by dawn."

"I'm surprised," Haydon said, "that you seem to be taking her death . . . so well."

Dr. Grajeda nodded. "I understand what you mean. Grief, where is this man's grief, if he loved her so much?" Grajeda raised his head and looked up at the canopy of the jungle. "Do you hear those cicadas? They never stop in the jungle. Never. They are among my earliest memories of life in Guatemala." He paused, looking up into the dark, listening with a vague smile. "I have a theory," he said, lowering his eyes to Haydon and seeming, perhaps, to be a little wary of going on. "I have a theory that from the first day God made this country, millennia before it came to be known as Guatemala, he made a starving child to live here, a creature, as it were, who would be the visible conscience of his people. As long as lies and cruelty prevailed in the people's hearts, the child would starve. That was his fate, to be a silent symbol, an 'outward and visible sign of an inward and spiritual corruption,' proof of the people's will to evil. And I also believe that on the same day that God made this child, he made the cicada to be his voice. Starving is a silent activity and a hungry child is easy to forget, so God made the cicada to cry for him. God knew even from the beginning that man had a secret weakness for, almost a love of, forgetting. So the cicada's voice became the voice of remembrance, reminding man that the great cruelties of his heart do not always come from something as grandiose as his evil imaginings, but just as often, perhaps more often, they come from something as simple as forgetting. And from that day to this, the voice of the cicada has never ceased in Guatemala."

Dr. Grajeda had finished his coffee, and the little bit left in his cup had gotten cold. He turned and tossed it out into the darkness. He paused again before going on, looking into the fire. He sighed.

392

"One day—I can't even remember exactly how it was—I decided that God was cruel. I could look around me and see his cruelty everywhere. I decided to devote my life to helping the people he had turned his back on. So I have done that. I haven't had a long life; I am still a young man, relatively speaking. But I did not anticipate the staggering cost of living such a spiritual arrogance. From the very beginning I encountered exhaustion, and I have been tired every moment of my life since. So deep is my weariness that I am tired even of my future. And so it is with the cicada. He is weary of his future too, because by now, after all these generations, he knows that man will never change."

Dr. Grajeda's eyes dreamed on the fire. "Grief is a luxury, Mr. Haydon, and God has taken all such comforts out of my life. He allows me nothing in that way anymore. Perhaps, I don't know, but perhaps death is arranged in such a way that the dead are allowed to forgive the living for their stupidities. I think it must be that the moment you die you receive wisdom and you can do this; you can forgive. I hope this is so, because I love the idea of forgiveness. But as for me, in my ignorance, I cannot do it. Not in this life."

Chapter 52

The walk out of the rain forest with Lena's crude coffin was a gruesome journey that took half an hour longer than the two-hour trip coming in, and this time there was no stopping to smoke. Aside from the four men who volunteered to carry the coffin, there was the nameless woman who had brought them from Cobán and who took the lead on the trail, and there was Dr. Grajeda himself, who brought up the rear. All of them carried Uzi's, the compact little weapons hanging over the bearers' shoulders and banging against the *lepa* coffin as they struggled and maneuvered the box through the dense forest, over the swift streams, down slippery slopes, and up slippery slopes. Three times during the trip the woman in the lead stopped them, and the coffin was lowered to the jungle floor while she waited to reassure her senses. Each time the coffin was lowered the bearers grunted under the strain and then panted like hounds in the darkness as they knelt against the box in the mud. Each time they raised it, they grunted again and then plowed ahead into the undergrowth.

Janet once again followed Haydon and occasionally gripped the belted waist of his trousers for support as she had done on the trip in. She had spent the rest of the time they were in the compound with Lena's body, insisting on helping the Indian women transfer the body off the chairs and into the narrow box, and she was the one to cover Lena's face with a layer of folded cloth just before the lid was nailed into place.

In no time at all Haydon's clothes were completely soaked through once again; his street shoes quickly accumulated three times their weight in heavy jungle gumbo, and once again the butt of the automatic he had kept wedged into his waistband, rubbed an enormous blister just below his last rib on his left side. But none of these distractions was enough to take his mind off the leg of the trip from Calvario to the Cobán highway. Whatever was going to happen was going to happen there, somewhere between those two points, during the hour it would take them to get from one to the other. The uncertainty of that coming hour was enough to have taken Haydon's mind off a great deal of personal discomfort.

When they finally reached the truck, Haydon was not surprised to find that the driver they had left behind was gone. No time was wasted. The bearers walked straight to the back of the truck with the coffin and set it on the ground. Still keeping their Uzi's strapped to their shoulders, they climbed into the truck and began moving the large burlap bags of coffee until they had cleared a space large enough for the coffin to rest on the flatbed. The coffin was then loaded and wedged into place with sacks of coffee, with two final sacks stacked on top of it. The tailgate of the truck was chained closed, and the tarpaulin flap was laced tightly over the rear opening.

It was all done with a minimum of conversation, with Dr. Grajeda watching every move and instructing them to make adjustments here and there until everything met with his satisfaction. When they were through the bearers moved away from the truck with the woman and waited under the black canopy of a giant *amate* tree that stood near the

395

trail that would take them back into the rain forest. Without speaking to anyone, Janet crawled into the truck on the passenger side and closed the door.

Dr. Grajeda took Haydon by the arm and casually walked with him a few paces away from the truck.

"It has been my privilege to meet you, Mr. Haydon," Grajeda said. "Give us a thought now and then, the people you have met here in Guatemala."

Haydon could barely see the doctor's face in the darkness. He had no way of knowing what emotions the man's features might have betrayed.

"I'll do that," Haydon said lamely, and he reached out and shook Grajeda's hand. But the doctor surprised him.

"In Belize," Dr. Grajeda said, holding the grip, not letting Haydon go, his voice calm and concentrated, "the authorities will require an autopsy and embalming before they will release her body to be returned home." He paused. "Do not feel badly for her. Remember what I told you about death in Guatemala? Each one is a message, a letter to the living. Even Lena's."

Then Grajeda clasped Haydon's hand in both of his and squeezed it tightly. Though they were close enough in the thick night for Haydon to feel the doctor's penetrating eyes, he could not actually see Grajeda's face, rather only a hint of a visage in the narrow gulf between them. Then Haydon caught a dull, gray light, a ghostly glint of the two discal surfaces of Grajeda's glasses, and the doctor let go of Haydon's hand. Grajeda turned away, and in a matter of a few steps the darkness and the cicadas had swallowed him.

Haydon waited without moving in the humid jungle heat until even Grajeda's footsteps had faded, feeling an inexplicable affinity with the erudite doctor-rebel. It was an unlikely alliance that Haydon could explain only in the context of this particular time and place and circumstance, as though he had lived the last few days in a dream that, like all dreams, was a world unto itself.

At the end of his thoughts, he turned back to the truck and climbed into the cab. Janet was crying, her head leaning against the glass. For a brief moment Haydon thought of Germaine Muller, leaning her head against the car window spattered with winter rain, and he felt an odd sense of loss himself, for never having actually met the girl who had been the source of so much emotion in others.

He started the truck—the keys were still in the ignition, a sure sign that the guerrillas commanded respect in Calvario—and flipped on the lights. Immediately he checked the gas tank: it was three-quarters full. Good. He backed around, making several efforts at it to avoid the boggy ditches where he knew he would spend the rest of the night if he wasn't careful, and finally got the truck headed back up the long sloping stretch toward Calvario, several hundred meters distant. Though the town was not far away, the lights of its houses could not be seen clearly because a fog had moved in and the amber lights that dotted the hillside came and went with the shifting strata of the low-hanging cloud.

The worst part of the long, upward-sloping road was the first three or four hundred meters. Here, at the end of the line, great eroded gashes ate away at the roadbed as the rain forest persisted in its ceaseless efforts to reclaim the hill where men had built Calvario. Haydon never shifted out of low gear as he let the truck ease down into the rifts and then creep out of them again, as though he were painfully scaling a wall, hand over hand. Then there were a few meters to the next hole and then ten meters and twenty, until they were moving at a fair pace, though still in the lower gears because they were continually climbing. Finally the gashes became potholes, and then the potholes were shallower, until Haydon could actually say they were on a street of sorts, with houses rising up steeply on either side, their lights hovering above the truck in the floating mist.

When the street turned and grew suddenly steeper, Haydon realized they were on the bottom leg of the switchback. He threw the headlights on low, trying to see the edge of the road in the thickening fog, and slowed to a crawl again. He thought about the coffin and what would happen if the chain across the bed of the truck was not properly secured. He thought about that all the way up to the actual switchback itself, and then all the way up to Calvario proper, his mind playing out the entire drama of the consequences of such a macabre occurrence, until the nose of the truck leveled off into an immediate turn and they were instantly into the *plazoleta*.

Everything looked different from behind the steering wheel than it had from underneath the tarpaulin in the back of the truck. But the place was small, the church where they had stopped was to their left, the main entrance and exit to the teardrop-shaped *plazoleta* was to their right. Haydon turned right into the narrowing top of the teardrop, realized they were on pavement, and within seconds they were leaving the town on a sloping paved road. In his headlights, Haydon could see the poor cinder-block houses on either side of the road. They seemed more scattered than he had remembered them from his seat behind the cab, and more isolated, and if there were barking dogs, the roar of the truck's motor drowned out their strident voices. Again he looked at his watch and noted the time.

As he pushed the truck down the long glistening ribbon of pavement, dropping meter by meter out of the cloud that hovered over Calvario, his headlights reached out farther and farther. It was clear for a while, the jungle and the road looking as if they had just been washed, but Haydon's luck didn't hold long. At first the fog came from the green wall on either side of the road in little tonguelike penetrations at the height of his headlights. He drove in and out of them until they became so numerous they pervaded, and then he had to slow the truck. Not only had the fog closed in, but the road changed too, leaving its straight descent from Calvario and beginning its serpentine course through the cloud forest.

He didn't know whether Janet slept or brooded, her head against the window, wrapped in silence. For his part, Haydon was almost weak with exhaustion. His mind fought the powerful urge of his body to quit. He rolled down his window and let the clammy fog whip across his face and into the cab. Constantly passing through alternating waves of dense and light fog was unnerving. He slowed when he could see only a few meters past his headlights, concentrating on the black margin of the road, and accelerated when he could see farther. It seemed that every kilometer or so he adjusted speed, corrected his distance from the cusp of the pavement, adjusted his eyes to a different depth of field, all of it drifting, wavering gray and silver.

But even in his bleary exhaustion, Haydon was nervous about what lay ahead. He knew something was waiting for him, a resolution of one kind or another with Cage or Pittner or General Azcona's death squads —or even some unimaginable amalgam of all three. The confrontation was inevitable, but the anxiety he felt at its approach was a peculiarly placed apprehension, perhaps not focused specifically on himself, despite the unbelievable experiences of the last twenty-four hours. Navigating the truck through the swirling veins of fog, he felt more like Charon, who, being only the boatman who ferried souls across the Hateful River of hell, had no fear himself of the torments on the other side. It was Lena they wanted. But they weren't going to like what he was bringing them.

The first stream caught him by surprise, and he plowed into it with a crashing roar that threw water up over the top of the cab. Horrified that he might have drowned the motor, he jammed his foot down on the clutch, hit the accelerator until the engine whined and smoked to life, and then he let out the clutch again and continued through the water and out the other side, more awake than he had been going in.

As the truck emerged dripping from the water, he allowed himself to take his eyes away from the headlights and saw that Janet was awake, staring sleepy eyed, her elbows raised as she ran her fingers through her hair. Haydon didn't bother to explain what had just happened. He assumed she had figured it out, and if she hadn't and didn't care enough to ask about it, he wasn't going to waste his time. She rode awhile with her eyes open, peering out across the headlights just like Haydon, but then the constant rush of fog wore her down and once again she slumped against the door, her head leaning on the window.

They were half an hour out of Calvario—Haydon had just checked his watch—when he thought he saw a faint rosy cast in the fog ahead. But it disappeared, or he thought it disappeared, if in fact he had seen it. And then it was there again. He was so tired his reaction was immediate confusion. Rose light? Was he hallucinating? Baffled, he took two deep breaths and reflexively lifted his foot off the accelerator. Suddenly he hit a pocket in the fog, and the light was brilliant ruby, and instantly the world was carmine, the color dancing off the particles of suspended fog until he felt as if he were entering the veins of a red planet.

"Jesus Christ!" Janet screamed, suddenly sitting bolt upright, her hands out in front of her bracing against the dash. "Slow down . . . for God's sake!"

Haydon hit the brakes, and they started sliding, the bed of the truck drifting. He let up and fought the steering wheel to correct the fishtailing and they straightened out, and then he eased down on the brakes again to slow the hurtling truck, and up again as he felt the rear end drifting. It seemed to last a long time, this unchecked plunge toward the heart of the brightening ruby light.

But the truck actually stopped in plenty of time, maybe twenty meters short of it, and Haydon, trembling and wide awake now, looked over the steering wheel at the roadblock, two cars nose to nose across the glistening pavement, each with ruby spotlights burning into the fog. Leaving the lights on, he cut the motor and sat there. For a moment no one showed himself, and Haydon heard nothing through his open window except cicadas and frogs.

"God, what's happening?" Janet wondered hoarsely. She was sitting

399

forward in her seat, hands on the dash, her eyes so wide Haydon could see the red reflected in them when he looked at her.

"Just sit tight," he cautioned her softly. "Give it time."

He hardly had finished speaking when someone moved between the two cars, and the solitary, barrel-chested figure of Taylor Cage emerged through the mist and stopped squarely in the middle of the road, a red world at his back.

And then a slow drizzle began to fall.

Chapter 53

"Haydon," Cage shouted, ignoring the drizzle. "Is that Janet in there with you or Lena?"

"Stay put," Haydon said to Janet. He opened the door and stood on the running board, his arms on the top of the door of the cab, and looked out over the hood of the truck. "Both of them," he said.

"Bullshit. We only see one. Janet."

"Lena's in the back."

"Yeah, well, the back's the problem." Cage wiped his face on the upper arm of his guayabera. "See, I've got people behind the truck there, in the woods, and they're looking into the back of the truck with night scopes and things, and they tell me"—he held up a hand radio for Haydon to see—"that they don't see anybody. Now, either nobody's in there or there's someone in there hiding, maybe with Uzi's or something, waiting to blow the shit out of us." He paused. "We can't have that, Haydon."

"I'm the only one who's got a gun," Haydon said. "The same one you gave me." Haydon reached down to his waist and pulled out the 10mm and held it up.

"Throw that thing out here," Cage said.

"No, I won't do that," Haydon said.

Silence.

The drizzle was peppering down on the truck's hood and cab and making deep, finger-drumming sounds on the tarpaulin stretched over the back of the truck.

"Nobody's in the back?" Cage said, lowering his voice some. It wasn't necessary to yell. Theirs were the only human voices in the cloud forest.

"Lena's back there, I said."

"Why isn't she in the cab with you two?"

"She's dead." Haydon did not care to put it any more kindly, and if he could have thought of a crueler way to tell him, he would have.

Cage just stood there.

"Bullshit," he said tentatively.

Haydon was tired. There was no reason for this drama. He stepped down off the running board and slammed the door, and immediately heard the collective clacking of automatic weapons cocking in the dark-ness. He stepped around in front of the truck.

402

"Come on, Cage," he said, motioning at him with the gun, deliber-ately not putting it away safely into his waistband. "No one's going to shoot you, come on around to the back of the truck."

Cage barked something in an Indian dialect as Haydon turned his back on him and headed for the rear of the truck, and suddenly men poured out on either side of the road, high-powered flashlights snapping on, lighting up the back of the truck and Haydon with it. He knew he was in the sights of every gun behind the lights.

Cage came stalking around the truck to where Haydon was already unlacing the rope from grommets in the tarpaulin. He got it open and threw back the flaps on either side. Finally stuffing the 10mm into his waistband to free his hands, he unchained the gate and took it off and tossed it on the pavement. When he turned, the lights were all around him, a couple of meters away, and Cage was standing next to him, looking at him, rain dripping off his nose, his guayabera soaked through to the skin. He held a radio and his own handgun and was staring at Haydon with an expression of cold skepticism.

"She's in a coffin under the coffee sacks," Haydon said. He reached up and grabbed the side of the tarpaulin, put his foot on the flat bumper and pulled himself up into the back of the truck.

Again Cage barked something in Indian, and the men moved up closer, and Haydon heard someone open Janet's side of the cab. Then someone else was beside Cage.

"Get up in there and look," Cage said, and Haydon looked down into the round face of Lita.

She was wearing quasimilitary garb, much like the woman who had brought them to Grajeda's compound. She grabbed the side of the tarpaulin as Haydon had done and pulled herself up into the back with him. She avoided looking at him directly but unsnapped a flashlight from her belt and shined it around in the truck.

"*Hay nadie aquí,*" she said.

"*¿Pero hay un ataúd?*" Cage asked.

"*Sí, es una caja.*"

Cage grabbed the tarpaulin flaps and climbed into the back too. He looked at the coffin, the foot and head of which were showing from under the two coffee sacks that had been placed on top of it. He stared at the box a moment, and Haydon thought he could detect in Cage's hesitation a true and threatening fear, the kind of fear that had nothing to do with an anticipation of danger.

"*Traéis las luces,*" he yelled out the back of the truck, and quickly two men mounted the bed and held their lights down on the box as Cage, without asking for help, grabbed the first sack and wrestled it off before Haydon could even assist him, and then together they removed the second one. Cage felt around the edges of the lid. "Crowbar," he said, looking around frantically as though there would be such a thing among coffee sacks.

"There's a tire tool," Haydon said, remembering one under his feet

403

in the makeshift seat behind the cab, and he crawled over and got it. Cage jerked it out of his hand and jabbed at the seam where the lid joined the sides until he gained some leverage and began prying, the nails groaning from the wood until Cage could get his fingers under the lid. With both hands in the crevice, he stood, pulling with his hands and wrenching the lid off in one ripping movement. The cloth that Janet had carefully folded over Lena's face came flying off with the lid, snagged on a splinter of the rough *lepa* boards, and the beam from Lita's flashlight fell squarely on Lena's pallid face. Cage grunted as if he had been hit in the stomach and sat down hard on the coffee sacks beside the coffin.

Lita snapped something in Indian to the men standing at the end of the coffin, and they quickly exited out of the back of the truck into the drizzle. Cage sat with his forearms resting on his knees, his hands dangling, staring at Lena's face a few feet away. No one said anything, and as the rain tapped on the tarpaulin, Cage leaned forward and rested his head in his hands. He began shaking his head slowly and emitted a sound that seemed to issue from deep in his barrel chest, as though he were trying to swallow back a wrenching nausea. Lita was motionless, and when Haydon looked up at her he found her eyes were fixed squarely on him. He tried to read her thoughts, but her round Indian face was as indecipherable as if it had been carved of dark wood. Then something made him look at the rear window of the cab. Janet was watching Cage's slumped figure with a loathing she could not have disguised if her life had depended on it.

"Who killed her?" Cage did not look up.

It was a question that summed up the cruelty that had become second nature in Cage's life. He did not ask what happened, rather, who *killed* her? Whatever he was feeling now, it was an aberration. Taylor Cage was irredeemable.

"She died in a car crash eight or ten hours ago," Haydon said. "I think she was coming down off the switchback at Calvario. She was pushing it."

"A car crash," Cage said, his head still in his hands.

"That's what they told me."

Cage said nothing at first, then, "Is that what you think happened?"

"Yes."

"You're such a stupid fool, Haydon," Cage said, swallowing. He ran his fingers through his short, brindled hair, let his hands drop to his legs, but kept his head down. "What about the documents?"

404

"I don't have them," Haydon said. "They wouldn't let go of them. They knew you'd be waiting for me, or Pittner would be, or the G-2. You screwed it up when you tipped your hand in Cobán."

"Did you see the documents?"

"No."

Cage nodded. "Do you know what's going to happen to Grajeda?"

"Happen to him?"

"Grajeda has a problem . . ." Cage wiped his brow on the shoulder of his guayabera and looked up at Haydon. "Their compound back there is a kind of way station for the guerrillas traveling in and out of the Petén jungles. There's a small permanent population that runs the compound, but most of the people there are transient, passing through on one mission or another. A group went in there yesterday, on their way through. One of them is an infiltrator, a Kaibile who joined one of the guerrilla groups six months ago, a sleeper, just waiting for the opportunity to cross trails with Grajeda. Tonight is the first time that's happened. Pretty good timing."

"He's going to kill him."

"That's right."

"I don't see the relationship between the documents and the 'problem.' "

"Grajeda's heard rumors about his impending assassination. They've beefed up their protection, of course, but . . . he knows the odds. He knows he's on short time. He considered Lena his last good chance of getting the stuff out of Guatemala." Cage looked around the truck. "So, why don't I believe you when you tell me you don't have the documents?"

Haydon looked at Cage. Like Grajeda, even sitting beside her coffin, close enough to breathe on her, he didn't have time to grieve for Lena Muller.

405

"They didn't give them to me," Haydon said. "I don't know what else to tell you."

"I want those documents real bad," Cage said. He was breathing heavily, almost as if he were doing control-breathing, trying to keep from hyperventilating, trying to keep his emotions on an even keel. "You know why those documents are so hot? Azcona's kidnapping crap, sure. That's enough right there, isn't it. State will be pissed if that gets around town. But there's more. Real embarrassing stuff that's been happening on Pittner's watch . . . they've known about Azcona's kiddie trade for a long time, just looked the other way because, you know, well, he's such a valuable asset. I mean, he has his bad points, but . . . If the great American public gave a shit about Guatemala—which they don't—that could be a scandal that would make some heads roll . . . nobody here wants to take any chances . . ."

Cage stopped. He was through explaining. He stood up and shouted something out to his Indians. He stepped over to the rear of the truck and climbed down.

"Lita, Haydon, come on out." Haydon got the lid to Lena's coffin and laid it back onto the box, lining up the nail holes as best he could aided by the beam of Lita's flashlight, and tried to bang a few nails back in with the tire tool. "Hurry the hell up," Cage yelled.

Haydon gave one quick look at Janet through the rear window and then followed Lita out the back and onto the pavement. As soon as they were out, four of Cage's men grabbed the canvas flaps and swung up into the truck bed and started throwing out the burlap bags of coffee beans. Two men on the ground began ripping them open with knives, scattering the beans all over the wet pavement.

"I'm going to empty the truck," Cage said.

Haydon stood in the drizzle and watched Cage's men scatter the coffee beans from an even dozen sacks, dumping the beans onto the roadside, down the pavement, wherever they happened to fly as the sacks were ripped open. They were throwing out the thirteenth sack when they heard cars coming from the Cobán direction on the road, and they all stopped and grabbed their Uzi's. Furious, Cage stalked around to the front fender of the truck and stopped. The fog lightened and grew bright as the cars approached and pulled up behind the roadblock. They, too, left their lights on so that this small point in the narrow Calvario road was lighted like a film set.

Car doors opened and closed, whump, whump, whump, whump, whump, muffled in the dense fog, and the long shadows of men in street clothes and carrying the ubiquitous automatic weapons stretched out toward the truck and played weirdly on the moving screen of mizzle. Lita moved up to the front fender, in Cage's shadow.

"Cage, this's Pitt." Pittner's voice was somewhere back among the headlights and the silhouettes moving across the rank of lights. "Let's talk."

"Fine with me."

Pittner threaded through the cars and moved out into the twenty-meter space between the front of the truck and the roadblock. He was wearing a cheap, gray plastic raincoat over his suit, and it glistened in the mist like the surface of the road. He wasn't carrying any weapon.

Keeping his gun in his hand, hanging straight down at his side, Cage moved away from the front fender and joined Pittner in the no-man's-land of headlight beams. Lita stayed at the front bumper of the truck.

"What's the deal here?" Pittner asked.

"Lena's dead," Cage said. Their voices were clear.

"Yeah," Pittner said. "I know that."

"Hard luck," Cage said, his voice a bit tight.

"Is everybody all right?"

"Janet's in the truck. Haydon's back there."

"You find anything?"

"Not yet. But we're emptying the coffee sacks."

Pittner nodded. He seemed to think a moment.

The two shots were so close together that one sounded like the immediate echo of the other. The first came from the headlights behind the roadblock, a little to Cage's right, blowing his head apart. He fell heavily right where he stood, like a fear-disdaining water buffalo. The second one came from behind Haydon and caught Lita in the back of the head, but she was lighter and the velocity of the hollow-point bullet snapped her off her feet and pitched her out onto the bright pavement. She lay on the front of her head where her face used to be. Not ten meters apart, their bodies bled in the drizzle long after their lives were gone.

Chapter 54

Janet was immediately taken out of the truck, and two of Pittner's men, from the embassy, put her in one of their cars and started back to Guatemala City. Haydon wasn't allowed to speak to her.

The traitorous ex-Kaibiles who had worked for the burly American —and one of whom had fired the single shot that killed Lita—were paid off by one of the G-2 officers and drove away toward the Cobán highway.

While Cage and Lita's bodies remained where they had fallen in the rain, the G-2 men in street clothes finished searching the truck—a formality, Pittner said—emptying the rest of the coffee sacks on the side of the road while Haydon and Pittner watched from one of the cars where they sat alone, staring over the two bodies in the road.

Haydon looked at the bodies in the rain and wondered how much this sort of thing happened in the world that Pittner and Cage occupied, and he wondered in how many third-world countries similar scenarios were played out in how many different languages, wrecking how many different lives.

"The poor bastard," Pittner said as they stared out through the rainy windshield. "When the decision finally came down that he just couldn't be allowed to go on, everyone was surprised how quickly his people were bought off." Pittner snorted. "Crazy thing is, Cage would have understood that. They went for the better money."

"What about Lita?"

"We didn't even try. You couldn't have bought her. By Cage's standards she was a failure, putting her life on the line for abstract ideas like fealty and love and respect."

"Did he care for her at all?"

"If he did, I'm not sure he ever understood it the way . . . other people would understand it." He paused. "Of course, I don't really know. I knew the man a long time, but . . . that doesn't mean anything."

He took his eyes off the grim scene lighted by the headlights and gestured toward the glove compartment in front of Haydon. "Open that thing up, will you. There's a flask in there."

Haydon opened the small door in the dash and took out a silver flask, not a hip-pocket-sized one, but a rather heavier one with a good capacity.

"Go ahead," Pittner said.

Haydon unscrewed the cap and took a drink. It was Pittner's beloved bourbon. He passed it to Pittner.

409

"He told me about Grajeda," Haydon said. "About an assassin. Is that true?"

Pittner nodded. "Yeah."

"Is there any chance it will fail?"

"Oh, sure. Happens all the time."

"But it didn't happen here tonight."

"No."

"Janet carried the transmitter for you, didn't she."

Pittner didn't answer immediately. He took another sip of the bourbon, his gaze resting on Cage's body in the rain on the pavement. Then he nodded again. "We had to get him here. I figured you would do your best to get out of Guatemala City without being followed, so . . . she agreed to offer to 'help' him. His people rigged the purse—he had access to good electronics people."

Haydon didn't try to satisfy his greatest curiosity about this crucial aspect of the arrangement—*why* did she agree to set Cage up for his execution. He knew the answer anyway. Revenge was ever a potent emotion. He supposed that Janet Pittner had gotten what she wanted, but he didn't believe it was what she had most desired.

"Then the taxi ride to El Salvador, switching the Land-Rover for the Blazer, none of that worked?"

"It fooled the G-2, the ones who weren't working with us. As usual, Azcona played with us and also ran a string on his own. His own string went all the way to El Salvador and all the way to Panajachel."

"How did you know?"

"We wouldn't have except for the bugs in Janet's house. That's the only way we knew." He paused a while, his plastic raincoat making the same crinkling sounds that Germaine Muller's coat had made four days ago in a colder rain. "Which reminds me, I'll need to get Borrayo's notebooks from you. You know, the clandestine prison business."

"What are you going to do with them?"

"Come on, Haydon," Pittner said, passing the bottle back to Haydon. "Don't start that."

Haydon took another drink and handed the flask back to Pittner. Then he leaned back and pulled the 10mm out of his belt. He popped the clip out of the handle and reached down between his feet and unzipped the flight bag. He tossed the clip into the bag and then the gun, and zipped it up again.

410

"Everything's in there," he said.

"Thanks," Pittner said. In the headlights the G-2 were crawling all over the truck. The doors were open, and the hood was up.

"What if they don't find anything?" Haydon asked.

"Then that's it, isn't it."

Haydon couldn't tell anything about what Pittner was feeling. He appeared as lugubrious as always, but Haydon knew that with Pittner appearances didn't mean much.

"Are you clear about it, in your own mind, why you had him killed?" Haydon asked.

Pittner reached up to the dash and turned on the windshield wipers. He let them make a few swipes and then cut them off again. The car had filled with the sweet, smoky fragrance of the bourbon on their breath. Pittner sat slump shouldered, his body reflecting that he was either completely relaxed or exhausted. It wasn't easy to tell which.

"We had tried to pension him out all kinds of different ways," Pittner said. "Did he tell you he'd quit us?"

"Yes."

"He didn't. We had to cut him loose. He was a rogue, Haydon. It was that simple. He was doing outrageous things. We tried to defang him, transfer him back to Langley, ease him out. We offered him the max allowed in benefits. After all, after you've run someone as long as we'd run Cage, in the places we'd sent him, in the circumstances . . . and he goes over the edge, you feel half responsible. So we tried hard. I did, personally. Then he started operating as if there had never been any rules. He was doing outrageous things, playing us and Azcona, the Israelis. To do what he was doing—it was like stepping out in front of a truck. It was provocative. The reason he's lying out there right now is more his doing than anyone else's."

"And the girl?"

"She was hit in the cross fire."

Haydon turned to Pittner.

"Metaphorically speaking," Pittner said.

Haydon studied Pittner's profile. "You're satisfied, then, with all the reasons."

"Satisfied?" Pittner's eyes drooped, and he cleared his throat and took a good swig from the flask and screwed the lid on and laid the flask on the car seat. "I haven't been satisfied with anything since I was twelve years old, Haydon. And I'm sure as hell not satisfied with any of this."

The only remaining man from Pittner's office was standing at the back of the truck, the short collar of his suit coat turned up against the drizzle as he talked to several of the Guatemalan agents. He shook his head, and they shook their heads, and then he nodded and turned and jogged across the pavement, past Lita's body, past Cage's body to Pittner's car door. Pittner rolled down the window.

"I think we're through, Pitt."

"Nothing."

"That's right."

Pittner looked at Haydon. "Come on," he said, and the two of them

411

opened their doors and stepped out into the rain. They proceeded past the bodies again, stepping in the blood and rainwater, and went to the back of the truck where they walked on a layer of crushed coffee beans that had been ground under so many feet that they had become a thin paste covering the pavement. Pittner grabbed the tarpaulin flaps and pulled himself up into the back of the truck as did Haydon and several of the men, including the American. The back of the truck was aromatic with the fragrance of coffee, and it was empty except for Lena's coffin.

Pittner stood a moment under the canopy of the tarpaulin, the flashlights pointed to the canvas roof to provide indirect lighting.

"Get a couple of those guys to open it up and lay her out on the truck bed here," Pittner said.

It had to be done, Haydon realized that, but knowing it had to be done didn't make it any easier. The lid came off without effort since Haydon hadn't been able to nail it on very well with the tire tool. They put the lid aside. The coffin was too small, something Haydon hadn't noticed before, and the guerrillas had had to roll her shoulders forward a little to get her in. Because of this the easiest way to get her out was simply to turn the box over and let her own weight do the work. They did this carefully, more carefully than they would have if the girl hadn't been Anglo or if the Anglo men hadn't been standing there.

She didn't come out while the box was on its side, so they had to turn it on over on its face. When they pulled it off of her, she lay facedown on the bed of the truck, her arms wrapped tightly against her sides with yards of gauze, a large amount of which was crusty with blood. They righted the box expectantly. It was empty.

No one said anything, they simply stood there looking at the dark stains in the bottom of the box and at Lena's long blond hair spread out over the dirty boards of the truck bed. Pittner stood there a long time, his rumpled suit seeming even more rumpled than usual under the cheap plastic raincoat. It was his move, but he wasn't moving. Haydon saw several of the Guatemalans exchange glances. It was almost humorous, as if the longer Pittner was immobile, the more important it was for everyone else to avoid even the slightest twitch or sound.

Finally Pittner said, "Before you put her back in the box, make sure there's nothing wrapped up in there with her." He turned away and got out of the truck. Haydon followed him.

The rain had slackened to a heavy mist, falling in a light, sparkling drift. Pittner walked past Lita and Cage without even hesitating, their blood spreading all over the pavement, enormous amounts of it, melting in the rain.

When they got to the cars, Pittner stopped and leaned against one of the fenders and looked back at the truck.

"Was it really a car crash?" Haydon asked.

"Christ. Yes," Pittner said, almost as though he could hardly believe it himself. "We had observers up in Calvario, and they saw it. She was with a man, one of the guerrillas. The guy was on the switchbacks, driving like hell, and went over. The son of a bitch lived, but Lena was thrown out of the car." Pittner shook his head. "It's . . . incredible."

Almost immediately the men began coming out of the back of the truck, their job finished. No one said anything about finding "documents" in Lena's shroud. Pittner watched them as they picked up Lita and carried her around to the back and loaded her in the truck as well, and then he watched them take Cage. It took four of them.

"You know what I was thinking back there in the truck?" Pittner asked. "I was thinking . . . that this was what I would remember of her . . . the back of her head, her hair spread out on the rough wooden bed of a truck, her body wrapped in bloody gauze. I was stunned, didn't want it to be that way . . . not that one image. Any of the many other ways . . . that I had known her . . . would have been preferable. But then, I didn't want to see them turn her over, see them . . . handle her . . . so, God help me, I'm left with that."

Pittner cleared his throat. He was growing maudlin and seemed to realize it. He was staring down at his feet on the black asphalt, the light drizzle stippling the toes of his shoes.

"I'm sorry I never met her," Haydon said.

"The thing is," Pittner said, "sometimes you can live whole decades of your life and miss the point of it all. It's so damned easy to do that it's scary. Knowing Lena was like that. We all wanted something from her, but we never really understood the real value of what she had to offer. We never got past the superficial, her beauty and her sexuality. When we looked at her we saw a pretty woman dancing with the devil, and we read it wrong. All we wanted to do was cut in on the fun. We were too sophisticated, too grasping, too corrupt ourselves to recognize that what they were engaged in was not a dance but a struggle. The truth of it is, we had no real understanding of what she was all about. And that was our fault, not hers."

413

Chapter 55

It was no trouble getting her body on the plane to Belize. The airstrip was little more than that, a strip of tarmac and a couple of cinder-block buildings painted turquoise and occupied by a couple of guards who almost fled when they saw the caravan pull up to the runway where the mysterious plane had been waiting all night. Pittner and the ranking G-2 officer with him had conversations with the two guards, and Haydon's plane was airborne while the sky was lightening to gray in the east.

The flight was a little more than two hours and at an altitude that allowed Haydon to watch the changing terrain as they crossed over the Sierra de Chamá and dropped down into the vast Petén lowlands of hardwood forests and dry jungle with thin columns of smoke rising straight up from the fires of the slash-and-burn farmers, seasonal swamps, and broad, sprawling savannahs. In no time at all they turned toward the Caribbean, which they first saw as a gray haze that proceeded to turn every shade and gradient of blue and green with the changing light until they circled and landed over turquoise water on a private strip in Belize City.

Haydon arranged for Lena to be taken to a private mortuary where she remained while he made inquiries through his pilots to people who knew people who knew a discreet pathologist who would be able to perform the autopsy in the presence of an equally discreet police captain who was authorized to draw up and sign all the proper Belizean documents necessary for Lena's departure from the country. By the time all this was arranged, it was late in the afternoon when the pathologist began the autopsy, but it was only minutes after beginning that he extracted a small plastic envelope from beneath Lena Muller's sternum, where a gash caused by the car crash had been crudely sutured. It seemed that Dr. Aris Grajeda had used Lena Muller for his purposes after all, as Taylor Cage had predicted, though not quite in the way Cage had imagined. None of them could have imagined it, Haydon guessed, but the infamous files of General Luis Azcona Contrera were finally out of Guatemala. And Germaine Muller's daughter finally came home.

Lena Muller's story, however, did not end for Haydon for many months to come. On behalf of Mari Fossler and her sons, he handled all the red tape required to recover her husband's body. It was a cruel and shabby affair, with official corruption causing promises and delays, and when it had reached absurd proportions with outrageous "requirements" of funds, Haydon got word to the Political Section of the American embassy that they had better step in and stop the farce. Fossler's body was back within days, the paperwork cleared, the ordeal at an end. Haydon could never understand why Pittner hadn't done something about it from the beginning; he hardly could not have known what was happening.

The loose ends of the story that were being played out back in Guatemala came to him like a recurring dream that presented itself in intermittent scenes in the form of anonymous mailings from Guatemala City. The first to arrive were two news clippings, one from *La Prensa Libre* and the other from *El Gráfico,* the two leading dailies in Guatemala. They were brief and recounted the death of a forty-three-year-old American tourist, Taylor Lee Cage, who had suffered a heart attack while deep-water fishing in the Bay of Amatique just off Puerto Barrios in the *departamento* of Izabal. Mr. Cage was visiting from Spokane, Washington, and was survived by a brother, Robert Cage of Fort Myers, Florida, with whom he was fishing when he died. The articles were brief, and identical in both papers.

The second mailing arrived a few weeks later, again two articles from *La Prensa Libre* and *El Gráfico,* which recorded the accidental death of a free-lance American journalist. John Baine died from injuries he sustained when his car crashed while traveling "at a high rate of speed" on the northern shores of Lake Atitlán. Mr. Baine, the articles said, had lived in Guatemala only a few years and specialized in stories about "Indian crafts" and articles for tourist magazines. Both stories were brief, and identical in both papers.

In early July, when the short but potent winter was long-since gone and the sweltering heat had returned to Houston and settled in for the long term, Haydon received the printed program from a funeral mass for Dr. Aris Grajeda, who had just been buried, in the drizzly heart of the rainy season, in Guatemala City's Cemetery of the Cypresses. The program was a cloying document of several pages that gave the order of the service, the hymns sung, the prayers offered. There was a picture of Jesus Christ praying in Gethsemane, eyes cast heavenward. There was a brief biography of Dr. Grajeda emphasizing his academic awards in college and his achievements in medical school, including a special grant awarded him by Johns Hopkins University Medical School to study tropical diseases upon his completion of his internship. After listing his academic achievements, it was simply stated that he practiced medicine in his native Guatemala City. His good friend Dr. Bindo Salviati gave a eulogy. Dr. Grajeda had died of complications following an appendicitis attack he suffered while vacationing among the Mayan pyramids in the Petén.

The six months that had passed between the time Haydon had left Guatemala with Lena Muller's body and the announcement of Dr. Grajeda's funeral made Haydon believe that the Kaibile assassin had in fact missed his mark that rainy night back in January. And what had happened to Dr. Grajeda in the meantime? Haydon had heard nothing in the interim and assumed Grajeda was dead. How had he lived in those six months? And how had he really died? It made Haydon feel odd that he already had grieved for the doctor and that many times over the past six months he had thought of him in the past tense while he was actually still living. Now he had to grieve for him all over again. And he felt guilty as well, for the earthshaking reaction that Dr. Grajeda had antici- pated upon the publication of the microfilmed documents that Haydon had carried out of the rain forests of Alta Verapaz had not occurred. Dr. Grajeda must have waited tensely in the ensuing months for the thunder- clap of media attention to the scandal that his papers exposed, only to realize after months and months that nothing was to come of it at all.

The grim fact was that Haydon himself had spent considerable time and expense to make sure the documents got to the most respected jour- nalists and specialists interested in Central American affairs in every branch of the media. But the media was a mistress much in demand, and a mistress who demanded much of her suitors. Guatemala? There was the maelstrom of Eastern Europe, the upheaval in the Soviet Union, there were the firestorms of hatred in the Middle East. The sins of General Luis Azcona Contrera were washed away by the blood of other horrors in other places, places where the United States had invested far more money and had far more at risk. Besides, Guatemala had already been converted from its heathen ways. It was already a democracy.

Dr. Grajeda must have realized all of this with suicidal despair as he hid and sweated in the jungles of the Petén. It must have haunted him as he lay awake in the dark, cicada-ridden nights and remembered his brief time with Lena Muller and how, together, they had dreamed of assem- bling a truth so powerful that its revelation would bring forth a redemp- tion of children.

417